The Hummingbird Saint

The Hummingbird Saint

Hector Macdonald

W F HOWES LTD

This large print edition published in 2003 by
W F Howes Ltd
Units 6/7, Victoria Mills, Fowke Street
Rothley, Leicester LE7 7PJ

1 3 5 7 9 10 8 6 4 2

First published in 2003 by Penguin Books

A CIP catalogue record for this book is available
from the British Library

ISBN 1 84197 655 5

Typeset by Palimpsest Book Production Limited,
Polmont, Stirlingshire
Printed and bound in Great Britain
by Antony Rowe Ltd, Chippenham, Wilts.

To Emily and Bruno

The people who make wars, the people who reduce their fellows to slavery, the people who kill and torture and tell lies in the name of their sacred causes, the really evil people, in a word – these are never the publicans and the sinners. No, they're the virtuous respectable men, who have the finest feelings, the best brains, the noblest ideals.

Aldous Huxley, *After Many a Summer*

CHAPTER 1

Before I get to Hoppner, I should probably say something about my own morality. I like truth – telling it and hearing it. Funny to think you'll have to take my word on that, but then I'm told humour is a virtue. What else? Temperance? Simplicity? Prudence? All good things in moderation, I suppose. Some bastards really test my tolerance, others my sense of justice and my willingness to forgive. And though I used to believe I was reasonably courageous, I have to admit none of this would have happened if I'd had the courage to deal with my own demons.

Has it changed me, this brush with virtue? The odds are against it: our vices are pretty deeply rooted. Am I a better person? Perhaps it's a sign of humility that I don't think I'm in a position to judge. But then if I was truly humble I wouldn't be congratulating myself on my humility, would I? Work that one out.

Think too much about right and wrong, try too hard to be good, and you end up going crazy.

★   ★   ★

1

There is only one flight a week from London to Santa Tecla. The day I chose to fly, the plane developed a small technical problem. What exactly the problem was, I never discovered. But it caused a delay, and the delay led to a meeting. And who knows how different things might have been without that?

'Ladies and gentlemen, this is the captain once again. We've made a few tests and I'm afraid the situation remains the same. Our instruments are indicating a potential problem in the cargo hold.' His announcement, delivered a long way above the Atlantic, might have been expected to induce a minor panic among his passengers, but the captain's voice was so reassuringly calm that most of us barely blinked. Was there a fire? Had the cargo shifted dangerously? No one seemed to care.

'It's unlikely to be anything serious, but your safety is our primary concern, so we've taken the decision to divert to the nearest airport.'

It was hard to imagine anywhere solid enough in that ocean to land our troublesome machine. But in fact we didn't have far to go. The nearest airport, seven hours along the flight path from London to the centremost point of Central America, turned out to be located on the island of Bermuda.

The real trouble started when we touched down.

The entire cargo hold would have to be emptied for safety checks, explained the captain. And because of the time that would take, the crew would not be able to complete the journey within their permitted operational hours. A new aircraft and crew had been hurriedly requested from Newark, but they wouldn't arrive for another six hours.

The benign acceptance of several hundred passengers switched in a second to belligerent irritation. Stewardesses were harangued. Watches were consulted. Whispers and mutters on all sides. Everyone but me, it seemed, was in a hurry to reach Santa Tecla.

Bermuda was hot and humid, the air-conditioned transit lounge icy cold. With the time difference it was still only ten o'clock in the morning, although most of us were already well into a London afternoon. Several of the passengers had identified each other as delegates bound for the Santa Tecla reconstruction conference and had already begun networking, scrolling through the tired list of introductory questions used wherever their taxpayers sent them. Clearly, the event was going to be a big one: I'd tried to book the previous week's flight, only to be told it was already full – packed with junior delegates sent on ahead to prepare the conference.

A look of glacial disdain met me as I passed the plump, unforgiving woman who'd occupied the aeroplane seat two along from mine. Mine, that is, until I'd discreetly asked to be moved. The seat between us had contained her bouncy, equally plump young son, and I knew she'd taken it as a personal insult that I hadn't wanted to sit next to him. I'd offered my politest, most

3

self-effacing smile to assure her the fault lay with me rather than with her son – that I avoided being close to any child, not hers in particular – but she was determined to view my relocation in the worst possible light. Resisting the urge to return her stare, I assumed an inwardly troubled expression I'd first developed to mollify Chinese border guards in Tibet, and walked quickly by.

At one end of the lounge was an odd little half-row of seats, stuck at an irregular angle to fill the awkward space between a wall and a pillar. It appealed to me. Well away from plump mum and plump son – what was she doing taking a child to a war-torn chunk of Central America anyway? – and comfortably removed from the bulk of the delegates. Sitting down, I stretched out my legs and wrapped my jacket tight around me to keep out the artificial chill.

Airline staff were wandering amongst the unhappy passengers like medieval priests ministering to a leper colony. As one stewardess passed me, I added my own logistical woe to the mountain of problems her passengers were laying at her door. Bermudan officials in knee-length shorts looked on impassively from the other side of a glass wall. Beyond them, a scrap of Bermudan sea was visible, pointedly beyond the reach of our band of uninvited refugees.

The novel I'd chosen was failing to hold my attention. I was about to embark on a more or less criminal act that would ensure the exclusion from my life of the only two people who meant anything to me. Fiction offered little comfort. After five pages I gave up, replacing the book with the only other reading material in my bag: an old *Sunday Times* magazine with a coy close-up of Madonna on the cover.

I never did read the Madonna article.

About ten minutes had gone by before I noticed a man staring at me from the nearest row of seats. He looked away when I stared back, a sudden flick of the head sending his blond hair flopping the wrong way. Still facing the blank wall beside him, he brought a flattened palm up to smooth his hair, with two natty flicks, back into position. His ears, I remember noticing, were tiny. Everything else about him looked overlarge on his rather short body. His chin and nose stuck out and his shoulders seemed too wide, a flaw augmented by the cut of his pale linen jacket. But he wasn't ugly. Somehow the bits and pieces of mismatched anatomy came together to produce a quick, seductive face and confident posture.

The next time he caught my attention, he was standing right beside me.

I hadn't noticed him move. I'd lowered my eyes to the magazine for perhaps a minute at most before I felt his presence and spotted his tasselled loafers out of the corner of my eye.

He was gazing at the magazine. I closed it sharply.

'Good readage?' he asked.

5

'Good what?'

His head rocked forward. 'You looked engrossed. Is that this week's?'

It was a strange question; I ignored it. 'Got to pass the time somehow.'

He took that as an invitation, though it wasn't and he knew it wasn't. A second later he was on the seat beside me.

'I'm Freddy.'

'Mark.' One of the very few things I can remember doing as a young child was telling people my name. Except, I think I used to say Marcos. I have a feeling that's what my mother called me: Marcos.

'Nice to meet you, Mark,' he said, hand already floating between us. 'Are you going to the conference?'

'No.'

'So what takes you so far afield? Mayan ruins? Rainforest conservation?'

'Business.'

'Oh, that,' he said, smiling. A pause, just long enough for me to notice the strange intonation he'd applied to those two brief syllables. He gestured towards my magazine. 'Interesting?'

'Just something I had lying around.'

'This week's?'

Again that question. I glanced down at the magazine. The date wasn't showing, but a sizeable chunk of Britain must have seen the Madonna close-up a month earlier. 'No,' I said.

'I've got nothing with me. Mind if I borrow it?'

The guy's presumption might almost have been funny if it hadn't been focused on that particular magazine. Instead, it was mildly alarming. 'I'm still reading it.'

'When you've finished, I mean.'

Shrugging, I nodded as lightly as I could.

Another passenger was wandering towards us. A woman, very pale, with wavy dark hair cut short, and a pair of inquisitive brown eyes. Like us, she was in her late twenties. For a moment, I had the disconcerting impression that she too was staring at the magazine. She stopped still when we both looked up at her, then – perhaps encouraged by Freddy's immediate grin – continued on towards us with a jauntier step.

'Not more delegates, I hope?' she said.

'Not us,' Freddy answered.

'Can I join you? I'm so bored.'

She dropped to a crouch in front of us. I might have offered her my seat, but she'd already assumed a posture so relaxed and natural that the gesture would have felt ridiculously formal. A silver cross hung at her throat, perfectly framed by the V of her black sweater.

'Hello,' she said to Freddy. 'Alice Williams.'

'Nice to meet you,' he said. 'I'm Freddy Greenock.'

She avoided shaking his hand by raising hers in a kind of mock salute. Then she shifted her gaze to me. I was so disconcerted by what I'd just heard that for a moment I was speechless.

Before I'd even reached Santa Tecla I was in trouble.

'And you are?'

'Mark.' In my confusion, I rushed the word out.

'That's it?'

I said nothing.

She lowered her chin, stared at me through her upper eyelashes. 'You don't have a surname?'

I stared back helplessly – perfectly prepared and yet so unready for this moment. I should have quickly made up something, but my uncle's relentless instruction in honesty had had more effect on me than perhaps even he'd intended. For me, lying was something that had to be practised in advance. Unfortunately, the name I'd rehearsed over and over again was now completely unusable.

Alice's gaze turned quizzical. I said the only thing I could, in the circumstances: 'Weston. My name's Mark Weston.'

Her mouth drew closed, as if she was about to repeat my name. But before she could, Freddy was leaning forward.

'So, Miss Williams, what takes you to—?'

'Mrs Williams.'

'Mrs Williams?' He leaned minutely back. His smile, though, didn't waver. 'Bereaved, abandoned or estranged?'

'Excuse me?'

'Mr Williams isn't with you?'

8

'Leonard's over there.'

The line of her finger led us to the far corner of the lounge. A stick insect of a man was spread out across four seats, his jacket bundled under his head and his gangly legs hanging off the end of the row. His fingers held the strap of a shoulder bag in a tight grip, but his eyes were closed and there was a blankness about his freckled face.

'He's very tired,' said Alice. 'Poor thing, he finds flying a nerve-wracking—'

A tannoy announcement interrupted her. At the entrance to the lounge, a stewardess was speaking into a microphone: 'Could Mr Greenock please come to the information desk.'

'What now?' muttered Freddy, rising. 'This had better be an upgrade.'

'Mr Mark Greenock to the information desk, please.'

He paused, halfway out of his seat. 'There's another Greenock on this flight?' he said. 'What are the odds, hey?' With a peculiar, somewhat uncomfortable laugh, he dropped back into his seat.

I kept my head down, praying they were too busy to pursue inattentive passengers. It didn't work. A moment later, the stewardess was standing over me.

'Mr Greenock? Didn't you hear the announcement?'

I looked up, trying to avoid eye contact with the other two. 'Sorry,' I said weakly.

'Don't worry. We're all a bit exhausted,' she

chirped. 'I just wanted to let you know we've contacted your driver and she's aware of the delay. She said not to worry, but that you'd have to stay overnight in Santa Tecla, as the road to Miraflores isn't safe in the dark.'

'Thank you,' I muttered dutifully, although at that moment gratitude was the last thing I felt towards her.

She leaned forward, confiding. 'Make sure you put in a claim for any accommodation expenses. The airline will pay.'

'Thank you.'

'You're welcome, Mr Greenock.'

As she straightened up, Freddy caught her arm, his fingers light and intimate on her sleeve. 'Look, do we really have to stay in here? The new plane won't arrive for hours. Can't we go outside – get a bit of fresh air?'

'I'm sorry, sir, it's Bermudan regulations. Not us.'

'Could you at least ask?'

She looked doubtful, but she gave a noncommittal nod and walked over to the entrance. I kept my eyes on her, unwilling to see the inevitable questions in the faces of my new acquaintances. After a few moments of whispered consultation with a Bermudan official, the stewardess waved us over.

Freddy and Alice stood up.

'I'll just see if Leonard wants to come,' said Alice, walking over to her collapsed husband.

'Coming, Mr Greenock?' said Freddy, the beginnings of a smirk on his lips.

'I . . . no, I think I'll—'

'Oh come on, friend, I promise I won't bring it up again. I'll buy you a drink. Christ, you look like you need one.'

His eel-soft hand was already on my elbow. Reluctantly, I stood up. On the other side of the lounge, Alice was crouched beside her husband. His lips moved slightly and his hand reached out to caress her cheek, but he didn't get up. With an affectionate smile, Alice left him to his nap and rejoined us.

'So, let's go,' she said.

The café recommended by our taxi driver was an airy, vine-smothered place on the edge of a golf course, overlooking the glistening beaches and turquoise sea of Tobacco Bay. I was glad to get out of his car: something about it was unsettling – a combination of the sun-warmed brown leather seats, the heavy, old-fashioned dashboard and the invasive smell of hot oil and burnt rubber. We'd passed several horse-drawn buggies on Bermuda's narrow, winding roads, and each one had made me wish I could swap over.

With three hours to kill, I would normally have wandered down to the beach and tested those inviting waters. Sunbathers were slumped in striped deckchairs; snorkellers drifted lazily over the reefs. But that stupid mistake with my name kept me glued to Alice and Freddy, if only to prevent them discussing me behind my back. I'd recovered from the initial shock of meeting another 'Greenock', but I wasn't looking forward to the lies I would have to tell to explain myself.

We were greeted by a hunched, bearded proprietor and given a table on the terrace, a menu, and permission to use American dollars but not credit cards. An array of terracotta tubs surrounded us, planted with flowers moulded in coloured glass. Each one was an exquisite piece of craftsmanship: not tacky, not mass produced, but individually shaped with delicate pointed leaves and tissue-light petals. Still, I couldn't help wondering why ersatz blooms should be necessary in sunny Bermuda.

The proprietor disappeared inside with our order. For a few seconds the respite afforded by the presence of strangers – airport officials, the taxi driver, the proprietor himself – endured. Then Alice turned to Freddy and said, 'I suppose it's safe to assume Mark really is called Mark, isn't it?'

'Who? Mr Greenock, you mean?' laughed Freddy. 'Sorry,' he added to me. 'Won't mention it again.'

It really wasn't a big deal. I smiled warmly, sharing the joke with them. I'd learnt a useful cautionary lesson, and it wasn't as if I was going to see either of them again. The only thing that bothered me a little was the interest Freddy had shown in that magazine.

'Are you actually travelling as Greenock?' asked Alice. 'What a strange name to choose.'

'I'm a journalist,' I said lightly. 'Sometimes I have to use a false name.'

'An undercover journalist? How exciting!'

'Better than working,' I grinned.

'What isn't?' she said.

A chocolate Labrador bounded up to us and sniffed at Freddy, tail wagging. Something didn't suit him, however, and he moved speedily on to me. When I rubbed his ears, he dropped his haunches and laid his muzzle on my knee. At an eager 'Here, boy!' from Alice he looked up momentarily but then sank back down against my leg. A small victory.

'What are you covering?' asked Freddy. 'The conference?'

'It's a secret, I'm afraid.'

'No, it wouldn't be the conference,' said Alice. 'He's going to . . . where was it? Miraflores?'

'Actually, that's a good point. I was thinking of heading that way myself,' said Freddy, scratching his nose. 'Any chance of a lift?'

He managed to bring it off perfectly casually, but I wasn't going to let him get away with that. The tiny fleck of suspicion I'd entertained in the transit lounge had just received a significant boost.

'And what are you doing up there?' I asked, trying not to smile.

'Soft drink distribution,' he replied smoothly. 'My firm's looking for vendors throughout the country – doing our bit for the reconstruction effort.'

Not bad. But I was on to him.

Over his shoulder, I noticed a deeply tanned blonde emerge from a ritzy mansion and saunter out on to a terrace a little below our own. As she stripped off her aquamarine dressing gown and arranged her perfect limbs over a sun lounger, the twin of our chocolate Labrador trotted out of the house and settled itself by her side. For a moment I was tempted to point out this matching dog, but I'd already got the measure of Freddy and the last thing I wanted was to have him grow noisily excited over the sybaritic beauty next door.

'Isn't Miraflores where that guy lives?' said Alice. 'That American guy?'

I glanced at Freddy; his face was stupidly blank. Mine was probably much the same.

'You know,' she insisted. 'The one who owns all those porn magazines. Benjamin something the third something. Hopper, was it? He was hounded out of the US and ended up in . . . I'm pretty sure it was Miraflores.'

A painful silence met her expectant gaze. The first to crumble was Freddy, who muttered, 'Really?'

It simply wasn't credible that neither of us had heard of Benjamin Sword Hoppner. Every American knew his name, as well as almost anyone else with half an eye on the newspapers. Once a favourite public enemy in the United States, he'd become such a figure of fun that endless cartoonists, sketch writers and stand-up comedians had at some point caricatured his ludicrous hypocrisies and moralizing proclamations. So, with Freddy still claiming ignorance, it fell to me to clear us both of suspicion by admitting a little knowledge.

'Hoppner. His name is Hoppner.'

'That's it!' she said, delighted. 'Are you going to visit him?'

'Why would I do that?'

'Didn't I read somewhere that he's offering handouts? Oh, I forgot: you're an undercover journalist, aren't you? I bet you're going to interview him.'

Her playful, seemingly naïve questions were getting too close to the bone. I realized I was pressing my hands deep into my jacket pockets – a subconscious defensive action. Under the Bermudan sun the jacket was too hot, but its worn leather had always represented something of a protective layer for me.

That jacket had been everywhere: it shared a lot of memories. I'd won it off a yacht captain when I'd spent a summer working the Mediterranean. Delighted to find a crew member as large as himself, he'd challenged me to a wrestling contest: first man to throw the other into the sea won. He was after my smuggled case of Jamaican rum; I bet it against his jacket. A prized possession for him, but he didn't expect to lose. In fact, he wore the jacket for the fight – his idea of an amusing

15

taunt – so it was sodden when I first, exultantly, tried it on.

Impregnated with salt, pounded by storms, left to bake on Landcruiser bonnets, muddied, scratched, scuffed on volcanic rock, that jacket had survived a lot of abuse. In patches, the suede had worn down to the base leather; it varied in colour from dark brown beneath the collar to pale coffee at one cuff. The effect should have been scrappy – a mess – but instead it suggested a rather elegant world-weariness. Occasionally I'd admit to myself that that was an image I relished.

I leaned towards Alice, casually easing off the jacket. 'And why are you going to Santa Tecla?' I asked, preferring to attack than defend.

'Oh, we're just hitting the beaches. Leonard's hardly ever been out of England before, so we don't want to be too adventurous.'

'He seems a bit dull,' said Freddy. 'Sleeping all the time.' He tried a wide grin. 'Why don't you give him the slip for a few days – come up to Miraflores with us?'

Alice just smiled. 'It's our honeymoon,' she said. 'We got married yesterday.' In an instant, her hand was in front of us, a boulder of a diamond nestling beside a plain gold band. 'What do you think?'

'It's . . . big. Congratulations,' I offered.

Freddy slouched back in his chair. 'Well, I tried. Can't blame me for trying. Why are you going to a war zone for a honeymoon?'

16

'It's not a war zone! The war finished six years ago.'

'But there are more obvious places to choose. It's still a ruin.'

'It's cheap,' she shrugged. 'Leonard's a teacher. Besides, who wants to sit on a Caribbean island with a million other newlyweds? At least we'll be special – get lots of attention wherever we stay.'

Alice didn't look like the kind of girl who needed attention. She had a manner that suggested she wasn't too worried what the rest of the world thought. I found myself wondering if Mr Leonard Williams knew exactly what he'd taken on. His new wife was what my grandmother used to call the tricky sort.

Imagining Alice lying on a beach was difficult. She was so pale that her skin would turn a painful scarlet within half an hour, unless she coated herself in sun block. The thought of that thin figure burnt and blistered was not appealing. To compensate, I pictured her on the same beach at night, her soft, bloodless skin catching the moonlight and turning silver. Beneath a delicate silk sarong those slim, nimble legs would dance through the sand to music only she could hear, her eyes closed, her mouth lightly smiling. For some reason I could only imagine her alone; the gangly husband asleep in the transit lounge just didn't fit the scene.

The fantasy was a harmless one: she was a newlywed whom I would never see again. At some

17

point I was going to have to get back into the dating game, and dreaming about other women was the first step in that process. It was good practice after four years of near-marriage. But the more I looked at Alice, stripping away our current surroundings and setting her in that tropical beach moonlight, the more I appreciated what a striking beauty there was in her flawless complexion and the sharp lines of her cheeks and temples.

It took a while for me to realize exactly where my imagination had chosen to locate her. She was out on the moonlit sands in front of the ramshackle bar I helped set up on Bequia's Friendship Bay.

Bequia, the largest of the Grenadines, was not on the Caribbean honeymoon circuit that Alice had so wisely avoided. Most of its visitors were yachties, and most of them headed for the smarter bars on Admiralty Bay, close to their moorings. Having said that, our best customers were three dapper yachtsmen, formerly Surrey-based millionaires who'd grown to favour tax savings over families and fixed abodes. Every afternoon at four, they would traipse in from their boats for the first of many cocktails. To entertain ourselves, each day we would select one of the jolly three to target with extra-generous measures. It was a point of honour to ensure that our boy was the first to tumble from his barstool.

One time it got complicated. I'd chosen my victim, only to discover that one of the others was celebrating his birthday and was determined to drink himself senseless. I couldn't allow that to happen – not until my target had collapsed. The birthday boy, remembering how effortlessly he'd found himself stupefied on previous evenings, grew steadily more dismayed at his enduring sobriety. The only effect his mountain of refills had was on his bladder. It was illegal, of course, even on Bequia, to serve short measures, but sometimes honour has to come before the Law.

I still held such affection for that bar, even though I'd lost what little savings I had there, that to find Alice – if only in my imagination – occupying a corner of it filled me with an irrational but nevertheless genuine warmth towards her. She gave me a curious look and I returned it with a smile. When she smiled back, brighter and faster than before, her whole face lit up.

The proprietor reappeared, bearing a polished silver tray: freshly squeezed orange juice for her, coffee for me, Black Seal rum and ginger beer for Freddy. The bill was a staggering sixteen dollars.

'Ah, damn,' said Freddy. 'I was relying on my credit card. Mark – do you mind?'

Both Alice and I produced a twenty-dollar bill at the same time. I put on a stern face; she laughed, returning the money to her shirt pocket.

'Why don't you try to sell him some of your soft drinks?' she suggested to Freddy, when the proprietor had gone. 'What are they, by the way?'

Freddy managed to name a minor brand without hesitation, but he made no move to follow her advice. Already, he'd spread himself wide across his chair, rolled up his sleeves and undone his shirt to expose as much of his shapeless white stomach as possible to the sun.

'If you go to Miraflores, you'll have to visit Mr Hoppner,' she continued. 'I read that he pretty much runs that town, so you'd better be polite to him.'

How had she come to know so much about Hoppner?

'That isn't how it works in my business,' Freddy announced to the sun, his eyes closed, the last of the rum cocktail balanced against his stomach. 'We turn up and they're begging for our product. Particularly in the armpit of the world.'

The shadow of the proprietor across his face made him open his eyes.

'I'm sorry, sir, I must ask you to dress properly.'

'What? We're the only people here.'

'All the same.'

Sullenly buttoning his shirt, Freddy cast a black stare at the departing man's back. 'Victorian values with an American accent. Unbelievable.'

I've always had a tendency to judge too quickly. It's a problem, I know: the nicest people can be hiding behind a veneer of irritating habits, bluster and unfortunate conversational openers, thrown up to protect their shy inner selves. One of my best friends was a fellow guide in the Torajaland region of Indonesia – an Aussie who introduced himself with a loud fart and the drunken words, 'I'm Jesus

Christ. You?' Amazingly, when sober he turned out to be the most thoughtful, considerate guy I've ever known – though he still liked to be known as JC. He had depth; he had an inner self. Freddy, on the other hand, as far as I could tell that first morning, simply did not.

A full hour before our deadline, we caught a taxi back to the airport. Our friendly Bermudan official was waiting to greet us and return us to the transit lounge, though he insisted on putting us through a full security check. When his turn came, Freddy waved us on before handing over his bag.

'I'll catch you up,' he said.

'No rush – we'll wait,' I smiled. I had a hunch about this.

He looked uncomfortable. I leaned against the X-ray machine and waited for him to open the bag.

'Hey-ho, security again,' he said to no one in particular.

'Please open your case, sir.'

'Yup. Sure.'

With a furtive grin at me, he pulled the zip halfway back. Impatiently, the security official brushed his fingers aside and opened it the rest of the way. Freddy was leaning oddly forward, but I still had a clear view of the bag.

The first item that emerged in the official's gloved hands was an old *Sunday Times* magazine with a close-up of Madonna on the cover.

21

The Man Who Would Be God (excerpt)

Interview by Sandra Collins

SANDRA COLLINS: Why did you leave the States?

BENJAMIN SWORD HOPPNER: The question is, why anybody remains in the States. The country has become a vipers' nest controlled by a clique of two-faced zealot-warmongers.

SANDRA COLLINS: So you chose to leave? You weren't forced out by the swell of popular opinion against you?

BENJAMIN SWORD HOPPNER: Popular opinion is a joke. Do you know how popular opinion is formed? Of course you do – it's your profession. The lawyers and the politicians get together and decide that, as of tomorrow, the people will think X. So they call in their pals at the newspapers and have them print X. Then, three days later, they hold a poll of fifty news-reading Washington households and discover – to their great surprise, of course – that popular opinion is now X.

SANDRA COLLINS: Were you surprised when your attempts to buy influence in Washington and New York failed?

BENJAMIN SWORD HOPPNER: You're misrepresenting what I've set out to accomplish. The money is not intended to win me friends. All I expect from my donations is a change for the better, somewhere in the world.

SANDRA COLLINS: Better as defined by whom?

BENJAMIN SWORD HOPPNER: By myself.

SANDRA COLLINS: Even when the rest of the world thinks your conception of morality is somewhat warped? Possibly even fanatical?

BENJAMIN SWORD HOPPNER: Again, you invoke public opinion as if there were some coherent world reaction to my Code. I wish there was, let me tell you. I wish the world would take the trouble to study my Code before passing judgement on me.

SANDRA COLLINS: Then let's hear it; sum it up for us.

BENJAMIN SWORD HOPPNER: It is not a sound bite. You can read the full Code in my book or on the Internet.

SANDRA COLLINS: Why have you chosen to make your home in Miraflores? Is it because the people here are more susceptible to the propagation of your ideas than in the States?

BENJAMIN SWORD HOPPNER: Why do you load your questions with such hostility? How can you hope to find truth using language associated with infectious disease?

SANDRA COLLINS: Then let me defer to the language of others: how do you answer critics who claim you're building a cult here, with yourself as the godlike, omnipotent leader?

BENJAMIN SWORD HOPPNER: There is nothing divine here; a well-lived, moral life has no need of a god. And any allegation of cult tendencies is insane: cults suck money out of their followers; I give money to mine.

SANDRA COLLINS: Bribing them, in fact, to follow your prescription for model behaviour.

BENJAMIN SWORD HOPPNER: It is no more a bribe than is a salary.

SANDRA COLLINS: Surely there is a very great difference. You are using your considerable wealth to buy behaviour.

BENJAMIN SWORD HOPPNER: We live in a market economy. Money is central to all endeavours, good or evil. But it is only ever the means. Yes, I use money to achieve my goals, but it is the goals themselves that matter. Forgive me for teaching you your job, but you should be concerned with the good I am doing the world rather than the precise mechanics of how that good is achieved.

SANDRA COLLINS: But how can you claim to be doing good? You peddle sleaze, you've raked in billions from pornographic magazines and television channels—

BENJAMIN SWORD HOPPNER (interrupting): This is what makes me so angry ... why don't you people ever look beyond the headlines? I've explained a thousand times, but no one wants to ... I'm sorry, this is a waste of time. [Mr Hoppner terminated the interview by leaving the room.]

CHAPTER 2

Santa Tecla. One of the most damaged capital cities in all Latin America. I'd seen it occasionally on the news in the eighties, but never imagined I'd actually go there. Blurred footage shot by reckless camera crews had brought us sights more graphic than any child should be allowed to watch. Public executions, tanks shelling the houses of rebel snipers; by the time full-scale war reached Santa Tecla in the nineties, most of us switched off at first mention of the place.

Stepping off the plane into this black-spirited world, I moved fast. Freddy was way behind me in the Immigration queue, and I kept myself tucked out of sight to avoid giving him any excuse to move forward. But the baggage handlers stymied my attempt to get rid of him. Nothing appeared on the carousel for twenty minutes, and by the time the first London suitcases were emerging from the airport's bowels, Freddy had planted himself beside me.

'Bloody typical, isn't it?' he said, mopping the sweat off his neck. 'Boiling temperatures and no air conditioning.'

One of the delegates standing beside us was foolish enough to challenge him: 'They've had a few other things to think about,' she said indignantly, a finger tugging at the damp silk scarf around her neck. 'Running water and hospitals are a higher priority after thirty years of war.'

'Bollocks.' Freddy was too hot and irritated to be polite with this busybody. 'The amount of aid pouring into this country, they could have built a gleaming metropolis by now. But the air-conditioning money – and the running-water money, and the hospital money – is probably already stashed in el Presidente's Bahamian accounts.'

Neither Freddy nor Alice had been seated anywhere near me on the flight from Bermuda, and I'd pulled out the *Sunday Times* magazine to look again at the cover. 'A Madonna for All Seasons', it proclaimed. Then, in smaller letters that I really don't recall ever having seen before: 'The legend talks to Adrian Greenock'. It was that simple. A million possible names, and Freddy and I, quite independently, had both fallen victim to the same subconscious suggestion.

On each pillar in the baggage hall was taped a black-and-white poster image of Daedalus Foy, the British journalist who went missing around the time I was booking my flight. His was a household name, at least in a certain class of southern British household, and his disappearance had unleashed a flurry of speculation about the dangers of Santa

Tecla and the country as a whole. But the stories of kidnappers, drug gangs and reborn guerrilla groups didn't worry me. The only hard part I anticipated in this whole business was the lying. Life, once I'd got what I'd come for, would be a lonely hell, of course, but there was nothing much I could do about that.

From our position by the carousel, we could see Alice and her husband descending the stairs from Immigration, past the advertisements that featured grinning, airbrushed locals using Avis cars, Siemens computers and Motorola telephones. Leonard still looked exhausted, moving as if he valued Alice's grip on his arm more for support than postnuptial affection. They were trailing the last of the delegates down the stairs. Very few of the passengers appeared to belong in this country – the Latin faces were mostly limited to baggage handlers, customs officials and the military.

Soldiers were everywhere: not in the state of high alert that accompanies sudden crises, but sauntering along the corridors or leaning against baggage trolleys as if they'd been doing this beat for years. Which they probably had. In the six years since the official guerrilla ceasefire and the formation of a new government, the army had paradoxically continued to expand. Former guerrillas had been given uniforms and set to work patrolling the streets of Santa Tecla, the rebuilt factories and the emerging tourist centres. The new government suffered from the old delusion:

that an armed presence was a reassurance to visitors.

For me, soldiers bring out the worst of moods. Anywhere in the world I've been – and that's a lot of places, in search of a lot of different things – the sight of a soldier with an automatic weapon has always spoilt the moment. The one time I tried to organize a romantic weekend in Paris – Hôtel de Vendôme, dinner on Île St Louis – it fell apart because of a soldier and two gendarmes. They wandered into Eurostar's Gare du Nord first-class lounge and walked slowly between us, guns casually pointed at us for no reason. They can go anywhere they like in France, the Eurostar management pathetically explained. The whole journey back I was furious; the girl – she was called Katie, though it was a name I was now trying hard to forget – eventually turned her face to the window to cry.

A year later, I had a shouting match with a soldier. I won – he didn't say a word. It was past midnight and Katie and I were walking home along Buckingham Gate, full of good spirits of all kinds, when I happened to glance through the railings into the darkened grounds of the Palace. The soldier was down on one knee, his face black with cam cream, his rifle aimed directly at us. I'm generally sensible: I wouldn't raise my voice to a soldier in Africa. But I yelled at this man – kept yelling until he melted away into the royal shrubbery. Christ, they have live ammunition in those guns, and they kill time by drawing a bead on passing civilians?

I loathe it all.

Freddy hardly noticed the military presence. He chattered away about the appalling state of the country and the ugliness of the busybody delegate, and all the time I was thinking of that driver waiting outside. Freddy was like a leech: undetachable by any means short of outright confrontation. Somehow I couldn't quite bring myself to do that to him.

As it happened, all four of us cleared Customs at the same time; all four of us were waved through with barely a glance at our luggage. Perhaps the authorities were under special presidential instructions to extend extra courtesy to foreigners during conference week. Aid money can have useful side effects.

Smiling their goodbyes to us, Alice and Leonard – the spanking new husband who still hadn't spoken a word in my hearing – set off towards the car-hire counters.

'A whole week with her,' mused Freddy. 'Lucky bastard.'

'A whole lifetime with her,' I said. 'Still appeal to you?'

'Sure,' he said breezily. 'I'm a romantic. And if I could have only one girl, she's . . . I mean, look at that arse.'

Off to one side stood the woman with the sign. 'Mr Greenock' was scrawled in thick purple ink on a yellow board, underlined twice. I started moving towards her, but Freddy was quicker than me.

'*Buenos días, señorita,*' he called, his brash voice dragging heads round from every corner of the concourse. 'I'm Mr Greenock. This is Mr Weston.' He had his hand out and a big smile in place before I had a chance to say anything.

'Welcome to Santa Tecla, Mr Greenock. I am María.' The driver shook hands, then looked up at me. Her English was steady and confident, if strongly accented: 'You are a colleague of Mr Greenock?'

I stared at her for a moment, noting the reduction in respect her eyes accorded this additional baggage. She was a young woman, sombre-faced, with skin that was dark brown and curiously mottled around the left cheek. Thick wiry hair was scraped carefully back, secured over her neck with a fierce-toothed clip. Apparently she wasn't the sort of driver who adapted easily to unexpected passengers.

'I hope it is possible to book another room for you,' she said, taking out a mobile phone.

'Excuse us a moment,' I said brusquely.

Dumping my luggage at her feet, I grabbed Freddy's arm and hauled him off to the edge of the concourse.

'What are you doing?' I snarled, as soon as we were out of earshot.

'What? What's wrong?'

'My name here is Greenock! That's my driver.

30

If I give you a lift to Miraflores, I'm doing you a favour, understand? Not giving you licence to usurp me!'

The concourse was a noisy place, but in the pause after my outburst I swear I could hear my own heartbeat.

'Calm down, Mark,' he rasped, looking up at me with pleading eyes. 'I'm sorry, all right? It was just a little joke.'

'That woman is going with me to Miraflores and she knows my real name. That's funny to you?'

'Look, come on, friend, you can't expect us both to go as Greenock, can you?'

'I don't give a shit what you call yourself.'

'Let's just calm down, shall we? Get ourselves to a hotel and have a nice cold drink. Come on – I'll buy you dinner and we can talk it over. Fair's fair?'

I didn't reply. María had put away her phone and was watching us with a concerned tilt of her head. I started back towards her.

'Just keep calm,' whispered Freddy from somewhere behind me. 'They always think we're in control, so long as we're calm.'

The streets of Santa Tecla, at one time the epicentre of the civil war, were still a mess. The roads themselves were new smooth tarmac, courtesy – so a blue-starred sign informed us – of the European Union, but the shops and houses that lined them were shattered relics of a forgotten

31

Spanish age. Some of the shops had new glass in the windows, but their walls remained blackened by fire or streaked with propagandist paint. *FNR* scrawled in huge letters. Great chunks of stonework were missing from the corners and pillars of many buildings, where explosions had torn through the city's fabric. Bullet holes in the plasterwork were too numerous to count.

Rickety wooden scaffolding had been erected around a few wretched buildings, but no one seemed prepared to trust their life to it and it lay empty, like a decaying exoskeleton grimly clinging to a condemned carcass. One row of stately houses had been completely flattened, only a grand, balustraded marble staircase still standing to hint at the gentry that had once called this heap of rubble home.

A crucial element was missing from the usual cocktail of city life. The crowds that packed Santa Tecla's narrow streets had a muted, lethargic air, as if nothing in the city was worth rushing for. The only bustle came from the occasional group of children kicking a plastic football between abandoned cars. Traffic was minimal. Most of the vehicles were stationary, collapsed at the side of the road, many of them missing doors, wheels, windows or engines. A few were burnt out. All had that rusted, decrepit look that age and neglect bring so much faster in the tropics, barring the occasional gleaming SUV imported from the States by some lucky member of the new elite.

Freddy and I sat in silence, listening to María's sporadic observations on her gutted town. She drove us past the port, still out of action after a lucky guerrilla missile had holed an Argentinian cargo ship right in the harbour mouth. American cranes mounted on American flatboats were stationed around it, as they had been, without obvious result, ever since the ceasefire. Up the hill from the port, the old congress building was little more than a shell. It was the brutal artillery battle that had raged here which finally brought to the negotiating table a government forsaken by its former US allies.

We passed a funeral carriage, trundling reverently along in the shadow of a collapsing, desecrated cathedral. Polished black ornate wood, drawn by two ancient horses mantled in loosely knitted white wool nets. The driver was dressed in a black waistcoat, black bowler hat and black trousers. In his hands, a black whip. Next to the intricately carved flowers, cherubs, trumpets and crosses that decorated his carriage, he seemed dour – too humourless even for this job. Behind the glass windows, the plain coffin looked desperately cheap against that frilly ensemble. Freddy gave the carriage a second's glance before turning his attention to his fingernails.

To the west of the city centre was the district of Las Palmas. What had once been a quiet residential suburb was rapidly becoming the new commercial and political focus for the restructuring effort: Largely untouched by the fighting, beyond the usual wartime pillaging and graffiti, it alone still had the accommodation, services and infrastructure required by the new elite and the ever-expanding international community. At the heart of this district was the Via España, and it was on this elegant, tree-lined promenade that María had found us a couple of rooms.

'You are lucky,' she explained. 'The Buena Vista is the best hotel in Santa Tecla. It is completely booked up for the conference. But the Australian delegates cannot get here until tomorrow.'

'We're going to be surrounded by delegates? That *is* lucky,' said Freddy.

Irony was something María understood well. 'Who knows? Maybe they will do some reconstruction this year,' she said with a soft smile.

On the pavement opposite us, when we stopped for a red light, two women sat beside a fragment of torn sacking on which a few paltry offerings of vegetables wilted in the sun. A hotdog seller stood haughtily over them, haranguing them. Great tangles of electricity cables hung from the poles above. Three children, in scraps of T-shirts, were sucking at little polythene bags filled with pink and orange fluid – the cheapest means of getting the cheapest flavoured drinks to market. Behind them was a pharmacy; a guard, not in uniform, stood at the entrance, shotgun balanced against his hip, a belt of cartridges strung around his waist. His mirror shades were permanently fixed on the children.

The racial divide was evident: the beggars and the street vendors were Indian; the guys with the cars and the guns were all Hispanic.

'Nothing's improved yet?' I asked.

'We cannot complain. If the rest of the world is willing to give us money, we are grateful.' She shrugged, then, in a slightly mischievous voice, added: 'But it would be nice if, when they promise money, they give it to us before our children are grandfathers.'

'What about the roads?'

'Yes, the roads. We are happy with the roads. But, señor, do you know how many European goods we must promise to buy in return for this "gift"?'

Even philanthropy has its price.

The Buena Vista was brand new, its swimming pool and shopping mall still unfinished. Each passageway was carpeted in light blue, each room in steely business grey. The reception, lifts and corridors were packed with delegates speaking a dozen languages. Hotel staff, newly trained and unaccustomed to occupancy rates above twenty per cent, were scurrying about in barely concealed states of stress and panic.

Freddy's room was on the top floor, mine just below. I opened the French windows on to sweeping views of a bay filled with small fishing boats – the only vessels able to operate without the facilities of the port. The Pacific glowed gold, the sun hanging just above the horizon. Really, this whole business had begun on the other side of that ocean – the other side of the world. In Indonesia, the water had been cerulean. Katie taught me that extraordinary word. She loved hearing me misuse it whenever I could: cerulean neon lights in Ujung Pandang airport; feeling cerulean when she went off to work each morning; little Christopher's cerulean eyes.

After a long, wonderfully cold shower, I put on chinos and a new short-sleeved shirt and wandered down to Reception. Freddy was already there, waiting.

'Just popping out to buy something,' he said, dusting down the lapels of his linen jacket.

'Oh? What?'

'Why don't you have a drink at the bar? I'll meet you there.'

His hair was wet and combed hard back. He too had showered, but already sweat was breaking out across his forehead. The air in Reception was unpleasant: muggy and humid.

With Freddy gone, I found a corner of the bar directly under a ceiling fan and ordered a beer. Out of habit I checked it was a child-free zone, not that any families were showing their faces around the Buena Vista. Most of the people in the bar were men, most of the conversations cynical takes on reconstruction.

'The point is, it's no good just handing them a bag of cash and telling them to build five new hospitals,' barked the delegate at the table beside me.

'Of course not – their accounts are still all over the place,' agreed his colleague.

'No, we need to set up transparent procurement procedures, checks and balances, even census-data systems first. No point building a hospital in the wrong place, is there?'

What to do about Freddy? He was a nuisance: a dislikeable individual who had, in almost no time at all, wheedled himself into my life, hijacking my plans and threatening my anonymity. I would have liked nothing more than to abandon him. But if I left first thing in the morning, giving María some plausible explanation, how long would it be before Freddy got himself to Miraflores? From what I'd read it was a small town: we were highly likely to cross paths again. If I left him behind he would be upset, certainly, but would that make him a threat to me when he reached Miraflores? Not physically, perhaps, but the inescapable fact remained: he knew my real name. Nothing would kill my chances with Hoppner more quickly than to have an angry Freddy turn up and denounce me.

Three new arrivals took a table near by.

'I'm not even covering the conference,' said one. 'Just trying to find out what's happened to Daedalus.'

'We're all keeping our fingers crossed,' muttered another.

Slick Latin men were gathering in the bar,

already groomed for the night clubs, with powerful belts around tight waists, aviator mirror shades and shining steel-capped cowboy boots. Some were sidling, some stepping confidently up to their foreign prey, promising the best war sights, the cheapest currency, the most accommodating whores. Not all of the delegates were refusing their services.

The place was suffocating.

One of those abrupt decisions, born of irritation and sudden intolerance: I picked up my beer and walked out. Out of the bar; out of the hotel. Already it was dark. I hadn't noticed the transition. First nights in the tropics are always disorienting. The Via España was nearly empty – this was not a place of convivial street nightlife – although a few groups of shadowy figures stood huddled together at intervals along the promenade. Some of them were eating from small packages; the smell of chilli, rancid grease and burnt maize filled the street.

Away from the bar's ceiling fans, the air was hotter still. No wind in this enclosed lowland spot. Sweat dampened the back of my neck, but I felt better for being outside. No one here was bragging, scorning or pontificating. The darkness of the promenade swallowed me up, its meagre scattering of streetlamps barely intruding on my quiet anonymity.

I wondered if Alice and her husband were still in Santa Tecla. Had they set off immediately for their honeymoon resort? For a fanciful moment, it occurred to me that they might be staying in one of the other hotels on the Via España, that Alice might even step outside, like me, for a few minutes. A trivial thing, which possibly took place only in my imagination: as we boarded the new aircraft on Bermuda, I thought I felt her warm little hand brush mine. The sensation of that touch, real or not, had lingered.

Taxis came and went, drawing up just yards from the Buena Vista entrance to minimize the time their delegate passengers were exposed to the harsh realities of the country they'd come to reconstruct. From my dark corner at the edge of the hotel, all I saw of them was the occasional flash of polished shoe or styled hair as they slipped from car to marbled entrance hall.

Only one other gringo was walking the street. Like me, he was quite a bit larger than most of the local guys, and perhaps he too derived a complacent sense of security from his size. Yet he stood out far more than I did, and when I saw him pass through the first pool of lamplight I couldn't help wondering if his evening walk wasn't a little foolhardy. Whereas my hair is thick, dark brown and could almost pass for Hispanic, his was blond and clipped short. My nose, cheeks and chin have a roundness to them and my skin is reasonably dark for an Englishman's; his face was unmistakably Nordic, the sharpness of his cheekbones visible even from across the street. Most revealingly, whereas I stood slouched against a corner of the building like any number of the locals around me, this man was walking fast, head turning from side to side as his cold eyes scanned the Via España. His movements radiated energy – quite out of place in that town.

But while I might have been better camouflaged to the casual observer, the blond guy was clearly more at home. As he reached the first group of men, he stopped and said something to them. What it was I have no idea, but he was using their own language. A Spanish-speaking delegate out looking for local feedback on the reconstruction process? Hardly. In his sharp black leather jacket and heavy boots, he couldn't have been less like the suits who filled the hotel. The men he addressed were shaking their heads and already he was walking on.

It was the movement that drew my eye back down the street. While the blond guy was putting the same terse questions to the next group of loiterers, I became aware of another man following silently in his tracks. This one blended completely with his environment. He was very dark – pure Indian blood was my guess – with lanky black hair, and despite the heat he wore a long black woollen coat. Whereas the blond guy walked confidently down the centre of the promenade, his tail was careful to avoid the streetlamps, cutting from doorway to tree trunk with cat-like agility. Only the swish of his coat gave away the urgency of his apparently casual progress up the road.

The blond guy had no idea he was being followed.

At first I was just curious about this odd, secretive dance moving along the Via España, the big gringo stopping at every group of men to repeat his questions, the Indian slipping from shadow to shadow behind him. But it didn't take long for me to work out how the stalking might end. Further up the promenade the lights were fewer, the people more scattered. What if the blond guy headed off down one of those narrow side streets? What would happen when he reached that dark, empty patch of urban terrain that is found in every city – particularly in war-torn, tropical capitals? Even a simple mugging could be dangerous. Quite possibly the stalker had something worse in mind. A knife in the guts, a kidnapping at gunpoint. The blond guy's obvious strength wouldn't help him then.

Already the two men were moving beyond the relatively well-lit area around the hotel. Two policemen leaning against heavy motorbikes chatted to the four Buena Vista security men and idly watched a couple of prostitutes work the hotel entrance. None of them noticed the stalking; possibly none would have cared. It seemed to me that the Indian was drawing closer to his target.

I began strolling up the road.

An easy pace – I didn't want to attract attention. It was exciting, of course, the slight edge of fear only heightening the thrill. I'd played this game

41

before – prowling through Asian cities at night, senses alert to all the dangers of an urban battlefield – but never with such clear purpose. On this occasion, it was just possible that the blond guy's life was at stake. I felt a surge of adrenalin course through me.

As we moved beyond the main concentration of people, I gradually picked up speed until I was level with the Indian across the street. He didn't see me; his eyes were locked on his gringo target.

Ahead of us, the blond guy stopped to talk to another local. The Indian dropped into a doorway to wait; I walked on ahead. When the blond guy received the usual shrug and continued onwards, I stepped into his path.

He stopped still. No surprise, no reaction.

'You're being followed,' I said.

At first, he didn't reply. Nor did he turn round. His grey-blue eyes were fixed, unblinking, on my face. I was very slightly disappointed: I'd expected at least to freak him out a little. I had the better understanding of the situation – it was my responsibility to teach him not to walk alone at night in a place like this.

'Do you speak English?' I asked.

'Where is he?' His voice was whisper soft, but there was nothing weak about it. Each word clearly enunciated, the urgency in his tone vivid.

'Just over—'

'Don't point.'

Again, a whisper, but a command of such force

that I dropped my arm immediately. Suddenly I didn't feel so sure of myself. I could smell his sweat – not stale, but warm and alive.

'What is he doing?' Completely calm, his eyes machine steady. Thirty-five, maybe forty years old. British accent – efficient, classless.

I dropped my voice to match his: 'Staring at us. At me.'

'Don't stare back.'

I nodded silently. Somehow this man's authority was unquestionable.

'Look at me. Smile like I'm an old friend. See him through the edges of your vision. How far back is he?'

The Indian had edged forward from the doorway and now stood partially obscured by a tree, watching. A plastic bag, shredded refuse carried by a slight gust, caught against his leg.

'About forty yards. Level with the last side street you passed. I thought he might try to mug you.'

A flicker of a smile. 'Describe him.'

'Quite short. Thick black hair. Long black coat. Dark skin.'

'Is the coat patched? Blue denim patches?'

I squinted into the darkness, trying to see while still keeping my eyes on the blond guy. 'I can't tell. Possibly.'

'On his left boot. Silver duct tape.'

Looking down I saw a slight glint. 'Yes,' I said in surprise. 'How did you know?'

'I gave it to him.'

'You know him?' I said. Then, as the figure behind the tree moved, 'He's running to the side stir—'

The blond guy didn't wait for me to finish. With a speed that astonished me, he whipped round and sprinted towards the Indian. It wasn't fast enough. Already the black coat was disappearing into the side street. A double pounding of boots on tarmac. The blond guy charged round the corner and out of view. For a moment, I just stood there, too amazed to do anything. What the hell was he thinking? The sound of sprinting feet grew fainter. My heart was beating double time on his behalf: I dreaded to think how the chase might end.

Hurrying over to the side street, I peered into the narrow blackness and glimpsed the blond guy walking back towards me. Alone.

'A maze,' he muttered as he reached me. 'Impossible to find him in those streets. Thanks, anyway.'

'No problem.' I found myself taking deep breaths to calm down again. 'I thought he might be dangerous.'

'He is.'

'So you do know him.'

'Neighbours,' he said cryptically. 'Little bastard must have heard I was after him and guessed the only place I wouldn't look was right behind me. You here for the conference?'

'Yes.' Uncomfortable to lie, but I didn't want to initiate a lot of awkward questions. 'You too?'

He smiled again at that. Not a warm smile. 'Just visiting. Anyway, thanks for your help. I have to check a few places our friend might try to spend the night.' He turned away. As an afterthought he called over his shoulder, 'You shouldn't walk around here in the dark.'

Then he was gone, striding away down that shadowy side street.

Freddy still hadn't returned by the time I got back to the bar. When he finally appeared, twenty minutes after I'd ordered a new beer, it was with a spring in his step that suggested he'd been shopping for either cocaine or women. I didn't ask which. We found a spot at the back of the hotel restaurant, well away from the three vast banquet-style, flower-laden tables reserved for the delegates. White wine was already cooling on ice for them, while a dozen waiters laid out their first course: a concoction of avocado, shellfish and sun-dried tomatoes.

Freddy immediately ordered the same, followed by 'whatever they're having next'; I chose tortillas stuffed with peppers and chicken.

'That's it. Get into the local spirit,' he said. 'Although you'll probably look more suspicious eating that rubbish than if you just stuck with hamburgers.'

'Suspicious?'

'You're supposed to be an undercover journalist, remember?'

'Supposed to be? That's what I am.'

'Sure,' he grinned. 'Course you are.'

Our waiter, wearing a badge that identified him with 'Hello, my name is José', brought us two new beers and promised to take good care of us.

'Tell me something,' I said to Freddy. 'Doesn't your company organize transport for you?'

'My soft drinks company, you mean?' he giggled. The action curled his upper lip grotesquely towards his nose. 'Come on, friend, you saw the magazine. You know what I'm up to.'

'And what's that?'

'Same as you, obviously.' He raised his beer. 'Paying a visit to Benjamin Sword Hoppner.' When I didn't reply he took a swig, then fixed his creased eyes on me. 'Friend, undercover journalists don't tell people they're undercover journalists.'

His starter arrived and I watched him eat in silence. The sun-dried tomatoes were picked off first, skewered all together on the fork and consumed in one single, oily mouthful. The avocado went next, similarly wolfed down. Only the shellfish got serious attention, each piece of crab or shrimp being savoured individually.

'I knew a journalist once,' he said, while his mouth was still finishing off the last of the crab. 'Sold him a house. Famous chap – Larry something. Been rude about the Queen on *Newsnight* so I "forgot" to tell him the owner was prepared to take fifty grand less because he'd found subsidence. Larry Muir – that was his name. You're not a bit like him.'

46

'You're an estate agent?' I could just see it: the easy charm, the comfort with blurred truths. Not that I was in any position to criticize, never having held down a job for more than a few months – until the visa ran out, the tourist season ended, or the urge to hit the road became irrepressible. I always did some kind of work – living with Katie, I made sure I paid my way – but I just couldn't handle the serious, high-salary jobs with their grey uniforms, desk diaries and career ladders.

He answered with a different question: 'Why did you choose Greenock, by the way? I've been thinking about that. Bloody odd us both picking an unusual name like that. Me, it just popped into my head.'

'Really?' I smiled. 'So what's your real name?'

'Come on! Hey, call me Freddy.'

José returned to clear away his plate just as the delegates started pouring into the room. Some walked stiffly to their places, still unsure of their new colleagues. Others had already become best friends or flirting couples, perhaps resurrecting illicit relationships begun at the last conference. Another waiter – 'Hello, my name is Simeon' – arrived with my tortillas and a bland stew for Freddy.

'Yours looks so much better,' he muttered.

I nodded sympathetically, concealing my delight. The tortillas were delicious. Even if they hadn't been I would have enjoyed pretending they were.

'OK, cards on the table,' Freddy declared

abruptly. 'I'm travelling under a false name to Miraflores, where I plan to spin a tale of deserving good deeds to Mr Hoppner, after which I expect to walk away with one of his famously generous handouts. You're using a false name, you have the *Sunday Times* article. I'm assuming you're after the same thing?'

'So you're a con man?'

'I'm an opportunist, like you. The money's there; he wants to give it away. All we have to do is take it.'

'If it's so easy, why aren't thousands of people visiting him?'

'They will, friend, they will. Once the word gets around. Won't be so easy to pull the wool over his eyes then, I'm sure, but you and I are early birds. We deserve our prize.'

'I don't see things quite the way you do.'

Freddy was chewing at the edges of a grainy roll. Now he let it drop on to the tablecloth, where it lay between us like a mauled rodent.

'You're not feeling bad about this, are you? It's porn money, Mark. Ill-gotten gains. He wants to give it away. That's his whole aim in life. Maybe it's his way of making good – repenting for a life of sin. Maybe he really is a philanthropist. Maybe he's just plain mad. Who the fuck cares? The point is, he *wants* us to come knocking on his door.'

'I doubt he has what you call "opportunists" in mind.'

'OK, so maybe we'll make up a few things when

48

we talk to him, but anyone that stupid deserves to be taken for the occasional ride. And what difference will it make to him to lose a couple of million? Whereas for us – for me, at least – that kind of money would mean a cataclysmic improvement in my standard of living.'

'Faster car?' I suggested. 'Plusher house?'

'Sure, why not?'

'Fancy clothes? Luxury holidays?'

'It's OK to want these things, friend. And it's not going to hurt anyone if you reach out and take them.'

I couldn't help smiling at the innocent, flawed way he justified his guilt. His victimless crime. 'Sorry to disappoint you, Freddy,' I said. 'I'm just not interested in Ferraris.'

'Look,' he sighed, apparently not believing me. He turned to indicate the delegates, while his other hand came up to smooth back a strand of unruly hair. 'See these guys? All these smart intellectuals come to raise the new country out of the ashes of the old? Think about who they work for: the World Bank, Oxfam, Christian Aid, endless other NGOs. Every one of them a saint. Devoting their lives to the poorest countries in the world.

'But now see what they actually do, day to day? Eat well, drink well, use hotel rooms paid for by charities or government aid to shag each other in, and all the time they're working out how many scuba dives and jungle safaris they can get away with on expenses. These are the saints, Mark! Why should we ordinary human beings be any better?'

By now his eyes were almost pleading, less trying to persuade me than to convince himself that what he was doing wasn't fundamentally wrong. God knows, I understood that urge – I'd been having the same unwinnable debate with myself ever since I'd set my sights on Hoppner. And although I could tell myself I had better motives than Freddy – that the money wasn't for me but for the son I would never see again – I couldn't deny we were both setting out to rob a philanthropist.

I looked away, spotted Simeon and beckoned him over. The noise from the delegates' tables was approaching a roar. Waiters were continually reappearing with new bottles of wine. At the end of a table, one delegate was slumped back in his chair causing his neighbour to prod him with a stubby finger. Such a distance from the outside world where a quietly self-confident Englishman had chased a vagrant Indian through the deserted, shadowy side streets of Las Palmas. Why had he been looking for him? What was the deal with those two men? Were they friends? Employer and employee? And why had the blond guy said the Indian was dangerous?

'The bill, please,' I called to Simeon.

'Christ, I was going to pay, wasn't I?' said Freddy. 'Would you mind taking care of this one? I spent all my cash just now.'

'Oh, that's OK, Freddy. They accept credit cards here.'

'Yeah but I can't use mine – they're in my real name. Wouldn't want you to discover that now, would I?' he smirked.

At that precise moment, finding out his name seemed to me the most urgent thing in the world.

'You could put it on your hotel bill,' I said, as Simeon brought the slip of paper.

'Tell you what. You pay this time, I'll go to the bank tomorrow and the rest of the trip's on me. Fair's fair?'

I let him dangle on his own plea for a while, then scribbled my room number on the bill and left a few dollars on the table. As I walked towards the lobby I looked back. Freddy was following me, a quick grin on his face. The dollars were gone. Simeon was nowhere near the table.

'Thanks, friend. Wish I could say it was a good meal, but . . . too bad. Why not join me for a nightcap?'

'I'm off to bed.'

'Come on. Just a little whisky from the minibar. I don't want you sleeping on bad feelings.'

Shaking my head, I walked across the lobby to a waiting lift. Freddy slipped in next to the buttons. He pressed the top one, waggling a forbidding finger up at me.

'Mark, really, it's not nice to refuse a drink with someone. We're travelling to Miraflores together – even if you are an undercover journalist, it's only right we should be friends.'

I simply didn't have the energy to argue, let alone

push him out of the way. The lift arrived at the top floor and I followed him along the corridor to his room.

'You'll love it. There's a terrace and everything. You should have seen the view in daylight.'

'I did see it.'

'Not the same, though. Not like up here.'

He pulled open the minibar and found a couple of Jack Daniel's miniatures. I don't particularly like whisky but I took the glass he offered without a word.

'D'you want ice? I have to have ice. I should have thought of it on the way up.' He deposited his glass on the television. 'There's a dispenser on the fifth floor. Make yourself at home.'

Pointing me to an armchair by the bed, he scooped up the ice bucket and hurried out of the room.

The silence that followed Freddy's departure was so conspicuous I realized his insistent voice had completely overwhelmed my senses for the last hour. It had a lazy twang that I've heard described as mid-Atlantic, though I've never known what that's supposed to mean. His speech rhythms too were unusual: unbalanced, sometimes slow, sometimes fast, but with no real logic as to the choice of one or other.

The effect of the time difference was making itself felt. It was something like four in the morning back in England. Just thinking about that made me sway slightly on my feet and I moved quickly across to the armchair. Sinking into its new feather cushions, I closed my eyes.

When I opened them again, I was staring straight at Freddy's hand luggage. Freddy Greenock, whose real name was . . . Where would he keep those credit cards? Had he brought his real passport? I only had to reach forward a few inches.

The bag was open. At the top was the *Sunday Times* magazine. Beneath that, a folded jumper. I glanced at the door. Freddy had left it slightly open; I'd hear him coming back. He'd only been gone a minute; the ice machine was six floors away. Quickly, I turned back to the bag and ran both hands down the insides, searching for pockets.

What the hell was his name?

I found something. A hard, thin shape inside the lining of the bag. And there was a zip. I turned round.

'Oh, friend, what are you up to?' he asked sorrowfully.

I froze. He'd left the ice bucket outside. He was holding a gun.

'What are you doing?' I stammered.

'What are *you* doing?'

Kicking the door shut, he walked across to the bed and sat beside the travel bag, staring up at me. I eased my hands out of the bag.

'Just . . . looking,' I said, my voice unsteady. 'Where did you get that thing?'

'What were you looking for?'

He raised the gun slightly. It was an automatic,

I knew that much. Rusty streaks ran the length of the barrel. I looked back at his eyes, trying to work out my chances. I had no idea how to handle him. Surely he wasn't going to shoot me just for snooping? But what if the gun went off by mistake? Did he have any idea how to use it?

'I wanted to know who you were.'

Freddy nodded slowly. He used his left hand to move the bag aside. 'Can't you trust me as Freddy Greenock? It would help a lot if you could trust me, you know.' There was a pause as we gazed at each other. 'I trust you, Mark.'

Very carefully, as if handling precious crystal, he laid the automatic on the bedspread between us and drew back his hand. We both stared at it for a moment.

'Is it loaded?'

'Yes.'

The gun had a bevelled grip around the handle, worn and stained. Overall, it looked more bleak than threatening.

'Does it work?'

'I tried the mechanism when it was empty, and it seemed all right.'

'You bought it when you went out?'

He stroked his chin, still looking at the gun.

I rubbed my eyes. The jetlag had temporarily dissolved in the sudden terror brought on by that thing. Now I just felt exhausted.

'Why the fuck are you buying guns, Freddy?' I yelled. 'What kind of stupid idiot are you?'

Unperturbed by my outburst, he continued staring at the weapon, his expression at some uncertain point between lust and superstitious fear.

'Maybe it was a bit stupid,' he admitted. 'I read about this guy who bought a gun the moment he arrived in any banana republic, although I must admit I've never done it before. But I just thought . . . this is quite a dangerous place, isn't it? Wasn't there some journalist who disappeared here the other week? And, you know, they're so easy to get hold of.' He looked up, suddenly pleased with himself. 'We could get you one, too. Tomorrow morning. It's so simple, you just go up to the stallholders and make a sign with your hands like . . .'

He broke off in the middle of forming a child's finger pistol, dropping his arm.

'I wasn't really threatening you,' he muttered. 'I was expecting you to have a look. That's why I went out.'

'This is crazy.'

'Don't you see? It means you're exactly the kind of person I hoped you were: nothing ventured, nothing gained, hey?'

I stood up.

'Friend, be sensible. We're in the same boat. Why not join forces? We'll be much more convincing as a double act. If two different Brits turn up on Hoppner's doorstep around the same time it could all get very messy, but if we work out a plan together . . . look!' He lunged for the travel bag and pulled out some papers. 'I've already got letters of reference and full details of the good works I'm planning. You could join me in that if you want.'

The idea of doing anything in partnership with this man was repellent to me. But at the same time the sense of what he was saying was clear. Much as I disliked him – didn't trust him – a joint approach to Benjamin Sword Hoppner was far more likely to succeed.

'I'll think about it,' I said.

'That's great,' he beamed. 'That's really great. Let's drink to that.'

Flicking his hair out of his eyes, he reached for my glass, pressed it into my hand, then grabbed his own. His eyes turned serious.

'Wait! One thing.' He put down his glass. 'Your passports. Where are they?'

My passports. Plural. I produced them from my back pocket. One genuine Mark Weston passport and one made-in-Ilford Mark Greenock passport.

'What about them?'

'Well, we can't both be Greenock,' he said. 'You'll have to get rid of that thing.'

'Why me? Why don't you change to your real name?'

He giggled a little. 'Friend, you don't know much about this business, do you? Tell me the truth. Is this the first time you've tried anything like this?'

I nodded.

'I thought so. Well, it won't be the last. Once you get a taste for it . . .'

'It will be the last.'

Chuckling, he inclined his head – an ambiguous gesture. I could just see him conning little old ladies out of their pensions. 'If you want to use a false name, you have to protect that name every second of the day and night. You have to live that name and never once let anyone know your real one. It's like a sealed container underwater: it works fine as long as there are no holes, but just one puncture and no amount of patching will ever make it totally secure again.'

'So?' The lecturing annoyed me even more than the cajoling or the pleading.

'So you didn't protect it. First time we asked you what your name was, you gave away your real identity.'

'I could hardly say Greenock after you'd just come up with that name.'

'Makes no difference. Your false identity is punctured. No amount of patching can save it. Mine is still intact. See, that's just experience, I'm afraid.'

The passport had cost me two hundred pounds. The forger had even given it an authentically battered look to complement the three Immigration stamps he'd randomly awarded me for Morocco, Singapore and Thailand. It felt comforting between my fingers: a shield against the uncertain world I was about to enter.

Freddy was holding a cigarette lighter.

'It's got to go. I'm sorry, Mark. If it's any consolation, you'll probably find it easier using your real name the first time.'

My fingers remained tightly closed around the passport. He tried tugging, let go, gave an uncertain laugh and held out the lighter.

'You should do it. Really. It'd be good for you to do it.'

The lighter was chrome – polished and loved. It hadn't occurred to me that Freddy smoked. Thinking back, I remembered him getting through at least two cigarettes in that Bermudan café. But he hadn't smoked once in the hotel. Perhaps it was a social thing, an affection he liked to exhibit around women he wanted.

'Really. It's got to be done,' he said.

I flicked open the lighter and touched the flame to the edge of the passport. It was a remarkably painful thing to do. The moment the red cover began to singe I wanted to pull it away. Freddy brought an ashtray over.

'Actually, friend, we should take this on to the terrace.' His eyes flashed upwards. 'Smoke detector, I mean.'

It wasn't catching. I followed him outside, moving the flame from cover to inside pages, fanned out to allow the oxygen to circulate. The thin paper caught immediately and I almost dropped the passport as the flames rose up around my hand. Hurriedly, Freddy placed the ashtray on a

58

low table. As the flames grew hot, I laid my dying identity to rest.

'You owe me,' I told him.

'It's OK.' He rubbed my back with his flattened palm. 'It's going to be OK.'

Hello. My name is Benjamin Sword Hoppner. My mission is the propagation of Good at the expense of Evil. I have spent my life examining what it means to be good and what it takes to encourage Good. My confident belief is that the world contains many more good people than is usually apparent. People who want to help others, who want to promote peace between all human beings, who want to live – and encourage others to live – by a strong moral code, regardless of race, religion or culture.

Regrettably, many good people are frustrated in their laudable ambitions by one thing: money. For every Peabody or Getty, there must be a thousand people who would like nothing more than to devote their lives to good works, but who do not have the funds to bring their dreams to fruition. If you are such a person, I would like to help you.

My door is always open to good people seeking financial or spiritual help. The journey to <u>Miraflores</u> is not an easy one, but the effort is worth making. Not only will you be able to see the work I am doing with this model society, but my associates and I guarantee you a warm welcome, an attentive ear and extremely generous support. But please, come only if you are absolutely sure of your moral goodness. Any person who is truly good will know it in themselves, but should your modesty leave you uncertain I suggest you consult my <u>Code.</u> If you see yourself reflected there, then I very much look forward to meeting you.

CHAPTER 3

Until Freddy got involved, my undertaking had seemed straight-forward. Somehow I had to raise two hundred thousand pounds for Christopher – lump-sum maintenance – and the most promising source by far was Benjamin Sword Hoppner. The moral dimension bothered me, but I envisaged no other problem or risk: how dangerous can an American philanthropist be? The prospect of travelling through one of the most backward parts of Central America might have deterred others, but for years I'd sought out exactly that kind of environment. I loved what others hated about the Third World: the anarchy, the disorder, the dirt and spontaneity. For me, a visit to Hoppner was a chance to see a new corner of the globe – not exactly a high price to pay for the potential windfall that would resolve my miserable quandary.

Besides, I really had no choice. To some people, a couple of hundred grand might be small change. But when you're earning at most fifteen thousand a year from a medley of casual and seasonal jobs, that kind of money is simply not in the picture.

My parents had lived too easy a diplomatic lifestyle and died too young to bother with savings, and Foreign Office support had come to an end with the schooling they had paid for. My aunt and uncle were lousy money managers, keeping their capital in treasury bonds throughout the stock-market boom and resisting the temptations of the Internet bandwagon until exactly the wrong moment. The only money they had now was in their house and pensions. No way was I going to ask for any of that.

My friends, scattered around the world, were always short of cash, and no bank would have lent that kind of sum to a wanderer with zero credit rating. To earn two hundred grand through serious employment – the only honourable solution, I suppose – would have meant a decade shackled to some soulless desk. I know that would have been the right thing to do; I also know it would have killed me. Short of hoping for a spectacular streak of luck in Vegas, or bursting into a bank with guns blazing, I was completely out of ideas until Hoppner made his announcement.

When I read about his offer, I considered just telling him my situation and asking for the money. He might almost have approved of my 'cause'. But a little research made it clear that Hoppner's bequests were offered only to people organizing charitable projects. He never just handed cash to individuals, however troubled their circumstances. So a little fabrication became necessary. It felt like a challenge: to play the saint long enough to scoop the jackpot. It was even a little exciting. A new name, a convincing story and an air ticket – that's all it would take.

Freddy was a complication, of course, but it wasn't until our first morning in Santa Tecla that I had my confidence truly shaken.

Our brand-new hotel had an unusual feature: an immaculate garden of potted plants that extended right out into the Via España. A cordon of steel wires went some way towards protecting the minia-ture palms, orchids and fountain from the general public, but it was a patrol of six armed security guards that kept the street vendors and beggars away from our al fresco breakfast tables. At any one time, if a guest cared to look up from his croissants, it was also possible to count at least eight policemen scattered around the Via España, every one of them ready to run to the assistance of the private security team.

I'd already watched one scrawny boy try to approach our table, a string of cheap watches and pink plastic mirrors clutched in each fist. As he reached the taut steel wires and, with an angelic smile on his thin face, made his charming English pitch – 'Here, for your lady, for your lady' – two security guards descended on him with frightening rapidity and plucked him and his tiny livelihood away from our luxurious enclave.

On this particular morning, a further dimension

had been added to the security arrangements. On the opposite side of the Via España stood the gleaming glass façade of El Palacio de Congresos José Delgado, built two years earlier and thus far only ever used by the reconstruction mafia. Santa Tecla had not yet made it on to the list of attractive venues for international business jamborees. Now, in readiness for the first plenary session of the conference, a line of polished policemen stood to attention along the third step of the building, waiting for their honoured guests to dab away the breakfast crumbs and shuffle across the promenade.

The salty morning air was bristling with official weaponry.

The civilian residents of Santa Tecla were also out in force. A sizeable crowd of onlookers was building – the well-shod and the dispossessed rubbing shoulders to catch a glimpse of these all-important foreigners who held the future of the country in their hands. As the Via España filled, more police arrived to exert some kind of control over the chaotic assembly. Breakfasting in style before all these observers was becoming embarrassing.

'Friend, you're not eating. Got to get your strength up. Big day.' Across the table from me, Freddy had already demolished a large plate of eggs Benedict, which he'd doused with Worcester sauce, followed by four pancakes swimming in maple syrup. Now he was leaning back, cradling a globular cup of coffee in one hand and stroking a palm leaf with the other. 'Is the sun at tanning strength yet, d'you think?'

I turned back from the busy street and took a bite of toast. Freddy smiled approvingly. A moment later, he was staring over my shoulder, eyes wide with concern.

'Oh, Christ, what are they doing to that poor kid?'

Some way up the Via España, two police-men had the watch-and-mirror vendor gripped between them, and were taking turns to beat him across the shoulders with their batons. The boy looked little more than ten years old. He was stumbling from one foot to the other as each blow knocked him forward. Not a sound came from him; the only noise audible over the hotel's piped music was the chatter of the crowd and the hum of a thousand dripping, rattling air-conditioners.

I lowered my tight fists below the tablecloth and looked back at the news articles Freddy had brought. A lot were duplicates of my own, but he'd managed to find a few Hoppner stories I'd missed in Internet archives.

'Bloody thugs,' muttered Freddy.

'Have you actually met anyone who's received a grant from Hoppner?' I said in a slightly uneven voice. That boy's face was not going to be easily forgotten. 'I called some of the projects listed on his website – the water purification team in Mali, the school for the blind in Canada – but I didn't get a chance to visit them.'

'He gave them the money, right?' Freddy mopped a dribble of coffee from his chin with the corner of the tablecloth.

'You didn't bother to contact any?' I asked, slightly incredulous.

'What would I talk about with a blind-school teacher? Where's the common ground?'

I couldn't answer that. 'I spoke to three people who'd visited Hoppner. Apparently, it's very simple: he just wants to meet you, find out what you're like. Then – if he's happy – he writes you a cheque.'

'See? Nothing to it,' grinned Freddy.

The smell of disinfectant wafted across our table. All around us, delegates were buried in their newspapers, enjoying the last few rays of sun before internment in the conference centre. None of them seemed interested in the little dose of justice that had been dispensed for their amusement. I couldn't help looking once more towards the boy. But he and his uniformed persecutors had disappeared into the crowd. There was nothing I could have done, I told myself.

I was about to turn back when a different figure caught my attention. About a hundred yards up the Via España, disappearing and reappearing intermittently as the crowd milled around him, was a short man in a woollen coat. The distance was too great to see the silver tape on his boot –

or even the blue denim patches the blond guy had mentioned – but I knew from his bent posture and the thick black hair tumbling over his collar that this was the same Indian I'd watched creep along this same street the night before.

The only thing different was the ice-cream trolley he was pushing.

What had the Englishman said? *He's dangerous.* Why? Scanning the crowd, I looked for the blond guy, but every head in the street was dark. The Indian was moving slowly, careful not to knock anyone with his trolley. His eyes were fixed on the ground – surely an ice-cream vendor should be engaging with the public, drumming up business?

What was he doing here, anyway? He was from out of town, the blond guy had implied. He was behaving, the previous night, like some kind of criminal. And now he was selling ice-creams? It didn't add up.

For a moment, I considered speaking to one of the many policemen on hand. *He's dangerous.* But in what way was he dangerous? What could I possibly say to the police? Even if the blond guy had been chasing him, that didn't mean the Indian was guilty of any crime. Perhaps there was simply some vendetta between the two men. As I watched, the Indian pushed his trolley past a policeman, his eyes still firmly down.

Stepping forward, the policeman put a hand on his shoulder.

The briefest of conversations, and the Indian

removed the lid of his trolley to extract an orange-wrapped ice-cream. The policeman did not pay him, just took the ice-cream and waved him brusquely on. Replacing the lid, the Indian lowered his eyes once more and vanished into the crowd.

How ridiculous it would be to run to the police now. What on earth would I say? Be careful – that ice-cream may be poisoned. *He's dangerous!*

I concentrated on the articles. 'Did you read this one from the *Tulsa Post?*' I passed it across when Freddy looked blank. 'They ran it the first time Hoppner was prosecuted. It's a useful summary of his early life – explains a little why he thinks the way he does.'

Flicking the print-out back across the table, Freddy reached for his sunglasses. 'Your enthusiasm's great, really, but we don't need to know what Little League team he played for.'

'Yes, but it talks about his—'

'Mark, relax. This isn't complicated. He's going to be a pushover: a naïve Yank who actually believes there are such things as Right and Wrong. We'll breeze in with our charming English accents, nicely dressed – you might want to do something about that jacket – polite, educated . . . he'll be eating out of our hands.'

I glanced round. A starved, limping dog was wandering hopefully along the edge of the street, past the Via España regulars: a broken crone, missing an arm and most of her teeth, huddled beneath the swaying aerial roots of a fig tree; strutting taxi owners and import warehouse managers – fat men fuelling their bellies with hotdogs and contempt for the rest of the world.

There were three more articles. The shock came in the last one. My eye caught that word straight away.

'Jesus,' I said. 'What's this about suicides?'

I looked up at Freddy. His calm was unperturbed.

'Oh, that article's ridiculous,' he chuckled. 'So melodramatic.'

It wasn't the reaction I had expected. I re-read the short text. Minimal information. 'It refers to an earlier *Newsweek* story.' I flicked once more through the print-outs. 'Do you have it?'

'I think I meant to look but never got round to it. Low priority. What's the connection to Hoppner?'

'Five suicides in Miraflores. His home town.' It astonished me that Freddy could be so unconcerned – uninterested, even.

'Listen, Mark, this is a fucked-up country. A lot of very desperate people. That boy we just saw. He gets hauled off to prison – what if he never comes out? How's his mother going to feel? His father? Hell, I'd be tempted to get out the sleeping pills if I had to live here.'

A guilt-stricken delegate returning to the hotel paused to drop a coin into the lap of the crone. Such generosity must have been rare in those parts for she stood up to thank him, though her legs were so thin it seemed impossible they could support her. A squeak of gratitude made it out of her sagging throat and she reached out to grip the wrist of the suddenly alarmed delegate. But the ever-vigilant police seemed unwilling to harass her – this creature who could be somebody's mother, somebody's sister, could have been theirs if the ghastly randomness of war had played out a fraction differently.

'He probably doesn't have any parents,' I muttered.

'Not the point, friend. What I'm trying to say is there're suicides every day, all over the country.'

'This is a Catholic society. It's against their religion to kill themselves.'

'Right. And I'm sure they're all sending tithes to Rome every month, as well.'

I lifted the article. 'This doesn't bother you?'

'Of course it bothers me. I'm human, aren't I? But it's got nothing to do with Hoppner. You don't commit suicide just because an americano moves in next door. The man's a gullible fool – they're probably clapping their hands with glee at all the dosh he's dropping in their begging bowls.'

I let the article fall among the others. The proud face of Benjamin Sword Hoppner stared up at me from three different images. In each one, he looked directly at the camera, challenging it, not giving an inch. An immaculate side-parting ran ruler-straight through the silver hair, but his throat was a network of deeply etched lines where the flesh and skin were tiring of life.

Suicides. Hoppner effectively controlled that town. A town which, according to his website, was supposed to be one of the happiest on earth. So why were people killing themselves? Before we reached Miraflores, I had to find that earlier article.

'What time is María due?' Freddy asked.

'Nine thirty.' If I went online straight away in the hotel's business centre, I should be able to locate the original *Newsweek* article before then. I found my eyes flicking across the crowd, unconsciously searching again for that Indian in the woollen coat. Something about his presence here made me feel deeply uneasy.

Freddy glanced at his watch. 'Great. Just time for another pancake.'

'Aren't you meant to be going to the bank?'

He hesitated, midway to summoning a waiter. 'You're right. Good thing you reminded me,' he said, rubbing his nose. 'Wouldn't have wanted to sponge off you the whole way.'

Pushing back his chair, he tossed his napkin into the centre of his large, syrupy plate. Around us, the delegates were starting to move. Freddy found himself part of a slow drift towards the street. On a signal from the police, the Santa Tecla crowds parted to let them through. Once outside the haven of the hotel garden, the few female delegates – as if sensing the testosterone overload from police, onlookers and security guards – adopted tense, nervous expressions and longer strides, keen to get across this no-man's land – this man's land – into the conference centre. I suddenly had a worrying thought.

He was halfway across the Via España when I called to him: 'Freddy, wait!' He stopped and I ran over, lowering my voice as delegates streamed past us. 'Have you got that gun with you?'

He nodded happily.

'Christ, Freddy, you can't take it into a bank!'

'Why not? I'm sure everyone else here does.'

'What if they have a metal detector? What if you get searched? They might march you straight off to the police.'

His smile disappeared. Instinctively, he pressed a hand to his jacket pocket. The lump of the automatic, now that I knew where to look, was obvious.

'Be sensible,' I continued. 'I'm not waiting if you get into trouble. Leave it in your room.'

'That's on the top floor! I'm not slogging all the way up there. Here,' he said, whipping the automatic out of his pocket and balancing it on his hand. 'You take it.'

I recoiled immediately. 'Put it away! Jesus, I'm not taking it.'

'Why not? What harm's it going to do you to look after it for twenty minutes?' The gun was still out in the open, for every passing delegate to see.

'Put it away!'

'Friend, you're being hysterical. Just take the damn thing.'

We were attracting attention. Several delegates, slowing to survey the cause of our dispute, hurried on the moment they spotted the gun. Infuriated, I snatched it up, pulled back my shirt and stuck it in the waistband of my trousers.

I took it out again half a second later. 'Is there a safety?'

'Yes. It's on.' He was grinning again.

He touched a finger to the side of the gun. The cusp of steel was unmarked, but I felt a little reassured. Gingerly, I returned the weapon to my waistband and smoothed my shirt over it. The metal felt alien and angry against my stomach. I knew I was scowling still, but I couldn't help it.

'You're a champ,' said Freddy, dusting his fingers against my shoulder. He set off down the promenade towards the conference centre and the shops and banks that lay beyond. I watched him go.

'Take out as much as you can,' I called after him.

'That's about fifty bucks,' he shouted, grinning through the crowd of delegates.

'Then you'd better hope Mr Hoppner's feeling generous!'

With a toss of his head he turned away, and I found myself looking at a very different face.

Unconsciously, I must have been aware of the man hurrying through the delegates, away from the conference centre. I must have seen him out of the corner of my eye when he passed Freddy. But it was only as I shouted those last words and the man's whole body froze in mid-step that I realized who it was.

For a second we just stared at each other. He knew me too – I could see the recognition in his eyes as he remembered me talking with his blond quarry the night before. Close up, the blue denim patches were immediately visible. Silver tape around his boot. His eyes were wide open, terrified. On one cheek was a smear of dirt, continued down the side of his coat as if he'd spent the night sleeping on rough ground. The ice-cream trolley was nowhere to be seen.

He began shaking his head.

I felt suddenly scared. *He's dangerous*. 'What?' I demanded. 'What is it?'

He seemed frozen to the spot. As I moved towards him, I saw a tremor in his cheek.

'What's wrong with you?' I said, taking hold of his arm. 'Where's your trolley?'

My touch unleashed a torrent of Spanish and desperate gesticulations. I glanced around, searching for someone to translate. The delegates were hurrying past, careful not to catch my eye. Fifty feet away stood a pair of policemen. Still holding the man, I began waving to them.

The moment he saw what I was doing, the Indian broke away and marched quickly in the opposite direction. The significance of the missing trolley was just starting to register in my subconscious. A fragment of the truth; a glimpse at the future. The international conference; talk of guerrillas once more becoming active; the blond guy searching the streets of Santa Tecla for this man. *He's dangerous.*

'Hey!' I called. Though I knew it was too late, though my mind was already throwing up barriers in preparation for the inevitable horror, I hurried after him. 'Wait!'

He broke into a run.

A barrage of sound erupted behind me. The air itself seemed to stretch and buckle. I stumbled forwards, knocked almost off my feet by the blast. A second later my hearing was gone, the whole world taking on a monotonic hum through which that explosion repeated and repeated.

Burnt rubber; seared flesh.

Dreamlike impressions: a streetlamp smashed above me, the glass tumbling harmlessly off my shoulders; two trees swayed violently as debris rocketed over my head and burst through their branches; something hard struck my thigh. A fine rain of powder fell around me, sheets of typed paper floating through the unsettled air. My lungs felt saturated with the stench of some noxious chemical. Turning round, pitching drunkenly, I saw a carpet of fallen delegates scattered across the promenade. Beyond them, thick brown and wispy white smoke.

Oh my God, I found myself saying. Oh my

God, over and over, oh my God. I couldn't even hear the words. A terrifying stillness. Everywhere deathly, deadly stillness. How many killed? How many torn apart by that horrific act? For all my world-weariness, all my traveller's savvy and my tough-guy confidence, I felt like a little child before that atrocity. The urge to hide myself away, to flee to some safe refuge, was overwhelming.

He's dangerous, the blond guy had said. That tough, serious Englishman had been scouring the streets of Santa Tecla for an Indian in a woollen coat. Now, too late, I understood what he'd been trying to prevent.

As I turned again towards the Indian, I found him watching open-mouthed. But his eyes weren't on the bomb-blast. He was staring at me.

I began running.

He was quick, his body spinning away and his legs kicking into action, but my fury – my absolute wrath at what I'd just witnessed – carried me smashing into him. I was enraged, I was beyond control. Images of what might be – broken bodies and slaughtered children – tore through my mind. The Indian's small body collapsed under my weight, his arms splaying out to break his fall, and we were rolling across the tarmac, hands gripping, pushing, punching until we came to a halt by a lamp post.

I fell across his chest, pinning him down. The craziness of fighting hand-to-hand with a terrorist was only just starting to dawn on me. He was wriggling and screaming like a lunatic. His nails tore at my face until I had to roll away to protect my eyes. Immediately, he was up on his feet. I kicked hard, catching his ankle with my boot and sending him crashing into a bench.

With blood running slippery warm from the scratches on my cheek, I wrenched at my shirt and found Freddy's automatic. I had it pointed at the man before he could move again.

'Stay still,' I shouted above the humming in my ears. 'No move!'

Chancing a split-second glance at the gun, I found the safety catch and flicked it off. The weapon was an alien object to me, but my action looked competent and that was all that mattered. The man was silent now, eyes fixed on the gun. Forcing my breathing to a slow, controlled rhythm, I climbed to my feet.

All around us, I now realized, was mayhem. People were running, screaming, away from the promenade. Sirens were blaring; shouts came from an angry and terrified crowd. Many of the delegates were standing again, some too dazed to move, others fleeing back into the supposed safety of the Buena Vista. A great commotion everywhere, but that part of the promenade closest to me was empty.

I shouted to two men running past. My voice was strained – croaking and off-key. They ignored me. On the bench, my captive was starting to wail again.

A policeman appeared on the promenade, arriving at the run through an alleyway and racing towards the blast site.

'Hey!' I yelled. '*Policía!*'

He didn't hear me. I straightened up, turning to face him.

'Help! *Policía!*'

For a moment I thought he'd picked up my cry in amongst that cacophony of disaster. He slowed, seemed to look around. Then a hard blow struck me in the ribs and I sprawled sideways.

The gun stayed in my hand, clattering against the tarmac where I fell. Winded by the impact, I had to suck in air for one crucial second before I could move. By the time I'd flipped over, the man in the woollen coat was racing away down the promenade.

It scared me how quickly my arm came up with the automatic pointed straight at his back. In that brief moment, I think I might have shot him. But I allowed myself just the slightest hesitation, and after that nothing could have made me pull the trigger.

As the Indian disappeared into the labyrinth of side streets, I heaved myself upright, returned the gun to my waistband and began to shake.

Freddy was standing by the shattered entrance to the conference centre. Most of the bodies draped over the steps and the pavement wore police uniforms. I counted three others that could have been delegates – there wasn't much left of their faces – and one in the rags of a beggar. Total death toll: twelve.

I could have prevented it. That was the terrible fact I would have to accept. I'd seen the terrorist, knew he was suspicious. With all the police around, how hard would it have been to get him checked out? But I'd been too afraid of the ridicule – the laughter when I demanded in the wrong language that these busy officers harass an innocent ice-cream vendor. Too afraid they would find nothing.

Amongst the mess of concrete shards, broken glass and blood were the buckled remnants of the ice-cream trolley. One half of one rubber wheel was still attached to the twisted metal. It had been so easy. He'd simply wheeled the bomb up to the front of the conference centre, sold a few token ice-creams to put the police off guard, then walked away.

'The fuckers nearly got me, too,' said Freddy. He glanced up at my scratched face. 'What happened to you?'

'Shrapnel,' I muttered.

'Good thing we didn't chat any longer,' he went on, not listening, 'or I'd have been in the middle of that.' He ran a sleeve across his forehead. 'Should we cover them up or d'you reckon they'll cart them straight off? No point getting blood all over ourselves if they're just going to ship them straight to the morgue.'

Several delegates were clutching handkerchiefs and jackets to their wounds. I started towards the most seriously hurt, but already the staff of the Buena Vista were running out into the promenade clutching first-aid kits and bottles of water. A hasty police cordon was being set up around the dead. Shocked, drawn faces stared down from the smashed windows above. The screaming and shouting was all but over now, leaving the chorus of sirens the undisputed masters of the morning air.

'Freddy, I want you to take this gun back now.'

'Can't, friend. Still got to go to the bank.'

Somehow, he even produced a warped grin.

'Well, hurry up,' I found myself yelling at him.

He lifted two surprised palms. I looked away.

A pair of ancient cannons – relics of a buccaneering age – stood guard at the front of the Santa Tecla central police headquarters. The building was huge, lumbering and decrepit. It was hard to imagine enough crimes being committed in the city to occupy its multiple wings, but I suppose they might have had other uses. Substantial sections appeared to have no windows at all.

A monument to 'La Revolución' – which one it didn't specify – served as leaning post to three officers just outside the entrance. I couldn't tell whether they were on duty or cigarette break. One of them straightened up at our approach, exchanged a few truculent words with María, then ordered her to remain outside while he led me in.

Policemen were everywhere – all of them armed, some carrying automatic rifles. The broad central corridor was lined with tiny windows, behind which sat the anonymous keepers of rubber stamps, the granters of permits and the extractors of fines. The real business lay upstairs. I was escorted at a brisk pace past the unmoving queues of petitioners and petty criminals, past the broken lifts and the posters of Daedalus Foy, and up a series of dank metal staircases that boomed at every step.

The Santa Tecla police force apparently didn't believe in female cops, or even female clerks. The only two women I saw on the maze-like upper floor wore handcuffs. Here, the police stalked their territory with menace in their eyes. Blood had been spilt and they wanted it avenged. Not a good time to be an outsider in that den of localized absolute power. What is more dangerous than a group of angry men who can do anything they like only in the place you happen to be? I kept very quiet, made myself as invisible as possible: I'd already, briefly, seen the inside of a Third World gaol and I had no desire to repeat the experience.

A hundred doors led off the airless corridors, some perhaps to soundproofed rooms. The ceiling fans turned so slowly I couldn't work out whether they were moving the air or vice versa. By the time I'd filled out a witness form twice – on the initial attempt I'd perversely stated my first name first, in brazen contravention of the minutely printed Spanish instructions – I was close to walking out.

Volunteering my assistance, something I'd felt a moral obligation to do, was starting to look like a particularly bad idea.

Three different officers interviewed me in three different offices. Each time, we required the services of the same interpreter. Not only was he struggling to translate any of their questions into English, he seemed permanently surprised by my answers, even on the third hearing.

'I have a driver waiting outside,' I said at one point. 'She speaks good English – perhaps I should bring her in to help us?'

That suggestion wasn't even translated. The interpreter just sniffed and waited for the next question.

'You say you hit this man?' the last and most senior officer asked through the interpreter.

He'd offered me a collapsing seat of chipped wood on rusting steel legs, before sitting back in his own padded swivel chair. His name, according to the lettering on his door, was Vilas. Capitán Vilas. A fastidiously groomed, bespectacled man, he was all the more threatening for his diminutive size. I couldn't help suspecting he made up for his lack of stature by a greater application of brute force on any prisoner unlucky enough to fall into his hands. A terrifying calmness pervaded his round face. All the time I was in his office he kept a ballpoint pen clasped in each hand. They were not held in a manner suggesting he intended to write with them.

'Only once,' I said. 'To stop him running away.'

'And that was enough? He stayed still, this terrorist who killed eight policemen, because you hit him once?' One of Vilas's thin eyebrows lifted minutely.

Before I'd gone anywhere near the police I'd promised myself two things: I wouldn't try to explain the first occasion I'd seen the Indian – I still didn't fully understand that whole business with the blond English guy myself – and under no circumstances would I tell them about Freddy's gun.

'I'm offering to describe a suspect for you,' I said with growing irritation. 'Do you want the description or not?'

'I have the description,' said Vilas, tapping a copy of my statement. 'You don't need to repeat yourself.' That immediately put him a class above the other two officers, who'd both embarked on a laborious discussion of the silver tape and blue denim patches. 'I am more interested in his behaviour.' He smiled thinly. 'And yours.'

'Why is my behaviour relevant?'

'You are a large man, Mr Weston. A strong man. Are you also a violent man?'

I felt as if he was gazing straight into my past. The occasional fight I'd got into in recent years was irrelevant. It was the violence committed many years ago – my original sin – that came instantly to mind. Not that it was ever far from my thoughts.

Some nights I dreamed of nothing but that non-descript car seat on which I'd wrecked all chance at a life of untroubled normality. Blinking, I said, 'I'm not going to answer questions like that.'

'You have been in our country less than twenty-four hours, but already you are hitting people. Are you a violent man?'

With his elbows resting on the desktop, he brought his fists together, the two ballpoints clicking against each other like knitting needles.

'I'd like to go now.'

Capitán Vilas considered the request for an uncomfortable length of time. 'Yes, you can go,' he conceded at last. 'But you must stay in Santa Tecla until we finish our investigations, and tell us your hotel arrangements for—'

'I'm not staying here. Why do I have to stay here?'

'To identify the suspect, of course.'

'Well, I'm sorry, I can't. I'm travelling to Miraflores today. You can contact me there, at the San Isidro hotel.'

The round face remained inscrutable throughout the translation. If anything, he seemed a little amused by my defiance.

'Why do you go to Miraflores?'

'For personal reasons.' I'd learnt a little discretion from the fiasco in Bermuda.

'To visit Mr Hoppner?' He nodded to himself when I didn't reply. 'That is not a good idea. Not for someone like you.'

'I'm on holiday.' Lying was unpleasant; not being able to probe that puzzling caution was worse.

'Then I recommend a different destination. Quiros is beautiful. And we have many fine beaches.' He was playing with me: he knew I wasn't on holiday.

'I like high altitude.'

'Do you also like high risk? The people who do this bombing, they are from Miraflores.'

'The whole town is a nest of terrorists?' I laughed.

'It is a small town, señor. A dangerous town. There are no police there to protect you.'

'After this morning I don't feel particularly well protected here. Anyway, I've heard Miraflores is very peaceful now.'

'Is that all you've heard?'

Was he talking about the suicides? After the attack on the conference centre I'd completely forgotten to look up that crucial article. Now there wouldn't be time before we had to set off. Another thing I would have liked to ask Capitán Vilas.

'Just that it's a good, law-abiding society,' I said instead.

'Excuse me, but this yanqui "Code" is no real law.' He used the tip of one ballpoint to scratch the back of his neck. 'Have you heard of a man called Daedalus Foy?'

I nodded. 'The missing journalist.'

'I have been trying to find him,' he said. 'He was

86

last seen in Santa Tecla fifteen days ago. Using a false name.'

'So?'

'Did you know he was interested in Mr Sword Hoppner?' Opening a drawer, he took out a battered pink file. From it, he pulled a single sheet of paper which he passed to me. 'You can keep that. It might be useful to you.'

I allowed myself only the slightest glance: a news clipping from a British daily, dated three weeks earlier. Not one I'd come across in my research.

'Why don't you ask Mr Hoppner if he's been to see him?'

He smiled at that – a silent laugh that had his shoulders gently rocking back and forth. 'It's very difficult getting information from Mr Hoppner. He has powerful friends.'

'You are the police.'

'I mean he has very powerful friends.'

I wasn't quite sure what he expected from me. Having thrown the deeply disconcerting fact of Foy's involvement with Hoppner into my lap – or at least Foy's focus on Hoppner shortly before his disappearance – he now seemed content to sit back and observe my reactions in silence.

'Well, if I meet Mr Hoppner, I'll ask him for you.'

It was meant as a joke, but Vilas just shook the pens at me like warning fingers. 'If you meet him, you must worry first about yourself,' he said.

All the way out, down the endless claustrophobic

corridors, past the interrogation rooms, the holstered sidearms and the dead-eyed, pitiful boys waiting to be locked up, I had to struggle to control my breathing.

The Truth and Nothing but the Truth

by Daedalus Foy

Benjamin Sword Hoppner has been a puzzle for quite a few years now. Every time we think we understand him, something new surfaces to challenge our assumptions. At one point we all thought he was a regular porn baron, until a forthright letter to the Washington Post from the women's rights activist, Pamela Martinsen, set the record straight. Then we reckoned he was running for office – why else show so much interest in public health and education? – until he moved to Central America. Now, just when we've got our heads round his dream of a 'model society', he complicates matters by offering the world his money.

What I don't get is what's stopping you or me going out there and taking it.

Hoppner seems to believe that every Tom, Dick or Harry who extends a begging bowl in his direction must be genuine. I'm not for a moment suggesting some aren't, of course; in fact, I've interviewed a couple of real gems. Dan Kosic, who's already trained fifty Kosovan nurses with Hoppner's grant, and Sunita Bal who's spent two million of Hoppner's dollars building wards for mentally disadvantaged children around Kerala. I've visited both projects and, I tell you, it's lovely to see those kids play, just as it's a joy to watch those eager young nurses save lives.

But this is the odd part: both Dan and Sunita just turned up at Hoppner's front door and asked for the money. Hoppner didn't check out their plans; he simply believed they'd do the right thing with his cash. When I pressed them, they both talked vaguely of a 'morality test', although their modesty prevented them describing in much detail a hurdle they must both have cleared with ease.

So here's my question. What's to stop any of us wandering out to Central America and claiming we need a couple of million for sick bears in Kazakhstan? The morality test, you say? Well, who couldn't tell a few fibs to get past that? Only the virtuous have to be honest all the time.

Honesty is one of the fifteen key virtues at the heart of Benjamin Sword Hoppner's moral Code. I decided to ask him a bit about it in an email correspondence we've been conducting. I began provocatively:

FOY: Spinoza says truth has no moral value.

HOPPNER: Spinoza died a while back. Let's move on.

FOY: So you don't agree that we label truth morally good because we love it, rather than loving it because it actually is good?

HOPPNER: Cute sayings are generally unhelpful, but I think this one raises an interesting question about what makes a virtue 'morally good'. We've evolved biologically to love truth because human society depends on it. Cooperation is impossible without trust, and trust will collapse in the prolonged absence of truth. Another way of stating the point is to say that truth is 'functionally good' for human society. In my book, 'morally good' and 'functionally good for human society' are the same thing. Religious people, on the other hand, believe something is morally good only if their god tells them so. Spinoza was Jewish and relentlessly focused on God, so we must allow him to get a little confused.

FOY: Then are we morally obliged to tell the truth all the time? Should I tell my cleaner she's fat? Should I let my son's bully know where he's hiding?

HOPPNER: The examples you choose suggest you already know the answer. Honesty is one of many virtues, and a good person will have all of them in mind when faced with a difficult decision. It is the tragedy of our existence that not all virtues are compatible all of the time. To call someone fat without good reason would be to lack gentleness and compassion. To assist your son's bully would be imprudent and unjust. Truth is important, but should not take precedence over the other virtues.

FOY: Here's a more complicated example. Suppose I am writing an article about you. I admire the good your money makes possible but I suspect you are not being wholly responsible in the way you allocate grants. Perhaps I worry you could unwittingly be funding a terrorist organization that puts all our lives in danger. Should I tell the world my fears, even though my piece might have a negative impact on the genuinely worthwhile projects that you fund? How much truth should I tell?

HOPPNER: Are you a journalist?

FOY: Yes I am. Freelance.

HOPPNER: I'm sorry, we cannot continue this discussion. I no longer talk to journalists.

Despite repeated attempts, I was unable to persuade Mr Hoppner to answer any further emails. Clearly if I want to find

92

out any more about him, I'll just have to try a different tactic. Would creating a fake email identity be morally wrong? I'll keep you posted . . .

CHAPTER 4

Three new road blocks – two police, one military – had been set up on the highway out of Santa Tecla. By the time we'd cleared the last, it was already midday. The soldiers and policemen had investigated every corner of María's car, searching for anything that might be connected with the morning's atrocity. I'd kept silent, moving when they told me to move but otherwise not engaging at all with the angry men in their wilting uniforms.

'Bit over the top, that lot,' was Freddy's comment as we finally made it out into open country. We'd already agreed not to discuss Hoppner in María's presence, but even Freddy was finding it difficult to think up alternative conversation leads.

'They have to do their jobs,' said María. 'Our country will see much trouble now.'

'Why would anyone want to blow up the conference?' I asked.

'The government has not kept the ceasefire promises. Many guerrillas agreed to surrender their weapons and believed they would be safe. Instead, the army is taking revenge – slowly, unofficially, but it is happening. People are attacked, their jobs are taken away. Especially Indians. At the ceasefire, also, the government promised to return the land that was stolen. But the army commanders will not give it back and now the guerrillas have disbanded they can do nothing. So they build bombs as protest.'

An explanation that made sense. But I couldn't help thinking of that blond Englishman in the Via España. How had he known about the imminent attack? Was he in some way involved with those ex-guerrillas? Vilas had claimed the Indian terrorist came from Miraflores. If true, did the blond guy also live there? Did he have some kind of link with Hoppner? The thought reminded me of Foy's article: he'd suggested that Hoppner might unwittingly be funding terrorists. Did he know something unpalatable about Miraflores? I started to wonder what kind of a world I was getting myself into.

The first stretch of the road followed the coast, running parallel to the high plateau further inland. The ground was very dry, the few patches of crops desiccated, the greenery limited to snaking bands along the rivers and streams that ran off the plateau. Up there, conditions were quite different, with a fat layer of cloud perched unmoving on the higher reaches, running the length of the continental spine.

Few solid houses still stood outside the city limits, although a couple of untended building sites suggested that some would one day be reinstated. Mostly, the people trying to make something of that parched ground lived in shacks by the side of the road. As in Santa Tecla the tarmac was excellent, but everything else was torn and destroyed. Many stands had been made by the retreating government forces along this route, every one of them devastating to the surrounding communities. Evidence of recent war was not so much in what was there as what wasn't: no fences, no wire between the lurching telegraph poles, no goalposts on the football pitches, no organized agriculture.

Six years of peace had brought some small changes. Advertising placards were appearing, led as always by Coca-Cola, with a smattering of tyre, beer and soap logos to keep the god of soft drinks from loneliness. Many of them were simply nailed to the sides of shacks or on telegraph poles, and I wondered briefly what the suits in corporate headquarters thought of the tiny sums they were being asked to pay for this most basic of communication channels. Hard to think in terms of a few cents per placard when you're sponsoring NBA stars.

We'd turned inland, silent for perhaps thirty miles, watching the roadside communities grow steadily more shrivelled, when María suddenly announced, 'You must be going to meet Mr Hoppner.'

Freddy and I stared at each other, then quickly

back at María, although her ever-cautious eyes hadn't once left the road.

'Why do you say that?' I asked. Capitán Vilas had assumed the same, as if anyone going near Miraflores became the victim of some inescapable gravitational pull.

Freddy elbowed me in the ribs, his scowl reprimanding me for my failure to deny. But it was clear to me from the start that María saw nothing unusual in her question, implying that nothing could be suspicious or out of the ordinary in an affirmative response. More than that, her words had been less query than statement. Our intentions may as well have been printed across our foreheads.

'Why else would any foreigner go to Miraflores?' she shrugged. 'I have driven three there before. All visited him.'

'Who?' said Freddy sharply, apparently forgetting his own strategy of silent denial.

'An Australian woman. She was called Dorothy.' María smiled. 'Like in *The Wizard of Oz*. But she was very much older.'

'Than us or than Dorothy?'

'Both. I think she was perhaps seventy years old.'

'God!' said Freddy. 'What on earth was she doing here?'

'She was very . . . nervous? No, shy. She was shy. I think she was afraid to bother me while I was driving. But I talked to her and after one hour, or maybe two, she started smiling and telling me about her project. That was the only thing she liked to talk about, but she liked to talk about it very much. All about these . . . I don't know the word . . . black children in Australia?'

'Aborigines.'

'Yes! She has many Abor . . . black children living with her. Because they don't have any parents.'

Just hearing about philanthropic Dorothy and her little orphans made me feel sick at myself. But this was information we couldn't afford to pass up. 'And she was going to ask Mr Hoppner for help?' I asked.

'Yes,' smiled María. 'Is that what you're going to do?'

'That's exactly what we're going to do,' said Freddy, all caution out the window.

'That's wonderful,' said María. 'I also do some work with children. Street children in Santa Tecla who are sick. There is not much I can do for them, but I try.' She fell silent for a few seconds as an oncoming truck overtook a sick tractor, threatening to push us off the road. Her fingers minutely increased their grip on the wheel, ready to steer the car out of the truck's path if it became necessary, but otherwise she retained her calm poise. When the danger was past, she continued smoothly: 'What is your project?'

Leaning forward, Freddy was about to launch into his pitch. Then he stopped himself and, turning to me, said, 'Why don't you tell her, Mark?'

It would be good practice for me, of course. But it was also a test, to see if I'd picked up enough of the details of his fictional cause for him to feel confident approaching Hoppner with me. In his position, I'd have done the same.

'Well, it's . . . also children,' I began, coughing awkwardly. 'In Malawi. Schoolchildren.'

Freddy's eyes were on me, unrelenting, but I addressed the rear-view mirror. Although María regularly glanced up, it was always to inspect the road behind her, never to watch me. It should have made my task easier, yet somehow I would have felt more comfortable lying to a face.

'Malawi's the fourth poorest country in the world and many of its schools depend on the Christian churches which helped found the nation. The government of the country is largely Islamic and the Christian funding is under serious threat. But the government is too poor to replace it. We want to set up a new, non-religious fund to support education at primary and secondary level all through Malawi.'

At the edge of my vision, I could see Freddy nodding approvingly. For now, it seemed, I'd passed.

'Mr Hoppner will like that,' said María confidently. 'He hates religion in schools.'

'Really? You know about Mr Hoppner, then?'

'Only what I hear. And what Dorothy told me, of course.'

99

'After she'd seen him? What did she say?'

María started smiling. 'Ah, she said he was . . . what word did she use? Odd!' That little adjective seemed to cause her linguistic skills real difficulty. 'Very odd.'

I glanced at Freddy. He was looking disappointed.

'So he didn't help her?'

'Yes! He did! She was so happy on the way back. She said he was very kind, a very lovely man, very charming and lovely. But . . . strange.'

'You mean she got the m—?' Freddy began.

I interrupted him: 'Why strange? Did she say?'

In the mirror, I saw María's eyes frown momentarily, as if struggling to remember. 'No. No, she didn't say. Although . . .' She brightened again. 'Although she said she'd kept her Bible hidden because she knew Mr Hoppner does not like bibles, but he saw it anyway and it was all OK. He was very polite – very kind.'

A charming picture. Both Freddy and I were smiling.

'What about the other two?' I asked. 'You said you took three people there.'

Might one of them have been Daedalus Foy? What had he come here for? To meet Hoppner, even though the pornographer was refusing to talk to any more journalists? No wonder he'd used a false name.

'Mr Smith and Mr Brown,' said María happily. 'Such polite men.'

Had they honestly used those names? Were they that stupid? I could only hope Foy had assumed a more original identity if he really had gone to Miraflores. Odd to think a real undercover journalist might have taken this same route just a couple of weeks earlier.

'And did Mr Hoppner help them, too?'

'Who knows?' said María. 'They went home a different way.'

I frowned. 'But there's only one road to Miraflores.'

Shrugging, María gazed briefly back at me in the mirror. 'I mean when I went back to collect them, they weren't there.' She lowered her eyes to the road. 'I do not mind. They had already paid.'

Just as I had decided the overwhelming, blanketing heat and humidity of the coastal plain were becoming unbearable, we began to climb. The foothills consisted mainly of scrub and patchy grassland. The lower hillside had once been a magnificent mango plantation, María explained, but none of the trees had survived the fires started by retreating government troops desperate for clear lines of sight. The despoliation of an entire region was just one of the prices paid by the country for its participation in the twentieth century's greatest ideological debate.

María's car was a product of Detroit, circa 1975. It had seen an awful lot of better days. Tired, punctured brown upholstery in a heavily rusted frame. Neither the radio nor the air vents worked. As it took the incline, the engine began to growl. The sound was not a healthy one, but María seemed unperturbed. The miles of low-gear work that it would take to reach the plateau were apparently not a concern to her. Perhaps I was exaggerating the frailty of our transport. Cars in the Third World have an almost supernatural ability to keep going, whatever punishment is inflicted on them, whatever industrial waste spews out of their exhaust pipes, and whatever inappropriate tools and spares are used to service them.

Even allowing for the poor state of the vehicle, it was unusual for me to get quite so bothered over a car. Something about the long, empty road, the smell of burning rubber and the heat was generating a sense of foreboding in me that I couldn't explain. In a slight daze, I even began to imagine that the car itself was a kind of malign spirit, leading me towards some unseen menace. This strange fantasy irritated me. Between fighting with terrorists and deceiving billionaire pornographers I had enough to worry about, without conjuring up mechanical demons.

'Would you like to stop for viewing?' María asked, as we groaned our way to the top of the hill.

'God, yes,' said Freddy. 'I need to stretch my legs.'

Where the road levelled out on to the plateau, a solitary minibus was parked on the verge. A handful of tourists had walked the ragged path to a viewpoint, and now stood in a huddle aiming long lenses at the coastal panorama below. María pulled up beside their vehicle and we stepped out into a fresh breeze that whipped the dust into dancing patterns around us. The endless cloud we'd seen from the coast had blown further inland during our long climb, leaving the air clear and surprisingly cold.

'Where are those people going?' I asked as we walked towards the tourists. 'Not Miraflores?'

'No,' laughed María. 'This road leads to Quiros – with the volcano. We turn off in twenty miles. The surface is not so good then.' She smiled apologetically. 'Europe pays for roads in cities and roads for tourists, but not roads to little towns like Miraflores.'

The loud, excitable chatter of Texan voices felt incongruous in that otherwise empty landscape. *Just think, honey! Real guer-rilla shootin', right here!* With the whole coast laid out in front of us, I searched for Santa Tecla and found a grey smudge in the distance. No other cities visible. The coastline itself was surprisingly beautiful, with white beaches, greenery and sparkling water, quite unaffected by the war. I looked down: a drop of several hundred feet below us. No guardrail, of course, but who could complain about safety short-comings in a country barely able to feed itself?

'You know Miraflores well?' I asked María, moving back a little from the drop. Freddy, of course, placed himself right on the edge, even leaning forward slightly into the wind.

'Yes, yes.' She looked down and added, almost shyly, 'I wanted to live there.'

'When?'

'When it started. I mean . . . when Mr Hoppner started rebuilding it. The promise of a clean, safe town was very nice for me then.'

'So is it? Clean and safe?'

'Of course!' She laughed a little, gently, at my ignorance. 'You can say it is a paradise, at least for this country. Good water, new buildings, electricity, fridges in every house, coffee farms that are the way our grandfathers knew them.'

The wind changed direction and a scrap of dust flew into my eye. Blinking hard, I used the tip of a finger to remove it, but the scratching sensation remained.

'Wouldn't you have missed Santa Tecla? Your family?'

'My parents died a long time ago, and—'

'I'm sorry.'

'That is no problem,' she shrugged. 'It is natural.'

'Sometimes.'

She looked at me curiously for the briefest moment. 'It was my husband's death,' she went on. 'To say, my husband's disappearance. It is the same thing here. The soldiers . . .'

She fell silent. There was no response I could

give. The Texan tourists were packing their expensive cameras away in padded bags and wandering back to the minibus. Their conversation had shifted to nachos and cheese puffs.

'So why didn't you move there?' I said instead.

She changed her tone to one of casual indifference. 'Who knows?' she said. 'It didn't . . . It felt wrong. For me, I mean. Miraflores felt wrong for me.'

Again I was reminded of that tantalizing reference. 'Did you ever hear anything about . . .' I hesitated. 'About suicides?'

As if she hadn't heard me, María coughed lightly and turned back to the road. 'I'll wait for you. Take your time,' she said.

An oddly fake note from this straightforward woman. Now I wished I hadn't asked. With suicides and a terrorist connection heavy on my thoughts, I was coming close to turning round and heading straight back to England.

Freddy and I were left alone on that windy viewpoint. He walked over to me, forcing his unruly hair behind his ear. A second later the wind had tugged it free again. For him, small matters of bombs and premature deaths were quickly forgotten.

'Friend, if everything goes well we must hit the beaches for a few days after this,' he said excitedly. 'How about it? Party on the beach? To celebrate, touch wood. Bit of fun. Blow some of the cash?'

I shook my head. 'I don't think so, Freddy.'

'Friend . . .'

'But thanks for suggesting it.'

Seeing his downcast expression, I couldn't help feeling a little mean. It was a friendly gesture that he hadn't needed to make. My instinctive revulsion at the idea must have shown on my face, even if just a little, for him to take my rejection so personally.

'I need a piss,' he said sullenly, moving off.

His footsteps receding down the path behind me sounded forced and aggressive. I shut him out, letting the view fill my mind for a few seconds longer.

Quite a landscape. Somewhere on that coastline, Alice and her new husband would be lounging by a pool or wandering hand in hand along the beach. Had she danced on the sands last night, as I'd imagined? I couldn't remember if there had been a moon. She would have looked good in moonlight.

I stepped forward to glance over the edge of the plateau one last time. A long way to fall.

I turned round. Freddy was standing right behind me.

'Actually, friend, I think you're right,' he grinned. 'Probably jinx us if we count on success.'

The shock of finding him just an arm's length away was so disorienting I nearly stepped backwards. His hands were hanging loosely by his sides.

'What are you doing?' I stuttered.

'How's that?' he said, tilting his head to one side.

'I thought you went for . . .'

'Too public here. I can hold on.'

I was still so close to the edge. Standing between Freddy and the void. No guardrail. I stumbled past him, knocking against his shoulder.

'Careful, Mark!' he laughed. 'You'll have me over the edge. Are you OK?'

He'd come back so quietly. So unexpectedly.

'I'm fine,' I said, shaking my head. Crazy thoughts. A second to reconsider, and I couldn't believe I was being so paranoid. There was just something about Freddy that made me wary.

I smiled my apology.

Tulsa Boy Makes . . . GOOD!

by Dan Barnaby

Well, what do you know? Tulsa has a famous son at last. For a small city we haven't done so badly, nurturing Garth Brooks, Jeanne Tripplehorn and Daniel Patrick Moynihan. But now, after a hundred years of eager anticipation, we've finally gotten ourselves a genuine, platinum-quality, A-list celebrity the whole world knows: none other than Ben Hoppner! Oops, sorry, Mr H. – forgot you don't like the informality. Mr Benjamin Sword Hoppner: our distinguished ambassador to the rest of the universe. Other towns get Nobel Prize-winning scientists and Presidents. We get a porn king. God digs up a sense of humor when he's passing through Oklahoma.

What's real sad is some folks here still remember Mr Hoppner Senior. For any of you school kids who weren't around October 25, 1944, he was one of our naval heroes who went down with the Saint Lo, the first ship ever sunk by a kamikaze. In hindsight we might say – and it's a sad thing to even contemplate saying – Mr Hoppner Sr. was lucky he never set eyes on his ill-destined child. Of course, a shrink would tell us it was the absence of a father that sent young Ben round the bend. But that would be an insult to his lovely mother, Rachel, who worked tirelessly to raise him right, from the day he was born, January 12, 1945, to the day she died, fifteen years later. This was not a boy who was ever allowed to wallow in the vice he later made his business. So what went wrong? Why is Tulsa's foremost celebrity now standing in the dock on five counts of peddling obscenity?

Curiously, Mr Hoppner claims he never indulges in his company's products – printed or televised – any more than he did when Mrs Hoppner held sway. This is no Larry Flynt or Hugh Hefner. When I first interviewed him, back in the days when he still graced our little town with his Olympian presence, he went to great trouble to show me what a virtuous life he led. A single bed, no alcohol, no ashtrays, no dirty magazines, no playing cards . . . his momma would have been proud. And even after he moved to the big-time cities, our Ben allowed himself only the simplest of homes. All that money and no Jacuzzi? What's wrong with the guy? Is he nuts?

Apparently so. Mr Hoppner, let us not forget, has repeatedly and publicly stated that pornography is bad! And he doesn't limit his opinion to interviews. He prints it on the front cover of every one of his adult magazines. Is this the first voluntary moral health warning in the history of pornography? But then maybe he's not so crazy. How many tit-hungry boys are going to let a little thing like that stop them handing their money to Mr Hoppner's empire? Our lad can claim some weird kind of moral high ground while raking in the greenbacks.

The high ground sure is important to him. He's made a life's work of developing and living his 'moral Code,' and now hopes to bring it to the rest of America. What does he want? Only to make the world G.O.O.D.! God bless him. But while we may smirk at such naïveté, the one thing we cannot do is deny his sincerity. While other boys were burning rubber or chasing tail, young Ben would spend his evenings helping out at the Old Folks' Home on Ashbury. Long before he'd made serious money, he was writing checks to every worthy cause in town. This is the man who canceled his own wedding to his high school sweetheart because he claimed she 'couldn't assure me of her fundamental goodness.' Oh, how she must have laughed (or wept?) when she watched him make his first million from nudie pix.

There's no denying Mr Hoppner's flair for business. After his mom died, he was out and running a home-decorating service within days, later forgoing a college scholarship to set up his first paint store. He learned the Harvard stuff the hard way. Now, anyone trying to estimate his wealth gets a headache from all the zeros. Enough to say that, seeing as how he doesn't like to spend it on anything, he must have plenty of cash lying around to fix himself the best legal services money can buy.

Assuming he gets off, with a little help from the First Amendment, what next? What's he going to do with so much dough? With all the coverage he's getting, Mr Hoppner may feel unwelcome in Chicago these days. So will he head back to little old Tulsa, build himself a nice fat mansion and retire amongst us? Well Mr H., if you're reading this, don't take it personally but: no thanks!

CHAPTER 5

We had moved into a wide belt of forest. Notwithstanding the clear blue skies, the higher rainfall up here was evident. Lush flora was abundant, houses and cultivated fields increasingly rare. María's car was a new-born force, zipping along the flat with a deep, satisfying purr.

Freddy was staring out of the window, shoulders turned away from me. I didn't know him well enough to interpret his mood. At times in Santa Tecla, he'd seemed not just dissolute but threatening. Then he would suddenly become insecure, craving friendship and approval. I tried not to speculate about what had just happened – or not happened – on that viewpoint.

Closing my eyes, I let my mind drift ahead. The way we'd arranged it, we would spend a couple of days in Miraflores, just getting a feel for the place and the people. Freddy had been all for jumping straight in; I'd argued that a longer preparation period would be sensible. We'd compromised. It was at least a positive indication that we could work together.

What would happen after that was still unclear. I knew nothing about Malawi, but Freddy claimed to have been there once. I couldn't imagine him on an overland truck or backpacking trip, and it seemed unlikely he'd have gone to that thin scrap of Africa for any other reason. Still, he had assembled a reasonably convincing set of statistics, names and references – all falsified or fraudulently acquired – which should satisfy a trusting mind. Of course, if Hoppner was the kind of donor who checked every detail, telephoned every Malawian teacher, then the pretence would fall apart. But we were counting on this fanatic's unquestioning belief in 'good people' to protect our story from serious inspection.

It wasn't the strongest position to hold, but then no story would be invulnerable to examination. My own had taken many days in a library to construct, and even though I'd thrown myself into the task of creating a credible good cause, I could never have prevented a dedicated auditor from picking apart its foundations.

We both knew there was a strong possibility we would be leaving Miraflores in embarrassing, perhaps even humiliating circumstances. That had been the risk ever since I first considered approaching Hoppner. I could almost imagine him standing, outraged, on his porch, shaking his fist at me and calling me a . . . what do righteous Oklahoma gentlemen call liars and cheats? Scoundrel? Scallywag? For some reason, in this imaginary sketch it was always raining as I sloped off, tail between my legs, cheeks burning. Now, revisiting the sketch, the only difference was Freddy, walking beside me, sharing the burden of shame.

Actually, there was one other, important, difference. Before, this humiliated future self had been nameless. Now I didn't have that safe anonymity. Hoppner would know my real name. Would he use it? Could he use it? What possible comeback could he throw at me from across the Atlantic?

More worrying was the money. I'd calculated exactly how much I needed – and it was a modest sum, stacked against Hoppner's other bequests. I'd assumed fifteen years of maintenance for Christopher at a more than adequate thirteen thousand pounds a year: one hundred and ninety-five thousand in total. Rounded up to two hundred grand, it was a manageable, reasonable sum to request, from which I could deduct the trip's expenses before handing the rest to Katie and walking out of her life for good.

Freddy wanted more. Much more.

With dreams of a house in Spain and a champagne lifestyle, Freddy was after a straight million. Quite a charitable contribution to expect in one bite. Whereas I didn't care if I had to wait on tables, crew yachts or operate ski-lifts for the rest of my life, Freddy had made up his mind that work was for other people. I suppose, to his credit, he was honest about it. But his greed was the single biggest danger I foresaw in our uneasy alliance.

One point two million pounds.

'For God's sake, we'll say two mill,' he'd breezed. 'Hardly fair if I take five times more than you, is it?'

'We'll never get two. We're very unlikely to get half that.'

'Nothing ventured, nothing gained.'

'The bigger the number, the more likely he is to check up on your famous Malawi schools project,' I'd objected.

'Heaven's sake, friend, if you don't like it we'll do your story. What was it again? Inner-city what?'

Full of good will, happy to compromise – just not on his share of the money. The target remained one million two hundred thousand pounds sterling. Nearly two million dollars.

For Malawian schoolchildren.

That rainy, shame-drenched sketch was growing more and more real. *You scoundrel, Mr Weston. Did you think you'd get away with this? Scoundrel!*

Miraflores was perched high up on the side of a valley that ran, green and hidden, through the central plateau. The road from the coast to Quiros crossed the valley at its shallowest end, and it was here – a few miles before the turn-off to Miraflores – that we stopped for lunch.

The restaurant was basic and unprepossessing: just a small kitchen building beside a wooden terrace, with a scattering of plastic tables and chairs. But the view down the valley was magnificent. The valley floor fell away quickly, a narrow river dropping at intervals over splashing cascades between ancient, imposing hard-woods. With the terrace so close to the road, the few cars passing on their way to Quiros were a minor irritation, but I soon forgot about them.

At first it looked as if the restaurant was closed, but María insisted it operated round the clock. She installed us on the terrace – balanced precariously on long, thin stilts above the valley – then wandered across the road to a rudimentary house.

'Nearly there,' said Freddy, a little awed as he gazed down the valley. 'Hard to believe, hey?'

The silent emptiness of that view made me wonder, fleetingly, whether Miraflores and its eldorado promises weren't some elaborate joke – a blank space on the Central American map that the comedian Hoppner had decided to liven up. It also occurred to me, as a rather less amusing afterthought, that the unknown quantity we were letting ourselves be drawn towards was an awfully long way from the nearest anything.

A man emerged from the house, dressed in an immaculate white chef's jacket, torn jeans and blackened trainers. He smiled at María and followed her across to us. A young child, perhaps three years old, tottered out of the house to stand watching him go, a finger lodged thoughtfully in her mouth.

'Welcome,' said the chef. The rest of his words were in Spanish.

'He says you can have anything you like,' translated María, 'so long as it is chicken or beef, and doesn't require any vegetables except tomatoes, onions and chillies.' She wasn't sure whether to be embarrassed or amused.

I looked at Freddy. He shrugged lightly. 'Great,' I said. 'Er, beef? However he wants to do it?'

'Same for me,' said Freddy.

María looked relieved. She spoke again to the chef, then disappeared into the kitchen with him, returning a moment later with two bottles of beer.

'What about you?' said Freddy, as she handed one to each of us.

'I'm driving,' she said.

It was the last place I expected to hear such responsibility voiced. I looked again at the road, empty except for a white car parked on the verge. The chances of having an accident on such uncluttered highways, even with a beer or two inside, were minimal.

I smiled a little.

'What is funny?' asked María.

'Nothing.'

'You're not laughing at our excellent driver, friend?'

'No!'

I shot Freddy a look, half chiding, half conceding. He winked back. María saw it, alternated her quizzical gaze between us both, then leaned back in her chair and called towards the kitchen.

'I think maybe I will have a beer, too,' she added in English, the beginnings of a grin emerging.

'Just one, now,' said Freddy sternly, with another ill-concealed wink towards me.

When I looked, some time later, and with a plate of delicious fried beef in front of me, the tiny child on the other side of the road was still standing all alone, staring at us. She would disappear occasionally behind a passing car, but her expression of deep curiosity never changed. Following the direction of my gaze, Freddy lowered his fork and turned towards the house. His face brightened immediately.

'Oh, she's adorable!' he cried, instinctively raising his arm to wave at the child.

'Freddy, don't . . .'

But she'd already started moving. It was as if she'd been locked to the spot, waiting longingly for permission to come running over.

Running over the road.

It was no motorway, but a couple of cars were racing along the tarmac towards that tiny creature. If the drivers weren't concentrating, if she happened to trip . . .

Freddy and I leapt up together. The plates rattled on the table, flecks of salsa spilling on to the cloth. María turned in her seat. Already, the little girl was across, happily oblivious to the danger of the road. While Freddy trotted forward to scoop her up, I sank back into my place.

'Felipe's daughter,' smiled María, who'd had her back to the house until now.

'Felipe's nearly dead daughter.' I picked up my fork. 'Isn't it a bit stupid letting her near the road? And what if she fell down there?' I added, looking over the edge of the terrace to the valley floor thirty feet below. 'She'd break her neck.'

'But what can he do?' She held up her hands as if to apologize for the state of the country. 'Should he lock her in that little house all day? Should he build an expensive fence all along the road?'

'Her mother?' I watched her expression change, and answered my own question. 'Dead.'

Somehow the food didn't taste so good any more.

'It's difficult here,' she said sadly. 'Very alone. Very exposed. Difficult for all the people living outside the cities. The army passed by here one night. They were drinking. Felipe's wife, she wouldn't let them . . .'

The depressing inevitability of it all suddenly overwhelmed me. 'Difficult outside of cities, even worse – if this morning's anything to go by – in the cities,' I snapped. 'Christ, is it safe to live anywhere in this bloody country?'

'Oh, yes,' she answered. 'Miraflores.' When I said nothing, she met my stare with an impassive nod of her head. 'That's what it is. That's . . . why it is.'

119

I'd been vaguely aware of Freddy mumbling his own special form of baby talk to the little girl in his arms, and now he came over to the table and sat down beside me, balancing her on his lap.

'Good girl,' he said delightedly. 'Good girl!'

I wasn't sure what it was she was supposed to have achieved, but I knew Freddy wouldn't leave me in the dark for long. Sure enough, before I'd eaten two more mouthfuls of rice and beef, Freddy leaned across and jabbed my arm.

'Isn't she pretty? Isn't she the most lovely little girl?'

His enthusiasm was quite genuine, his eyes alight at the sound of her trusting laughter.

'Come on, pretty little thing. Say "Freddy". Say . . . "Fred-dy".'

'Why the hell would she want to learn your name?' I said.

'Mark,' he complained, drawing the word out as far as it would go. 'You'll upset her.' He put on a look of exaggerated worry – wrinkled brow, big eyes – for her. 'You're not going to let that stuffy man upset you, are you, angel?'

Her chirpy laughter reassured him and he laughed with her, taking her little hand and waggling it from side to side.

'That's my angel. Lovely angel. Isn't she so beautiful, Mark?'

'Uh-huh.'

'Put some enthusiasm into it, friend! Tell her she's beautiful.'

120

'She's beautiful.'

'No, tell her. Say, "You're beautiful".'

'Freddy, we're trying to eat.'

'You're being stuffy again. Isn't he being stuffy, angel? Come on, Mark, tell her she's beautiful.'

I threw an exasperated glance at María. She smiled back, understanding as always, if perhaps not sharing, my irritation.

'Would you like to hold her?' suggested Freddy. 'Angel, you don't mind if—'

'No thanks.'

'Oh, come on, friend. She's so lovely.'

'Freddy, I don't like children.'

He didn't hear me, or if he did his brain refused to credit my blunt honesty. Something inside me was building, engulfing, strangling my lungs in a web of clammy silk; suffocating me.

'Here, just take her for a minute,' he continued, blindly unaware of the danger. Suddenly he was thrusting her towards me. 'She won't bi—'

'I don't want to hold the child!'

I'd thrown my fork hard against the plate: the memory of that sharp clatter filled the ensuing silence. Vicious rebuke. I looked away, gazing out over the valley. Somewhere in the distance, something was thrashing around in the great trees that lined the river. A monkey, most likely, but it could have been a sloth or even a giant bird, for all I knew of the region's wildlife.

'Jesus, Mark,' Freddy said. 'You didn't have to do that.'

The girl, silenced at first, with an expression of astonishment on her little face, began to cry.

'See?' said Freddy.

I turned back in time to catch the dirty look he threw me as he stood up, cradling the child against his shoulder.

'Hush, angel, hush,' he said, patting her back while he carried her away towards the house.

Maria and I turned our eyes to our food. She ate a little; I forked a piece of beef, then let it drop back on to the plate.

'I'm sorry,' I said.

'No, no.'

'I'm not very good with . . .' I waved, too brusquely, in the direction of the houses.

Somehow, without replying, María managed a smile which simultaneously absolved me of my sin and contradicted my admission. It left me feeling particularly sick at myself. Barely noticing what I was doing, I drained my beer.

'I'll bring you another one,' María offered, standing.

'I can get it.'

She put a hand on my arm to keep me seated. 'It's no problem.'

What her gentle manner conveyed to me, whether or not she intended it, was a deep pity – pity for my inability to enjoy, even to love, children like any normal human being. Part of me wanted to shout after her, call her back and tell her I was fine – absolutely fine – the way I was, and thank you

122

but I didn't need any pity. I could have told her a million things I liked doing, places that made me happy without any need for little 'angels' running about to – what? – *complete* me? The protestations sounded shrill and defensive in my head, and that just made me angrier.

It wasn't a phobia, although the end result was much the same. How difficult it was to put into words. Occasionally I'd got close enough to someone to want to confide in them; with Katie, an explanation had become absolutely crucial. But to state the truth – that it wasn't a fear of what children might do to me but, terrifyingly, the exact opposite – was a near-impossible thing to do. Friends, girlfriends – especially Katie – would say sweetly, *Don't be ridiculous, Mark, you couldn't possibly harm a child!* And I would never be able to counter, never explain the hard facts behind my fears, although every time I would think silently, achingly, *Oh, but I have* . . .

How many people would have still wanted to know me if I'd come out and said that?

Perhaps they would have viewed my crime more sympathetically if I'd explained that I myself had been a child when I . . . But that was the difficulty: I had no idea what I'd actually done. My memory of those early years had always been poor; that particular incident was no more than a jumble of sensations and shocked emotions. Even the name of my victim – a shivering, terror-stricken boy the same age as me, hiding himself under a man's blue cotton jacket – was lost in the confusion my mind had subsequently thrown up around the scene. I'd been zealously protected, by my subconscious as well as by those who loved me, from all but the slightest knowledge of my own brutality.

Whether any of this would have made sense if I'd suddenly, madly, decided to unburden myself to María, I don't know. In any case, I didn't get the chance.

The first crack of noise, I didn't even understand. Sharp, loud, coming from the road, it seemed to my preoccupied mind to be the noise a tree makes as it falls. Yet, too quick, too precise. I knew it wasn't a tree. Nor the exhaust of a passing car, nor any other normal, unthreatening thing. But it took a second shot for me to understand.

The thud of bullet into wooden rail beside the table so surprised me that for a moment – possibly only a fraction of a second, but to my bewildered brain it seemed the longest of minutes – I simply stared at the splintered, torn wood.

Bullet?

Before I knew what I was doing, I was on the floor of the terrace, thrown there by some unconscious survival instinct. Shooting . . . someone was actually firing a gun at me? I had to spell it out to myself before the incredulity could give way to terror.

Another shot, louder, now that I was listening for it. As the sound rocketed out across the valley, my whole body went numb with fear. Though I tried to move, nothing would respond. The thought of a bullet carving, tumbling through me, held me paralysed. All I could do was twist my head round. Where was it coming from? Was I out of sight now? Who was it? Who would . . .?

That gun.

'Freddy!' I screamed. 'Stop!'

He'd pointed the gun at me in his hotel room. Had he meant to use it? Had he been about to pull the trigger when the incriminating consequence – a corpse in his room – made him reconsider? And what about that silent approach at the viewpoint? There, it might even have looked like an accident.

My eyes flew back and forth, searching frantically, but I couldn't see anything through the maze of tables and chairs. A fourth shot sounded, then a fifth, and the floor in front of me blew apart in a shower of wood fragments. In panic, I recoiled, rolled backwards and struck a wooden post. The edge of the terrace. Trapped.

'Please, Christ, Freddy, stop!' I cried.

Even in the midst of that terrifying chaos, it wasn't hard to guess why he might do it. Two Englishmen – he'd said it himself – turning up at the same time: *it could all get very messy.* Competition for Hoppner's funds. Perhaps the danger of one of us revealing that the other was a fraud. Endless complications that could be instantly swept away by eliminating the rival contender.

Another shot.

The numbness had passed as quickly as it had begun. But still, I couldn't move. Where could I go? Where could I run to? I'd imagined being shot at before, the bullets flying in clear paths from an obvious source. But now I had no idea of direction. A thudding impact here, a splintering of wood there. Where was safety? Fatal ignorance. If only Freddy were visible, I might stand a chance. Instead, I was imprisoned in a tiny area of terrace no better than a shooting gallery, with only one possible way out.

I flipped my body back and round the post until I was hanging half off the terrace. Pounding footsteps: someone running towards me. Gripping the post, I rolled myself right off the edge. Hanging by one hand, I looked down.

The drop must have been thirty, maybe thirty-five feet. At the bottom was patchy grass and sharp rocks: hard ground. I would break something, for sure, possibly paralyse myself for life. The footsteps were crashing towards me – almost upon me. I closed my eyes, whispered the kind of prayer only desperate agnostics can, looked down once more and prepared to let go.

A hand grabbed my wrist.

'Mark! Oh God, Mark!'

Freddy. His eyes stretched wide. Already, he had both hands round my arm, body wedged against the post, bracing himself to pull hard. The gun was nowhere to be seen.

'Get off me!' I yelled. 'Get off me, you fucking psycho!'

In the first second of pulling, he hesitated. Frozen in that position, gripping my arm, he stared at me in apparent confusion.

'Mark, what . . . what are you . . . ?'

'Let go of me!'

His grip weakened a little, but his hands remained glued to my arm. Swinging myself round, I reached up with my other hand and found a second hold on the edge of the terrace.

'Let go!'

Finally, he backed away. María came running up.

'What has happened?' she cried. '*Válgame Dios!* What has happened?' In a flash she was on her knees beside Freddy, leaning forward to grab my arm.

'This bastard just tried to kill me!'

'Me?' Freddy blinked, almost in parody of perplexity. 'Mark, someone just shot at you.'

'Yeah!'

'You mean . . . me? Why would I . . . ? Why do you think I would . . . I would shoot you?'

'Mr Weston,' said María. 'You must be calm. You are saying terrible things.'

I pulled myself up so that my shoulders were pressed against the terrace. 'Get away from him, María. He has a gun.'

I swung my legs up and on to the terrace. Freddy was still motionless, staring at me with

127

mouth limply open. When I lunged forward and grabbed him by the throat, he rolled meekly back on to the floor.

'Where is it? Where's the gun?' I demanded.

'My jacket,' he wheezed under my grip.

'A handgun?' María said. 'This was not a handgun.'

I yanked the automatic out of his pocket. 'You're mad, Freddy! You're completely mad! You think it's worth killing someone over this? Is that what you think?'

His face was turning a strange colour. Unsure whether it was owing to fear or a lack of oxygen, I loosened my grip slightly, but kept the gun pointed at him.

'Mr Weston, please. It wasn't that gun. Look at this.' She was pointing at the hole in the floorboard. 'This is a rifle.'

'It's a hole,' I snarled. 'It could have been made by any gun.'

'No,' she insisted. 'Please, I know about this. The gun you are holding does not fire a bullet to do that.'

Someone else had joined us. The chef: the man who'd lost his wife to rapist soldiers. He was standing still, watching one man point a gun at another, with an expression of such resignation on his face that I found myself wavering for the first time.

'Look at the clip,' begged Freddy. 'It's still full.'

'So you reloaded.'

'Let me, please?' said María.

She had her hand out, calmly, respectfully. I stared at her for a moment, then gave it to her, increasing my pressure on Freddy's throat as I did so.

'Mark. Please,' he gasped.

I ignored him, watching María closely as she examined the barrel.

'This gun has not been fired,' she murmured. 'Not today.' Removing the ammunition clip, she extracted one of the bullets. 'Look,' she said, holding it up to me. 'Too small, you see? Too small to make this hole.'

When she'd slipped the bullet back in place and reinserted the clip, she handed the gun to me. Reluctantly, I let go of Freddy. He stayed where he was on the floor, jacket hanging open, legs sprawled round the edge of a table.

'I'm keeping this,' I said, standing up and sticking the automatic into my waistband for the second time that day.

The chef was speaking, his Spanish slow and careful.

'A car drove off,' translated María. 'He says, after the shooting, a car engine started near by. He didn't see it. He was in the kitchen.'

I looked towards the road. The white car I'd noticed earlier was no longer parked on the verge. Had it been empty? I couldn't remember. The possibility of an unknown, unexplained assassin was even more frightening than a murderous Freddy.

'It's OK,' murmured Freddy as María helped him up. 'I understand; you were in shock.'

'Shut up,' I told him.

'I just don't understand why you thought I might have wanted to kill you.'

I glared at him. 'I still think you might want to kill me.'

'But you know it wasn't me! It was a rifle—'

'So, I've seen your handgun. Who knows what else you have in your luggage? Who knows what you were doing when you went off just now?'

'You do know!' he cried indignantly. 'I was taking that little girl—'

'Just shut the fuck up, Freddy.'

He seemed about to speak, but María laid a hand on his arm and he glowered in silence.

I turned away, dropped some money on the table, and walked back to the car.

The American Dream: Part 2

by Father Jeremy Morris

There is not much time in most people's working day to think about ideals anymore. Today's Americans work longer and harder perhaps than any free people have ever done throughout the history of the world. Still, one ideal survives, indeed thrives, in this environment. We call it the American Dream.

The part of the Dream that everyone remembers is highly motivating: anyone, we like to think, who works hard can make it in the United States of America. He or she can start with nothing and end up as rich as a king. The American Dream promises full reward for perseverance, diligence and honesty.

But is that all the Dream is about? Taking a different point of view, one might say that our country's central ideological tenet is nothing more than selfish greed: its only end is making money for oneself. Can that really be the value that the greatest country on earth was founded to uphold? Why, then, did Andrew Carnegie, possibly the most successful entrepreneur of all time, declare that 'the man who dies rich dies disgraced'?

I believe there is a second part to the American Dream – a part we do not often remember. In its entirety, the Dream might read, 'Any American can start with nothing but through hard work achieve great wealth, with which to help those less fortunate.'

One of the few Americans I have watched live this dream in full is Benjamin Sword Hoppner. I look at this man and I see the essence of what once made America great. He has started from nothing, built up a great fortune, and is now generously using it to help the poor, the sick, the young and the old. Why, then, do so many wish to shoot him down?

I've heard all the objections: he's a non-believer, and he made his money from filth. Well, I'll tell you, if the occasional adult magazine was the only vice I ever heard about in confession, I could retire. So Benjamin Sword Hoppner doesn't believe in God? I'm pretty sure God not only respects those who are honest in their skepticism but looks more favorably on a generous, compassionate atheist than a churchgoer who nevertheless is selfish and vain. Mr. Hoppner may not have much time for me or the institution I serve, but as long as he keeps up the good works, I have a lot of time for him.

CHAPTER 6

None of us spoke for the first part of the journey down the rutted track to Miraflores. Whether Freddy would have tried to break the silence at all, I don't know; I had made up my mind not to respond to anything he might say. In fact, I didn't expect to have anything more to do with him. Once we reached Miraflores I intended to put as much distance as possible between us: go to Hoppner alone, make my request, then get out. The bullets hadn't come from the automatic – I accepted that. But I also knew, white cars parked on verges notwithstanding, that the only person who could possibly want to kill me was Freddy.

Except all that changed when we rounded a bend and found two foreigners – one tall and gangly, the other thin, pale and brunette – standing all alone beside a white car.

'Bloody hell, it's Alice,' cried Freddy. 'María, stop! We know them!'

And that's when everything got much more complicated.

★　　★　　★

133

I'd already searched Freddy's luggage. Before even letting him back in the car, I'd gone through his grip and his suitcase, checking everything for weapons. The fact that I found nothing didn't lessen the possibility he'd had a rifle by even the slightest degree. All around us were bushes. Any one of them could have held a discarded gun. *They're so easy to get hold of!*

Now Alice and Leonard, whose surname might or might not have been Williams, who were supposed to be honeymooning in a tourist resort, just happened to be standing a few miles from the restaurant where I'd almost been murdered. Was it the same white car? I couldn't be sure, but it looked identical.

'The engine,' exclaimed Leonard, still astonished, it seemed. 'It just . . . stopped.' Somehow, even though I'd never heard him speak before, I knew Leonard was going to sound the way he did: endlessly surprised by anything inconvenient or unfair, yet never seeing the need to introduce the slightest anger into his voice.

'We've been stuck here for ages,' added Alice. She, on the other hand, had a definite touch of venom about her. 'That bloody hire company told us it had just been serviced.'

'God, you poor things,' said Freddy, leaping forward to hug her. 'It's so lucky we were—'

'What are you doing here?' I demanded.

Freddy looked at me, as if to say, 'Can't you see they've suffered enough already?' only to change

134

his mind as he began to appreciate the huge discrepancy between Alice's honeymoon story and her presence on the road to Miraflores. He turned back to her.

'You're not . . . ?'

But his usual confidence must have been badly shaken, because he didn't feel able to finish the question.

'With permission?' murmured María, taking the keys from Alice and slipping behind the wheel of their car. The ignition worked, but the engine refused to catch.

'What are you doing here?' I said again, no more warmly.

'Nice to see you too, Mark,' replied Alice, a definite strain in her voice.

I said nothing. Neither did Freddy. Already, María was under the bonnet of the car, checking leads, spark plugs and fuel pipes.

'This is a very remote spot,' Alice went on in quite a different tone. 'I keep thinking someone's watching us. Are you going to offer us a lift or leave us stranded here?'

'Of course we're not going to leave you here!' cried Freddy.

Only half-satisfied, Alice turned to me for agreement. I looked away. María lowered the bonnet of the white car, shaking her head in defeat. While Leonard and Alice transferred their baggage across, I glanced through the windows of the white car. No guns. Just Leonard's tweed jacket, folded on the back seat. I shuddered a little at that.

I called Leonard over to collect his jacket and returned to our car. Alice had just closed the boot, and was slipping into the back next to Freddy. She could easily have been carrying a weapon, but then I too was armed now. Besides, with María present, I felt reasonably certain no one would try anything more. Leonard, lightly built but absurdly tall, I directed to the front seat. As María restarted the engine, I climbed in beside Alice and discreetly slid the gun across my waist, away from her.

I knew one of them had to be innocent. Alice or Freddy. I just didn't know which. There was no doubt in my mind that Alice and Leonard were heading to Miraflores for exactly the same reason as Freddy, and so would have the same motive to eliminate the competition.

Freddy had been conveniently out of sight during the shooting at the restaurant, had behaved strangely at the viewpoint and in his hotel room, but that look of innocent, hurt surprise would have been difficult to fake. Alice, by contrast, was behaving nervously, jerkily. Maybe it was simply embarrassment at being caught heading for Miraflores. But it could easily have been guilt.

The main factor in her defence was Leonard. To imagine him wielding a gun, attempting murder, was impossible. Where Alice was crafty, probably deceitful, definitely evasive, Leonard looked incapable of speaking anything but truth or doing anything but good. If she had been responsible for the shooting, Leonard must have been elsewhere at the time.

He twisted round in his seat and said, 'We're really so grateful, you know. We haven't seen a single other car on this road. If you hadn't come along we might have been waiting all day.' Looking back at María, he added, '*Gracias, señora.* Um . . . *gracias.*'

'She speaks English,' I told him.

'Oh!' He blushed, the colour spreading through his boyish, freckled cheeks in an anguished flood. 'Oh. Of course you do. Sorry. Thanks,' he said to María.

'This is Leonard,' muttered Alice. 'Leonard, Mark and Freddy.'

'Nice to meet you properly at last,' said Leonard, glancing nervously at his irritated wife.

'And you,' I said. 'Are you enjoying your honeymoon?'

'Y-yes, very much. I . . . well, it hasn't really begun yet. Santa Tecla wasn't really . . .'

'And you're hoping Miraflores will be?'

'What? Will be what?' Again, that nervous check with Alice.

'We're very much looking forward to it,' she said calmly, resting a hand on Leonard's shoulder.

'That's great,' I said. 'When did you decide to go there? Sorry to pry, but you certainly didn't seem to be planning a trip this way yesterday morning.'

'We changed our minds. Our hotel on the coast had overbooked.'

'Really? Which hotel was that, Leonard?'

He spun his head round, almost terrified by the question. Alice's hand gripped his shoulder hard.

'The Marriott at Jupa Beach,' she answered for him.

'What bad luck.' I couldn't help smiling.

'Not at all. I'm sure Miraflores will be just as nice.'

She was not smiling. Slowly she released her grip on her husband's shoulder, but didn't let her gaze drop from my face.

'It's going to be great having you there,' said Freddy.

'You're forgetting they're on honeymoon,' I said. 'We won't see them at all. I doubt you'll make it out of the hotel, will you, Alice?' This got no reaction. I turned to Leonard. 'Tell me, did you stop anywhere on the way here? I mean, before you broke down?'

'Why on earth do you care where—?' Alice began quickly.

'I'm asking Leonard.'

'Well, I'm answering for him.'

'Why don't you let him speak for himself?'

'Why don't you stop being a fucking jerk?' she shot back, straightening up like a cobra preparing to strike. 'What is it with this interrogation? We've just been sitting on a deserted roadside for an hour. Back off! Has it even occurred to you to imagine

138

how frightening it was to break down in the middle of nowhere?'

The way she said this, totally straight, apparently unaware of any irony, raised in me my first serious doubt. Could she honestly have come out with a question like that after trying to shoot me?

'I'm sorry,' I told her. 'It's been a difficult day.'

'For all of us.' She stared ahead for a moment, then her face softened. 'Let's just get to Miraflores. We can talk it all over then.'

The road continued level along the side of the valley, so that as the valley floor fell away beneath us we had the impression of climbing. Plant life here was diverse and abundant: creeper-laden trees, clearings filled with rich grasses, occasional tiny patches of cultivation in which the manioc and peppers grew sturdy and rich. Gradually the occasional tiny islands of human habitation petered out, the trees grew closer and taller until the light dimmed and solid forest surrounded us.

Freddy was fidgeting. Silence always seemed to make him uncomfortable. I interpreted every new gesture or mood in the light of the shooting. Alice and Freddy might both be good actors, but surely the shooter's guilt would eventually become apparent.

Predictably, Freddy spoke first.

'So, Lenny, how did you meet Alice? Can I call you Lenny?'

Leonard twisted round. 'Oh, of course. You

can call me whatever you like,' he said. But the accommodating smile grew decidedly shaky. 'Although, I mean, I do prefer Leonard.'

'Sure, no problem. Leonard it is.' In the presence of the other man's timidity, Freddy's confidence was returning fast. 'How did you meet each other?'

For a moment, I expected Alice to intervene, answer for him again. But she was sitting back, quite relaxed, watching her husband with a gentle smile.

'We've always known each other,' said Leonard. 'I mean . . . since university. We had rooms next to each other in Halls.'

'Leonard was my only constant friend,' added Alice, 'right the way through university. The only person I didn't once stop trusting.'

'So you weren't together then?'

'Oh God, no,' said Alice. 'Leonard was far too sensible to have me in those days. I was a nightmare.'

'Ali . . .' Some kind of warm signal passed between the two of them, and while it lasted Freddy and I were simply not part of their universe. Then Leonard shook his head: 'It's not true, of course. Ali was easily the most popular girl in Halls. I was just lucky she liked sharing the odd cup of hot chocolate with me.' His uncertain grin would have seemed ingenuous on most men, but Leonard's humility was genuine.

'So you only loved him for his hot chocolate,' I suggested.

'I think I mostly loved him for his shoulder,' said Alice. She gazed back at Leonard. 'I'm sorry, darling. It got very damp.'

Calmer now, she started to let her body relax. Her leg, constrained by the back of Leonard's seat, brushed against mine.

'Ali was always having these stormy relationships. Great excitements with the latest man, then a few days later she'd be round to my room for more hot chocolate . . .'

'And floods of tears . . .'

'I used to try to comfort her with Nietzsche,' said Leonard. Yes, he actually said this. There was, I believe, a tiny flash of embarrassment in his eyes as he made the admission.

'Leonard is a lecturer in philosophy,' explained Alice, as if that were sufficient excuse.

'Nietzsche?'

'Yes, you know: "Pleasure and displeasure inextricably linked together",' said Leonard. 'You must have heard philosophy undergraduates going on about it at some time or other when you were—'

'I never went to university.'

'Oh . . .' Leonard's magnificent blush returned in full force. 'I'm so sorry.'

'That's OK. I managed to find a couple of other things to do instead.'

'No . . . I mean, obviously you would have, but . . . I'm sorry I . . . presumed.'

141

'Presumed?' I couldn't help smiling, even though I knew this sweet, blundering man would misinterpret it as a gesture of contempt.

Alice intervened to rescue her husband: 'He used to tell me that we had a choice: avoid suffering but lose all chance of real happiness, or take the pain and from it build great pleasure. It made me feel a bit better about each heartbreak.'

'Of course, Nietzsche was really talking about building talents,' Leonard quickly added, in case I was an expert in disguise just waiting to catch him out. 'How great artists, politicians and engineers are born out of their bad luck and their failures. But the same principle could apply to bad luck or failure in love.'

'Meaning that because Alice dealt well with her earlier bad luck in love, she's now found greatness in you?'

'Oh, no, I'm not saying I'm any—'

'Yes,' interrupted Alice. 'Why not?' She leaned forward and kissed Leonard's cheek. 'I messed up before; now I've found the perfect relationship.'

'Ali!'

He couldn't help smiling in delight, and I began to wonder if maybe, just maybe, the honeymoon was genuine. The freshness, the uncertainty: it all suggested new love.

'It's kind of you to say it,' Leonard told her, 'but, really, to extrapolate from Nietzsche's theory that greatness usually has difficult, strife or even evil at its root to suggest that anything that begins in difficulty, strife or evil must become great would be an inexcusable fallacy.'

I couldn't help laughing. 'Now I'm really getting confused.'

'I'm sorry,' muttered Leonard. 'Look, it's not worth worrying over. Most of Nietzsche's ideas were nonsense, really: he himself went mad.'

'Don't apologize. I'm fascinated. Although, I can't promise I understood any of it.'

'But it's so simple,' he said, his lecturer's enthusiasm rushing back. 'We all have bad patches – bad luck, work that we know is poor, behaviour that we're ashamed of – but what distinguishes us is the way we react to those bad patches. The way we harness them – turn them around – to . . .'

'To achieve greatness,' I finished for him, feeling stupidly pleased with myself for having understood even such a simple principle from a subject I'd always viewed as the exclusive preserve of the educated elite.

'Exactly! I mean, take this Hoppner fellow in Miraflores. He had a pretty dismal start: his roots are about as black as they can be. But somehow he's forged a kind of greatness out of it. He had the strength of character to persist in his ambition to be a good, moral individual, even though frequently he succumbed to temptations of vice.'

No one said anything for a moment. Part of me wanted to challenge his extraordinarily naïve armchair analysis of Benjamin Sword Hoppner.

143

But that urge was quickly forgotten in the fascination of seeing Alice swamped by embarrassment. Whatever she'd said earlier about honeymoons and coastal resorts, Hoppner was clearly, irrefutably, her target.

She raised a hand to her mouth and managed a fairly convincing sneeze.

'Please don't tell me I'm allergic to some plant around here,' she said, sniffing furiously.

Immediately, Leonard's academic wanderings were forgotten as he turned solicitous and bizarrely apologetic.

'Are you OK, darling? Is it making you feel bad?'

'Just . . . it's only that it's a bit itchy.' Focusing on María, she asked, 'How much longer is it?'

While María was assuring her we were almost there, I caught Freddy's glance towards me, behind Alice's back. He wasn't very subtle, but no one else was watching. His message was clear: Alice was *in the same boat.*

Around the world, the approach to a town can be signalled in any number of ways. In the West, the signs are deliberate: text on metal welcoming you, commanding you to slow down, entreating you to stay in a particular hotel. Elsewhere, the signs are more haphazard, although no less reliable: a marked increase in plastic refuse, a greater concentration of shacks, a police roadblock.

For Miraflores, it was a bomb crater.

To be honest, I might not even have realized what it was if María hadn't pointed it out. Beside the road, in a small gap of sunlight squeezed between the endless trees, the hole made by a five-hundred-pound bomb was a perfect bowl, lined with grasses and tiny saplings. In a softer light it could have passed for a rustic English hollow.

'The town had an anti-aircraft battery here,' explained María. 'They shot down two helicopters before the army located them.'

'Poor bastards,' murmured Freddy.

'No, they were fine. The battery was on the other side of the road,' grinned María. 'They were a little muddy, only.'

She might have come from Santa Tecla, but it was clear with which side María's sympathies had lain.

'The army bombed the town?'

'They tried to. But this is cloud forest here – most days you cannot see anything from the air. Even with President Reagan helping them, they couldn't blow away the clouds.'

Beyond the crater, the forest continued right up to the edge of the town: thick, dark, laden with creepers and epiphytes. Then suddenly we were driving over cobbles and on either side of us the sun was reflected off bright white plaster walls and polished doors. Rounded ochreous tiles covered each low, sloping roof, projecting several feet out over the pavements on ornately carved hardwood beams. Miraflores was a Spanish-colonial gem.

As we moved slowly through the tranquil, sloping streets, variations appeared in the architecture. Some of the houses had bow windows, flanked by wrought-iron lamps. Others tentatively rose to a second storey, with a balcony reaching out across the road. Colours grew more adventurous too: adobe walls painted pastel blue or mustard yellow, and the occasional doorway brought into sharp relief with a lick of pale green.

The delicate beauty of those old buildings was so striking that it took me a while to appreciate their condition: to realize that every window was glazed and polished, every roof tile in place, and – under the fresh paint – every wall intact. On the roads, each cobblestone had been precisely arranged to form subtle geometrical patterns – parallel tracks, diamonds or crosses – while above us electricity cables ran in taut, regimented lines.

Even before I'd noticed all this detail, I knew what kind of people we were going to find here. None of them were in cars: ours was the only motor vehicle in sight, and María acknowledged the fact by driving almost at walking pace. Instead, the inhabitants of Miraflores moved about on foot, bumped along the cobbles on bicycles, or coaxed sleepy donkeys and horses up the steep inclines of this hillside town. As we passed, some of them watched us with excitement, others with a kind of bemusement, as if surprised that we should choose such an ungraceful mode of transport. But all of them looked on with warmth.

'They're smiling at us,' said Leonard in confusion. 'And waving. Ali, they're waving!'

'So wave back,' she grinned.

'And you didn't want to live here?' I muttered to María.

'I wanted to live here very much.'

'God, look at those girls!' Freddy cried, vigorously returning their waves. 'Hey, is this anywhere near the hotel?'

In fact, all of Miraflores was near the San Isidro. The only real hotel to have survived the war, it stood at the centre of the small town, on the western edge of the Parque Central. This was not a park, as such, but a breezy cobbled square dotted with tall trees, on a gradient like the rest of the town, with a crumbling but ornate church on the east side and gleaming white colonnaded buildings to the north and south. A domed structure – some kind of bandstand perhaps – took central position in the square, and on its steps lounged a scattering of young couples, holding hands and lazily intertwining ankles in the late-afternoon sunshine.

The hotel, like the rest of the square, was built in the classic Spanish-colonial style, with an imposing archway through to a central courtyard, two storeys of large square windows and a flat, balustrade-lined roof. The gates in the archway were fixed permanently open, studded with wrought-iron rosettes,

147

and had that impressively robust feel that only the hardest of woods, weathered for three hundred years, can convey. Between them stood a tall, angular man, dressed in a grey fitted suit that emphasized his heavy shoulders. Thick black hair was gelled back into snaking locks. A small, untidy scar halfway up his neck was the only detail out of place.

'Welcome,' he said, stepping forward. 'I am Francisco José Sánchez. My hotel is at your service.'

I'd been in my room for less than five minutes when Alice knocked on the door. She walked straight in and sat on the bed, facing me.

'We have to talk.'

My case was open; my arms were full of clothes, halfway to the wardrobe. Outside, in the square, an old woman wearing a white apron made of overlapping layers of braid was wandering between the lovers on the bandstand. She beamed at each embarrassed couple in turn, perhaps dispensing observations on the weather, grandmotherly tales, tips for natural contraception.

'About what?'

'You know perfectly well.'

'Are you really on your honeymoon?'

'Leonard doesn't know about Hoppner.'

I dropped the clothes back in the case. The wardrobe hadn't looked all that clean, anyway, although the rest of the room was exemplary in its minimalist, airy comfort. The only decoration on the walls was a woven textile of abstract, blue-grey design: a twin to the rug on the polished floor.

'Remind me who he was talking about in the car?'

'He doesn't know what I'm hoping to do here. What you're hoping to do here, for that matter.'

Her eyes hadn't left my face for one second. The stare wasn't aggressive, but neither was it particularly friendly. There was a probing, testing quality about it, as if she was trying to decide how far she could trust me.

'You're assuming I'm—?'

'Really, Mark, don't bother. You're a crap liar.' She stood up, paced to the window, looked back. 'You want to talk here?'

'Will Leonard come knocking?'

'No. Will Freddy?'

I nodded. 'Better go out.'

She stared down at the Parque again, pressing her face up against the window. When she pulled away, her nose left a tiny spot of oil on the pane, above a flood of ephemeral condensation. 'All our rooms face the square. I don't want them seeing us.'

'There's a back way.'

She followed me out on to the gallery that encircled the courtyard. Everything here was white fluted columns, balustrades and tumbling shrubs in hanging baskets. Several hundred years before Hoppner came to Miraflores, the town had been the regional centre for coffee production, and the San Isidro the Spanish Governor's personal residence. Ancient grandeur, founded on colonial riches derived from a noble crop, had finally been restored thanks to the bounteous generosity of a pornographer.

We hurried past Freddy's room and her own, then down the curving staircase. The back entrance lay through the bar, perhaps to provide easy access for local drinkers. Señor Sánchez and his staff were nowhere to be seen.

A gentle silence hung over the hotel, as it did over the rest of the town. It was as if the people of Miraflores, enjoying their afternoon siesta too much, had decided to postpone their re-emergence until the following morning. As we wandered from back street to back street, the most we saw was an occasional old man shuffling along the centre of the road and a couple of children chasing each other around a lamp post.

'How much are you after?'

We hadn't spoken since leaving the hotel, so my blunt question came across all the blunter. Her eyes when she turned to face me carried no rebuke, but her delay in answering felt calculated to underline my indelicacy.

'Three million pounds.'

'You're joking.'

'Have you noticed how none of the windows here have bars over them? Every house in Santa

150

Tecla had bars on the windows, but not here.'
She wandered away from me, towards the nearest
house. I watched as she ran a finger over the
window sill, finding old indentations regularly
spaced under the new paint. Walking back to
me, she glanced at her fingertip as if checking for
dust. 'Do you think I would joke? In this situation?
With you?'

'What's the cause?'

'Does it matter?'

'So long as it's not Malawian children.'

'No.' There was a touch of the Bermudan smile
back in her eyes. Perhaps I was starting to seem a
little less threatening, acting a little less antagon-
istically. 'I think there's something very sad about
you, Mark.'

'Sad?'

'In the old sense. Melancholic, perhaps.'

Ahead of us, the road curved, heading downhill.
Dark shadows sketched two-dimensional trees and
houses over the cobbles. A solitary horse – thin,
but less so than many of the walking skeletons
we'd seen on the coastal plains – was nibbling
at a weed growing out of the pavement. From
its neck a frayed rope dangled to the ground and
trailed several feet behind it. As we walked past, the
animal raised its head and followed in our tracks,
its hooves clipping against the cobbles at a slow,
comforting pace.

'Aren't you worried how your husband will react,
when he finds out what you're doing?'

151

'Leonard lives in a world of his own. He's too happy thinking complicated thoughts to notice my murky dealings.' She glanced sideways. 'But I need you to back off: stop insinuating things in front of him. And tell Freddy the same.'

'We're going to have problems,' I sighed. 'Three of us turning up at the same time.'

'Hoppner's invited the world: it isn't an excessive response.'

'We'll be falling over each other in his anteroom. He probably hates signing more than one cheque a month.'

'We can vouch for each other. That's a real advantage, don't you see?' She stopped walking, putting out a hand to turn me. Behind us, the horse kept moving until its nose bumped against my arm. 'Each of us has spent years working for different charities, and we've all met each other countless times on the fund-raising circuit. What could be more reassuring to a donor than that kind of network?'

She had a point. Which implied she had no interest in seeing any of us killed. Once again, the balance of probable blame for the shooting swung towards Freddy. I wondered if this enthusiastic, faultless logic wasn't just a clever pretence by Alice. With a slight sense of unease, I found myself longing to believe her. 'Be careful of Freddy,' I muttered.

'Freddy? I don't think he's going to make a move with Leonard around,' she laughed.

I didn't know how much to say. There was still no proof that either of them had been behind that rifle. 'He's . . . A couple of odd things happened today.'

'Am I supposed to guess?'

I shook my head, then lifted my shirt. 'He bought this gun. In Santa Tecla.'

For the first time, I'd surprised her. Tilting her head to one side, she gazed at the worn handle protruding from my waistband. With uncharacteristic hesitancy, she reached for it, her fingernail lightly scraping my navel.

'And now you have it,' she murmured, lifting it high to examine the trigger, the barrel, the clip. 'I wonder why.'

There was no one in sight, but I was keenly aware of the number of blank windows facing us, the half-open doors with curious observers invisible in the cool darkness beyond. 'I don't think this is a good idea.'

She misunderstood me, but her concern was equally valid. 'No. No, it isn't. You must get rid of it. Toss it into the forest.'

'What if some kid finds it?' I waited for a quick answer, hoping it would override my other, less worthy objection. But she said nothing, and I couldn't stop myself adding, in a smaller voice, 'What if we need it?'

Her laughter was so loud, I grabbed the gun and thrust it back under my shirt, convinced that every hidden pair of eyes was on us.

'Mark! Oh, Mark, where did you grow up? Vietnam?'

'We don't know these people. We're at the end of a very empty road. Who knows what the hell—?'

The creak of a heavy door interrupted my flow. We both looked round. A woman – an exact replica of the chatterer on the band-stand, with layered apron and bundled hair – was dragging a goat out of a house, tugging on a cord round its neck. As the animal reached the threshold, it dug its hooves against the flagstones and began to bleat. The woman threw us a happy grin and yanked harder, sending the animal in an undignified scuttle out into the street.

'I think I'd like to know,' said Alice, suddenly serious, her eyes all the time on the goat, 'whether you've used guns in the past.'

'Never.'

Still pulling the goat, the woman passed us with a congenial, incomprehensible greeting. To my surprise, Alice smiled and spoke back to her in Spanish. Delighted, the woman rattled off a few more words, then forced the goat on to its knees in the gutter, produced a knife from her apron and slit its throat.

The noise was worse even than the blood, which shot in pulsating bursts over the cobbles. A kind of rasping, gasping panic of a noise, direct from the severed windpipe. I'd heard it before, from animals far larger than this one, but never so unexpectedly.

The smile on Alice's lips faded. Swallowing, she turned quickly away. 'I want to go back,' she said. 'I want to go back now.' Already she was walking up the street towards the Parque Central.

I caught her arm. 'You speak Spanish?'

'Don't you?' There was more than a little scorn there.

'Wait. What about the gun?'

'Mark.' She stopped to face me. 'It's your problem. You deal with it.'

'It was just a goat, for God's sake!'

A side alley lay to our left. Keeping hold of her arm, I led her across to it. Darker than the street, late-afternoon shadows obliterated all traces of sunshine in the narrow passage. A faint smell of stale urine made me appreciate how untainted by normal urban pollution the rest of Miraflores was. I looked around for a manhole cover, a loose paving stone, anything. Four feet above our heads was a line of metal boxes, half embedded in the walls. I pointed to one.

'Electricity meter,' she said.

'Hiding place,' I replied.

She nodded. Without further discussion, she held out her hand for the gun. I crouched down and clasped my fingers together over my thigh. Somewhat carelessly, she planted a foot in my hands and balanced her weight against my shoulder. It took hardly any effort to lift her. By the time I could look up, she had the tiny door of the meter box open and the gun inside.

155

She slammed it shut. 'Let's go,' she said, not waiting for me to lower her, but jumping to the ground and striding off ahead of me.

Whether as a result of the goat's untimely end or some irritation with me, Alice didn't reappear from her room until after dark. When I'd returned to the hotel, five minutes behind her, Freddy had been slumped in one of the garish woven hammocks that hung like links in a chain around the courtyard. He'd leapt up at the suggestion of a drink.

We sat on a couple of stone benches beside the courtyard fountain: a very straight, very vertical fish, spewing just enough water to wet its half-moon scales and produce a light tinkle against the terracotta basin beneath. The courtyard was cobbled like the streets, and almost claustrophobic in its greenery. Banks of red and orange flowers in large stone troughs clashed violently with the Indian dyes of the hammocks, the effect mitigated only by the abundance of tumbling vines and potted coffee bushes.

'This is bloody great,' exclaimed Freddy, not referring to his surroundings. He clinked his beer against mine. 'I thought you'd turned snotty on me. Now you're buying me drinks!'

'Someone has to,' I said, shaping it as a joke – humouring him, even though I knew there was a good chance this man had tried to kill me.

'Uh-uh, friend, you mustn't worry about that.' He patted his jacket pocket. 'I went to the bank while you were chatting to the cops. Quite prepared to stand my rounds.'

It took a couple of minutes for him to settle down. Three times he assured me in various ways of his fairness and generosity. Then I told him about Alice.

'Bloody hell,' he laughed. 'Thought so. She's a cunning one, isn't she? All that nonsense about honeymoons. Maybe she'll be amenable to a little Freddy charm after all.'

'Leonard doesn't know,' I told him. 'So for God's sake, don't say anything.'

'Even better,' he winked.

'Oh, grow up, Freddy.'

'Friend,' he whined, his hurt expression back.

A firm tap-tap of heavy footsteps signalled the arrival of Señor Sánchez. He stopped at a polite distance, arms linked behind his back, elbows at right angles. 'Everything is to your satisfaction?'

'Very pleasant,' I said. 'Are we the only guests?'

'It is a quiet time,' he said, 'and a small hotel.'

There was a certain hollowness to his dignity. The clothing was immaculate, the hotel a fine domain for any man, but this would never be Mustique. It was hard to imagine a busy time for the hospitality industry of Miraflores. Yet Francisco José Sánchez carried about him an air of laudable determination to make the best of God's bequest – to build a solid, decent life in this place of age-long conflict.

I wanted to demonstrate a little respect for

his efforts. 'Will you join us for a drink?' I offered.

Freddy shot me a tetchy look. 'Thank you,' said the manager, 'but I never drink alcohol.'

'Then something else.'

He was reluctant, but he was a professional and well aware of the more subtle obligations of his position. Nodding graciously, he turned towards the bar. As he did so, I noticed that the small scar two inches below his chin was replicated on a larger scale at the back of his neck. It didn't take much imagination to guess how the two wounds might have come about. A chilling thought.

In a voice that remained understated yet some-how carried the full distance to the barman, Sánchez placed his order in Spanish. An orange juice arrived a few moments after he'd sat down.

'You've always lived here?'

'Not in the hotel,' he said with a slight smile. 'This is a luxury we only recently have. But, yes, I am from Miraflores.'

'I'm curious. There are no cars here.'

I don't know why I brought that up. A psychological thing. After Santa Tecla, the lack of cars on the streets of Miraflores had lent the town an unexpected air of sanctuary for me.

'Some, yes. But they are not used so much. This is a farming community. We have little need of cars.'

'And it is a successful farming community?'

'The coffee we are planting now will soon be

158

in great demand, I am sure. No one starves here.'

'How much of that is due to Benjamin Sword Hoppner?'

A chiding cough came from Freddy, though he seemed more eager than I to hear the answer. I wondered if Daedalus Foy had stayed here, had perhaps even asked this man the same questions. There was a guest register, but of course the name Foy would not appear in it. Mine was probably the first genuine name to be written in the book since Dan Kosic and Sunita Bal visited. Alternatively, Foy might have driven straight up to Hoppner's gate, not bothering to stop at all in Miraflores. There was a good chance he was still there, calling himself Jennings or Derbyshire, probably, and luxuriating in one of the billionaire's whirlpools, blissfully unaware of the international search for him.

Sánchez placed his orange juice on the bench beside him and spread his hands over his knees. 'There are many ways to make a goal,' he said. 'We tried one way for twenty-eight years and it brought us only suffering. Now it is time to try a different way.' Some kind of mental shift took place behind his eyes. 'If there is anything I can do to assist with your activities in Miraflores. As I said, there are cars available if you need transport.'

'Thank you.'

Somehow he'd avoided suggesting anything very much about our reasons for coming to his town.

159

Yet why else, as María had said, would we be there? I wondered if his delicacy was a desire not to appear intrusive or a more deep-rooted reluctance to discuss further the man who'd paid for it all.

'So, did you fight in the war?' asked Freddy, perhaps to prove that delicacy is not a universal trait.

'I regret we all had to fight in the war,' said Sánchez. 'Even my daughters.'

'Actually, there is something you could do for us,' I said quickly, steering us away from that precipice. 'Do you have an Internet connection here?'

Finding the story was easy. The *Newsweek* website held most of the articles published in international editions during the last few years, and once I'd used my credit card to pay a subscription, I had full access.

Sánchez had left the office door wide open, and as I read the article on the screen I kept an ear alert for his return. While the text was cautious, it was clear what lay between the lines. *No previous inclination. Unexplained fatalities.*

The desk was empty. Sánchez had left nothing lying about. Had he read the article? On a board above the computer, sixteen hooks held thirteen keys, each suspended on a loop of beaded leather.

What kind of reaction would that article have provoked in Benjamin Sword Hoppner?

A printer sat beside the computer, one little green light burning with reassuring steadiness. I hit the *Print* icon on the browser.

Nothing happened.

I checked the cable between hard drive and printer. Everything was connected. Again, I clicked on *Print*.

Mine is the kind of haphazard understanding of computers that falls apart when basic functions don't work the way they're supposed to. Katie would have known what to do. My approach, on the other hand, is to keep pushing in the hope that something will give. I tried one more time.

'Something else you need?' said Sánchez, just behind me.

I hadn't heard him come in.

Jerking the mouse across the desk, I clicked the browser shut.

'No, that's fine,' I said, standing hurriedly. 'Thank you.'

When I looked back, from halfway across the courtyard, he was watching me curiously.

'Katie?'

'Hello?' Her voice was distant, sleepy. 'Mark, is that you?'

Unable even to answer that simple question, I sat back on the bed and stared at my watch. Six eighteen: it was already past midnight in London. How stupid not to think of that! Her precious sleep: she got so little these days, and now I'd gone and interrupted it. Yet one more thing to feel guilty about. I was tempted to hang up without another word.

'Mark? Are you all right? Where are you?'

'I'm fine.'

I could hear the rustle of hair against linen, the thud of pillows being shifted, the lamp with the broken switch being turned on at the wall. My imagination filled in the gaps: the second finger of her left hand rubbing life into her eyelids; the unruly collar of her blue-striped pyjama top curled up under her chin; perhaps an unconscious glance towards the Indonesia photographs in her grandmother's heavy silver frame. Which side of the bed had she been sleeping on?

'I got so scared when you just . . .'

'I'm OK.'

The monosyllabic responses were cruel – hurt me as much as I knew they were hurting her. Once, she'd told me I could talk more fluently, more beautifully, than a poet. That wasn't something either of us had pretended for a while. The shutters had come down so quickly, as I'd known they would have to, after that pivotal day.

'Was it . . . something I did? Something I said?'

'Katie, no. I just . . .'

She waited patiently, hoping for some kind of reassuring explanation. When none came, she spoke in a whisper: 'Christopher misses you. I miss you.'

'I just can't . . .' I closed my eyes. 'How is he?'

'He's well, Mark.' A swallowing, hesitating sound made me picture the shape of her chin, pressed protectively against her chest, leaving the nape of her neck stretched and vulnerable. 'But I've been so scared, and he can tell.'

'I'm sorry.'

'Please, just please come home. Whatever it was, whatever you've been doing – whoever you've been with – please come home.'

I stood up. The square outside was a pale, steely blue as the light slipped away. The lovers on the bandstand had all gone.

'There's something I have to do here. For Christopher.'

'But there's nothing either of us wants except you. Back here.' Her voice was higher now, the tears almost audible.

'I can't come back. Not yet,' I added weakly, though I hated myself for offering that false suggestion of hope.

'Where are you? At least tell me that.'

Outside, a line of coloured bulbs lit up, then another and another, criss-crossing the Parque Central, strung between the branches of the tallest trees. A clattering sound made me look down: two waiters were setting up tables and chairs in front of the hotel gates, annexing a substantial chunk of the square.

'It doesn't matter.'

'Please, Mark. I have to know.'

I never could lie to her. Ever since an early morning climb up Mount Sesean when she'd looked out over Torajaland and asked me what I was thinking.

'I have to go,' was all I could say, the receiver shaking in my hand.

Her voice, reduced to a poignant fragment of sound, was just audible as I hung up.

A Code for Life, Section 8: Forgiveness

Long claimed by Christianity as a cornerstone of its teachings, forgiveness is a virtue prized by most oriental and occidental philosophical traditions. Like many virtues, we find it difficult both to want to exercise and to know how to exercise. Forgiveness is not about letting a wrongdoer off his punishment: that is clemency, which must be practiced with an eye to justice and effective deterrence. To talk of 'forgiving a debt' is to misunderstand the root verb.

Forgiveness is a state of mind – an intellectual choice that carries greater consequence for the forgiver than the forgiven. As such, it is open to all of us to forgive – not only those who are strong or powerful enough to entertain the option of retribution. And as such, like all virtues, it is ultimately far more rewarding than the alternatives – in this case vengeance or seething resentment.

To forgive is not to forget. Nor is it to deny or erase the truth of the wrong-doing. Rather, it is to understand and accept. The concept of absolution, dear to Catholic confessors, is a very different business than forgiveness. If an omnipotent god exists then perhaps he does have the power to wipe the slate clean, but we can be certain no one else does.

Forgiveness is an intellectual effort to understand the reasons behind a wrongdoing followed by an intellectual choice to eliminate rancor and discount vengeance. It is not an emotional act. That is why, unlike Compassion (see Section 5), which depends on a kind of love, it is within everyone's grasp.

Let me give an example. When I lived in Tulsa I had a small yard in front of my house, and I let it be known that children from the neighborhood could play there whenever they liked, just so long as they did no damage. One of the kids who loved spending time there was a boy named David. Like me, he'd lost his father, but he had a sense of joy about him that cheered me every time I saw him swing from the apple tree or chase another kid across the grass. I must also mention – though it is a fundamental of this Code that such genetic descriptors carry no significance – that he was black.

One day I came home from work to find the yard empty except for David. He was huddled up against the porch, his arms and legs covered in bruises, and his head hidden between his knees. At first he wouldn't lift his face. When I persuaded him to tell me what had happened, he dropped his legs and showed me where they'd cut him: two slashes across each cheek and one across his forehead. Three white boys – seventeen or

166

eighteen, maybe – had held him down while a fourth 'marked' him with a buck knife. David was eleven years old.

We called the doctor and the police. They found the boys and David testified against them. That was straightforward, if terrifying, for him. The difficult part came next. There was so much anger in David's young heart, such a sense of humiliation burning for revenge, that I thought we might easily lose him. For the rest of his life, David would harbor a resentment against all white people, perhaps even take an opportunity when he grew up to even the score. But, worst of all, a part of him, of that sweet, kind child, would die inside.

I spent many afternoons talking with David. He trusted me for some reason, and he let me guide him slowly back through the experience. It was painful for him. The words didn't come easily. We talked over what he remembered, and we discussed why those boys might have done what they did. 'Because they hate blacks,' was his initial answer. It wasn't surprising he thought that, and he may have been right. But I asked him again: why? Why would they feel that way toward a race?

It took awhile, but eventually he agreed to something brave. He came with me to visit the mother of the boy who'd cut him. And he heard direct from this good woman how she had been minding her husband's convenience store a few weeks before when two black teenagers came in and demanded money at gunpoint. It was wrong what her son had done, she said, but he was only trying to avenge his mom.

David made the effort to understand why those boys cut him. And once he'd done that, he found he wanted to forgive. Part of him still felt hatred and wanted vengeance, but he took the commendable decision to push that longing out of his head. And he felt better for it. He understood that he'd been cut only because that woman's son could not forgive, and he felt so strong knowing he had achieved something his persecutor had not.

Does a human being do wrong because he doesn't understand it is wrong, or because he is fundamentally wicked? And if he is wicked, was he born that way or has his upbringing made him so? Whatever the answer, he deserves our forgiveness, if only because we are spared his fate purely through good fortune. That we have a better understanding of morality, that we were born with certain genes, that we grew up under certain conditions – these are matters of luck, not personal achievement. If we hate people because they are unlucky, if we seek retribution against Fortune's fools, what does that make us? Forgiveness is understanding – it is an intellectual virtue. And yet, without forgiveness, we lose far more than intellectual contentment: we lose our soul.

CHAPTER 7

It was Leonard who came to find me. The darkness was complete now, the ceiling of my room flecked with wavering colours from the strings of bulbs outside. Though I was vaguely aware of voices, laughter, the gradually increasing bustle of people down in the square, my mind saw only the bedroom in Pimlico.

Katie, her face a warm gold in the soft light filtering through the scarf she's draped over the lamp. The rigid corner of her briefcase, hastily pushed aside, digging into my thigh. The pen she's been using to mark up a contract still uncapped and drying between her teeth – between her smiling, frowning lips. And as she cleans the caked blood from my face, I try to convey the exhilaration of the moment – the sense of coming alive as I took the punch and still got the guy out of there. Her laughing protest that she will never marry a man who fights for a living; my objection that it was precisely because it went beyond the call of my duty as a barman to play bouncer that it was so intoxicating, and, anyway, I don't believe in marriage because why oh why do we need it? She

169

goes quiet then, silent for a moment. And then she tells me why.

'Mark?'

The knocking, despite its tentative politeness, seemed suddenly very loud. I wondered how long he'd been out there.

'We were about to . . . we were hoping you might come down. For a drink.'

Rolling off the bed, I pulled open the door. He hesitated at the darkness.

'I'm sorry. You were asleep.'

'Just thinking.' I flicked the light switch, rubbed my face. 'Drink sounds good.'

'They seem to be having some kind of . . . what would one say here? Fiesta?'

A door slammed further along the gallery. Alice appeared at her husband's side. 'You look like shit,' she observed.

When I went downstairs, a couple of minutes and some cold water later, Freddy was just pulling himself out of a hammock. A succession of American pop hits was drifting through the courtyard. Outside in the square, the music was louder still, courtesy of two large speakers set either side of the hotel archway. Swarms of people had materialized since the sun went down and it took a moment to readjust to this crowd.

The tables around the hotel were all occupied by chattering, laughing men, but as we approached, two different groups stood and offered to give up their places. All of them were smiling warmly at us, that is until each group noticed the competition from the other table. One group waved the other back into their seats; when that had no effect, they started remonstrating with them. The other group, apparently just as determined to be generous, shot back angry retorts.

'I don't believe it,' I muttered.

Before the argument could grow too intense, Alice picked one of the tables and spoke to its occupants in Spanish, nodding gratefully all the time. Immediately that group were all smiles again as they picked up their drinks and moved away to the edge of the square, leaving the table empty for us.

'Carlos Juárez,' said the last of them, bowing and pointing to himself as he exited backwards. A black, very bushy eyebrow ran the length of his forehead. 'Carlos Juárez.'

'*Gracias*, Carlos,' we all managed, with more or less straight faces, before he bowed once more and walked off.

The table occupied by the other contenders was now a sour nest of resentment. They sat in silence, not looking at us, each clutching his beer tightly in his hand.

'Gosh, aren't they nice here?' exclaimed Leonard. 'To give up their table like that. I can't see it happening in England.'

Señor Sánchez came over with a set of laminated menus, and took our drinks orders. Every now and then, while still giving us his full attention, he would send a little nod towards one or other of the men sitting around us. This small gesture was enough to bring delight to the faces of the recipients.

'What's the occasion?' I asked him after Freddy had made up his mind which cocktail to try.

'No occasion,' he shrugged. 'It is just that we do not have many dry evenings in Miraflores. These hills are normally full of cloud. You have brought the sun with you.'

'Then maybe it will last as long as we're here,' said Alice brightly.

Sánchez offered a more restrained reflection of her smile. 'It won't last.'

It wasn't just the men who'd come out to celebrate the clear night, though with true Latin machismo they dominated the tables, slapping backs and roaring with laughter, each talking over his neighbour and accompanying his loud words with wild gestures. A number of women were scattered at the fringes of our improvised street café. While the men were mostly in their forties and fifties, the quieter conversations taking place around them were between women of all ages.

The young lovers were back on the bandstand, perhaps exploiting the dark shadows to take matters a little further than before. Around the rest of the Parque Central, children ran from tree to tree or took turns riding shiny new bikes and metallic scooters. This world bore no relation to the slums and war-ravaged ruins of Santa Tecla. Each child was neatly dressed in ironed jeans, trainers and colourful T-shirts or sweaters. They could have been running around any mall in Middle America, if it weren't that the skin was too dark, the hair too carefully brushed, and the smiles a fraction too generous.

All of us felt it, I know: that beautiful warm glow that comes from seeing not just a family but an entire social system – a community, for want of a less clichéd word – relaxed and happy. I'd always enjoyed watching kids have fun from a reasonable distance. That was the paradox: I could have loved children just as much as Freddy; I did love Christopher – my Christopher – more than anything, with the possible exception of his mother. But I was just so damned terrified of hurting them – of hurting him. Better to lose the people I loved than risk injuring my son.

How lucky those untroubled Miraflores parents were.

It took a while for me to notice the anomaly in that vibrant, companionable setting. We'd been talking for half an hour, carefully steered by Alice towards neutral topics made fascinating for the brief moment they held our attention. She sat with her arm threaded through her husband's, drinking only mineral water, smiling at his observations and squeezing his hand whenever he turned to her. Every now and then she'd glance at Freddy and me, as if to check that we were equally impressed by Leonard. And, to be honest, he was impressive. I found his opinions thought-provoking and revelatory – if largely too abstract to be of much practical use – and if I hadn't glanced for just a second over his shoulder, I don't think I would have ever noticed the silhouettes, those black figures, in the building across the square.

They were quite still, most of them, painted against the yellow glow of their cells, their faces impossible to distinguish. Several arms were visible, a couple of hands clutching the bars that separated them from our little utopia. Despite the blackness, I had no doubt that every unseen set of eyes was turned towards us.

'Señor Sánchez,' I called vehemently, surprising everyone. As he walked over to us, I still couldn't tear my gaze away from the building. 'Is that a prison?'

Immediately, the other three twisted round. Incredible that none of us had seen it before. But then our arrival in Miraflores had been a feast of new sights, and our brief time outside the hotel had been taken up by an unexpectedly emotional farewell to María. Dark men in dark rooms don't catch the eye in daylight with the same immediacy as silhouettes; bars on windows seem unremarkable until experience has taught otherwise.

'God,' breathed Freddy. 'Are we safe here?'

'Poor bastards,' said Alice. 'Look at them!'

So much information the posture of a body can convey, we all silently agreed with her – even

Freddy, once he'd reassured himself that none of them could make it through the bars.

'It is our gaol,' admitted Sánchez, with obvious reluctance.

'What the hell's it doing here? In the middle of town?'

He didn't answer straight away. He, too, stared at the gaol – one end of the long white colonnaded building that had seemed so elegant in daylight – as if needing to remind himself of the reason for the presence of convicts at the heart of this quiet society.

'The Spanish built it,' he muttered.

'And no one's thought to close it? To move it, at least?'

'Yes. It was closed in 1893. It became the library.'

'Then why—?'

'Mr Weston, I am sorry, I would prefer to discuss happier things. We have spent too much of our lives here drowning in sorrow.' He paused, let a little of the rigidity slide from his shoulders. 'Perhaps another drink?'

Before I had a chance to push him further, he was calling to a waiter, ending the conversation by moving away.

With a deep sigh that was part apprehension, part gloom, Freddy turned back from the gaol. 'That's bloody weird, that.'

No one disagreed. But then, no one else was saying anything. The spectre of the gaol had affected

175

all of us in the same way, dousing our spirits, killing all inclination to make small talk. The other three, their backs to the prisoners, probably felt it even more than I, unable to monitor what those distant, mournful shapes were doing.

Our silence went unnoticed by the men around us, who continued drinking and laughing, apparently unconcerned by the shadowy proximity of their incarcerated sons and brothers. Not one of the prisoners made a sound, a peculiarity that disturbed me. Weren't they allowed to speak? Wasn't it inhuman to prohibit that most basic need? What were they guilty of, anyway?

'Of course, it's easy to see the logic behind it.' It was Leonard who ended our chilled silence. 'Putting your gaol in the centre of daily life not only inflicts on the inmates a public shame that may help convince them of their wrongs more effectively than conventional punitive measures, but also reminds the rest of the society what the future would hold for them should they transgress.'

'It's Hoppner's doing,' muttered Alice.

I nodded. 'I think it must be. That's what Sánchez is so carefully not telling us.'

Freddy produced his chrome lighter and a pack of cigarettes from his jacket pocket. He offered one to Alice and, when she refused, gave her a playful nudge: 'Better hope he doesn't stick us in there, eh?'

She flinched at his touch, glaring at me. 'Did you talk to him?' she demanded.

'Yes,' I sighed.

'What?' said Freddy, lighting a cigarette for himself. 'Come on, I haven't said a thing! That was just a little joke,' he added to Leonard, as if the hole wasn't deep enough already.

'I don't follow,' said Leonard.

'Exactly,' said Freddy, 'I—'

'Will you shut up?'

Alice's exasperation caught the attention of the nearest tables far more effectively than our earlier silence. For a moment we were the focus of a lot of curious stares. To Alice, this was a blessing as it distracted Leonard. His only thought was to protect his wife from the public embarrassment she'd caused herself. Smiling uncomfortably, he waved at the other tables as if to assure these concerned strangers of her well-being and sanity.

'Darling, really . . .'

'Sorry, darling.'

Already the surrounding curiosity had reverted to welcoming, understanding smiles, and that tiny fragment of domestic dispute between Leonard and Alice was over before it had begun. He leaned forward to kiss her, chastely on the cheek; she accepted the gesture with just the right measure of tenderness and gratitude.

A slim figure – almost androgynous, but coming down marginally on the side of masculinity – approached our table with a cautious grin. In his delicate hand was a clutch of tapered sticks, a hunk of brittle white cheese impaled on each one.

Delighted to discover a Spanish speaker amongst us, he embarked on a long description of the wonders of flame-grilled cheese, until Alice produced a bank-note and ordered one for each of us.

'Wasn't he sweet?' she said after he'd scurried off to the edge of the square, where his brazier stood waiting. 'He said we should eat the cooked, melted bit on the outside, then give the rest back to him to barbecue some more.'

'I do hope the manager doesn't mind,' her husband murmured. 'I think he's expecting us to eat in the hotel.'

'I doubt he'll shoot us for it,' said Alice tartly.

The barbecued cheese was surprisingly delicious. I'd visualized an amorphous glue, dripping with painful globs of molten fat, but instead the surface was a golden crust that yielded to the bite with just enough resistance to make the rich, white warmth beneath taste silky light.

Freddy ate the whole thing, including the hard, cold core. When the brazier boy returned to collect our cheese kebabs for their second firing, he stared at Freddy in confusion.

'Bloody good, friend,' grinned Freddy. 'Let's have another.' He tossed his stick on to the ground behind him, only to have the boy get down on his knees to retrieve it. 'Oh, for God's sake . . . Alice, ask him to get me another, will you? On a clean stick, if that isn't asking too much.'

For a while now, the sugar-coated musings of an endless string of boybands, popchicks and dancebabes had been swamping us from the San Isidro's speakers. But now – as one compact disc came to an end and Sánchez dispatched a waiter to start another – a new, much more welcome sound started up. Walking towards us from the direction of the bandstand, a man had begun to play a guitar.

Beside him were three other players, with a second, smaller guitar, a violin and a tiny drum. One by one they joined in. Like all the men around us, they were dressed simply: pale clean shirts over worn jeans and cowboy boots. This was no mariachi band of flamboyant costumes and disciplined routines; it was just a group of friends who liked to make music together.

And it was beautiful music. Simple, perfectly rhythmical, yet hauntingly reflective of this gentle, alien evening. The melody was uncertain at first, as if its makers hadn't quite decided which direction to take. But then, to a burst of applause from all around them, a lively tune – an old favourite, presumably – emerged.

They got half a minute more before the hotel speakers came alive again, and an ex-Spice Girl in search of a solo career drowned them out.

The protest was immediate. Arms flew up and chests puffed out with Latin indignation. From all sides, Sánchez was assaulted by pleas for silence. Despite their volume, the shouts were good-natured, the complaints respectful. Most of the men were smiling as they lifted open palms in mock-astonishment at this tasteless interruption of their home-grown bards.

'I don't know what they're saying,' I whispered to Alice, 'but did I just hear Sánchez called "Comandante"?'

'Twice,' she nodded. 'And look how careful they are not to upset him.'

No one was putting up a real challenge that might embarrass the hotel manager. In fact, when Sánchez finally relented, ordering the recorded music to be switched off, it came across as the action of a benevolent leader indulging his people's whim rather than as any kind of defeat. His reward was a cheer and a rush of new drinks orders.

It was impossible not to feel uplifted by the general mood. Alice, as she gazed around the tables, was grinning so naturally and joyfully that I felt myself begin to smile. When she caught my eye, the pink tip of her tongue appeared briefly between her teeth – an unconscious movement, I think – and her chin lifted a little higher. That slender neck, held straight and steady, was pale gold from the coloured lights above. I had a strong urge to lean across the table and touch it.

She was wearing a single diamond stud in each earlobe. I didn't notice them until she turned to answer a question from Leonard. Only then was I reminded of the earring in my pocket. Katie preferred plain silver, wrought into some complicated, delicate design. The earring I'd taken, as I went one last time into the bedroom and buried my wet face in the pillow beside her, was a Celtic knot. I wondered if she'd miss it. Reaching into my pocket, I closed my hand around it. My smile faded; I no longer wanted to look at Alice.

A man at the table behind me stood up, glancing towards the edge of the square. At this signal, a woman who'd been chatting to a group of children hurried over. Without a word, the two came together and began to dance. Their movements were lively, if a little ragged from the occasional stumble on the cobblestones, and soon several other couples were joining them.

Leonard was sinking lower and lower in his chair.

'Let's,' smiled Alice.

'Oh no.' His head shaking was emphatic.

'Please, darling!'

She was already on her feet, holding out her hand. He didn't stand a chance. Reluctantly, he got up, his body unfolding to its great height like an awkward crane. A new melody had taken over, a more complicated beat, and for a moment I thought Alice might relent. But she drew Leonard close to her, perhaps conscious of the many appraising eyes around them, smiled up at his lost face and led him into the first step.

'Poor bastard's hating it,' said Freddy with relish. 'I'd love to have seen the first dance at their wedding.'

'You very nearly gave everything away with that little prison joke.'

'Friend, see, this is how amateurs react: all twitchy, even at the slightest oblique reference to their plotting. You need to learn to relax into this. You and Alice. Does she want to be part of the Malawi thing, by the way? Perhaps she could pretend to be my wife . . . I mean, Lenny's not going to be there, is he?'

It annoyed me to see how quickly Freddy had recovered his arrogance. While he'd been cowed in the aftermath of the shooting, I'd enjoyed a comforting sense of security. Probably an illusion, but preferable to a newly confident Freddy, yet again on the lookout for ways to get ahead.

'You'll have to talk to her.'

'Yes, I will. When, though? Lenny's awfully protective, don't you think? Always hovering around her. Bit desperate, in my opinion. He should set her free, and if she comes back—'

'Christ, you're such a dick,' I told him, eliciting a stunned, open-mouthed silence.

Leonard's performance on the cobbled dance floor was deteriorating. Far from gaining confidence as the dance proceeded, he was straying further and further from the beat until it was too painful even to watch the faces watching him. None of the residents of Miraflores needed proof that Englishmen couldn't dance like them, but they were enjoying it all the same. Their smiles were amused rather than scornful, as if Leonard were putting on a comedy turn for them and inviting them to laugh with him.

'What have you done with my gun?' Freddy had turned surly; with reason, I suppose.

'What?'

'My gun. I want it back. It's mine – I bought it.'

I ignored him. With a stunning gallop of fingers across strings, the lead guitarist drew the number to a close. Alice hugged her husband, but made no attempt to prevent his headlong retreat to the safety of our table. She followed more slowly; before she could reach her chair, Freddy had bounded up and grabbed her arm. The next tune was a familiar Brazilian song, given a more languorous air by the insouciant bowing of the violin.

'May I have the pleasure?'

She stifled a laugh and allowed herself to be led back into the music. I glanced at Leonard.

'I really am hopeless,' he said. 'Poor Ali.'

'I don't think she's too bothered by technical skill,' I offered. 'She'd love dancing with you even if you stepped on her feet.'

'I did,' he replied miserably.

'Oh. Well, then . . .' I said feebly, as if that somehow proved my point.

The gentle charm of the music was lost on Freddy, who was trying to throw Alice through all kinds of jive turns and spins, moving at double time to compensate for the slow beat. Like the men at neighbouring tables, I couldn't help flinching as Alice was forced to negotiate the cobbles while keeping up with Freddy's energetic but graceless demands. Twice, a grimace of pain crossed her face as he held too tightly to her hand during a spin, wrenching the bones in her wrist.

'She shouldn't really be dancing,' Leonard smiled. 'Poor thing's been jolly sick recently. Some kind of stomach bug that won't go away. She keeps fainting and throwing up.'

'She's not . . . ?' I glanced at his strangely child-like eyes and decided to drop the question. 'She's a lovely woman,' I said instead. 'I can see why you went for her.'

'Actually, she went for me more. Though, I've always adored her,' he added quickly. 'Long before she even knew my name, I used to watch her from the library roof while she sunbathed.'

Several ugly words for that activity, but none would have suited Leonard. The way he said it was so innocent – as if he had only behaved the way any love-struck, gallant hero might.

'What the hell were you doing on the roof?'

'Reading the Greeks,' he replied, with a shy grin. 'It seemed important to study Anaxagoras, Epicurus and the rest al fresco. Just as I've always preferred to read Aquinas in chapel, Montaigne in my aunt's farmhouse and Kierkegaard in winter. Sorry,' he muttered, 'that was almost a syllepsis, wasn't it?'

The incomprehension must have shown on my face, because he glanced again at Alice, straining to keep a comfortable gap between herself and Freddy, and said, 'I dedicated my

184

first paper to her, you know. An argument against incompatibilism, based on differential information availability.' When I didn't respond, he helpfully added, 'After Spinoza. I never ever told her about it. All those years, I never once dared tell her my feelings. You must think I'm such a fool.'

'I think you're the most intelligent person I've ever met.'

'Not a rebuttal,' he observed, 'but thank you, anyway. Regrettably, some of history's most intelligent men have also served as its greatest fools. I sometimes wonder if there isn't a level of intelligence beyond which we should be prevented from taking ourselves. A point at which one has trained one's mind for so long, understood so much, refined one's intellect to such a degree, that one becomes functionally incapable of most everyday tasks or ordinary human behaviour.'

'Never been a problem for me.'

A furrow appeared in his brow: 'Now, that's an interesting little paradox. If I were to agree with you, it would be an insult to your intelligence; yet to contradict would be to question your common sense along with my own. Oh dear, how did I get myself in that fix?' He blinked and said, 'I must tell Ali that one. She finds my little thought problems very amusing.'

'Does she?' I said, way too much surprise in my voice.

'Well, I imagine so. I can't think what else

she sees in me.' It was meant humorously, but somehow ended up as a serious admission.

'Don't you think she just loves you for yourself?'

'Sometimes I don't understand how she can.'

'You're a philosopher and you think any man ever understands why a woman loves him?'

Sighing, he looked away, his eyes seeking out his wife. 'It's easy for you, Mark. You're the kind of man woman are drawn to. Strong, active, forceful . . . a little dangerous. All I have to offer are soundly constructed but hypothetical arguments and speculations on the existence of a deity.'

It maddened me to hear the assumption in his tone. 'Do you have any idea how inadequate you can feel talking to a woman when you don't share her education? How hard it is to keep up with a qualified solicitor when you didn't even finish school?'

I suppose I expected him to fall silent, to apologize, even. But to Leonard, arguments were not emotive matters to be shied away from but academic tussles to be embraced. 'Why didn't you finish school?' he asked.

'I had some trouble at home. I decided it was best for everyone if I just went away for a while.'

'You fell out with your parents?'

'My guardians. Aunt and uncle.'

'Oh.' For a moment, we'd slipped out of his academic realm and back into the personal dimension, prompting a return of that extravagant blush. 'I'm sorry. Your parents . . . ?'

'In a car crash.'

'Mark, I . . .' He gazed helplessly around himself, searching vainly for the right words. I was used to the embarrassment my little personal revelation caused unwitting strangers and I waited patiently for whatever he had to offer. But instead of mumbling the usual sympathies he said, 'I want to thank you for being kind to Alice.'

That, I hadn't expected, and it reduced me to silence. As the music reached its climax and Freddy drew Alice into an exaggerated clinch, I looked away, wondering what the hell I was doing letting such a simple plan grow so complicated. The figures in the gaol were still motionless – live waxworks in latter-day stocks. If only the whole town would spontaneously pelt them with rotten fruit, then maybe Hoppner's brave new world would feel a little more reasonable. All these honest farmers, these ex-guerrillas whose aged mothers were seeping out of doorways in the side streets, positioning their rocking chairs on the pavement where they could view the festivities from a distance. For a second the contradiction of simple joy and overwhelming tragedy – in the town, in Leonard, in me, everything – made my head spin and my stomach contract.

A hand touched my shoulder. 'Mark? Your turn.'

187

I looked round. Alice was smiling down at me. 'Oh, no. Thanks, but . . .'

Freddy stepped up beside her. 'I don't mind giving you another twirl if Mark's being—'

'Mark.' The mild touch on my shoulder turned insistent. 'Come and dance.'

The next piece of music was quieter, slower still, an aching duet between guitar and violin that took on the sentiment of two doomed lovers in their final embrace. For me, at that moment, it was the worst tune they could have picked. We moved slowly, giving the music and each other space, Alice's hand resting lightly on my shoulder.

'I was just remembering how you kept staring at me in Bermuda,' she murmured. 'What a smouldering gaze you can put on when you want to. I'd love to have known what you were thinking.'

I kept my eyes on the table, watching Leonard watch me.

'He said something, didn't he?' whispered Alice, suddenly anxious.

Her head had moved slightly towards mine. I didn't reply. Another couple were dancing close by us, and Alice seemed to steer us round them, using them to block her husband's view.

'You have to remember, Leonard sees everything differently from the rest of us. His philosophy – sometimes he sees things so clearly . . . sometimes not at all.'

'He said nothing. You can relax. All of your various secrets are safe with each of us.'

I didn't mean it to come across so cruelly. Her closeness was confusing me – disturbing me. Her smell – sweet lemon, tinted with a disconcerting suggestion of sexual heat – soaked through my shirt until I could feel it, like a clasping, grasping presence all around me.

'Whatever you think, I do love him,' she said, forcing me with a quick shift of her arms to meet her gaze. 'When I flirt with you, it's just that. Nothing more.'

'You don't flirt with me,' I told her curtly, though I sensed an involuntary tightening in my fingers on her back.

'Then perhaps I've forgotten how.'

The first guitar was fading now, to be replaced by the second – the lover thrown out by the husband. Except there was nothing indignant in the higher pitch of the new guitar as it took up the duet with the violin. As if all three could coexist.

I let go of her; stared at her. A moment's uncertainty flooded that thin, drawn face, obliterating the tense excitement her own words had caused her. 'It's a foolproof curtain, then, your husband's philosophy? You can do anything you like and he sees nothing?'

'Mark . . . Don't, please.'

'Don't what?'

'Don't . . . Let's just dance a little more.'

She was holding her arms out, ready to slip back into the dance, and it is that image I will always associate with what happened next: two pale arms, thin arms, clutching nothing.

A scream came first, torn and terrified, from high up across the square. Every man, woman and child in the Parque Central froze at that bestial sound, their heads spinning round towards the roof of the church. The scream echoed around us, tripped down my spine, drove my fingers rigid. Even before the music had stopped, a body was falling in an arc that brought it crashing through the strings of coloured bulbs above.

Our eyes, already blinded from staring at the lights, were frighteningly useless in the new darkness. My incredulous mind could only piece together fragments of images to understand the horror taking place in front of us. All over the square, the tinkle of bulbs smashing against cobbles filled our brief, shocked silence.

Then the panic began.

Long before the hanged man had completed his oscillations and come to a rest, suspended from the highest tree in the square, Leonard was on his feet and rushing to Alice. But she didn't even see him. Her arms went straight around my body, her shuddering face pressed against my chest. Traitorous impulse. I stared wordlessly at Leonard, my throat drawn constriction-tight at the thought of that neck breaking – that body jerking against the sudden pull of the rope. Leonard's eyes flickered pleadingly between the back of her head and my face until I turned away, still gripped by Alice as if her life depended upon it.

Only seconds had passed. Women were running to their petrified, uncomprehending children, Sánchez was shouting at the men; Freddy had dashed immediately towards the suspended body, and now leapt pointlessly upwards, trying to grab the feet dangling just out of his reach. He was alone: everyone else had fled towards the corners of the square. Mingling with the shouts and wails, I could hear that wretched scream reverberating through my brain. And yet, despite all the noise, despite all the confusion streaming across the Parque Central, something made me look the other way.

The lights were out in the rooms above us. But there was a sliver of illumination in one of them, perhaps coming through an open door from the gallery beyond. My room, I realized with a shudder. And at the window, backlit in an eerie echo of the still-silent prisoners across the square, was the broad-shouldered, straight-standing figure of a man.

'What are we doing here?' screamed Alice suddenly into my shirt, her terrified embrace growing still tighter. 'What are we doing in this place?'

I turned back to Leonard. 'Come here,' I shouted. Reaching behind my neck, I seized Alice's hands in mine and tore them free. Still gripping them, I spun her round and transferred her to

Leonard. He sagged visibly as he took her weight.

'Thank you, I . . .'

I didn't listen to the rest. I looked round again, but the silhouette at my window was gone.

'Get him down! Get him down!' Freddy was screaming the same words over and over again.

No one was listening to him; his voice was just one of many – all shocked, all frightened. I marched over to him and grabbed him by the shoulders. 'For God's sake, shut up!'

I looked up at the body: a scrap of silver tape on one collapsing boot, a lolling head topped with thick black hair; a long woollen coat patched in blue. He looked so different from that angle, in that light.

'Christ,' I whispered.

'We have to get him down,' cried Freddy, his wide eyes boring into mine. 'Look at them all, Mark. They're children! They mustn't see this. They're just little children!'

On the table nearest us lay a farmer's machete in its tasselled sheath, its owner standing in stunned silence like his companions. All of them paralysed by the death of their terrorist friend. He didn't even notice when I picked up the knife and slung its strap over my shoulder.

The tree was in darkness; what light still came from the surviving bulbs was blocked by its thick foliage. I've never had a problem with heights, but locating hand holds on that broad trunk by touch alone was hard going. As I reached the first branches and began to move upwards more quickly, Sánchez started speaking.

I didn't look down at first, but I could hear his deep authoritative voice calming his people with an expertise born of long experience. By the time I found a clear view of the square, children were being dragged away by their mothers; those without parents were ordered home. Alice and Leonard stood where I'd left them, though now her face was raised, towards me, I think. No one had gone any closer to Freddy and the corpse.

The rope had a pale sheen in that weak light, easy to make out running tautly to the uppermost large branch. I'd been afraid that my weight combined with that of the dead man might be too much, but the branch was solidly unbending. Twelve feet along it was a shiny silver hook.

As I began to edge my way towards the rope I looked down at Freddy, standing all alone and desolate, and felt something close to guilt. It had seemed so clear that he'd been the one trying to kill me. He had the motive, he'd been out of sight at the restaurant, and apart from the slim chance it might have been Alice, there hadn't been any other explanation. Until now.

The man on the end of this rope had also travelled from Santa Tecla to Miraflores today – had driven past the restaurant. Whether or not he knew I'd spent the morning in a police station describing him, he was still a mass murderer whose escape I'd impeded. A killer with a grievance.

193

And now he was dead. Suspended, I discovered, from a kind of three-pronged grappling hook – the rope wrapped twice around the branch, one prong embedded deep in the wood. Drawing the machete from its sheath, I braced myself against the branch and slashed once at the rope. Fifty feet below, a dull thud signalled the drop of the body.

Quite a stunt: a dramatic way to go. Or to be seen to have gone? Why the scream? Was it a coincidence that a man had been watching from my hotel room at the exact moment this 'suicide' took place?

I pulled myself up into a sitting position, legs gripped around the branch. In front of me was the darkened façade of the church. I could just make out the shape of a bell tower; presumably a staircase led up to it. But however much I strained my eyes, I couldn't see anything else – anyone else – there.

The face of the blond Englishman came to mind – the man who'd pursued this dead terrorist around Santa Tecla. *We're neighbours*, he'd said. Was he here?

The grappling hook was a curious design. When I untied it, I found it was formed from three separate hooks – each with a sharp blade, a handle and an eye – that locked neatly together. Very new, technologically advanced, and inexplicably out of place in this backwater. Breaking it down, I dropped the three pieces into my jacket pocket.

'Mark?'

The voice was Freddy's, strained, frightened.

I twisted round and began edging my way towards the trunk. On the cobbles below, someone had covered the terrorist's face with a coat. Four men were standing around the body, arguing with one another.

'Mark?' The call was louder this time. He couldn't see me up among the dark foliage. 'Mr Sánchez says we must go into the hotel now. As a sign of respect.'

Most of the crowd – so recently dancing and laughing – was already disappearing down the back streets. The rocking chairs were gone, the brazier doused. Apart from the contentious voices directly below, there was no sound. The musicians had taken their instruments and their fount of good cheer and retreated from the scene. The evening was over.

One by one, the remaining lights were extinguished.

Driven to Extremes in Paradise

An alarming spate of suicides has rocked the small farming community of Miraflores, adopted home of pornographer Benjamin Sword Hoppner. The latest death occurred May 24, but, as with the preceding four apparent suicides in the last ten months, it went unreported by local or national press. This disturbing set of events came to light only by chance when this writer visited Miraflores to interview Hoppner.

According to Miraflores resident Martha Masaya, the five men had shown no previous inclination toward depression or suicide. All had been prominent members of the community and stalwarts of the recently disbanded guerrilla opposition to the former government. 'There is evil living among us,' said Masaya, a mother of three. 'We are all in fear now, every day and night.'

Hoppner relocated to his Central American lair three years ago, after his mauling at the hands of the Supreme Court, the Decency

League, and the New York Times, among others. He has claimed to be rebuilding Miraflores at his own expense, as a 'model paradise on earth, where all are free to discover the joy and satisfaction of leading a morally good life.' Hoppner, who still holds majority control of Sword Enterprises, did not wish to comment in connection with the unexplained fatalities.

CHAPTER 8

From the roof of the church, Miraflores was a delicate patchwork of tiled red and cobbled grey, floating lightly on a broad hillside of forested green. Television aerials were few, but so were derelict buildings and broken windows, although here and there a house stood out for its flaking walls and collapsed roof, contrasting oddly with the relative affluence all around.

The church itself was surprisingly dilapidated, given the painstaking renovation of the rest of the buildings in the Parque Central. The façade was a dirty yellow-brown, the few patches of original white paint spattered with musty growths of disfiguring black mould. Large chunks of the fluted pilasters that flanked each door were missing, as were many details of the baroque ornamentation, two of the four bells in the tower, and the original stone cross. A crude replacement, made of iron, had been bolted in its place.

The branch from which the terrorist had hanged himself – had been hanged, perhaps – was closer than I'd realized. It wouldn't have been difficult for a desperate man to stand on this parapet, fling a grappling hook out above our heads and anchor it firmly on that great bough. I could have done it easily. But it's not the way I'd have chosen to kill myself. To secure the anchor, tie the noose, scream and then step off into the void: anything but that.

In Britain, the church roof would have been treated as a crime scene, sealed off from the curious and the suspicious until a proper police investigation had been carried out. That was never going to happen here, of course, and although I did examine the surfaces of the rickety wooden stairs and the parapet before I stepped on to them, I had no reservations about contaminating any invisible evidence once I'd confirmed the absence of the visible. No footprints, no blunt instruments or indications of a struggle; only wind-blown, rain-washed tile and stone.

The Parque looked peaceful and inviting this morning, but although a few people walked through it, no one stopped to dawdle. There were no lovers, no vendors, not even the old woman with her layered apron. Just the ancient trees standing guard over empty cobbles, and the memory of a shocking death. There was nothing more to see here.

Walking back down the stairs, clinging gingerly to both railings when the planks groaned and bent under my weight, I saw a priest standing at the bottom. There'd been no one about when I came into the church soon after seven o'clock, and I hadn't seen anyone enter from the square. But presumably there were several back entrances, left open at all hours like the main door: that was something I wanted to check.

We smiled at each other: he warily, I unconvincingly.

'Good morning,' I said. I'd picked up a few words of Spanish, *buenos días* among them, but I didn't want to encourage a long burst of incomprehensible chatter.

He didn't reply, but smiled again while nodding his head. Protocol was satisfied, though his anxieties ran deeper. He gazed past me up the staircase, as if trying to remember what lay there. Then, when I started walking off towards the apse, he followed me. Without a common language it was pointless to challenge his movements in his own church, and, besides, it was unnecessary. There was nothing very much he could do to impede me. Together we made our way along the length of the nave, past lines of burning candles, dusty paintings and a lurid plaster Jesus gazing mournfully into the middle distance, while above us tiny birds fluttered around the peeling columns and the decaying wooden ceiling.

At the north-eastern corner was a door. Small, designed to be invisible to the casual eye, it was clearly intended for the exclusive use of the clergy. With a vaguely apologetic smile to the priest, I tried the handle. It wasn't locked. Moreover, a quick glance at the rusted, split mechanism suggested it hadn't been for a while. I pushed open the door and stepped out into the street behind.

As if his responsibilities extended only to sacred ground, the priest nodded a hasty goodbye and closed the door after me. I gazed around at the silent, anonymous street. What had I proved? Nothing at all, of course, except that it would be possible, hypothetically, to push someone off a church roof and then slip away via a back street, most likely unobserved. A dozen further streets and alleyways led off this one into the charming maze that was Miraflores. Escape routes abounded.

Had I heard the distant sound of a vehicle last night? I didn't remember it, but I hadn't been paying much attention to anything outside the Parque. Whoever had been in my hotel room – I hadn't been able to tell if he'd searched through my bags – had not left via the front entrance. Had two men walked, one from the back of the hotel and one from the back of the church, to a meeting point at the edge of the town? Hoppner and the blond Englishman perhaps? And if a car had been there to collect them, had it rolled silently down the hill before switching on the engine?

Really, none of those questions made a difference. All that mattered was that it would have been possible. More than that, it would have been easy.

I couldn't swear that Alice had been waiting for me. It's possible she'd simply woken early – as I always did – and decided on a pre-breakfast stroll. On the other hand, the roof of the church was visible from our hotel rooms, and it was a bit of a coincidence that she was hovering at that end of the Parque Central. When I appeared from the side street to the south of the church, she walked straight towards me, clearly unsurprised.

'Hi,' she said, continuing past me, effectively leading the way back out of sight of the hotel.

I followed. 'Hi.'

'God, sorry.' A sunny, broad, morning smile. 'Wasn't I pathetic?'

'Have you seen a man hanged before?'

She gave a cough of a laugh. 'Never seen anyone die.'

'Hardly pathetic, then.'

We walked on past a small street market: neat little stalls stacked with eggs, live chickens, sticky buns, and vegetables still plastered in dirt. An unnatural silence hung over the traders. Their clothing was sombre, and several of the men wore black armbands – a last salute to the dead terrorist, perhaps.

'Oh, but it's such a cliché,' she sighed. 'The weak woman, almost fainting – needing the men for support.'

'That bothers you?'

'I'd rather die than be dependent on a man.'

I stared at her.

'Shall we grab a coffee?' she suggested brightly. There weren't a lot of cafés in Miraflores, and the one we found – near the top of the town – was a little disturbing. Located beside a barber's shop, where bleary-eyed customers in heavy swivel chairs were shaved with real cut-throats, it had once had a quite different function. At one end of the long room, an eight-foot section was glassed off and lined with corrugated cardboard. On the back wall of this preserved shrine to revolutionary broadcasting was a torn green and orange flag with the letters FNR embroidered in red.

The microphone, cracked plastic mixer desk and red bulb were all still in place, together with a selection of variably focused black-and-white images of valiant, mud-streaked heroes, weighed down by AK-47s and mortars. Two or three of their faces were recognizable from the previous evening. Sánchez had a framed photograph all to himself. The glass partition shone: someone still cared, though the airwaves had fallen silent long ago.

The proprietor of the café – I couldn't help speculating on his former role in insurgency propaganda – was dressed in faded jeans and a banana-yellow shirt on which he frequently wiped his fleshy hands. His black armband looked almost farcical against that vivid background. A little moustache, shaped like a domino, collected the sweat that ran down the pockmarked sides of his nose. Every now and then, two fingers would transfer the damp residue from moustache to shirt.

Alice greeted him in Spanish. His name was

Iguana – just Iguana, apparently – and he was charmed by whatever she had to say. The coffee, when it arrived, was thick, powerful and very good.

'You seem almost at home,' I told her. 'Speaking such good Spanish.'

'Given that you don't speak it at all, you seem pretty comfortable.'

'I wouldn't say comfortable.'

'At ease, then. Not fazed by what is different.'

'I've had a lot of practice with "different".'

'A restless wanderer?'

'There were certain places I felt compelled to see. Once I'd seen them, I just kept on wandering. It's in the blood.'

'Your parents were explorers?' she smiled.

'Diplomats. I wanted to visit the places they'd been posted: Canberra, Delhi; Tokyo, where they met over a round of croquet on the Ambassador's lawn.'

'Not really?' She smiled in case she was being teased. I nodded; the smile slipped away. 'Leonard told me they were killed in an accident. Were you very young?'

'Four. I don't remember them.'

'Four years old?' she frowned. 'You ought to remember something.'

'Well, I don't,' I shrugged. 'Hence the pilgrimage: a tour of diplomatic missions, culminating in Washington.'

'The car crash?'

'It was embarrassing, really. I shouldn't have gone. A lot of uncomfortable but sympathetic faces at the Embassy when I pitched up unannounced. I think they must have called London five or six times for instructions before one of the junior diplomats was dispatched to escort me. Poor guy, he was only a few years older than I was. When we got to the anonymous bit of Georgetown tarmac where it happened, he was so wound up trying to say something meaningful that he started shaking. In the end I had to buy him a drink.'

'I'm sorry.'

'No need. I was being self-indulgent; easy when you're seventeen. I just thought the pilgrimage might exorcize a few ghosts.'

'Did it?'

'Sure.'

A small pause. 'I see,' she said, unconvinced.

She put her empty cup back on its saucer, pulled a paper napkin from the steel fold on the table and touched it to her lips. Like her cheeks, they were surprisingly pale. My chair creaked in the silence. The café's furniture was made of old, brittle plastic. Hoppner's benevolence hadn't yet extended to checked tablecloths or wrought-iron chairs.

Five smiling plastic suns gazed down on us, only their blue eyes and rosy lips standing out against the sponged yellow walls. I found myself looking away from her, fixing my stare instead on a misshapen bird – four feet tall, carved from gnarled wood and missing both tail and beak – that stood guard at the entrance to the café.

'Have I put you at your ease yet?' I asked.

'Excuse me?'

'You've had me getting personal.' I looked back at her confused face. 'How about telling me what's going on between you and Leonard?'

She shook her head. 'There's personal and there's personal.'

'Oh, that's the last thing I'm curious about.'

'We make you curious?'

'You say you love him . . .'

She was immediately tense, her expression defensive. 'Because I do.'

'Yet you treat him like—'

'Don't go there, Mark.' The tone was far more threatening than the words.

'You think he's happy?'

'Philosophers aren't supposed to be happy,' she shot back. 'They think too much.'

'That's a very glib answer.'

'You deserved it. The question was ludicrous!' An angry frown. Spots of colour appeared on her pale cheeks.

'I find it incredible you dare say that,' I told her, matching the rising hostility in her voice.

'Don't tell me what I should and shouldn't dare say,' she cried, rising half out of her chair in her fury.

'He's your husband and you think concern for his happiness is ludicrous?'

'He's not my husband!'

I waited for her to settle back in her chair.

'I know.'

'Well then, for Heaven's sake . . .' Waving a hand vaguely, she turned her face away, fixing her gaze on one of the plastic suns. 'How exciting for you,' she muttered. 'The skinny chick is available after all.'

'You're confusing me with Freddy.'

'Oh, fuck off.'

An absurdly happy splurge of music from the stereo in the corner: ecstatic notes beaten out on a xylophone while pan pipes wheezed away in the background. Iguana wandered over with fresh coffee, a basket of rolls and a quizzical smile. Alice didn't look up.

'What did you tell him?'

'That it would be exciting – romantic – to pretend to be married. That it wasn't really lying, because we were only doing it for fun.' The fingers of her right hand closed around the fake diamond and began kneading it. She must have grown conscious of her fidgeting because she abruptly dropped her hands to her lap.

'So, are you sleeping with him?'

'That's such a predictable male question.'

I ignored the jibe. 'Are you planning to take him along when you see Hoppner?'

'Of course.' She stared at me like I was some kind of imbecile. 'Why else do you think I brought him?'

That stopped me short. Until now I'd seen Leonard as a useful screen for Alice – an excuse for being in the country in the first place – and perhaps a safety measure for a woman travelling alone. But this was something quite different.

'You're using him,' I murmured. 'He's here as your pillar of goodness, is that it? You've exploited his crush on you to drag him halfway across the world because you're worried Hoppner will think you alone aren't virtuous enough.' When she didn't deny it, I shook my head in disbelief. 'You cold-hearted, manipulative snake.'

'Oh, I'm a snake? Because I actually bothered to prepare for this, I'm a snake? What gives you the right to judge me? You come to a remote corner of Latin America and you don't even bother to learn Spanish; you make up some half-baked story about undercover journalism; you flash that magazine interview around; you walk through town with a gun; and now you're going to rock up on Hoppner's doorstep without anything to satisfy the one criterion he's looking for. And you criticize me!'

Iguana had stepped forward, only to beat a hasty retreat. I wondered if perhaps he did speak a little English. If so, we were already in trouble. Or perhaps Hoppner had installed listening bugs along with the electricity. Was it him who had been in my room? Weren't there a hundred other windows in the square he could have chosen from which to watch a terrorist die?

'How is Leonard going to feel when you've got what you want and don't need him any more?' I said softly.

Already, her indignation was subsiding, as if her spare body could support only so much outburst. 'Isn't it better to have loved and lost than never to have loved at all?'

'Perhaps you should ask him.'

She looked down. 'I try not to think about that. I know he's enjoying the present, and that's enough for me.'

'I don't believe you're that short-sighted.'

'No.' Her fingers were tapping the wood of the table: fast, slow, fast. 'No, I know it will hurt him.' She caught my eye at last. 'But he'll get over it. Men always do. Maybe it will be a useful experience. God knows, he could do with a little exposure to the real world.'

'That's a pretty weak justification.'

'I'm so sorry I don't match up to your high moral standards.'

'What do you need the money for, anyway?'

'What business of yours is that?'

'I'm curious to know what drives someone to abuse a friendship.'

She stared at me furiously. 'You wouldn't understand. Men never understand.'

'Try me.'

'You probably think all women should just get married and settle down to have children under the protective wing of some rich husband, right?'

'You don't want children?'

'I want lots of children. I don't want the protective wing.'

I laughed at that. 'It doesn't cost three million pounds to bring up a bunch of kids!'

'Oh, sure, I could live on baked beans in an unheated council flat. Suitable penance for any woman not willing to play by the rules, is that what you think? You can be a single mum, but you're damn well going to suffer for it!'

'What have you got against men, anyway?'

'Try having a relationship with one and you'll understand. Unreliable, deceitful, prone to running off at any moment. If I find someone different one day, great, but I refuse to have my children depend on it.'

Her words hit a nerve. I couldn't exactly argue the point, given my own situation. 'But three million, Alice . . .'

'I want a proper house with a garden, in a safe part of London: that's half a million, straight off. Decent schools – the kind you have to pay for – will cost two hundred thousand for each child. Fresh, healthy food. The occasional family holiday. I'll need help with the children – that's expensive these days. Clothes, shoes, toys, furniture. A car every few years. Healthcare. It all adds up. Two million should cover me for the next thirty years, but Hoppner's a rich shit so I may as well try for three.'

'And this is all just good, careful planning for a hypothetical future?'

She looked uncertain. 'That's right.'

'I don't believe you.'

'You think I'm doing this to fund my drug habit?' she said lightly.

'Alice, are you pregnant?'

She'd been about to turn towards Iguana, to order some more coffee. My question froze her in her seat. 'What makes you . . . ?' Her voice was suddenly very small. No attempt to deny. 'How did you find out?'

'Leonard told me you'd been sick. Fainting. And you never drink alcohol.'

'He doesn't know,' she muttered.

'I guessed.'

Some of the tension went out of her. 'I don't stand much chance of pulling you now, do I?' She laughed to make it a joke, but her eyes stayed serious. 'Please don't tell him. It would really hurt him to know.'

'How many months?'

'Four. They say I'm so thin it'll start showing in the next few weeks.'

'And this is why you're here?' Having lived through the terror and exhilaration of a pregnancy, I was shocked that Alice could even consider coming to such a difficult part of the world in her condition – risking her child to tropical diseases and the stresses of long-haul travel.

'Mark, I'm Catholic. Anyway, I would never have given it up. But when I found out, I had this terrible panic. I knew that in a few months'

211

time I'd have this baby on my hands twenty-four hours a day. How could I look for money then? The father's nobody – certainly not someone I want to live with or beg child support from. My parents are living off a basic pension. Where was I supposed to find the cash?'

'The State, like anyone else?'

'No way am I bringing up my child in some council hostel. I told you, I need a serious nest egg. Not just for this baby but for the others I hope to have as well.'

There didn't seem much to gain by pointing to the thousands of single mothers in her position who managed perfectly well without stealing seven-figure sums. I was on decidedly shaky ground in that respect. 'So you saw that *Sunday Times* article last month?'

'Is that what gave you the idea, too? I'd been praying for something, some way to raise the capital. I'd thought about gambling; I even wondered if I could sell myself to some rich guy for a couple of months – that's how desperate I was. But then, all of a sudden, there was Hoppner handing out millions. My prayers answered. Such a simple way to solve this impossible problem.'

God, I knew that feeling. 'What about Leonard?'

'Hoppner's obsession with good moral character was the one thing that worried me: the only person I knew who would reliably fit the bill was Leonard. I had to move fast to pull this off before the baby started showing, so I signed up for Spanish classes during the day and spent my evenings with Leonard, gradually "falling in love".'

'That's pretty callous.'

'I need the money,' she said simply. 'If I don't get hold of that nest egg in the next couple of months, then the opportunity is gone for ever. My children deserve a good start in life.' She produced a wry smile. 'I plan to get through a lot of oil paints and canvas as well.'

A painter. For some reason I found that endearing, despite her selfish dreams. But I didn't share her smile. Katie, too, would be a single mother. She would work part-time to support her child, supplementing whatever I could get her by wading through contracts for her old firm. Why should Alice be free to pursue her hobbies and nurture her brood in her beautiful house while Katie had to work?

'And too bad if Leonard gets hurt?' I said.

Her smile disappeared. 'Everything in life is a compromise. I value my children's happiness above the wallet of an American pornographer and the heart of a British philosopher. If Leonard gets his feelings hurt, that's an unfortuante but necessary sacrifice.'

Towards the end, she lost a little of the conviction; trailed off a fraction.

'I'm not talking about his feelings,' I said. 'What if he gets hurt for real? What if he gets killed?'

'Don't be ridiculous.'

'Let me ask you something. Didn't you think

213

that suicide last night was a little melodramatic?'

'It was horrible and I don't want to talk about it.'

'But I do. See, I'm not convinced that man wanted to kill himself.' When she said nothing, I asked, 'What was it he screamed as he jumped?'

'Nothing. It was just a scream.'

Turning towards the back of the café, I waved to Iguana. He came straight over.

'Ask him who the man was,' I told her.

'I'm not going to start—'

'Ask him.'

She did – reluctantly, apologetically. As I'd expected, Iguana turned off his smile at a stroke.

'He says his name was Joaquim. Joaquim Tanadio.'

'Ask him why he killed himself.'

'This is . . .' But she let her objection crumble when my stare outweighed hers. As she spoke, I watched Iguana's face carefully. From his flickering eyes, I knew his response to be a lie even before she translated it. 'He says he doesn't know. Perhaps Joaquim was unhappy.'

'Was there any reason for him to be unhappy?'

His reluctance was getting to her. When she'd translated his noncommittal reply, she started pulling out her wallet. 'Let's go. I don't like this.'

'Ask him where we can find—'

'No, Mark, let's go.'

I turned to Iguana. 'Martha Masaya?' I said slowly and clearly.

His reply was swift, his departure following it even more so. Alice's hand froze on her wallet.

'Who is she?'

I stood up, dropping a couple of banknotes on the table. 'It doesn't matter.'

'He said she'd left. She's moved to another pueblo.'

'Yeah, I got that much.'

I walked back out into the sunshine, relieved to leave that mush of revolutionary radio, smiling suns, cutesy music and suspicious Latin reticence behind.

'Wait, Mark!' She came hurrying out after me, blinking in the new light. 'How? It was in Spanish. How did you understand? And who's Martha whatever?'

I shrugged. 'We should get back before Freddy starts making trouble.'

One odd thing happened on the way to the hotel. Our route from the revolutionary radio café took us down Calle 4 and past one of those few unrestored houses that I had seen from the church roof. As we approached it, not talking now, although Alice seemed to be struggling on that score, a bustling, big-chested woman came hurrying out, long torn skirts flapping round her bare feet.

In her hands was a platter laden with sickly sweet pastries, fudges and the like. She stopped in front of us and, with an encouraging nod, held out the platter.

215

'No. Thanks.' I held up one hand, smiling to soften the refusal.

'Is free. My generous for you,' the woman said in strongly accented English.

'Oh.'

I glanced at Alice. Sickly sweet or not, prepared hygienically or in a filth-encrusted rusting tin, a gift had to be accepted. She reached forward and selected the smallest piece of brown goo, flecked with brittle white pieces that might have been sugared coconut. I took a gelatinous orange lump. It tasted as bad as I'd expected.

'Thank you,' we both grinned, already turning away to avoid any further generosity.

'Thank you,' she parroted. 'Thank you. I am Lupita. Lu-pi-ta.'

'Thank you, Lupita,' I said, the edges of my smile beginning to tire.

'You tell him? Lupita,' she said, pressing her hand to her breast in a suddenly sickening echo of the man who'd given us his table in the Parque. Generosity poisoned by agenda. 'Lu-pi-ta.'

'Lupita,' I nodded, walking quickly on.

'Lupita. Tell him, please. Lu-pi-ta.'

Freddy had taken a bottle of J&B to his room to ward off the previous night's trauma, and was still lying in bed with a hangover. On the gallery outside, Leonard was neatly perched on a cane chair, an intimidating cloth-covered hardback in his hands. Neither appeared to have missed us.

Breakfast had been and gone; our absence had been noted by Sánchez, said Leonard, but no other comment made.

'I decided to have another look at Nietzsche,' announced Leonard, holding up his book. 'Our chat yesterday made me feel awfully rusty.'

'He brought a whole library with him,' groaned Alice. 'So much for our honeymoon.'

I looked at her curiously. Fascinating how comfortably and unselfconsciously she could continue to lie, even knowing I knew the marriage was a fraud. That kind of easy deception has always been impossible for me. 'Perhaps a walk outside town,' I suggested. 'Have a look at Hoppner's place.'

'God, no,' groaned Freddy. 'I'm not ready to move.'

'You stay here. We'll tell you what we find.'

'Now, friend, don't be silly. You're not going anywhere without me. Just give me a couple more hours.'

Alice was feeling a little nauseous, anyway, so we postponed the walk and spent the rest of the morning waiting in the uneasy atmosphere of the San Isidro. Twice I picked up the phone to call Katie; both times I left the number half-dialled. For much of the time, I sat with her earring in the palm of my hand, drawing my thumb along the curving silver, wondering how the hell I was supposed to move on. Outside, in the courtyard, Leonard and Alice faced each other across a chess

217

board: he coaching in a gentle voice; she hesitating with fingers on a piece, trying not to lose patience with the game. These imaginary lovers.

I stayed in my room, and it made me restless and irritable. I hadn't realized until Katie drew my attention to it, but I've always been happier outdoors. Once, when she had been due to go on a team-building course with her law firm, I booked a weekend of mountain biking in Wales. At the last moment, the course had been cancelled, so reluctantly I called off the Welsh trip. I was cooking dinner when Katie came home from work and the first thing she said was, 'Why aren't you in Wales?' The second thing she said, once I'd answered, was, 'Go away! I don't need you here every minute of my life. Go!' She sounded angry, but I understood the generosity behind the imperative. When I arrived back from the Brecon Beacons, muddy, exhausted and exhilarated, there she was, cooking us dinner, a knowing smile on her face. She understood exactly how I ticked.

Freddy made it out of bed, with the help of three aspirin, in time for lunch. He came downstairs dressed in a pink polo shirt and sunglasses, and walked straight into the dining room, rubbing his hands.

'Bloody hungry,' he muttered as we joined him. 'Starving.'

None of us had eaten anything other than the grilled cheese the previous night. After the hanging, no one had been particularly interested in food.

As only Leonard had made it to breakfast, Alice and I shared Freddy's appetite. Lunch was a fixed menu, though, and when Freddy saw what he was expected to eat, his enthusiasm collapsed.

The grilled beef strips, plantains and guacamole were delicious. What offended Freddy was the generous dollop of refried bean paste in the centre of his plate. Admittedly, its appearance hovered somewhere between chocolate mousse and dog shit, but its distinctive taste was oddly appealing. Freddy, however, was in no mood to believe me or to check for himself. He picked at the rice and beef furthest from the bean paste, his face set in a determined sulk.

'Can you believe they serve bananas with meat?' he muttered scornfully.

Alice glanced at me, smothering a laugh. She was eating ravenously; now that I knew why, I found it hard to believe no one else noticed.

'We should make a plan,' I said. 'Work out how to approach Mr Hoppner.'

'Isn't it just a question of paying him a visit and explaining about your charities?' said Leonard.

Freddy looked up. 'Oh, you know about that now?'

'Quiet, Freddy,' I said as casually as I could.

'We could all go together,' said Alice.

'I wonder if he'd feel overwhelmed.' I pulled a notepad out of my jacket pocket and scribbled a few dates. 'How long has everyone got here? I've booked ten days.'

'Two weeks,' said Freddy.

'Five days,' was Alice's reply.

'OK, then you go first. We'll send a note down this evening saying we're all here – let him choose times when he could see us.' I glanced at Alice. 'It's not a bad idea you trying first, seeing as you're asking for the most. If you're successful, Freddy and I should stand a good chance making our pitch a day or two later.'

'Wait a minute.' Freddy was paying attention now, his irritation over the food forgotten. 'How much does Alice want?'

It was Leonard who answered. 'Poor Alice, she's desperate to raise three million pounds for famine relief in Central Asia, but I wonder if even Mr Hoppner will be able to find that much—'

'Oh, sure,' snorted Freddy.

'Freddy!' My warning was a little too sharp.

'Fine, whatever.' He rolled his eyes at the uncomprehending Leonard. 'But three million? Christ, I should increase my—'

'The Malawi school project only needs one point two,' I told him firmly. 'We don't want to get greedy, do we?'

He didn't reply. I could feel the resentment building across the table. Despite the arrival of the terrorist Tanadio in Miraflores and my realization that it must have been his hand on the rifle at the restaurant, I was still glad Freddy no longer had his gun.

'Malawian school project?' said Leonard with a

polite tilt of his head. 'How interesting. You must tell me about it.'

I got up and walked out into the courtyard to find Sánchez. He was standing by the archway to the square, his black armband tight around his bicep. With him was Iguana. The café proprietor was doing the talking, and it wasn't idle chat. When Sánchez turned to look at me, I caught a glint of burning anger in his eyes. It quickly disappeared behind that courteous service mask, and he nodded briefly. I returned to the table.

'Yes, Mr Weston?' said Sánchez a few seconds later as he entered the dining room. Hearing my real name spoken with such regularity by a man who'd probably spent half his life killing was starting to get to me. Did the Comandante's influence extend beyond Miraflores? How would he react if he found out I was here to rip off his benefactor?

'We wanted to know how to find Mr Hoppner's house,' I said, after considering and rejecting a more roundabout approach.

'Certainly,' said Sánchez. 'I will drive you there myself. We must just telephone before—'

'No, I mean we just want to go for a walk. Have a look at the house at the same time.' I felt compelled to fill the subsequent silence with some kind of excuse. 'It's a beautiful house, isn't it?'

Sánchez seemed to tower over us as he considered this request. Was it unreasonable? Why did I – perhaps all of us – feel so uncomfortable?

221

'It is down the hill, past the coffee plantations,' he said at last, apparently with deep reluctance. 'Go down Calle 7 to the last house, follow
the track through the coffee and then through
the forest. There is only one road. It is very
muddy.'

'We'll be fine.'

I smiled up at him, as did Alice and Leonard,
waiting for him to slide smoothly away. But he
didn't move. Behind the mask, something was
agitating him.

'You went to the church this morning?'

My smile turned sour. 'The priest has filed a
report too, then.'

Sánchez reached into his jacket pocket and
brought out a set of folded papers. 'These are
yours, I think,' he said, handing me three copies
of the *Newsweek* article.

That damn printer. I didn't doubt he'd looked
at the text.

'Thank you,' I said calmly, laying them on
the table.

'May I ask what is your interest in Martha
Masaya?'

'Who?' muttered Freddy.

We were heading towards dangerous ground.
But with the print-outs in front of me and Iguana
standing outside, there was no point in denying it.
'I was curious,' I said.

'About what?'

'What happened to her?'

A second silence from Sánchez – perhaps intended to warn me against such direct questioning. But this time I was prepared to wait for an answer.

'Martha Masaya caused us many problems. The whole pueblo suffered for many weeks because of her. We do not want that ever to happen again. We make sure,' he said with greater emphasis, 'that it does not happen again.'

'She was kicked out, wasn't she? For what she said.'

He didn't answer.

'Worse?' I stared at him. 'Oh, Christ.'

Sánchez was in the act of turning away when his eyes fell on the small pad of scribblings in front of me. For a couple of seconds he froze, his stare locked on that scrap of paper. 'Mr Weston,' he said slowly. 'Are you a journalist?'

I heard the unmistakable metal in his voice, and for a fatal second I hesitated. Perhaps that alone would have been enough to condemn us, but at that moment Freddy's rambunctious voice burst across the table:

'Yes, didn't you know? He's an undercover reporter.'

'I'm not,' I said immediately, definitively, already knowing it wouldn't be enough to undo the damage. For the first time, I felt real fear for Daedalus Foy. 'He's joking. Just joking.'

'Oops, sorry, I forgot,' said Freddy with exaggerated drama. 'It's a secret. He's investigating very secret things – spying.'

'Freddy, shut up!'

My loss of temper couldn't have been less helpful to my cause – our cause. Sánchez was moving away, a chilling expression on his face. Foy was already forgotten, my fear now entirely reserved for us.

'Mark, what's going on?' said Alice, rightly alarmed.

I gazed after the departing back of Francisco José Sánchez. There was still food on our plates, but no one was eating. Even Freddy had finally appreciated that the Comandante's questions represented more than just an amusing diversion. 'Come on,' I muttered. 'Let's get out of here.'

On the Revolutionary Trail With El Tigre

by Heath Katzenbach

Three days ago, I witnessed sixteen men die. Theirs were horrible deaths: five were killed in a blast from a rocket-propelled grenade, seven more were torn apart by AK-47s, the rest were finished off with bayonet, rifle butt, and machete. In guerrilla warfare, it is hard to take prisoners.

El Tigre, one of the more legendary FNR commanders, showed some regret for the loss of life. 'They are our brothers,' he said, 'but we have no choice.' When he agreed to have me accompany his group, El Tigre warned me of the unpleasant scenes I should expect to encounter. The unfortunate army patrol that we ambushed was by no means the first to fall victim to this formidable fighter. Indeed, he and his men – fourteen deeply loyal comrades who have fought together for much of this seemingly endless civil war – are understandably jaded by the killing. 'The more soldiers they send up here, the more we have to send back in coffins,' shrugged one guerrilla.

Each man is heavily weighed down, with an AK-47, ammunition, grenades, food, basic medical supplies, commando knife and either a radio, a mortar, an RPG launcher or a machine gun. It's a truly tough existence. But not one of them has any doubts: 'They have burnt our homes, killed our livestock, tortured our parents, raped our sisters,' says El Tigre. 'We either submit completely or we fight to the death.' For El Tigre, death very nearly came a couple of months ago. An army bullet passed clean through his neck, narrowly missing his carotid artery.

These men face a much larger and better-equipped force. During my week with them, we were attacked twice by helicopter gunship and once by artillery. Although the FNR receives some support from Cuba – El Tigre has come a long way since the night when this one-time lawyer led a few friends into the mountains with no uniforms, no training and just a handful of shotguns, .22 rifles, and pistols – they will never be able to fight pitched battles against the army as long as the Pentagon keeps the weapons flowing.

Which is why the recent rumor that Congress may be about to pull the plug on military aid is so warmly welcomed in these cold, muddy quarters. If that happens, the FNR could well regroup and go on the offensive. Talk of a direct attack on Santa Tecla is not uncommon.

But until that happens, El Tigre will continue to lead his band of dedicated warriors through the forests and mountains of the central highlands, always moving, always hiding. This war is set to run a long while yet.

CHAPTER 9

About two weeks after we met, Katie and I were in Ujung Pandang for a day, waiting for a flight to Ambon. Her friend had already flown home, but I'd managed to persuade Katie to miss the start of the new term at law school. She'd left her travelling pack of compact discs on a bus – unusually careless for her – and while I was taking a siesta in the hotel, she slipped out to buy some replacements. The shopping mall was a couple of miles from the hotel and she took a taxi. On the way back, she forgot to agree the price with the taxi driver before getting into the vehicle. At the end of the short journey, she was informed the price was three times what the first driver had asked.

These were small sums – tiny sums, by London standards – but Katie believes very strongly in moral justice and hates being ripped off. Unable to speak the language, she could only gesture her outrage. The driver insisted. Katie handed him the same amount she'd given the first driver. The notes were thrown back at her feet. She turned and marched into the hotel, leaving the money in the dust.

When she saw the driver come after her – a big man with a nasty attitude – she got scared and ran. By the time she'd raced up two flights of stairs and charged along the corridor to our room, she was panting for breath and slightly hysterical. As I was calming her down, there was a thump on the door and I opened it to the irate taxi driver. He yelled abuse at her over my shoulder. I blocked his way and offered him some money. He pushed past me, and went for Katie.

I hit him once, then threw him out.

The police came two hours later. It wasn't a serious charge, I knew. But finding myself out of my depth, even for just a short while, was a frightening experience. They held me in a police cell for one night and largely refused to acknowledge my questions, though I asked them in clear Indonesian. They didn't lay a finger on me, but I spent most of the night imagining they would. Events had moved out of my control, and I hated it.

Miraflores was no police cell, Sánchez was more courteous and better dressed than any of the policemen I encountered in Ujung Pandang, yet that sense of vulnerability before unpredictable, threatening strangers was ten times greater now.

We stepped out of the San Isidro into a lively wind. It coursed through the streets and the Parque Central, lifting dust, setting leaves dancing around us, and banging windows. Although still sunny, the sky was disappearing at its western edge behind a wall of thick cloud.

Through the back streets that led towards the coffee plantations, we felt reluctant now to catch the eye of strangers, returning their waves and greetings with muted gestures. Sánchez's suspicion had spoiled our enjoyment of this friendly community.

Leonard's long legs, so ungainly when dancing on the Parque's cobblestones, were now in their element. However often Alice urged him to slow down, his speed would build up again until he was marching several paces ahead of us. The fresh, high-country air had brought a vitality and an energy to him that was hard to reconcile with the collapsed figure in Bermuda airport. As we left the town behind us and made our way down the hillside, he eagerly pointed out plants and tiny, shrill birds, barely noticing the steep incline and the deteriorating track underfoot.

Cobbles gave way to compressed rubble, and finally to mud, the road swinging round until it was running along the contour of the hill. I had to admire the neat lines of coffee bushes that extended right down the slope to the river at the bottom of the valley. Dark-red beans speckled every plant. A sprinkling of orange and lemon trees – all bearing ripe fruit – interrupted the perfect symmetry of the plantation. At one point, half an acre of tomato and bean plants had been carved out from the coffee.

The wind, out in the open, was growing stronger,

sending birds of prey skimming across the sky and tracing crazy patterns in the approaching wall of cloud. Already, a slight dusting of raindrops was falling, so fine that in that bright sunshine I could see them dance with each sudden gust, sweeping sideways, even funnelling upwards. The droplets were all around us, yet our clothes never seemed to get wet and our faces remained warm.

'I don't think Sánchez likes us very much, does he?' whispered Alice when Freddy and Leonard were momentarily out of earshot. 'Who is Martha Masaya, by the way?'

'She was quoted in an American news report, insinuating that the suicides here weren't suicides.'

'Oh no.'

'Quite.'

'Have you gone and—?' She choked herself off with an exasperated sigh. 'One more night, and then we must go to Hoppner. I don't feel comfortable being around Señor Sánchez any longer than that.'

'It's going to be fine,' I told her, without much regard for whatever the truth happened to be. Might Sánchez have caught Daedalus Foy phoning in reports to some newspaper? Had he perhaps found a journalist's notebook in Foy's room? What would the ex-guerrilla have done then? Exactly how allergic to journalists were these people? 'We'll just keep away from him. No more suggestion of nosing around.'

'Ali, this wind is so strong, any moment we'll be flying!' called Leonard.

She threw me a look, then hurried towards him. 'Brilliant, darling!' As she reached him, she scooped one arm round his waist and thrust the other out like a wing, propelling him forward.

The forest, at the far end of the coffee plantation, was thick and impenetrable: grand old trees that had seen out Spanish colonization, political ferment and civil war, and were now set to survive even Benjamin Sword Hoppner, their trunks as sturdy as cathedral columns, their branches choked by epiphytes that thrived in the moist cloud air. The road, now just a muddy track churned up by the thick tyre treads of a heavy 4X4, cut a remarkably narrow course through this tangle of giants. Huge ferns fanned out above our heads; to left and right, the calls of unseen birds mingled with the chatter of a far-off monkey. Cloud swelled and rolled through the tree tops, giving the higher reaches a half-sketched, ethereal quality.

With the wind muted, the mood of the forest infected each of us, and even Leonard slowed, falling silent within minutes of passing the first trees. The track here was wetter, the ground holding water like a sponge beneath us. Navigating the treacherous ridges and furrows carved by Hoppner's vehicles required ever more attention. Freddy slipped once, lunging out to grasp my arm, and nearly landed us both in the mire.

From then on, I kept a good distance away from him.

'Sod this,' he said. 'Let's go back and get a lift.'

'It can't be much further,' said Alice with determination.

'Yeah, right,' he muttered. But he kept walking, without further remark.

When it finally came into view, there was no doubt we had found Benjamin Sword Hoppner's house. More than a house, it was a groomed compound of pinewood bungalows, set on a terrace in the hillside with a view over a crescent-shaped lake at the valley end. But it wasn't ostentation, as I'd expected, that defined it: rather a sense of functional order. In this country of war, of Spanish elegance and Latin temperament, those modest, precise quarters could only have been assembled by a foreigner. An interloper.

'There are guards,' said Freddy morosely. 'There's a bloody great fence and armed guards. Like something out of James Bond.'

'You can't tell from this distance that they're armed,' I pointed out, without much conviction.

'Well, what did you expect?' demanded Alice. 'Of course he's going to have security in a country like this. Otherwise, what's to stop a couple of enterprising thugs wandering in and kidnapping the resident billionaire?'

'Is there something wrong with having guards?' asked Leonard.

We all looked at him. 'No, no,' Freddy muttered. 'Not at all.'

'It's a good thing,' said Alice firmly. 'It means we'll be safe when we visit him.'

'But surely that's going too far in the opposite direction,' said Leonard. 'If you thought the danger was significant without guards around, then we shouldn't be staying in Miraflores.'

He was smiling, enjoying his role as destroyer of faulty logic. Alice just stared at him, nodding wordlessly, unsure what she could safely say. I began to appreciate how much effort it was costing her to sustain this fictional romance.

'There's no danger,' I said, feeling a sudden urge to give her a little support. 'We're staying in a paradise created by a philanthropist. We've got nothing to worry about.' But a small part of my brain was still wondering what had happened to Martha Masaya and Daedalus Foy.

'Bloody creepy, though,' said Freddy, 'even if it's not dangerous. People hanging themselves in the middle of the town square.'

'Poor chap,' said Leonard. 'Do you think he had family?'

Freddy had fully recovered from the shock of the previous night and was now in judgemental mood: 'Any bastard who kills himself in front of kids deserves to die.'

For a moment I expected Leonard to pick holes in that warped assertion, but this time his humanity got the better of his intellectual instincts. 'It's just tragic that anyone should become so desperate as to lose hope altogether – no longer have a reason to live.'

'But you're a philosopher,' I couldn't help saying. 'What reason is there ever to live?'

'Of course. But I didn't mean "reason" in the strictest sense. I'm afraid I was speaking loosely – of motive . . . emotion . . .'

'What's wrong with saying we live because God put us on this earth to live, full stop?' demanded Alice.

The man of reason put his arm round the woman he believed to be his girlfriend. 'Nothing's wrong with that,' he smiled gently. 'Nothing at all.'

The sun had completely disappeared behind the cloud now. In its absence, the wind and the flurry of rain droplets had begun to chill. None of us wanted to stay any longer, staring down at a compound where the only movement came from the four grey-uniformed guards on the perimeter. We started back up that long muddy track at least five minutes before the rain reached us, but when the first torrents burst on the trees ahead we were still a long way from the town.

'Oh, great,' muttered Freddy. 'Wonderful.'

'We're going to get soaked,' said Leonard helpfully.

'Here,' I called to Alice, 'take my jacket.'

'I'm fine,' she said resolutely.

Slipping the jacket back on, I glanced at the forest on either side of us. With thick cloud and

235

an even thicker canopy blocking out much of the light, the undergrowth looked dark, damp and thoroughly unappealing. But only a fraction of the rain was penetrating the tree-top foliage.

'Let's wait it out in there,' I said.

My suggestion was not a popular one, but it was clear we didn't have much choice. None of the others was wearing anything waterproof; all of us were beginning to shiver in the bullet-hard rain. We couldn't even see more than fifty feet up the track. Fighting our way through the ferns and the treacherously exposed roots, we made our way to the biggest, leafiest tree in sight, huddled against its trunk and waited.

The tree was laden with creepers of all sizes – delicate green twine to thick mossy wood – that dangled over our heads, trickling raindrops down our collars and into our eyes. Gaps in the canopy glowed electric white against the blackness of the leaves.

We said nothing, avoiding contact. Four people stuck in the same uncomfortable – possibly even dangerous – position, yet reluctant to share any of it.

While I was passing the time gazing at the vast gardens of orchids, ferns, mosses and grasses that clung to the upper reaches of each tree, I noticed a much larger gap in the canopy further into the forest. Thoroughly fed up with standing still, I started walking towards it.

'Look at this,' said Freddy, bending down to

236

scoop a delicate golden frog the size of a penny off a leaf. He looked faintly ridiculous in his damp pink polo shirt, studying an amphibian in the middle of a Central American cloud forest.

'You shouldn't pick it up,' I told him over my shoulder. 'They die if you hold them too long.'

'Bollocks!' he cried. 'Where'd you pick up a superstitious idea like that?'

For a moment I hesitated, asking myself the same question. Then I walked on without replying.

The reason for the clearing was obvious the moment I reached it. In its centre, battered by the ever more forceful barrage of rain, was the crumpled wreck of a grey-green helicopter.

It had been lying there a long time. Only a few segments of the body were actually rusted, but the paintwork on the rest of the aircraft was tired and decayed. Vines and ferns smothered much of it; the belly and tail were buried in the mud of the forest floor; smashed lengths of rotor blade lay hidden in the undergrowth. The tree beside me bore a great diagonal gash, partly hidden beneath moss and scar tissue.

Despite the rain thundering down in the clearing, I stepped forward, drawn by that twisted remnant of a once-powerful fighting machine. None of the interior fittings remained: someone had carried off the seats, harnesses, guns, bodies; whatever bullet-proof substance might once have filled the windows was gone. Between rips and gashes, the battered metal skin bore stencilled markings – SUMP DRAIN, FUEL/PUMP – and a large red arrow, ironically marked DANGER, pointed down the fuselage towards a tail rotor that no longer existed. In places the outer skin was torn away, revealing an extraordinary honeycombed structure underneath. At my touch, the tiny hexagonal aluminium cells bent sideways and collapsed into distorted packs of crushed metal. I wondered idly if any of the government troops shot down had realized what fragile tissue shielded them from the gun emplacements of Miraflores's rebels.

'Mark!'

I looked round. It was Freddy calling, though he wasn't yet in sight. The idea of him coming upon this fallen bird disturbed me, and I hurried back under the shelter of the trees.

'You were right!' he cried, the moment he saw me. 'It just . . . stopped moving.'

'What?' Increasingly impatient with the endless rain, I was letting my frustration get the better of me. 'What are you talking about?'

'The frog. It just died, there in my hand.'

'Oh, for Christ's sake, it doesn't matter, Freddy.'

'But why? I don't understand.'

'The heat. Your body's too hot for it.'

He digested this idea for a moment as I walked past him, back to where Alice and Leonard stood pressed together for warmth. Both of them looked miserable.

Freddy trotted after me. 'How d'you know this stuff?' he marvelled.

'I've no idea. It's just something I picked up, OK?'

'Look, friend, there's no need—'

'Where have you been?' said Alice. 'You're soaked!'

'We should go back,' I said. 'Who knows if this rain is ever going to stop? It's going to get dark soon.'

'And now you're wet . . .'

'We're all cold. We'd be better off just heading back fast – the walk will warm us, and we can soak in hot baths when we get there.'

No one was disagreeing. The chill and wet were penetrating our brains.

It was hard to see much on the track, away from the protection of the trees, in rain that beat down with ever greater intensity. So when a little boy – dressed only in a pair of shorts – appeared out of the mist and gave a victorious shout, we were as surprised as he was. Immediately he spun round and ran off ahead of us, vanishing into the gloom of the road ahead, making little birdlike calls that grew steadily fainter.

'What was that about?' said Freddy.

'Do you think they sent him to find us?' suggested Leonard. 'We've been away a long time in bad weather.'

'If they did, why'd he run off like that? How are we supposed to follow him?'

Feeling a sudden shudder of unease, I reached into my pocket for Katie's earring and gripped it tightly between finger and thumb.

The force of the rain against the track was deafening, and we gave up talking. Within seconds, our legs were splattered with mud. Leonard began moving faster, and this time we matched his pace, all of us aching to get back to the warmth and comfort of the San Isidro. Even if Benjamin Sword Hoppner himself had appeared in the road behind us, chequebook in hand, I'm not convinced we would have slowed. By the time we reached the bend in the track that marked the halfway point through the forest, we were almost running to keep up with Leonard's great strides.

But the moment we rounded that bend, we all stopped dead.

Francisco José Sánchez stood at the head of eight men, all of them familiar from the previous night, fanned out across the road. They were drenched through, their hats sagging, their leather and woollen coats hanging limply from their shoulders, a sheathed machete suspended at each waist. Every one of them wore a black armband. Off to the side, the boy was standing on one foot, pointing eagerly towards us.

A single hiss from Sánchez sent him scuttling up the track towards Miraflores. None of the men moved.

'Is this a search party, or what?' I murmured.

Alice swallowed once. 'It looks more like "or what",' she said, her lip trembling very slightly. 'Hang on.'

She started forward, a smile appearing as if by magic.

'What are you doing?' I cried.

'Stay here. Let me talk to them,' she said without looking back.

'Ali,' said Leonard, half questioning, half fearful. I put a hand on his arm. Freddy had already taken a step back.

Thirty yards separated us. Alice walked the distance without hesitation. I heard her voice through the drum of the rain – cheery, unwavering – as she came to a halt two paces from Sánchez. A greeting: perhaps a traditional British observation on the appalling weather. Sánchez didn't react. Not a word; not a smile.

She spoke again, this time with more urgency. Again, there was no reply from the men around her. Water streamed off the brims of their hats, bouncing against jutting knees and knuckles that rested on machete handles. The fading light was turning oppressive.

Then, almost a shout: Alice was turning angry, demanding an explanation, citing a grievance. And all of a sudden Sánchez's hand had reached out and grabbed her arm. Her words turned into a scream. Two men ran forward at Sánchez's sharp command. Alice was thrown into their arms, and Sánchez started towards us.

'Ali!' yelled Leonard, almost collapsing from fright.

'Oh, Jesus!' cried Freddy.

As he turned to run, I gripped his collar. 'We stay together,' I shouted.

A commotion broke out behind Sánchez. My attention momentarily on Freddy, I didn't see what happened, but when I looked round Alice was tearing towards us, her feet sliding wildly in the mud. One of the men assigned to hold her was bent over, clutching his groin. The rest were racing after her.

'Run!' I cried, sprinting towards her.

Sánchez was nearly on her when he slipped and stumbled. One of his comrades caught him as he fell. Another man – heavy chested and long legged – ran past them and seized Alice's arm, sending her spinning to the ground. Remembering the tiny child inside her, I felt some reservoir of rage burst open in my brain. By the time I reached them he was standing over her, one hand round her neck, the other clutching her hair. Her face was half-buried in the mud, a bright red gash blooming where her forehead had struck a stone.

Without stopping to think I reached into my jacket pocket, seized one of the grappling hooks and slashed its honed blade across the man's arms. His blood spurted across Alice's back and he screamed horribly, yanking himself away and falling against his comrades.

A second hook was in my left hand before I'd even looked for the next assault. Against nine men armed with machetes, I wasn't using my fists. Already they were encircling us, Sánchez directing them to the left and right. When I glanced round for a split second, I was amazed to see Leonard and Freddy – tweed jacket and pink polo shirt – standing right there behind me. Somehow, both men had found a kind of courage I would never have expected of them.

'See if she's all right,' I shouted to Leonard, pulling myself up straight and turning towards Sánchez. 'Freddy, take this.' I pulled out the last grappling hook and tossed it back to him. He missed it in the confusion of rain and panic, and it fell in the mud at his feet. 'Leave it! Try to get one of their machetes.'

'My gun, Mark! Where's my gun?'

I had no time for that. I turned back to Sánchez, hook blades extended. He drew his machete from its sheath. Around us, his comrades followed suit. The man I'd cut was crouched in the mud at the edge of the track, moaning aloud. When Sánchez snarled a single syllable he fell silent.

'What do you want?' I shouted. 'Why are you doing this?'

'We cannot let it happen again.' Sánchez shook his head. 'Not again.'

'What? What did we do?'

'You saw Tanadio die. We cannot allow another journalist to report—'

'I'm not a journalist! None of us will say anything!'

He shrugged. Through the rain, his face seemed to carry real regret. 'So you say,' he murmured.

'Please! Think about what you're doing. If four English disappear, the whole world will come asking questions! They're already looking for Foy!'

It made no impression. 'People disappear here all the time,' he said. Then he gave a nod.

Four of the men behind me leapt forward, seizing Leonard and Freddy between them, forcing them to the ground beside Alice. Machetes were held ready, just waiting for Sánchez's signal.

With his eyes locked on mine, Sánchez waited for me to drop the hooks. I could sense the other men all around me, ready to strike at my unprotected back the moment the command was given. I had no choice: there could be nothing in store for us short of death. With a sudden roar of outrage, I leapt at Sánchez.

If I could only have got a grip on his machete arm and a blade to his throat, I believe I could have got us all out of that muddy battleground. Those men revered Sánchez – they would never have allowed him to be killed. But Sánchez, it turned out, deserved his following.

As I went for him his whole body twisted away until there was nothing but air for me to grab. I plunged forward, out of control, and felt a whiplash down the side of my ribcage where his machete struck me. The next moment I was in the mud,

Sánchez's knee across my back and the blade of his machete pressed against my neck. The grappling hooks had disappeared into the mire.

'Wait!' I yelled, unable to see, my mouth filling with grainy, filthy water. 'Wait!'

My voice sounded shrill, almost drowned out by the mud. Sánchez ignored me. He shouted his commands. There was nothing I could do to stop the massacre. Just because we'd been in the wrong place at the wrong time. Just because Freddy had made a joke to the wrong man. Just because . . .

A blast of sound – like a foghorn, like an explosion – burst through the air. The weight on my back shifted; Sánchez fell silent. I became aware of a motor, somewhere beyond the crash of the rain.

I lifted my head, coughing up mud. Sánchez was gone, his weight lifted. Rolling on to my back, I looked around for the source of the noise. Grit and mud half blinded me.

At the bend in the track, where we'd hesitated as Alice walked bravely into danger, a large black vehicle stood with doors open and headlights ablaze. In front of it were three figures, dressed identically in olive-green ponchos and wide grey hats. Through the rain, through my near blindness, those tented, armless shapes seemed frighteningly supernatural: wraiths that could have been angels or demons.

The nearest to us was the largest, and, as I rubbed the dirt out of my eyes, he lifted his head and barked at Sánchez in brutal, furious Spanish. His face was obscured by the hat, but his voice had an immediate effect on the men around us. All of them backed away, leaving just their leader standing over me.

The second man was shorter and slimmer, with a black face and fluid movements. He darted forward to the spot where the others lay pressed together in the mud. 'Are you all right?' he called, his voice a gentle American flutter that was more comforting even than the first man's evident authority. He glanced towards me, then waved at Sánchez. 'Go. Go,' he said, hardly raising his voice.

Not one of the new arrivals was carrying a weapon, yet their orders were obeyed instantly. Sánchez muttered a brief few words and his comrades fell into line behind him. I watched in near disbelief as the men who'd come so close to killing us walked meekly away towards Miraflores.

Then I turned back. The third man still had not moved, had not said a word. He stood rigid and erect, silhouetted against the headlights, just as he'd stood at my window the night before. I could barely see his face, but as I pulled myself out of the mud and felt the sting of the machete slash come alive below my arm, I sensed an anger in Benjamin Sword Hoppner darker than I'd ever known before.

A Code for Life, Section 2: Justice (excerpt)

Moral justice is not concerned with obedience to law. Too often the word justice is used to mean law enforcement. Yet if laws are unjust, it is our moral duty to oppose them. Moral justice is better thought of as fairness.

Sadly, it is often impossible for human beings to look beyond their own interests in deciding – even with the best of intentions – what is fair. Dreamers have invented perfect systems in which we make decisions about laws, societal structure, prices and punishment regimes without knowing what role we will play: ruler or ruled; buyer or seller; complier or transgressor. Perfect systems never come true. That is why, to figure out equitable solutions to our disputes, we must turn to judges.

But who should judge? Remember, this is moral, not legal, justice we are talking about. We cannot simply ask the guys with the wooden hammers. Our elected representatives have proven themselves endlessly corruptible wherever votes or election funding are at stake. Besides, democracy is not moral justice. Winning an argument by having more people on your side is no fairer than winning by having bigger muscles: it's simply a numerical version of Might is Right. Worse even than the politicians are the newspapers. Editors and journalists love to sit in moral judgment over whomever they dislike. Damning headlines sell copies, and give those faceless pseudo-judges the chance to shoot down anyone they resent, envy or hold prejudice against.

In fact, very few people are qualified to pass moral judgment – to say what is fair. These few are the students of morality – the people who have devoted many years to understanding secular morality from all its different angles. We need far more of these people.

Even the best judges will struggle with the dilemmas that trouble us from time to time. Should we sacrifice an innocent to save a city? Should we release a violent man once he has served his term, even if he declares an intention to continue his violence? But far better to place these matters in the hands of the morally enlightened than to let a corrupt politician condone the guilty, or an innocent be persecuted by the newspapers. Might – whether it be wealth, position, crowds, armory or daily circulation – cannot be allowed to dictate justice. Only the disinterested third party, well versed in virtue, can say what is truly fair.

CHAPTER 10

Like refugees from savage war we waited, each in our own cocoon of shock, for some kind of sense to emerge from this nightmare. We were all shivering. None of us spoke. Of the three men in their otherworldly green capes, only the slim black guy joined us in the back. The tall man removed his hat a second before stepping into the driving seat, and I recognized the blond terrorist-hunter from Santa Tecla. Hoppner took the seat beside him. Not a word from him, not even – in that driving, splashing rain – a smile of acknowledgement. The black man helped us into the back seats, slammed the door and leaned forward to confer with his master as the vehicle was thrown into an aggressive turn.

It was some kind of sports utility vehicle – metallic black, high off the ground, its interior spotless until we climbed in and spread our shaking, jellied limbs and mud-sodden clothing across the cream upholstery – and it took the track with a snarling, sliding brute force. The noise and jolting were a welcome restorative after Sánchez's primeval barbarity, and they helped take my mind off the disaster our endeavour had become.

We had, after all, just been rescued by the man we'd come to rob.

Within seconds, all the windows were steamed up. The blond guy's broad palm slapped out against the windscreen to clear a small patch of glass. Enclosed in that hot, claustrophobic bubble, I couldn't help thinking of another urgent drive down rain-drenched hills, this one with Katie by my side. Not touching yet, but brought together in a sort of adversity, with a comatose woman lying between us on the grubby floor of the local bus.

Her friend and travelling companion had collapsed. I'd seen it coming: I'd warned her, after she'd vomited at the sight of two dozen lively water buffalo having their throats cut for a Toraja funeral. But Liz was as stubborn as she was ill-suited to the realities of Sulawesi's death culture, and she refused to get anything less than her money's worth from her guide. It was already raining by the time I showed them the trees into which the corpses of babies had been sewn. The dripping coffins hanging from cliffs made her sway. And when, finally, I led them bent double into the black, decay-ridden burial caverns, she lasted just two minutes before the fit.

The black man looked round. 'I'm David,' he said, catching the gaze of each one of us in brief, sympathetic turn. The telltale scars of that childhood trauma in Tulsa were just visible on his cheeks and forehead. 'Are you cold? We'll have your clothes brought. While you shower.'

Leonard was searching his pockets for a handkerchief to clean away the blood on Alice's forehead. She was quite still, neck crooked forward. She didn't react as he dabbed the edge of his sleeve, for want of anything more absorbent, against the cut. It shook me to think he'd had his life on the line, might even have done something stupidly heroic, for a girl whose love for him was make-believe.

David leaned towards us. 'You deserve an apology. And an explanation. It must have been frightening. Terrifying. Please. Be patient now.'

Beside me, Freddy's left hand was stroking a torn strip of pink polo shirt back into place over his stomach. The material slipped away; he retrieved it: over and over. His face was empty – the basis of his whole personality was a confidence that now lay shattered. The slightest rustle of half-spoken words came from his slack mouth.

I looked back at David: 'Why did—?'

'Please.' His hand came up, lay briefly against my arm, then returned to his lap. Behind him, a slight tilt in the angle of Hoppner's head. A second later, his neck was perfectly straight again. 'We're there now,' said David.

The SUV was slowing. I rubbed a scrap of mist away in time to see the high fence, the gates, two of the guards. Unsmiling, solidly built and efficient in their movements, both carried ferocious-looking combat sticks, although there were no guns in sight.

As we came to a halt, Hoppner opened his door.

'Now. Gotta have been terrifying,' said David, suddenly strangely eager to talk. 'But not now. Let's see. You must be Alice. So you're Leonard. I'm gonna guess. Between you two?' As he glanced at Freddy and me, I got the distinct impression that he was slowing his staccato sentences even more than usual, allowing Hoppner time to get well clear of the SUV before he opened the back door. We were guests – not just rescued victims – but we were being carefully managed.

'I think you're Mark,' he said at last, warm almond eyes firmly, confidently on me.

Katie's earring was missing. I'd felt something was wrong in the SUV – the absence of that little jab of metal against my thigh. When I realized what it was, when in a panic I ran desperate hands into every one of my pockets, I nearly cried, so distraught was I to lose my last piece of her. Buried in the cloud-forest mud. Gone.

I stood in the shower for a long time, unwilling – as I suspect we all were – to be the first into the interrogations. Out of Sánchez's frying pan, into God knows what. How the hell could we even begin to come out with our lame stories now?

The wound from Sánchez's machete was more bruise and graze than serious laceration, but still it stung like hell. Although blood had rather dramatically soaked my shirt, the flow had dried up by the time I reached the shower. If it hadn't been for

252

the tough leather of my jacket, the damage could have been a lot worse. The jacket's world-weary look had just become a little wearier thanks to a seven-inch slit down its side.

My bathroom was pure North America. Whatever Hoppner thought of his country's morals, the depravity of its leaders, he clearly approved of its industrial products. Nothing excessively luxurious, but everything cleanly modern: wall-to-wall mirror, power shower and white plastic units. A stack of neatly folded white towels. It could have been the Hyatt.

The bedroom I'd been allocated was much the same: character-free, but guaranteed to offer an uninterrupted, pleasant sleep. True to his word, David had had my bags delivered, silently, while I'd been scrubbing the mud out of my ears, hair and nostrils. Had Sánchez brought them? Had David himself driven straight back to Miraflores? What kind of terse conversation might the two men have had in the aftermath of that murderous ambush? Even the toothbrush and comb I'd left on the hotel basin had been tucked neatly into the side pocket, wrapped in two scented tissues.

I put off the inevitable a little while longer, taking my time to comb my hair and button a pale-blue shirt, staring out of the window at the back of the house I believed to be Hoppner's. Like the other buildings in the compound, it sat four feet off the ground on robust concrete piles. A veranda ran round the sides, with wooden columns supporting a roof from which water flowed in great sheets – lit from behind by porch lamps – cascading down into muddy troughs that might once have been flowerbeds. The billionaire's grand residence.

Picking up my watch, I walked out to meet David.

He was sitting on one of the long sofas that lined the central hall of this capacious guesthouse – this supplicants' dormitory. Opposite him was Freddy, clutching a cup of steaming coffee two inches below his nose. David stood up to shake my hand, that sympathetic smile making another appearance. Behind me, a door opened and Alice and Leonard emerged.

'Good! All here. Hot coffee?'

Away from the battleground of the forest track, David was a brighter star – a courteous organizer and a charming host. Yet there was something inexplicably comic about the scene.

'With a slug of brandy?' I said, stifling a laugh.

David's eyes widened. 'OK. Why not?'

'Is alcohol approved of around here?'

'Certainly. In moderation. Mr Hoppner is no killjoy.'

As David walked to the open-plan kitchen area, Freddy perked up. 'Actually, if you wouldn't mind . . .' He hurried over with his half-drunk coffee. David saw him coming and reached into a steel-and-glass cupboard for the bottle. 'Oh, magnificent, friend,' muttered Freddy, when his cup was filled.

With the two of them occupied, and Leonard inspecting the framed watercolours of dazzlingly vivid tropical birds on the walls, Alice caught my eye. She had a large plaster stuck across her forehead. For some reason I wanted to stroke it. She mouthed, 'What now?'

I shrugged. The gesture irritated her, but, given that we'd just survived the Latin version of a lynching, I was quite happy to enjoy a hot coffee and brandy for a while without thinking about very much else.

'He thought you worked for us,' said David, suddenly, to me. He held three cups in his two hands. 'Sugar? Yes? No?' The coffee was too milky, but I didn't care. 'Joaquim Tanadio. He saw you with Hawken. In Santa Tecla.' Belatedly, I realized he was talking about the Indian terrorist and the blond guy. Hawken? I recalled those cold eyes. 'Then you shouted Mr Hoppner's name. The next day. Just after he placed the bomb.'

I thought back to the Via España, the morning of the blast: my last words to Freddy, a moment before the terrorist had re-entered my consciousness. About Hoppner's generosity. One meaningless little joke.

'He was terrified. Thought you were our spy. Would tell Hawken he did it. He wanted to stop you telling us.'

'You mean he wanted to kill me,' I said, nearly choking on the coffee. 'He tried to shoot me!'

'See, friend, I told you it wasn't me,' said

Freddy. For a second, the old self-assured grin was back.

'We know,' said David. 'He told us. He came here. When he couldn't stop you. He has a family in town. To protect them, he came to confess.'

'And then . . .'

I thought about that body swinging through the square. Before the ambush, I'd half suspected Hoppner of ordering the hanging. But if I'd learnt anything this afternoon, it was exactly who around Miraflores was prepared to kill. Had Sánchez taken the law into his own hands with Tanadio as well?

'Why was he so afraid of you finding out?' I said.

'This is a moral town now. Mr Hoppner is very clear. Murder is forbidden in all social orders. Mass murder of innocents cannot be tolerated.'

Hoppner quite rightly deplores murder, but under his system of governance the whole town gets punished for it. Just as in the case of Martha Masaya. Unless, perhaps, the town's leaders dispense their own justice first . . .

'It was suicide?' I asked.

David's eyes dropped for a split second. It was all the confirmation I needed. Sánchez, or one of his friends, had murdered the mass-murderer. Making it look like a suicide for the most important spectator of all. The terrorist dies, apparently at his own hand, and the town can rest assured of Hoppner's continuing benevolence. Once a dependence on another's money becomes established, there isn't a lot the dependant won't do to maintain the flow – as we had unwittingly discovered.

'Tanadio recognized he was a detriment,' said David belatedly. 'To his society. He removed himself from it.'

'How convenient.'

'Wait a minute,' said Freddy. 'Forget the terrorist bloke. What about that lot back there? They just about slaughtered us!'

'Mr Hoppner will take action.'

'But why did those people attack us?' asked Leonard. 'What had we done?'

He was sitting to my left, and as he turned to David I noticed a patch of mud below his ear. He'd put on a bright yellow jumper and brown corduroy trousers. His wet, combed hair brushed his collar in uneven tendrils.

'I'm sorry. They over-reacted. Mr Hoppner hates bad press. Stories that damage his work here. They thought you were journalists. They thought he'd want it.'

'Want us dead?' I said. 'He's given them the impression he wants all journalists murdered?'

'Who's been murdered?'

The voice came from the main door. I hadn't heard the woman come in: the heavy tropical rain clattering against the tiled roof obliterated all other background noise.

She repeated the question: 'Who's been murdered?' Another North American. She was soaked, but it was clear from her manner that the rain

didn't bother her. Dressed in Lycra shorts and a
thick fleece, she carried over her shoulder two coils
of bright yellow rope; in her hands she held a canvas
bag and a climbing harness. Streaks of orange mud
decorated her bare legs and her forehead below the
flattened curls of red hair.

'No one,' said David. 'A misunderstanding.
Sánchez was nervous. About these—'

'Nervous?' I sat up at that. 'He had eight men
armed with machetes. That's not nervous.'

'Try to understand. They—'

'They were about to cut us to pieces!' I couldn't
believe this.

Neither could Alice. 'Mark!' she cried, leaning forward, her face taut with her unvoiced
message. I was going too far, apparently, being
too blunt with our prospective benefactor's lieutenant.

A moment later, blood was oozing from the
plaster on her forehead. 'Shit.' She brought up
her hand, felt the sticky wetness.

'Ali . . .'

'Let me look at that.' The woman dumped her
climbing equipment at the door, picked up a roll
of paper towel from the kitchen area and walked
across to Alice.

'It's just a . . .' For a moment, Alice looked a
little faint.

The woman ripped the plaster off, dabbing a
handful of towels to Alice's forehead in the same
motion. Tiny pools of rainwater collected on the

258

carpet around her feet. I noticed she was wearing black rubber shoes, tight-fitting and tapered, specialized for climbing.

'You need stitches,' she declared. 'Hold this.'

Meekly, Alice took the paper towels, pressing them against the cut. The woman stalked off to a side room.

'That's Pamela,' said David, in her absence. 'She works mainly with the women. In Miraflores. She's Canadian. It's important to remember that.'

'What about Daedalus Foy?' I asked quietly. 'Did he upset Sánchez in the same way?'

'Who?' said David blankly.

Pamela was back within a minute, the wet fleece gone and a heavy towel wrapped round her shoulders. She was carrying a green plastic medical box and a jug of hot water.

'Oh! Are you a doctor?' said Leonard with an apologetic laugh.

'You're Leonard, right?' she said, without much interest in an answer.

'Yes, that's right. And this is Alice; that's Freddy, and—'

'Lean your head back.' Laying the medical box on the sofa beside Alice, Pamela drew a white flannel from the jug and cleaned away the blood. 'How did she do this?'

'We were attacked,' I said firmly, watching David. 'Sánchez organized a little hunting party to get rid of us.'

'Please.' David looked distressed. 'They were

259

guerrillas. For many years. Killing is different here.'

A small bottle of antiseptic came out of the medical box. Pamela soaked a cotton-wool pad and dabbed it against the cut. When Alice twitched at the sting, she looked profoundly unimpressed.

'A way of life?' I said.

The irony wasn't lost on Alice, even if David, nodding, seemed to take the words at face value.

'Mark . . .' Unable to see me, her face tilted back beneath Pamela's hands, she was nevertheless determined to put a halt to my outspoken bluntness.

David shook his head. 'They thought Mr Hoppner wanted it,' he sighed.

'Blameless, then. Like the knights who killed Thomas à Becket.' I got a confused look from David, but a nod from Leonard that was almost congratulatory. 'Does that mean we should blame the King?'

'No one's to blame. Really. Please. Understand. It's just—'

'If you're holding Mr Hoppner responsible for Sánchez's actions, you obviously know nothing about either,' said Pamela, eyes still on Alice's forehead. 'Sánchez is an animal I doubt we could make good of in thirty years of trying. Mr Hoppner, on the other hand, is as close to being a saint as it's possible for a man to get.'

Barely needing to look at the box, she selected a sealed packet and broke it open. Inside was a

260

long needle, already bearing a strand of thick black thread. The thumb and index finger of her left hand pinched the flesh on Alice's forehead, while the right pushed the needle through. Alice didn't make a sound. I watched the quick, practised strokes with morbid fascination.

Leonard coughed. 'I mean, he is doing jolly good things here . . . but surely there are one or two aspects of his past . . . the pornography, for one, and . . . I mean, it's not all completely saintly . . .'

He trailed off as Pamela looked up at him, needle paused in mid-stitch, buried in Alice's flesh. She took one deep breath in, one deep breath out.

'I used to think like that,' she said. Then she looked down at the needle. 'You're done.' She pulled it clear, snipped the thread with a pair of surgical scissors and twisted the end into a knot.

'Thanks.' Alice looked round at her healer, but Pamela was already standing up and walking towards the kitchen area. From her shirt pocket she produced a plastic case containing three slim cigars. She took one and stooped to light it on the gas hob.

'Pamela hated us,' murmured David with a small smile.

'Only because you seemed to go against everything I stood for,' she snapped. Picking up a bottle of mineral water, she came back over and stood with one foot balanced on a chair. The burning cigar hung loosely from her hand, resting on a heavily muscled thigh.

'I worked for Women Against Sexual Exploitation in Toronto,' she explained. 'Sword magazines were everywhere. They were a major target for our anti-pornography campaign.'

'Yet you think he's a saint.'

'I hadn't understood why he was doing it. It was only when I went to Chicago to lobby him – banners outside his offices, demonstrations – that I got what he was doing.'

'It's economics,' said David. 'Robin Hood.'

'You have got to speak in longer sentences if you're going to get the message across,' Pamela told him crossly. She put the cigar between her teeth and looked back at us. 'Not "from the rich to give to the poor". For Sword Enterprises, it's "from the bad to give to the good". Every part of the business is focused on sucking money out of immoral people.'

Did she really believe that? So simple. So unbelievably naïve. She was staring at a vastly profitable conglomerate and seeing only virtuous dreams. 'You're kidding,' I said.

'No.' And in fact, looking at her, I seriously doubted she'd ever cracked a joke in her life. Somehow, the wet, matted red hair just gave her convert's face an even greater and more urgent sincerity.

'The first thing Mr Hoppner showed me was the halfway houses that his magazines paid for,

262

helping prostitutes to get off the street and train for real jobs. Women who'd been forced to sell their bodies since they were teenagers, suddenly able to get free of that horrific trap.'

'But isn't photographing naked women for money just a form of pimping?'

She stared at me with something close to scorn, the cigar tip burning suddenly brighter as she sucked on it. 'It's good to see you don't know much about prostitution.' Taking the cigar between finger and thumb, she tapped a scrap of ash on to the bloody paper towels that still lay on the side table. 'Immoral men buy the magazines and grow poorer – their economic power diminishes. Meantime, we use the money to support charities, pay for good people to do good works, or – like here – fund a complete society based on morality. Money is drawn from the bad to the good, making the first weaker and the second stronger. And it's all down to Mr Hoppner.'

I wanted so much to tear it apart – to laugh at this appalling catch-all defence for participating in every profitable vice imaginable. But Alice was glaring at me, warning me against screwing up our chances with these deluded people. Sucking money out of bad people! It was absurd. And yet the more I thought about it the more I came to appreciate how attractive such a simplistic capitalist proposition could be to anyone obsessed by the great earthly battle between Good and Evil.

The main door opened again. This time it was

the blond guy: Hawken. I don't know if he ever used a Christian name. In Santa Tecla I'd told him I was there to attend the reconstruction conference. A blatant lie, he now knew. I wondered if it would count against me with Hoppner.

Pamela and David gave him their immediate attention. 'He wants us,' Hawken told them. Then a brief glance at me – silent recognition, not reassuring. In the light, out of the rain, he looked tougher still, his heavy shoulders sitting comfortably on a broad frame.

'What will happen?' David asked.

'The power. Off for two weeks at least. Maybe the water as well.'

'Nothing more?' There was a definite uneasiness to David's voice.

Hawken stared at him curiously for a moment, then shook his head. 'Come.'

I stood on the guesthouse veranda, the glassy sheet of water sliding off the roof falling an inch from my nose. Nothing to see in the darkness. Hoppner's house was silent, just a couple of rooms lit, their interiors obscured by blinds. I noticed something else: a row of red tubes hanging where the gutters should have been, bouncing about in the run-off. Two guards stood under a shelter by the floodlit gate. Two more, dressed in ponchos, were patrolling the perimeter fence. It was comforting to know they stood between us and Sánchez's men.

Freddy appeared beside me.

'I want to talk to you,' he said.

'So talk.' I didn't really have the energy to listen.

'My gun. What did you do with it? We needed that gun.'

'I threw it away.'

'You thr—! . . . What do you mean, you threw it away?'

'I mean I threw it away.'

He was spluttering now. 'That was my gun!'

'Yes.'

'Well, then . . . how dare you just throw it away?'

I sighed. 'Freddy, is there a point to this?'

He pulled himself up, straightened his shoulders. 'Yes, there damn well is a point to this! I paid for that gun. You can't just throw it away.'

Beyond Hoppner's house, the lawn disappeared into the darkness. To each side of us a scattering of other buildings probably served as stores and garages, a workshop perhaps; maybe even a conference room for the town elders. Sánchez, staring at a flipchart explaining the costs and benefits of murdering people versus being nice to them.

'You're going to have to pay for it, you know. That gun cost me four hundred dollars. You owe me four hundred dollars.'

I looked at him, unable to stop myself laughing at his absurd, pathetic lie. 'Four hundred? Is that right, Freddy?' I said.

His head bobbed a little from side to side, but

he managed a definite nod. 'Yes. Four hundred. In cash, please.'

'Oh sure,' I muttered. 'Whatever you say.'

Somewhere across the compound lay the source of many times that sum. The difficulty was in persuading myself it was still prudent to pursue it.

A Code for Life: Introduction (excerpt)

Our world turns on rationalization. We must have a reason to do everything. We must have a reason to be good. Some say it is our duty to be generous, to forgive and to tell the truth. Some say we should do whatever has as its consequence the greatest amount of happiness for the greatest number of people, regardless of whether the actions involved are intrinsically good or bad. I say, forget duty, forget consequences. We should be generous, forgiving and truthful because these traits are virtues, and virtues make the world a better place. That is sufficient reason for me.

CHAPTER 11

A silent mist hung over the compound on our second morning as guests of the reclusive Benjamin Sword Hoppner. The rain, which had endured more or less continuously since our arrival, had finally relented, letting the sounds of the surrounding forest fill the air. Early morning birdsong, the shrieks of distant monkeys, the slight rustle of canopy foliage. And all around, the mist – close and comforting – blocking out the world beyond my small patch of lawn.

'The man who drew first blood.' The voice was deep, yet light-hearted; breezy, yet rich in sincerity. 'How do you rate your chances when your reach the Pearly Gates?'

I turned. Without the cape, Hoppner was instantly recognizable. He looked exactly like every picture of him – razor parting, erect stance and pressed business shirt – except for one thing: he was smiling.

'Well, technically, the first blood was Alice's – a gash on the head when she was thrown to the ground.'

'Then we shall defend you in the celestial court

on grounds of chivalry,' said Hoppner. 'A Christian invention, let's not forget, and it always works with well-spoken Englishmen.'

'I thought you didn't believe in God?' I couldn't help returning his smile.

'There's a story that Isaac Newton, when asked if he truly gave credence to the horseshoe nailed above his door, replied: "No, I don't, but I'm told it works anyway."'

And already the ice was broken. This man, whom I'd spent weeks imagining as a sour-faced, eccentric schoolmaster, had made me laugh in less than a minute.

'So you're covering all the options?' I said.

'Newton was joking, of course. But I haven't yet found reason to deny the possibility of God; just as I never understood folks who consider Him fundamental to moral behaviour. What will the preachers preach if the scientists ever find the proof that we are alone? What message will be left them for the guidance of their flock?'

I thought about that for a moment, wishing that Leonard was there to take up the argument in which I would only flounder. Eventually I just held out my hand. 'I'm Mark,' I said.

Pornographer and con man were finally introduced.

Hoppner had been tied up, David had explained, for the whole of the previous day. Business matters, conference calls to Chicago, decisions to be made about Miraflores, urgent communications from the

269

government in Santa Tecla. Quietly, he'd added that his boss was not yet psychologically ready to see us. The actions of Sánchez and his comrades had left him shaken and enraged – he needed time to calm himself before he met the victims.

We'd spent the day listening to the rain beat its endless tattoo against the tiled roofs, watching the young saplings planted around the compound bend beneath the onslaught from the sky, and talking amongst ourselves about absolutely nothing at all. Alice had produced a sketchbook and water-colours, and had painted remarkably good portraits of each of us. David was endlessly solicitous, offering us drinks, books, food and movies, but he was also endlessly present. At no point could the four of us – or better still, the three of us, without Leonard – talk over this new situation. Instead, I watched Pamela disappear into the rain with her climbing equipment and wetly reappear six hours later, without being able to recall a single significant moment in between.

'How're they looking after you?' Hoppner asked.

I wondered if he always walked the gardens at dawn – if, like me, he found it impossible to remain asleep once the skies had begun to lighten.

'Great,' I said. 'David's been cooking delicious meals. Our rooms are very comfortable. I got told off for likening pornography to prostitution, but otherwise . . .' What on earth made me say that to this man? Was he really that disarming?

'You must have met Pamela,' he said, a wry

270

smile drawing out the creases in his face. 'I'm afraid she takes life a fraction too seriously. I've tried to explain that humour is a virtue but . . .' I think he might even have winked at that point. 'Come see the hummingbirds,' he added, to expunge any suggestion of criticism.

Pressing one veined hand to my elbow, he guided me across the lawn. His pace lengthened automatically to match mine, with no outer sign of discomfort or strain despite his age and his shorter build.

As his house emerged out of the mist, my gaze was drawn to a swarm of tiny bodies fluttering around the veranda. Hummingbirds, dressed in iridescent blues, yellow-greens or vivid reds, were darting around the wooden columns, occasionally hovering to drink from one of the red tubes.

'They're filled with sugar solution,' said Hoppner. 'I hang out the bait and they come swarming.' A short cough. 'What do you think of that?'

He wasn't looking at me, was still watching the tiny hovering miracles. Nevertheless, I felt myself under his scrutiny.

'I think both parties benefit,' I said carefully. 'You enjoy seeing them fly. And, at very little cost to you, they get what they most need.'

He turned then, and even though I had three inches on him I felt as if his sharp grey eyes were staring levelly into my own. 'You know, the girls we photograph and film do bother me. Of course, you're right, it is a form of prostitution:

paying women for a service that renders sexual gratification. The fact that I never approved of the service doesn't make my position any better.' His shoulders shifted minutely. 'But I always tried to choose the vainest girls – the proudest. These are women who adore to be photographed naked and exhibited around the world – who would do it for free. I have dirty hands, using vain women to draw money out of hypocritical, lust-driven men, but I've always persevered for the good it makes possible.'

'Not to mention the very comfortable lifestyle,' my rash tongue muttered before I could stop myself.

'What is a comfortable lifestyle?' He shook his head. 'So long as there is nutritious food on my plate and warm clothes on my back I am content. This crazed fixation with money that defines our society – that is more or less written into my country's constitution . . . what is it for? What purpose does that new Mercedes have other than to cast a shadow over the neighbour's older model? What advantage has a dryer over a washing line that could possibly compensate for its consumption of finite energy resources? Why do we insist on spending the same on a night out as a Senegalese doctor earns in a year, if not to impress those around us – to join the endless, circular and therefore futile race to be better than the next guy?'

It was too early in the morning for this. My brain was distracted by that amusing American pronunciation of the word 'futile', which seemed to deny the existence of any vowels in the second syllable. Yet one thing was clear: any suspicions I might have had about Hoppner's motives were misplaced. This was not a man out to make a fast buck for himself. The bad-to-good economic theory of Sword Enterprises may have been deluded, but it was genuine. Meaning Hoppner truly was a man whose primary concern was changing the world. That in itself was a frightening thought.

'Perhaps we just need something to aim for,' I said, turning away. 'Some meaning.'

'And that's the tragedy,' he murmured. 'For so much of the world, meaning is given to life only by the acquisition of money. Yet if they could comprehend the satisfaction that is found – that you and I find, in our different ways – by doing good. Making a difference. Sowing a seed in Miraflores that just might grow roots across the world . . . that's as much meaning as I will ever need.'

A hummingbird shot out from the mêlée around the feeders and sped past our heads. Hoppner looked at his watch.

'If you'll excuse me, I try to fit in a half-hour of exercises before the working day begins. Not as impressive as Hawken's runs up and down the valley, but it keeps me healthy.' He gave a little nod as he walked towards the house. Pausing momentarily, he looked back. 'I'd be glad to see you all for dinner tonight. Would you pass that on to your friends?'

He'd barely closed the door of his house when Alice appeared, dressed in a sober black pullover and blue linen trousers of impeccable decency. 'Was that him?' she immediately demanded. Then, at my nod: 'Damn. I missed him! What was he like?'

'Surprisingly good fun.'

She stared at me in amazement. 'You and Hoppner together: that was good fun?'

'That sounds insulting.'

'I just don't think of you as someone who has a lot of fun. Or him.'

'So it was insulting.'

'Sorry. I didn't mean it that way. It's just . . . you don't laugh much.'

Until that point it hadn't occurred to me, but what she said was true: I was so wrapped up in the tension and uncertainty of this business that I'd effectively closed down a large slice of myself. Where was that high-spirited boy who'd once carried a blindfolded, giggling Katie halfway across Cornwall just to show her a single, perfect view?

'I'd better start. Apparently humour is a virtue.'

'He said that?' She was the one to laugh. 'I don't believe it.' Turning to look at the house, she added, 'Are those hummingbirds?'

I started walking back towards the guesthouse, but she reached out and touched my arm.

'Wait, Mark. I wanted to catch you alone for a moment.'

'The grand plan? We're going to have to wing it, I'm afraid.'

'No, not the grand plan.' She brought a hand up to straighten the neck of her pullover. Her fake engagement ring snagged for a second in the wool. 'I've been wanting to say: when they attacked us . . .' She looked down.

'Are you going to be OK?' I asked. 'The baby?'

'Of course – it's fine.' She said, a little irritably. 'Please don't bring that up again. I don't want Leonard to know. Or Hoppner.'

'I'm sorry.'

'No. Don't be. Look, I'm trying to thank you!' she said in mild exasperation. 'When they were chasing me. You came to help me, I know, even though I couldn't see shit. Just . . . thanks.'

When she looked up again, I caught her sweet little chin between my finger and thumb. I have no idea what made me do that. 'You were very brave,' I told her.

'Really?' A hesitant smile appeared. 'I didn't expect them to grab me.'

'Still, it was brave. To go alone.' Especially when you're pregnant, I wanted to add.

I let my hand drop. Her chin remained in the position I'd left it, as if she felt some shadow of my fingers still holding her.

'We got off on the wrong foot, you and I,' she

275

said. 'I'd like to get to know you properly – see you when we're back in London.'

Her smile faded and I knew my face had changed. 'I'm not going back to London,' I said.

'Why not?'

'There's just too much there that I . . .'

'Memories?' She was watching me carefully now, chin lowered once more. 'A girl,' she guessed.

'It's better if I go somewhere else.'

She left a pause. 'You mean *anywhere* else.' When I didn't reply, she continued, as if on the same subject, 'Breakfast. Time for breakfast, don't you think? Another of those fantastic waffles.'

She strode off ahead. Almost by habit now I lingered, giving her a few minutes to enter the building, return to her room and caress her fake husband out of bed. I had no appetite for waffles. When she'd disappeared into the mist I looked back at the hummingbirds seduced by Hoppner's benevolence.

The satisfaction that you and I find by doing good.

Hawken did not hang around for pleasantries. I wasn't entirely sure what he did do, but it was clear he felt no obligation to share David's burden of hospitality. He lived in a small house near the gate, though I saw him on the first morning emerging from Pamela's room in the guesthouse. No guilty laugh or laddish grin, he acknowledged my presence that time with a flicker of his eyelids. I watched him cross to his house and reappear a few minutes later, dressed in a tracksuit and all-terrain running shoes. The guards already had the gate open for him, and they saluted him as he disappeared at a brisk trot into the downpour.

Given his elusive movements and minimal communication, I was surprised to see him walking towards me that afternoon as I once again paced the compound, feeling ever more like a caged animal. The mist hadn't shifted; in fact, I'd come to realize it wasn't mist at all but solid, cloaking cloud. It was getting to be a little claustrophobic.

'You gave up on the conference,' he said.

I had a suspicion he'd been waiting for me at this point in the compound gardens that lay furthest from any building. I'd followed the same route three times in a row; he'd noticed. I took his hand: a powerful, clenching grip that might have crushed one not tensed to receive it.

'Listen, about that,' I started, 'I just said yes because it seemed easier at the time.'

'A white lie.' That smile, devoid – as always – of warmth.

I just nodded. A slightly uncomfortable pause.

'I was impressed by what you did up there,' he said, surprising me with his sudden shift from a kind of chastisement to a kind of praise. 'Brave to take on a lot of men carrying machetes.'

'Not that impressive,' I said. 'I was lying face-down in the mud when you arrived.'

He nodded solemnly, missing the lightness I'd tried to bring to that uncomfortable memory.

There was something too focused about him: a penetrating spotlight on his subject that denied him a balanced awareness of his surroundings. It was easy to guess what he'd been. The stance, the polished black boots, the crisp, polite tones – a man at home on a parade ground. A man who once had lived with, cherished and depended on a gun. I wondered idly how Hoppner had found him, this English ex-military man. Had he been visiting the London subsidiary of Sword Enterprises? Perhaps hired a security firm that in turn hired former servicemen? Had Hawken, in some meaningless London scuffle – in back street or night club or paparazzo encounter – impressed the visiting billionaire?

'Does that bother you?' he asked quietly, his pectoral muscles shifting beneath the stretched grey T-shirt and black leather jacket. 'That Sánchez took you?'

I thought about that for a moment – not the question, but the fact that he'd asked it. 'I'm alive,' I shrugged. 'We're all alive.'

'All the same. I bet you'd like a second chance. Sánchez – alone.'

It was an offer. Unquestionably an offer. What kind of power did this man hold around here? Suddenly I really didn't want to know.

'That's not why I came,' I said, a little hoarsely.

Something closed down, as if from disappointment, in his expression. But still his eyes held mine. In his gaze was a suggestion of something disturbing – as if in me he was recognizing a part of himself. I had to stop myself from drawing back.

'What you did on the track,' he said, 'I respect that. So let me give you some advice: don't ask for it.' He breathed deep and turned away, half disappearing in the cloud already. 'Don't ask for the money.'

The first time I set out to raise funds for Katie was an unhappy patch for both of us. She was nearly eight months pregnant, but still working. A complex deal was in the making; her boss was pressuring her not to take maternity leave until the last minute. The flat was more or less ready – I'd cushioned the sharper corners at floor level, fitted catches on the cupboards and knife drawer, and cleaned the place until every surface gleamed – but we still needed to buy the cot. Mothercare on Oxford Street at five o'clock, Katie had said in a rushed phone call that morning. By 5.45, I'd examined every cot about a hundred times and was growing exasperated.

She arrived in a cab, her face flushed, ten minutes before closing. My greeting wasn't brilliantly chosen:

'Jesus, Katie, where have you been? How are we supposed to choose the right cot in ten minutes?'

'The meeting overran, we messed up a document and the client freaked out, and I'm sorry,' she said. She was hot and feeling sick, and the baby was kicking inside her. The weight, by this late stage, was killing her back. 'Let's just take this one,' she said, pointing to the most basic model.

'Wait a minute, you haven't even looked at the others.' I pulled her arm, leading her towards my favourite cot. 'This one's really good – look, if you press these buttons it makes all these sounds. And it's got a—'

'All we need is a cot, Mark. Let's just get the cheapest.'

'The cheapest? This is our child, Katie.'

'It's just got to sleep.'

'Please say "he". We know it's going to be a boy.'

'I really need to sit down,' she said. 'Can we just buy the damn thing and go home?'

'We can't go straight for the cheapest. How would you have felt if your parents only ever got the cheapest of everything for you?'

'Fine, Mark! If you want the fucking bells and whistles, why don't *you* pay for it? Oh, I forgot, you don't even have a proper job!'

Later that evening, she apologized unreservedly. The last thing she wanted, she said, over and over, was to see me put on a suit and tie. There was no need financially, she insisted, and she had never wanted to trap me into a career I hated when she'd decided to keep our baby. Nevertheless, that afternoon in Mothercare stuck in my memory long after I'd worked the extra bar shifts to pay for what we came to call the 'fucking bells and whistles cot'.

Katie repeatedly swore she would never need or want any money from me for Christopher. But of course that made no difference: I simply couldn't leave her with nothing.

Somewhere in the compound, there must have been a cook. I was aware from the beginning of the lack of staff: just the eight ever-vigilant security guards, a couple of PAs floating around Hoppner's office building – easy to spot by the array of communications antennae on its roof – and perhaps a cleaner or two brought in from the town on alternate days. This was a compound run on lean, self-servicing lines, with no one to pick up the resident billionaire's dropped handkerchief or fetch him a caviar and watercress sandwich at the click of his fingers.

But when he emerged from his kitchen bearing a large dish of baked chicken in barbecue sauce, I found it a step too far to believe that this business giant, this standard-bearer for Good, had taken an hour out of his day just to cook us dinner.

'I eat plainly,' he announced as he placed the chicken in front of us and returned to the kitchen for jacket potatoes, spinach and cauliflower in white sauce. 'I hope that suits you all.'

Leonard and Alice were nodding enthusiastically; Freddy looked delighted to be spared the refried beans of the San Isidro and the heavy use of chillies in David's cooking. And, in fact, the chicken did smell delicious: reassuringly North

281

American, yet maintaining its distinct flavours of garlic, soy and brown sugar. Was there a cook hidden back there? Would this man of honesty, justice and fidelity really try to pass off such a trivial pretence on us?

'Thank you all for coming,' he said, dishing out the chicken in generous helpings. 'We depend on visitors here to keep us sane. My fellow directors in Chicago keep wanting to fly analysts down to check me out.'

This was the first contact the other three had had with our host. No uncomfortable, ritualized pre-dinner drinks. Hoppner had whisked us straight into the dining room – wood-beamed, unfussy lighting, with just a couple of Grand Canyon photographs on the walls – and seated us at the rustic rough-wood table. Place settings were minimalist, wine glasses were capacious rather than elegant. The wine itself – a straightforward Napa red – was already sitting, opened, between the bottle of ketchup and a dented, worn, but probably much-loved pepper mill.

'We should be thanking you,' said Alice, holding a hand over her glass as he poured the wine. 'For saving our lives.'

'No,' said Hoppner. 'On the contrary. If I'd gotten things right here, they would never have been in danger.' He laughed a little sadly. 'Building the perfect society is trickier than it looks. Don't try this at home.'

'Isn't that the point, though?' I asked. 'Don't

you want people to take what you're doing and try it elsewhere?'

I didn't get an answer straight away. Hoppner had started eating, and he was not the kind of man to rush a mouthful to avoid an awkward pause. By the time he was ready to speak his brain had moved on.

'It depresses me so much when I look at what Western society has become,' he said. 'We won all those wars, those conflicts of ideology, and for what? A society based not on goodness – on kindness to and care for each other – but on rights. On each individual's selfish demands: "I have a right to consume as much as I like", "My behaviour may be hurting a lot of people, but I'm within my legal rights", "I want what's mine". A society, in fact, that breeds lawyers and strangles philanthropists.'

'Surely we need a system of rights,' said Leonard, 'if only to protect the weak minority.'

'That isn't true if the majority believes in virtue: if they practise compassion, justice and generosity on a daily basis, what need do the minority have of legal rights? Focusing on rights only draws attention to the individual at the expense of the community.'

Already, though he was still eating with relish, Freddy was bored. His eyes were flicking between his plate and Alice, with occasional deviations to the ceiling.

'How realistic is it to ignore the individual?' said

Leonard. 'After all we've learnt from the collapse of communism? Given basic human nature?' On this topic he was more confident than I'd seen him before: no hesitation, no blushing.

'It's a question of demonstrating to people, as I am trying to do in Miraflores, how much they personally benefit from living in and contributing to a virtuous society. Ultimately, there is no greater individual happiness than that.'

I thought back to the behaviour we'd witnessed: Carlos Juárez giving up his table; Lupita offering sweets. Both of them insistent that we tell Hoppner of their generosity. 'That isn't really what happens, is it?' I said. 'I get the impression that they only personally benefit because you pay them to be virtuous – reward them for good behaviour with paint jobs on their houses and new bicycles for their kids.'

'Mark.' Alice was glaring at me. I sensed a flutter in the left leg of my trousers, as if she'd tried to kick me but missed. 'We're guests!'

'That's quite all right,' smiled Hoppner. 'I welcome debate. No one with power should go unchallenged: it isn't healthy.' He laid down his knife and fork, leaving his meal only half eaten. 'I do operate a reward structure, it's true. Even a punishment structure for serious transgressions. But I do so for the sake of the virtuous society, never for my own benefit.'

'Although, of course,' commented Leonard, with a fair degree of timidity, 'as Kant said, true morality is found not in what we do but why we do it. If the people of Miraflores are behaving virtuously because you pay them to, that does not make them virtuous.'

'Mr Williams, we could throw dead philosophers at each other all night: Aristotle said if we do something long enough we become it – if we pretend to be good we will eventually become good. But let's not alienate our friends by falling back on the quotations of others. By all means use their arguments, but make them your own.'

Leonard, of course, blushed immediately. But he did not seem to object to this mild dressing down; on the contrary, it awoke some spark of intellectual excitement in him.

'So you really believe that getting them into the habit of goodness will make them good? Even after you take the incentive scheme away?'

'Remember, the Church operates in the same manner: it commands us to be good while hanging over our heads the carrot of divine paradise and the stick of eternal damnation to help us decide. Christians are good because it pays them to be good. Yet we don't question the virtue of the Saints. What would Kant say to that?'

Leonard didn't seem to notice the gentle strokes that Alice was applying to his arm. I wondered if her objective was to keep him sweet and inoffensive to the money man, or to demonstrate for

Hoppner's eyes the virtuous affection and selfless love she felt towards her 'husband'.

'I suppose what intrigues me most is the nature of the government you effectively run here,' said Leonard. 'We tend to view liberal models as the least damaging options available in the modern world, limiting their role to ridding society of avoidable evils – crime, ill health, traffic congestion. Yours delves deeper, driven by an active quest for a specific moral end – a trait shared with most fascist governments.'

He might have stammered and stumbled if asked to comment on the weather, but Leonard was no shrinking violet when it came to philosophical debate. Alice's strokes turned into a sudden grip of restraint, but Hoppner was speaking again before she could voice any admonishment.

'You're a fan of liberalism? How free would you want the people of Miraflores to be? Free to spread hatred and political unrest? Free to destabilize a fledgling democracy? Free to set off bombs in the capital?' For a moment Hoppner seemed genuinely angry. 'I'll tell you how free these people are: they are always free to leave.'

'I'm sorry,' muttered Alice. 'Mr Hoppner, we didn't mean to offend you.'

He shook his head. 'Morality is never easy,' he sighed. 'And applying something that most of us find hard even to define is near impossible. I have critics every day telling me that I'm wasting my time – that morality is a spent force; that modern life depends on a perfectly constructed set of compacts rather than some superannuated belief in absolute good.'

'They have a point,' said Leonard. 'If one doesn't believe in a god who could supply it, then it's difficult to envisage how such a morality might come into being.'

'Which is nonsense! We still care, even without God. We're still upset by injustice, even without God. Morality is intuitive. Are you going to tell me our ancestors had no sense of compassion or honesty before the prophets came along? That gratitude didn't exist on the plains of Africa? We are not simply selfish machines! Altruism – for whatever spiritless reason the scientists like to claim – demonstrably exists. Yes, it may have evolved to serve a selfish purpose – to induce reciprocal acts, or to increase reproductive success among genetically related individuals – but that doesn't diminish its importance for us. We are born with the ability to put ourselves in the shoes of others: natural empathy is at the root of our morality, not God.'

It seemed to me ironic that Hoppner's defence of his pornography business was as a dirty means towards a selfless end, whilst morality itself, he was suggesting, had evolved as a virtuous means towards a selfish end. I glanced at Leonard, wishing for some reason that I could share that thought with him – test my valueless, abstract idea on the philosopher to see if it impressed

– but his attention was entirely focused on the argument.

'The problem, surely,' he said, 'is in defining what is and is not virtuous. So many people – so many cultures – have different views. How do we choose an absolute morality – an objective morality that carries any sort of innate authority – once you remove God from the equation?'

'Easily. There are plenty of absolutes. What about charity? Giving to those worse off can only be a virtuous act.'

'Again, that must depend on your motives. If you are doing it to impress an observer, or even to salve a guilty conscience, then it is nothing more than self-interest.'

'With that logic, you could claim any virtuous act to be self-interested – virtue always brings greater happiness in the long run than pursuing selfish desires – in which case the concept becomes absurd. Pamela spends her days here teaching the local women practical skills they can use to work – to make themselves less dependent on their fathers and their husbands. She does this not out of duty but because she loves the crusade of liberating women from the male yoke. Does her enjoyment make her donation of time and energy any less generous?'

Leonard wasn't easily won over. 'But how do you decide where the lines are drawn? Is all deceit forbidden, or should we lie to save an innocent's life? If so, at what point does deceit become wrong? Who is to judge that giving a few coins to a beggar is worthy generosity but giving your house to a drunken gambler is recklessness?'

'You make good points,' said Hoppner. 'They are the standard objections of the intellectual to any practical action in the field of morality. Myself, I would rather form usable, if imperfect, guidelines than throw in the towel because nothing is conveniently black and white. The fact that we cannot say precisely how many hairs a man may have and still be classified bald does not imply the term has no meaning.'

'We already have guidelines: laws, constitutions, the Bible.'

'And you believe that no one can do better than nomadic Israelites, the founding fathers or the Romans?'

'The Bible is supposed to be the word of God,' Alice observed.

'Yet as a moral code for practical usage, it's a disaster of contradictions, confusing historical and fictional deviations, prejudices and anachronisms. Worst of all, it cannot evolve: while we grow more enlightened, it remains stuck in the Palestine of stonings and crucifixions. Mrs Williams, do you believe homosexuality is an abomination when the best scientific opinion reckons it to be genetically determined? Do you really agree with St Paul that women should never hold positions of leadership over men?'

'So you think you are in a position to improve on the Bible?'

That was positively bold for Alice. Her chin was set; her eyes locked on his. Something in her had been deeply stirred. Was her faith strong enough to derail her bid for the perfect family lifestyle?

Hoppner spread his hands. 'My Code is imperfect, I grant you. But so few people have spent their lives researching, analysing and dreaming about morality away from the skewing context of religion that I believe I am as close to being an expert as any man. I long for more secular moralists to step forward, to argue with me and to help me refine my ideas. My Code will always be in development, of course, as new information becomes available on controversial issues such as the redistribution of resources, abortion and—'

'What about suicide?' I said.

There was a silence. Alice was staring at me, horrified. Freddy was shaking his head in disapproval.

Hoppner took a sip of wine. 'I believe suicide is an admirable course of action, if you can achieve more by dying than by remaining alive.'

'So old people should take an overdose of sleeping pills to avoid wasting their children's inheritance on nursing homes?'

'Let's pick a clearer case. The Japanese pilot who flew his damaged plane into my father's ship was not only courageous but morally in the right. He could have baled out, would probably have been rescued, but he knew he could achieve more for his most precious cause – his country's war effort – by dying. Quite distinct from the suicide bombers of the Middle East and the World Trade Center, who saw their actions as the fastest route to heaven: if there is an afterlife, they will surely rot in Hell for taking so many innocent lives on their short-cut to Paradise.'

'And what about terrorists committing suicide after the act?' I said softly. 'Out of remorse, perhaps?'

Hoppner did not give a direct answer. Instead, he sat back and gazed at us all in turn. 'Question: Who among you wishes well for his fellow human beings?'

It was a little like going back to school. Once we realized the questioner expected an answer, our hands began to rise, just a little way above the table: enough to give a signal of affirmation without admitting a full regression to the classroom.

'Then who among you, if he came to realize that his presence here on earth had only a negative impact – *and could only ever have a negative impact* – on his fellow human beings, would not wish to terminate that presence?'

I think a shiver must have crept through us all at that moment. It is not often that one is forced to confront the question of what, ultimately, we contribute to or detract from our world. Answering it, or at least attempting an answer, is an uncomfortable moment of truth at the best of times. When

291

it is accompanied by a prescription of suicide for those who fall short of the measure, it is enough to turn any stomach.

Needless to say, none of us this time raised our hands.

'Mr Williams, you're fond of the philosophers,' said Hoppner. 'Perhaps you recall what Camus had to say on the subject?'

Leonard hesitated, then said, 'Concerning Sisyphus, wasn't it?'

'Exactly. Let me help you: "There is but one truly serious philosophical problem and that is suicide. Judging whether life is or is not worth living amounts to answering the fundamental question of philosophy."'

'I thought Camus concluded that it always is,' murmured Leonard. Bravely, I thought.

Hoppner smiled, acknowledging Leonard's small victory. 'Then I must be more precise. Most people kill themselves because they cannot see a compelling reason to live. Camus rejected that reasoning, perhaps rightly. However, I claim suicide is perfectly justifiable – is, in fact, necessary – when one has found a compelling reason to die.'

And that was the root of everything.

A little smile: friendly – reassuring. An apparent change of subject. 'You came here to ask for help,' said our host.

Freddy was the first to respond, at last spotting the chance he'd been waiting for all evening. His sense of the disturbing was less developed than in the rest of us. 'Only if it's not too much to ask,' he gabbled. 'You see, I have this dream to help the children of Malawi get a decent—'

'Oh, no, please,' said Hoppner, holding up his hand. 'This is not a sales pitch. I have no interest in judging the projects of good people. My only concern is to ensure that they are . . . good people.'

Freddy sank back into his chair. 'You don't want to hear about the schools?' The disbelief and disappointment in his voice was clear. All that work, he was thinking. All that effort.

'It's most important that I don't. At this moment in time I want to know as little as possible about your backgrounds, in order not to prejudge you. Perhaps you've noticed I've kept our discussion to matters philosophical, well away from anything personal. By all means, if we go forward, write me and let me know how you're getting along. I always like happy stories. But for now all I need do – if you'll forgive the suggestion of doubt – is confirm your natures, the strength of your goodness.'

I don't know what the others had been expecting. A checklist, perhaps; a set of criteria to meet: *there must be no opportunity for corruption, no excessive expenses or salaries, no open-ended financial commitments.* Certainly none of us imagined that our potential benefactor would dismiss out of hand even the slightest discussion of our good works. There was a certain logic to evaluating the individual rather than the act, but how on earth could he 'confirm our natures' if he refused to hear about our backgrounds and plans – real or imaginary?

'I'll make you a deal,' he said. 'I am willing to offer up to five million dollars to each one of you – the exact amount is your decision – to spend on whatever worthy causes and projects you see fit. My condition is that you must agree to undergo a morality test. If you pass the test, as any genuine philanthropist always will, then you'll have a cheque right away. If not . . .'

He paused, as if to ensure we were paying attention, though at that moment nothing short of an atom bomb could have distracted us from his words. 'If not – if you are found to have only a negative impact on your fellow human beings – then you must remove your presence from this world immediately.'

No one breathed.

For some reason, he was staring at me.

'Wait a minute,' I choked. 'You mean suicide? This is your cleansing exercise? Eradicating the bad, one by one?'

'You agreed, did you not, that you wouldn't wish to remain alive if only to have a negative impact on the world?'

'Yes, but . . .'

Surely he didn't believe that any of us would actually take our own lives just because we'd failed his test? Negative impact or not, did he honestly think the survival instinct was so easily subverted? His naïvety was almost laughable. I caught Freddy's eye: a smile was flickering at the edge of his lips. I threw him a glare: it disappeared.

'But what if we don't believe your test will give the correct result?' said Alice, again finding the indignation to confront Hoppner.

'Then don't take it,' he replied. 'Stay as long as you like – as my guest – but if you can't accept the principles of my Code, don't submit yourself to the test drawn from it.'

'We're not questioning the Code, but—'

'Why not?' Hoppner smiled. 'You should. Like I said, it is always in development. However, I can reassure you on the test: it deals only with those aspects of morality that are clear-cut – shared across almost all cultures. Truth, property rights, promises, treating others as you would be treated, assisting the disadvantaged – none of these is controversial. Those very few ethnicities that don't share such moral values are not represented at this table tonight.'

Another silence. I could see Leonard aching to launch himself back into the intellectual fray, but Alice's hand was gripping his wrist again, her knuckles taut.

'How does it work?' said Freddy finally, a tremor of anxiety in his voice. Yes, he had good reason to fear for his million-pound windfall.

'True character can be revealed only in the decisions we make,' said Hoppner. 'Specifically, the decisions we make when faced with tough choices. I will be inviting you to consider certain situations – dilemmas, where the morally right course of action will likely be at the expense of your own interests – and asking you to state what action you would take.'

'Oh.' Freddy's face brightened immediately. He was so transparent, I was amazed Hoppner didn't send him home straight away. 'Well, that sounds OK.'

Like a child who thinks he's found a cunning way round his parents' rules, he sat back in his chair, imagining the heartfelt stories he was going to spin – the tears he was going to shed. Then Leonard ruined it for him:

'How will you know we're telling the truth?' he asked.

Hoppner brought his hands together, folded them neatly on the table in front of him. 'Because you'll be under hypnosis.'

He glanced at his watch, sighed, looked back at us. No one else moved.

'It's late,' he said. 'I try to keep a regular pattern of sleep.' He stood up. 'Why don't you think it over tonight – have another look at my Code. You can tell me your decisions tomorrow.'

I don't remember anyone else speaking after that. I suppose we must have made our farewells, perhaps thanked him for dinner. A little forced laughter to soften the tension. But none of it registered. It was as though we were already hypnotized.

Our host was smiling kindly when we left, a little wave as we made our way across the darkened compound to the guest building. His door closed with a click that was clearly audible through that still, misty air.

The darkness grew a little darker.

A Code for Life: Introduction (excerpt)

We will look at many facets of virtue. We will consider courage, prudence, gratitude and a dozen other traits. We will go into depth and at times the ride may get confusing. But one simple idea will be of the greatest value to you throughout: virtue depends on the transcendence of the self.

We spend most of our lives thinking about ourselves or our families (which are effectively extensions of ourselves). We focus on the issues that affect us, we weigh up courses of action by reference to their benefit to us, and we see almost everything from a point of view that favors ourselves. We are self-centered because that is how we have evolved: to look after ourselves and our close family.

But the fastest road to virtue requires us to abandon this egotistic perspective, or at least to stow it for awhile. Imagine yourself as a neutral observer looking down on an interaction between your former self and another individual. Suddenly you're able to see both arguments, you can compare the relative levels of need, and you can take pleasure from the happiness of both people. The total benefit to two individuals is almost always greatest if they act pleasantly toward each other, help each other out – behave virtuously, in other words. By stepping outside your own self, you can enjoy this joint benefit and so work to maximize it.

Of course, relinquishing the self is a real hard thing to do. It goes against our natures. But you can work toward this noble goal step by step: take time to figure out the other guy's point of view, listen to his arguments, try to imagine being in his shoes and guess what he's thinking about you. This is empathy: a most valuable human skill. You will find it much easier to give generously or forgive once you understand other people's problems, just as you will find gratitude comes more naturally when you think through the effort others have made to help you. Those who step outside themselves cannot but he humble and truthful as they no longer have reason to boast or lie.

So when the theory gets complicated, or becomes overwhelmed by life's practical demands, try to make that mental jump out of your skin. You'll be surprised how straightforward virtue can be once you have that neutral perspective.

CHAPTER 12

Alice came to my room that night. Not to sleep with me – at least, that isn't what happened, although the possibility was in both our minds. Leonard used sleeping pills and ear plugs from long habit, she said. Their beds were five feet apart. It wasn't hard to leave, once he'd started snoring.

'I couldn't marry him,' she smiled. 'The snoring – oh, the snoring! I wouldn't sleep for forty years. I haven't slept . . .'

It was true, she looked drained. Behind the bright smile and lively manner, the pallor was deepening. I'd put it down to the stress of our situation.

'Can you hear it?' she said, stilling my restless movements with an outstretched hand. I sat down on the bed beside her, leaned back against the headboard, listening. 'There! Hear?'

With a finger she conducted the sound: ticking the air as each snore began, drawing it out, raising it to a climax, then dropping it as the noise abruptly cut out, ready to begin again.

I clasped my hand round the finger, ending

the mockery, though perhaps to her it was only harmless fun.

'Will you do it?' I asked.

She stared at her finger, disappearing into my fist. Together, our hands dropped to the bed between us, still locked together. A second's indulgence. Another. Then I loosened my grip and she pulled free. But our hands remained where they lay, a few inches apart.

'You have a mirror,' she said, gazing across the room. 'We don't. Only in the bathroom. They should have put the girl in here.'

'With Leonard, you mean?'

'Of course that's what I mean.'

It was a rectangular mirror, new and characterless like everything else in the room, with a frame of unpainted pine. I hadn't even noticed it.

'Perhaps they knew you weren't the kind of girl who likes a lot of mirrors.'

'That is so rude!'

'Keep your voice down!' I stared at her. 'You know I didn't mean . . .' Already she was smiling – a tease. 'You do know.'

'I do know you don't think I'm ugly, Mark, yes.' She glanced down at our hands, so close together. 'I do wonder, though, what else you think about me . . . when – if – you do think about me.'

She'd come in her nightshirt: white, with a black motif over her left breast; soft, worn cotton. Extending almost to her knees when she'd stood at my door, barely reaching her thighs after she'd

301

settled herself on my bed. The smooth whiteness of her legs, stretched out over the sheets, glowed a little in the weak light of the single lamp I'd left burning.

'It's hardly easy right now,' I murmured. 'I can hear your husband snore: he's very present.'

With her eyes narrowed and her mouth turned down, she lifted herself up and twisted round to straddle my legs. I was still wearing jeans, but the touch of her body on mine burnt straight through them. She brought her hands to the sides of my head, flattening her palms over my ears until I could hear nothing but the rustle of her skin against mine, loud as a storm. I leaned forward and kissed her mouth.

Hers was a demanding kiss.

'Don't call him my husband,' she whispered when she sat back.

We watched each other for a while. Her body, poised, resting lightly on my legs, spine straight and shoulders relaxed. I let myself slump back against the headboard.

'Does it bother you that I'm pregnant?'

I shook my head. Her groin was warm against my thigh. The situation called for a cigarette, a drink – some prop to catch our attention, to save us from going further.

'It's fine to have sex, in case you're worried. My breasts are a bit sore, but otherwise everything's normal.'

Leonard's snores re-entered my consciousness.

I lifted my hand, brushed the stitches on Alice's forehead with the tip of my little finger. She flinched, though I barely made contact. The area around the cut, around the coarse thread, was still an angry crimson – an island of colour on her pale skin. Hoppner hadn't commented on the cut, though he couldn't possibly have missed it. Was it considered bad manners in Tulsa to draw attention to a wound? Or had he been avoiding anything that might lead to open discussion of his flock's murderous tendencies?

'Will you do it?' I asked again. 'Will Leonard do it?'

'Of course he won't do it. You think I'd let him put himself in a position like that? The idiot would probably go ahead and kill himself if Hoppner decreed it. That's the trouble with Leonard: he gets so tied up in logic – ergo this, ergo that, deductions and hypotheses – that when a situation which actually matters comes along, he's liable to do something really stupid.'

And me? Would I do it? Something about that blunt warning from Hawken had unnerved me. *Don't ask for it.* Was he simply trying to stem the outflow of his master's wealth, or did he have some reason to aim that warning at me in particular? Could he see in me the one thing I'd always tried to hide?

Hypnosis. The word alone unnerved me. What if Hoppner was able to reach back into my childhood? What if he discovered, in my unwitting responses, the cruelty I'd once inflicted on a defenceless boy? Would he find a vicious streak running right through me? Could I do anything to suppress that one awful blot on my moral report card, or would it surface on his command to sink any hope I might have of reaching into his purse?

A small boy, cowering on the back seat of a car. What had I done to him to bring such paralysing fear to his eyes? Sheltering under a blue cotton jacket. I remembered brown leather seats, very hot – it must have been high summer. The doors of the car wide open. A slight breeze. What terrible thing had I done?

I'd asked, or tried to ask the question a thousand times. My uncle and aunt refused to talk about it. If I mentioned a blue jacket, or a car with brown leather seats, I would be silenced with a hug or an angry shout, depending on their mood. But just as they were committed to keeping my young mind away from its past, so they made sure I never got the chance to repeat my crime. Once, at a neighbour's house, my aunt found me chasing another boy with his plastic machine gun: she ripped the toy out of my hand and sent me home with a harsh smack. I wasn't allowed back to that house for two years. Often when a quarrel broke out between small boys, I was drawn out of the pack and kept in quarantine until the scuffle was over. I was, quite plainly, a walking hazard.

I could taste Alice's kiss still. An indefinable blend of flavours, not unpleasant particularly, it had surprised me only because I'd forgotten women could taste different from Katie. Could feel different; could be different – her weight on my legs was all wrong, her attitude unsettling. Katie would never have just sat there, watching. It was impossible for her to maintain eye contact with me for more than a minute without smiling. A game we'd often played. Four years of loving one woman had lulled me into a comfortable familiarity from which I was reluctant to be dislodged.

Alice's thumbnail traced a sketch on my thigh.

'What did you think of Hoppner's ideas?' she said.

I shrugged. 'I couldn't see much wrong with them. But I'm hardly qualified to judge. You should ask Leonard. I'm sure he could have torn them apart if you hadn't kept him on the leash.'

'Actually, he was quite impressed.'

Her thumbnail slowed to a halt. She rocked it from side to side, then slowly increased the pressure. I felt it dig into my flesh: no pain through the jeans, just a kind of erotic itch.

'You could kiss me again,' she said eventually.

I nodded, though I meant the opposite and she saw it in my face. She got up, walked stiffly across the room.

I leapt off the bed and ran up behind her, catching her as she opened the door. The bruise left by Sánchez's machete sent a flood of pain down my side. My body pressing Alice's body pushed the door shut again. A slight slam. The snoring continued undisturbed. Her shoulder blades felt awkwardly sharp. Taking her cheek in my hand, her back tight against my chest, I brought her mouth round to mine. Her neck was twisted – uncomfortably, perhaps painfully. She let me kiss her, though she didn't respond. That taste again.

When I let go, stepping back, she left the room without another word to me.

I overslept. Extraordinarily for me, I was still in a dreamless void when a knock sounded on my door at twenty past eight. Perhaps, after half a night of lying awake but seeing only Katie, my exhausted mind just refused to give up the safe refuge of unconsciousness. For some reason I'd been remembering her pregnant, the smooth dome of her stomach fascinating and repelling me in equal measure: the taut beauty of her, tainted by the terror of what lay inside.

A decision had to be made today. I stood in the shower, eyes closed, not making it, thought of course there was never any question what I would do. We had not come all the way here to give up at this last, bizarre fence. Committing to commit suicide: a matter of a few simple words spoken with a ring of sincerity. The idea that we would actually follow through was so ludicrous it hardly seemed like deceit to promise it. All of us would solemnly give our assurances, take our tests and then prepare to leave in disgrace.

A dark shirt seemed appropriate: a symbol of

willingness to mount the scaffold. I left my scuffed and machete-gashed jacket in my room as further acknowledgement of the gravity of our undertaking. Breakfast was not on my agenda: despite my readiness to make false promises in my bid for two hundred grand – hell, five million dollars if I wanted it, although I knew I would never request a penny more than I'd come for – anticipation of the hypnosis had left me too green to eat. The idea of Hoppner, of any of them, finding out what I'd spent so much of my life trying to conceal was terrifying.

She was standing on the veranda, alone. A grey skirt with the black pullover: she'd had the same sepulchral instinct. Her sleek white nape – the last part of her I'd seen the night before – held the same nervous tension. She knew I was there.

'Good morning,' I said – brightly, to dispel my own sense of foreboding.

'Mhmm.'

The cloud was gone; bright sunshine coloured every flower and glossy blade of grass. For the first time since arriving, I could see the compound in its entirety: the line of wooden buildings on their concrete stilts, the neat, sloping lawn, the low white balustraded wall that marked the bottom end of the compound and protected the unwary from the cliff drop down to the valley floor. Further east, the lake at the end of the valley was once again in view.

Strolling along the gravel terrace that ran the length of the cliff wall were Hoppner and Leonard.

Wooden benches were stationed at regular intervals on the terrace. Beyond, surreally, the tops of great fern-laden trees swayed back and forth in the gusting wind. Such a privileged view directly into a tropical forest canopy was an unusual feature in a manicured garden. From the size of the upper branches, I reckoned the height of the trees – and therefore the drop beyond the white wall – to be at least eighty feet.

'What are those two talking about?' I asked, more to get Alice speaking again.

'I don't know. They've been at it for an hour.'

'Really?' What about Hoppner's morning exercise routine? I felt an odd pang of jealousy that Leonard was able to hold our host's attention where I'd been politely dismissed after a few minutes of hummingbird viewing. The two men had their heads slightly bowed, matching pensive frowns drawing both sets of eyebrows down.

I turned to Alice: 'Listen, I'm sorry if—'

'I'm going to do it.'

I nodded silently.

'Fucking waste of time bringing Leonard, wasn't it? A lot of good his virtue's going to do me when I'm under hypnosis.'

'You could get him to—'

'No.'

With one sandalled foot curled sideways and tucked behind the other, David was leaning against the office building, chatting through the window. Or rather, given his way with words, listening to someone else chat. The skirt-clad thigh and matronly hip of a seated woman – a PA, presumably – were visible through an open door. So remote from a city office, yet the gossiping dynamics of everyday work were just the same. A reassuring normality.

'You know it's possible he may discover certain facts if you're hypnotized?'

'We all have things to hide,' Alice retorted.

Indeed.

A door opened behind us and Pamela came out on to the veranda. Once again she was dressed for climbing, Ray-Ban sunglasses added to the usual assembly of Lycra clothes and rubber shoes. I began to wonder if the women of Miraflores really did receive all that much of her time. Quite a nice life she'd carved out for herself here, with her sports, her muscled boyfriend and an occasional bout of good works to justify the more than comfortable board and lodging.

Alice, on the other hand, evidently saw a lot to admire in the serious-minded Canadian. I'd spotted the two of them talking together several times since Pamela had sewn up Alice's forehead. Some kind of bond beyond the obvious had been formed with that needlework. It had earned Pamela a respect that I would guess Alice rarely accorded other women, and she seemed to appreciate the compliment. Where I was still viewed with slight contempt for my pornography – pimping quip, Pamela was more than happy to greet Alice.

'You have the test today? Good luck,' she said sincerely, as, in fact, she said everything. 'I'm sure you'll do well.'

That prognosis was carefully targeted at Alice alone. For a moment, I imagined revealing to Pamela the scandalous truth of Mr and Mrs Williams's false marriage, just for the shock value. The poor, principled thing would probably faint in disbelief. A brief and pleasant fantasy.

'Thank you,' said Alice, slipping easily and unconsciously into Pamela's wholesome cadences. 'Any tips?'

'Just be yourself,' smiled Pamela, lighting a cigar.

Tobacco aside, they could have been Girl Guides.

More footsteps, and Freddy wandered out of the guesthouse, rubbing his eyes. So I hadn't been the last to get up.

'Hey, friend,' he said brightly to me. 'Big day. What do you think?'

Perversely, but probably unconsciously, he'd chosen to wear a sunny yellow shirt with some kind of fancy monogram on the pocket. Florid italics – perhaps the key to his real name, but I couldn't decipher the twirling, interwoven letters.

'I think you shouldn't try,' I told him seriously.

'Well, tough,' he said, misunderstanding my motivation completely. 'I'm going to.' Once again, he was aggrieved.

The strollers were approaching, their expressions still serious.

'It's true,' Leonard was saying. 'I, along with most of my colleagues, do tend to concentrate rather more on the hypothetical argument. Perhaps we suffer from a certain lack of practical experience. Practical wisdom.'

'*Phronēsis*,' Hoppner said.

'Exactly,' said Leonard in delight.

Hoppner smiled. 'I'm sure we can do something about that.'

Our host, this morning, was in high spirits. Was it the rare sun, or the prospect of new associates to join his worldwide philanthropic family? Would he still be good humoured if someone failed the test? If unpalatable facts about our past – my past, particularly – started to emerge during the course of the hypnosis? He raised his eyes to our veranda.

'Your husband is reading Nietzsche,' he called to Alice, indicating the book clasped in Leonard's hand. 'Be careful: Nietzsche's two pet hates were Christianity and women.'

'Thanks for the warning,' said Alice dryly.

'What was it Nietzsche said, Mr Williams? "Thou goest to woman? Do not forget thy whip." Pleasant fellow.'

'Oh, I don't subscribe to much he says,' blushed Leonard.

'I can assure you, Mr Hoppner,' said Alice, 'Leonard is the kindest, most loving husband any—'

'Stop!' The force in Hoppner's voice was startling. One forbidding hand was raised; the smile was gone. 'I mustn't hear any character traits. I mustn't hear any background. It's fine to discuss abstract philosophical matters, but if I'm to pass judgement fairly on your moral character, it's imperative I have not been previously biased toward or against you.'

'OK, I just meant—'

'It works both ways,' he said, the smile making a tentative reappearance. 'Imagine I heard a rumour before your hypnosis that you were a mass-murderer – how could I give you a fair test? You would be damned before we began. We would have to cancel the test. Fairness is more important to me than anything.'

'We understand.'

'Good. Have you made your choices?'

Hoppner was taken aback to discover that Leonard would not be undergoing his test. Perhaps, after what had clearly been a highly cerebral conversation, he had been looking forward to examining the philosopher under hypnosis. As for the rest of us, he accepted our decisions with a quick nod.

'I must be very clear about the conditions,' he said, in a voice that was the quintessence of clarity. 'If you commit now to take the test you may not leave this compound until it is successfully completed. And, of course, should the result be negative, you will not be leaving the compound at all. Are we clear?'

312

Each of us nodded, though I hated the lie I was being forced to share.

'You accept the conditions?'

'Yes,' we replied, one after another.

'All right. Mr Greenock, would you care to go first?'

It was exactly what I'd hoped wouldn't happen. Freddy could only spoil our chances. How could he possibly pass this test? And how could Alice and I expect Hoppner to give us a shot at the big prize after Freddy had refused to fulfil his obligation?

I didn't get much chance to worry about it. A sudden shout from David drew our eyes to the office building. From the window beside him, a flood of colourful papers were fluttering out on a sudden breeze. A startled screech from the panicked PA inside followed shortly after.

'Oh, dear,' sighed Hoppner. 'Those are the new photographs for *Venus Mountain*.'

He hurried forward to grab them, but the wind lifted the pictures up, spreading them wide across the compound.

'Gentlemen?' he called, snatching one as it sailed past.

All of us, gentlemen or not, dashed after the pictures. It hadn't occurred to me until I caught one what they would depict. Mine was a brunette, stretched, rather painfully I thought, across a glass coffee table, with one hand in her mouth and the other between her bare, perspiring legs. Her eyes

313

looked comatose to me, but presumably the effect was meant to be one of ecstasy.

'Oh, Lord,' I cried, choking on a sudden fit of hysterical laughter.

'I know,' said Hoppner, shaking his head in mock despair. 'Aren't they appalling? The board insist on faxing me every picture – you wouldn't believe the number of colour cartridges we get through.'

I caught two more; David plucked one off Hoppner's veranda and Freddy came running up with an impressive – one might almost say devoted – five.

'If you want my opinion,' he told Hoppner with a gleeful grin, 'this one's all right and this one's pretty stunning, but *this* one . . .' He handed the offending image over.

'Yes, I see what you mean,' said Hoppner. 'Not up to scratch?'

'I wouldn't want the artistic integrity of your magazine compromised,' Freddy told him.

'Right. What do you think, Pamela?'

Hoppner held out the picture, managing to sustain his innocently serious expression until Pamela scowled and turned away. Hardly Girl-Guide material.

'Oh, friend!' said Freddy, seizing the supine brunette from my hand. 'That's the girl. Mr Hoppner, this one you must promote.'

'Heavens, yes,' said Hoppner. 'Extraordinary talent!'

'What do you think, Leonard?' asked Freddy, passing him the photograph to elicit an unsportingly easy blush. 'Is Alice this good under her clothes?'

With Leonard coughing furiously, Alice came straight to the rescue: 'A true gentleman would never comment,' she said, holding out four pictures to Hoppner. 'May I submit, however, that the blonde in the cowboy boots is in a class of her own.'

Though I too was smiling, I found the whole business quite disturbing. It was like catching the headmaster smoking behind the bike sheds. 'Should we be doing this?' I asked, for some reason casting myself as the class wet blanket. 'Didn't you say looking at pornography is . . . bad?'

That fundamental, monosyllabic adjective seemed so weak, so vague on my tongue. Childish; way too simplistic. In fact, its very minimalism made my defining use of it feel almost neurotic, as if I were some crazed street preacher. Are we really so unused to talking in terms of right and wrong?

Tidying the pictures into a neat pile, Hoppner said, 'Pornography becomes immoral when men stare at and lust over images of women doing things they would never permit of their daughters. That is hypocrisy. A fine point, perhaps, but it is a kind of infidelity to the self. There is also the matter of intemperance: many consumers of pornography indulge so excessively that women, sex and love cease to have any real meaning for them – it is no different than immoderate consumption of alcohol

315

or doughnuts. On the other hand, there is nothing wrong with having a little joke over these ridiculous images – it stops us taking ourselves too seriously, and that's never a bad thing.'

Leading by example, he offered me a broad, humorous smile. But by the time I'd matched it, his had disappeared. He was staring at something over my shoulder. I turned round. David was walking towards us from the upper end of the compound. In one hand was a photograph, in the other something quite different.

'What is that?' demanded Hoppner.

'Thrown over the fence,' said David weakly. 'Just now. It wasn't there before. Ten minutes ago.'

It was the crudely severed head of a goat.

My first reaction, almost comically detached, was to wonder if it came from the animal we'd seen killed that first afternoon. A second later and I was experiencing the same nauseating shudder that had already struck David and Hoppner. The sense of menace. Its eyes were already half eaten away, the lips ragged and blackened. Straggly hair curled around its ears and horns. The severed windpipe and a clutch of torn vessels and muscles dangled below.

'Does it mean something? Who would do that?' demanded Hoppner, throwing the sheaf of pictures to the ground. He seemed suddenly taller. 'What does it mean?'

David could only look at him apologetically, shaking his head.

316

'Where's Hawken?'

Tearing our eyes away from that ghoulish harbinger – of what, we had no idea – we all turned towards the house by the gate. He was immediately distinguishable, standing nearly half a foot taller than the four guards who encircled him. All of them looked angry. What they were saying was lost to the distance between us.

'Hawken!'

The power of Hoppner's normally gentle voice took me by surprise. As Hawken looked round, the guards stepped back, revealing another figure previously hidden in their midst: a thin, hunched boy. At the sight of that forlorn creature, Hoppner frowned.

'What's going on?' he called.

Hawken walked swiftly towards us, dragging the boy along by his arm. It was an odd pairing: a burly, dispassionate ex-soldier, his face glowing from an arduous run, his T-shirt flecked with mud and patterned with sweat; next to him, a terrified Indian boy of fifteen or sixteen, struggling to keep up in his ill-fitting rubber boots and torn canvas trousers. The black armband seemed to be the only thing holding his shirt together. Approaching Hoppner, his face grew more and more distraught, until he seemed ready to burst into tears.

'I found him in the forest,' said Hawken. 'Tanadio's son.'

'I know who it is.'

Taking the goat's head from David, Hoppner

held it under the boy's nose. His question was in Spanish, but the nature of the interrogation was clear. A sudden tremor passed through the boy's frame.

Once the accusation being levelled at his detainee had sunk in, Hawken's expression changed from placidity to wrath. The boy was no longer merely a snoop but an adversary of some undefined nature. When he failed to answer Hoppner's question, Hawken slapped him across the face with the back of his hand.

The blow was severe: I winced at the hollow crack of knuckle against cheekbone. Staggering backwards, the boy lost his footing and only Hawken's grip on his arm kept him from falling. I glanced instinctively at the others: Alice had her hand over her mouth, while Leonard looked astonished; Freddy was riveted.

I turned back in time to see the boy suddenly wriggle free and sprint towards the gate. Why he did it, I don't know. Even I, a newcomer, could see what had to happen. Perhaps he was just too scared to think straight. When he reached the gate, two of the guards knocked him down, grabbed him by his arms and dragged him, stumbling and whimpering, back to Hawken. The red marks left by their vice-like hands seemed branded on his wrists.

Again, Hoppner barked his question. The boy's eyes sought out David – the warm, accommodating face of Hoppner's government. But David was inexplicably looking away, as if some detail of the guesthouse urgently demanded his attention. Losing hope rapidly, the boy dropped his chin to his chest and curled his free arm around his stomach. This poor child who'd just lost his father to the hangman's noose.

Hawken hit him again.

A gash appeared below his eye. By the time the boy's head had stopped reeling from side to side, a glistening streak of blood was smeared across his cheek. What kind of brute force did it take to cut flesh with the back of a hand?

'Please . . .' said Alice, trailing off as she, like I, weighed the instinctive demands of human decency against the diplomatic constraints of our situation. It takes a lot to interfere in another's barbarity when five million dollars are at stake.

Leonard looked too stunned to say anything. I realized he probably hadn't ever seen an act of deliberate violence before.

The boy screamed something. I glanced at Alice.

'He said he was told to do it,' she hissed.

When Hawken hit the boy a third time, I turned to Pamela, hoping that she might intervene. But she was observing the torture – there wasn't any other word for it – with a serenity that chilled me. How could she love a man who dispensed such savagery? Perhaps she didn't love him: there was no reason to assume that, because they slept together, any kind of emotional warmth existed between them. In this lonely, remote place, perhaps both of them just needed a little physical intimacy. An occasional fuck.

'Enough,' said Hoppner.

The word made no obvious impression on Hawken. Letting the boy sink to his knees, Hawken punched him full in the mouth.

'Hawken . . .'

There was a frightening energy about Hawken's eyes as once again he paid no attention to his employer's call. The punch had thrown the boy backwards; a scream came from his mashed lips as his head hit the ground. Hard to tell, with all the blood, but I think one of his front teeth had snapped off. I was horribly reminded of the young vendor in Santa Tecla, dragged down the Via España to a similar fate at the hands of the police. Was there really such a parallel between these two world-apart worlds? Reaching down to seize the boy's flapping shirt, Hawken was already drawing back his right arm for another blow.

'I said, enough!'

He did not look round at Hoppner's livid face, but he let his arm fall to his side and stepped back from the boy. The despicable cruelty of his act meant nothing to him, it was quite clear. If anything, I detected in his eyes something close to resentment at the intervention.

The boy pulled himself up and Hoppner tossed him the severed head. He missed the catch – the repulsive object slipped tumbling through his hands – but he bent to snatch it up as hastily as if it were a grenade. At Hoppner's curt order he tucked the head under his arm and started running towards the guards. A further, louder command, and the gates were thrown open to let the boy through.

Hoppner turned back to Hawken. A castigatory stare.

'I want security increased,' he said. 'Go wake up the nightshift. Six on, two off, until we figure out what this means.' He didn't wait for any acknowledgement, adding, 'And come right back. We have a test to do.'

It happened in a building at the upper east corner of the compound: a low, squat cabin consisting solely of one large room. Other than a scattering of hard plastic chairs, it contained no furniture. A ceiling fan emitted a low, constant hum. There was nothing on the walls or floor, and there were no windows.

'This takes concentration,' said Hoppner. 'Absolute quiet. You will shut your eyes and see nothing, hear nothing but my voice. You must relax, but you must concentrate. Are we clear?'

Alice and I stood in the darkness at the edge of the room, as far from Hawken as we could manage, watching Hoppner watch Freddy. Concentration was a lot to ask when Sánchez's thugs were possibly already on their way to add substance to the symbolism of that severed head. I couldn't help worrying that six guards and a fence would not be enough to deter them. But Hoppner commanded such attention that even murderous ex-guerrillas faded into the back of the mind. The two men sat facing each other beneath a single, central spotlight. Hoppner reached out and gripped Freddy's shoulders, pressing hard until the other man seemed to melt back into his chair.

'So, what do we do?' said Freddy loudly, perhaps trying to dispel the disquieting atmosphere, his laugh collapsing under the strain of his nervousness. 'Are you going to wave a pocketwatch at me?'

'No.' Hoppner shook his head slowly. Mesmerically. 'No, I simply ask that you let yourself slip back into your thoughts. Your underlying thoughts. What we think in life is what we are in life. Thinking is doing is being. It is possible for one man to be a dozen different people to his friends, colleagues, lovers, parents . . . but inside there is only one. We believe we have conflicting thoughts, but this is rarely true. Our brain is simply floating alternatives, allowing us to work through possibilities . . . simply . . . quietly . . . thinking without trouble or strain or effort.'

As he spoke, Hoppner allowed his voice to slow. The words became softer, more melodious. I don't remember most of the phrases and images he used to lull Freddy into a trance. The fan seemed to grow almost inaudible. Everything blurred a little.

'To a man with dreams, thoughts are the language of expression – they float across the landscape, taking him on a journey to places he might never expect to see. Beautiful places, strange places . . . places he has never known. Close your eyes now. Places that become as real as anything around him: cathedrals, the bottom of the ocean, a storm cloud, the palace of an emperor, the burrow of a mole. Dreams lift him, soar him out of his existence to these places . . . these otherworldly places. Can you see a place?'

At his command, Freddy's eyes had closed fluidly, as if they'd just been waiting for permission. Already his head had tilted a little, his chin closing in on his chest. To Hoppner's question, he nodded once.

'Tell me about this place. Where are you?'

'A factory,' whispered Freddy. 'A big factory.'

'You are in a factory. A big factory. What does it feel like, this big factory?'

'It's empty. Dark. No one here. Just long passages.'

'Let us walk down one of those passages. You have three to choose from. Can you see them?'

A hesitant nod from Freddy – an odd movement, as if someone else were controlling his head with an unseen string.

'You are going to take the left passage. You walk; it is dark; you walk, thinking through your thoughts, your dreams. Your mind is quite clear. There is water on the floor, puddles that you avoid.

The floor is concrete, greasy with oil. It is dark, but you can see the slight gleam of oil on water. Patterns form in the oil, curling, dappled shapes. You walk on; the passage comes to a junction; you go left. Here, there is more water, dripping from the roof, but the drips are soft, slow, noiseless. There is no sound at all, only a tiny flash of light where water strikes water. You walk on, turning right now, the passage is opening up, wider, colder, darker. You reach into your pocket; there is something there, something very special to you, something you have always loved and cared about, something deeply precious. What is it?'

'My lighter.'

There wasn't a second's hesitation from Freddy. His voice had dropped – a deeper, far-off register. The cigarette lighter that had destroyed my anonymity. Freddy's right hand was closing, the fingers pressing together, holding his mind's treasure.

'Tell me about your lighter.'

'It's mine – it's my lighter. Always has been.'

'Describe your lighter for me.'

'Silver. Works like a dream. Never let me down. Girls love it.'

And that was when I knew Hoppner had him. Freddy had regressed to being Freddy.

'You are walking on now, through the darkness. The passage is drying out, the water disappearing. As the floor becomes drier, the air becomes warmer – can you feel that? It is dry air, the passage is dry, and you are starting to feel thirsty. A single electric light ahead: strip neon, very white, very bright. After the darkness, it feels like a lighthouse, it is so bright, burning through you. You cover your eyes against it but it is so bright and you are so thirsty. There is no water anywhere, no puddles, no drips, not even any oil. The passage is covered in dust, in tiny shavings of metal, in plaster dust, fine dusty plaster. No water anywhere. You're so thirsty, you would drink out of a puddle if you could find one, but there's no water.

'You're under the neon light now and you can see in its light a million particles of dust, floating around in front of your eyes like a silent snowstorm. It is beautiful, but you're too thirsty to appreciate it. The dust is in your mouth and your lungs, drying them out. You want to spit but your mouth is dry, completely parched. You're afraid you might die if you don't drink soon.'

For a few short seconds, Hoppner paused. Freddy's right hand was still closed around the imaginary lighter, but now the rest of his body was tensing up. His mouth was open. He licked his lips.

'There is a door in front of you. It is open. You walk into a room. There is a man there behind a desk. He has a sign on his desk: his name is Arnold. Beside him is a large stack of clear blue bottles. Can you see what is in the bottles?'

'Water.' It was a gasp – of relief, of excitement.

'There is water in the bottles. Cool, refreshing mineral water. A stack of bottles, full of water.

Arnold looks up at you. Would you like to say anything to him?'

'Can I . . . ? Can . . . can I have some water?'

'He looks at you, he examines you, he sees you are dusty and thirsty and need water. But he tells you that you cannot have any water. He must save it for other people who are coming – people who need it more than you. People who are so dehydrated they will die if they don't get this water. He makes you leave his office. You are thirsty. You have to walk back out into the passage. How do you feel?'

'Angry. Thirsty and angry.'

'You look back. The door is still open, but now Arnold is gone. There is no one in the room: just a lot of water – his water, which he has told you that you cannot have. What do you want to do?'

'Take some water.'

'You understand that other people need it more than you do?'

'I need water!'

'You take a bottle and drink it. You throw the bottle into a trashcan. Arnold comes back in. He is suspicious when he finds you there. He counts the bottles. There is one missing, he says. He asks if you took it. He looks angry. What do you tell him?'

'I didn't take it.'

'He doesn't believe you. He is very angry. He grabs you and pushes you out of the room, throws you out, so that you fall against the opposite wall. As you collide with the wall, your hand opens and your lighter falls out. He slams his door shut. Your lighter falls, it falls through a hole in the floor, into a drain. You reach in but it has already been swept away, far away to the sewers. Your lighter . . . your lighter is lost, is gone for ever because Arnold pushed you . . .'

Freddy had turned white. His right hand was open, the fingers stretched taut. His mouth was moving, the muscles of his face drawn tight.

'Bastard,' he whispered.

'You notice something beside the door to the room. It is a motorcycle, polished, gleaming, much loved: it is Arnold's motorcycle. Arnold loves this motorcycle – it is expensive and special. Now you notice another door. It is open, and through it you see a street. Out there is sunshine, quiet, pleasant surroundings. You would be happy out there. You could leave, walk out and be happy outside in the sunshine. There is water to drink, there are people to talk to. You would be happy. What do you do?'

'The bike,' said Freddy, between tight lips. 'His motorcycle. For my lighter.'

'What do you do with the motorcycle?'

'I pick it up.'

Hoppner was frowning. Watching and frowning.

'What do you do with it now?'

'I throw his bike against the wall.'

A pause.

'It is dented. What do you do now?'

'I throw it again. And again.'

'It is broken. Arnold's motorcycle is broken. What do you do now?'

'I throw it against his door. I break down his door with it.'

Oh Christ, Freddy.

Hoppner nodded, crossed his legs. His voice was whisper quiet. 'You break down the door. You walk into the room and see Arnold. He is lying under the door. Under the motorcycle and the door. He is stuck. He cannot breathe. In a little while he will die because he cannot breathe. What do you do now?'

And Freddy hesitated. He sat there, eyes closed, seeing it all yet seeing nothing that mattered. Eventually, reluctantly: 'I take the door off him.'

'You try, but you can't. It is too heavy. You need help. You go to the outer door, look out. There are people there. They could help you. But now you hear sirens. The police are coming. Arnold is about to die and the police are coming. What do you do now?' The words fell heavy, like a judgement.

'The fingerprints.'

'What fingerprints?'

'I have to clean the fingerprints off the door. Off the bike.'

'What about Arnold? He's dying.'

'I have to clean the fingerprints!' screamed Freddy.

His voice rebounded through the room. Hoppner took a deep sigh. He glanced at Hawken.

'Thank you,' he said to Freddy. 'In a moment I'm going to ask you to wake up. When I do, you will slowly open your eyes. You can relax now. You are no longer thirsty. You have found your lighter – it is on the floor beside you. You pick it up and put it safely in your pocket. You walk out of the room, through the passage and out of the factory. You are in a peaceful, sunny place and now you wake up. Slowly, comfortably wake up.'

When Freddy opened his eyes I felt a strong urge to look away, out of embarrassment, perhaps. I'd seen him as he would have hated to be seen. He was smiling now, looking around him in some confusion, but smiling all the same.

'Did you do it?' he said. 'Was I hypnotized?'

'You don't remember?' asked Hoppner.

'I was . . .' Freddy looked around again, peering into the darkness beyond his pool of light to locate Alice and me. 'I was thirsty.'

'Are you still thirsty?'

'No. No, I'm fine. So what happened? Did I do OK?'

He was still smiling, but as the silence that followed his question lengthened, the smile began to slip. The drone of the fan now seemed unbearably loud. Freddy gazed into Hoppner's solemn face, reading his answer there.

'You're kidding,' he muttered. Again, he looked around, trying to see us. 'Mark? Alice?' He turned back. 'You're telling me I didn't make it? I came all this way and now you're going to tell me it's been a waste of time. Is that what you're telling me?'

'Mr Greenock, I'm sorry to say your responses indicated—'

'Oh, for God's sake! You don't honestly think I'm going to make any sense when I'm fast asleep, do you? I mean, it's ridiculous! It's unfair. I should be given a chance to make a proper bid. There's so many incredible things I can tell you about this project in Malawi. Those children, they deserve the chance to learn, don't they?'

'You are not the person to help them. I'm sorry.'

'I don't believe this,' he whispered. Then, much louder: 'I don't fucking believe this! I came all this way, put in all this effort and I'm going away empty-handed? How come that Dorothy woman gets the cash, and I don't? I suppose you're going to give it to Mark, as well? You think he's more saintly than—'

'Mr Greenock!' Hoppner was suddenly on the edge of his chair, staring into Freddy's eyes. 'You are not going away empty-handed. You are not going anywhere. You made a bargain. I expect you to honour it.'

Something in Hoppner's anger quelled Freddy's indignation immediately. In its place, I think I glimpsed a kind of shame. A squirming awkwardness, at least. He dipped his eyes.

'You mean, kill myself?' he said, with a little laugh.

By way of response, Hoppner stood up and walked to a cupboard on the far wall. It was too dark to see what it contained. When he returned to Freddy's side, he was carrying a device that at first I took to be some kind of futuristic pistol.

Startled, Alice reached out to grip my wrist.

'This contains sodium pentobarbital,' said Hoppner, his finger tapping a vial mounted on the pistol's glass barrel. 'It is a jet injector: not painful. There is no needle, just a burst of compressed helium to shoot the dose into your arm. Then, only drowsiness. You will lose consciousness soon after.' He held out the device, indicating the trigger. 'You should not be afraid of death: billions have taken this journey before you; most of them had no choice. You are lucky: you made a choice, and it was the right choice. It is a good and a brave thing you are doing.'

For an age, Freddy just stared at the jet injector, not quite believing, not knowing what to think. Perhaps, like me, he was asking himself if this wasn't some appalling sick joke. Then he looked up into Hoppner's eyes and shook his head.

'I'm sorry, friend,' he shrugged.

What else could he say, faced with such insanity? But even though I would have done just the same, I couldn't help resenting him a little: his refusal would derail any chance I had of raising Christopher's money.

Hoppner looked across at us. 'Mr Weston, Mrs

Williams – will you excuse us? Mr Greenock and I need to talk privately for a moment.'

About what? Did Hoppner honestly think he could convince Freddy to do the honourable thing – the lunatic, stupendously ludicrous thing – just by talking to him? Surely that was too much to expect of a man who had been shown through hypnosis to be a thief and a vengeful liar, a man who would rather see someone die than risk gaol.

A blinding flood of daylight filled the room. Hawken had opened the door and now stood beside it, waiting for us to leave.

'Mark . . .' Alice turned her worried eyes to me.

'It's OK. Freddy's not that suggestible,' I said, guiding her out.

'Be with you in a sec,' Freddy called after us.

The gardens seemed bizarrely vivid after the darkness of the cabin and the gloom of Hoppner's imaginary factory. The hummingbirds floating around the main house sparkled in the sunlight, flashes of lustrous green suddenly disappearing behind pillars to be replaced by flamboyant reds and purples. At the bottom of the garden, Leonard had put aside his book to watch the progress of a long-limbed monkey as it tumbled and bounced through the lush, quivering canopy.

'He's going to send us all home now,' growled Alice. 'With nothing.'

'I'm afraid he might,' I said.

'Damn! Why'd he have to pick Freddy first?'

Apparently only partially recovered from the shock of finding the goat's head, David was slumped on the steps of the office building, chin resting on his fists. The same thigh and hip were visible behind him, but if that unseen PA was talking to him he was showing absolutely no sign of listening. I had a brief vision of him crouched by Hoppner's Tulsa porch – younger, of course, but drawn in that same posture. How much did the memory of that meaningless attack still haunt him?

'Hi,' he said, jumping up as we approached. 'How's it going? Everything good?'

'Freddy's out,' said Alice.

David's smile collapsed. 'Has he . . . ?'

'No. He changed his mind. Mr Hoppner thinks he can convince him, but it's not going to happen.'

'Oh.' Glancing at the closed door of the cabin, David started biting a fingernail. 'Mr Hoppner wants to help. That's the main thing. Whatever he does. It isn't for his own sake. He's just helping out.'

'What do you mean?' I said, unsettled by the anxiety in his voice.

But before David could reply, his name was called from the direction of the guesthouse. Pamela was walking across the lawn, a pair of yellow ropes coiled over her shoulder. Her expression was marginally more irritated than usual.

'Has anyone taken my ibis hooks?' she demanded.

'They were hanging in my room, but now I can't find them.'

'Ibis hooks?' queried Alice.

'For climbing. Three of them are gone. Have you seen them lying around anywhere?' There was no disguising her exasperation. 'They might have been linked together like this.'

She reached into the bundle of ropes and yanked out a shiny silver grappling hook. Three sharp prongs.

It was unmistakable.

'That was your . . . ?' I stared at the hook aghast, knowing what it meant long before I was ready to accept it.

'Mark, is something wrong?' Pamela was looking at me curiously, almost cautiously.

Swung across the Parque Central, from church roof to tree top, a hi-tech climbing hook that had nothing whatsoever to do with Francisco José Sánchez. A hook taken from Pamela's room by someone with easy access.

Someone prepared to kill.

The dawning horror choked me, made my sight flicker.

'Freddy!' I shouted, twisting round and sprinting back to the cabin.

'Mark, no,' I heard David cry. 'Please! No.'

The door was locked. I wrenched at the handle, threw my weight against the unmoving wood, battered my fist on it.

'Mr Hoppner, wait!' I yelled through the door.

'Ask him some other questions. Do it once more, please! Ask him about children! Hypnotize him and ask him if he'd take care of children in trouble! He adores children! He's good, really good with children! Mr Hoppner, he has so much love for children!'

A click in the lock. The door opened. I stood back, feeling faint, as Hoppner walked slowly out, his eyes saddened.

'Love is not enough, Mr Weston,' he murmured. 'Caring for those you love is no better than caring for yourself.' He laid a heavy hand on my arm. 'Love is not virtue.'

An unbearable absence of noise from the cabin. The merest whisper from the fan as it slowed to a halt. I found it impossible to breathe. The touch of Hoppner's palm against my shirtsleeve seemed to suck the life out of me. His eyes were a muted grey, unblinking but strangely comatose, as if the thing I knew beyond all question he'd just done had taken a heavy spiritual toll on him.

Shaking him off, I pushed past Hawken into the cabin. Freddy was sprawled in the same chair, his arms hanging loosely by his sides, one leg stretched out, his head collapsed over his left shoulder. He was just about breathing, and the wretched, hopelessly doomed movement of his chest sent a searing wave of desolation through me. Beside him on the floor, his jacket was lying in a crumpled heap. His shirtsleeve was torn.

I dropped to my knees beside him, desperately

whispering God knows what, afraid to touch him, helpless, useless. Would resuscitation work? Could I pump life back into him? Slice open his arm to bleed out the poison? How could I be so fucking ill-informed? My own heart was pounding so fast, it seemed impossible that his was on the point of stopping.

Tentatively, I lifted his wrist, tried to find a pulse, but as I did so his body went still and the foul smell of an evacuated bowel filled the room.

I closed his eyes with thumb and finger. Letting his arm drop, I knelt alone beside his body in that single spotlight, fighting to control my terror.

It's always the good men who do the most harm in the world.

Henry Adams

CHAPTER 13

Alice sat huddled beside Leonard on one of the benches overlooking the valley and the forest canopy. Every few seconds, a shudder would run through her slight body. A tiny cry echoed in her throat. Leonard had an arm stiffly curled around her shoulders. He stared blankly into the tree tops, as if unable to accept even the barest of facts in this new, horrifying reality. His long legs were tucked self-consciously under the bench, knees almost scraping the gravel. The fingers of his right hand were threaded through the slats of the bench, distractedly kneading the rough, rain-warped wood.

'I wouldn't . . . I mean, I don't think we should jump to conclusions,' he said, his voice trembling.

'They killed him,' I repeated.

'But how is that possible?' He glanced up at me, his face tautly drawn. 'It goes against everything Mr Hoppner stands for. I mean, you weren't actually there, were you?'

'Would you prefer to ask Freddy?' I said coldly.

'Stop it, Mark!' cried Alice.

In her distress, her bony shoulders heaved a little under Leonard's clumsy arm. Her left hand moved briefly to her throat, her fingers brushing the silver cross. Did it bring her courage? Luck? Either would be invaluable right now.

'We're all in shock,' said Leonard, struggling to find a mental escape. 'None of us were expecting anyone to fail and actually have to . . . have to do it.' He lowered his eyes to the ground. 'But I suppose he had agreed to suicide in that eventuality, so the only honourable thing for him to do was—'

'What if I fail?' cried Alice.

For a moment he seemed truly terrified. A shake of his head, interrupted for a word that never made it out of his mouth. Then a weak laugh. 'Don't be silly, Ali,' he stuttered. 'How could you possibly fail?'

With sudden impatience, she pulled herself out of his rigid grip. 'Leonard, I need to speak to Mark for a moment,' she said, her voice empty of expression. 'Alone.'

His head turned, eyes confused.

'Darling, please,' she said, relenting a little. 'Mark and I are in a terrible mess. You're not. Please.'

Frowning, he muttered, 'All right.'

He rose in three ungainly stages to his feet. As I took his place I caught the hurt expression on his face. Did he begrudge me Alice's trust? Did he resent me? That was the least of my worries.

Since witnessing Freddy's death, my mind had been filled with one thought alone: the fear of Hoppner uncovering that unmentionable fragment of my past. A small boy, tears flowing, hiding from me under a man's blue cotton jacket. How could I possibly hide that image from his all-seeing hypnosis?

Alice waited until Leonard had walked to the far end of the terrace and settled on another bench, out of earshot.

'Will they let us leave?'

'No.'

'Can we get out of here?'

'That fence is twelve feet high, topped with razor wire. The guards are serious fuckers, well trained and presumably well enough paid to be loyal. Even if we could climb over the fence, even if we could persuade those guards to open the gate, we'd have no transport. The whole of Miraflores depends on Hoppner for cash. You want to ask Señor Sánchez for a lift?'

The earlier winds had died down; the tree tops opposite were calm. Sunlight filtering through the upper leaves drew broken patterns on the foliage beneath: light green splashes on a dark sea.

She took a long breath, ragged and broken. 'Oh . . . Lord,' she whispered. 'We're not going to pass that test.'

'We might . . .'

'How can we?' she almost shouted. Pressing her

trembling hands against her face, she rocked forward until her elbows were balanced on her knees. 'How can we?' she repeated softly. 'We came here to rob him. You saw how Freddy was.' Looking up at me with eyes red and wet with tears, she whispered, 'I'm so frightened, Mark. I'm supposed to be *married*!'

'You must tell Hoppner you're pregnant. He won't make you do the test if he knows.'

'I asked you not to talk about that.'

'It can get you out of here.'

'Oh, really? What happens when Hoppner congratulates Leonard only to discover he's not the father and knows nothing about any pregnancy? What odds of survival do you give me then?'

By chance – or was it some kind of sixth sense brought on by my fear? – I looked round in time to see Pamela approach, her rubber-shod feet silent on the soft grass. She was still cocooned in the coils of yellow ropes, her rock-climbing plans temporarily interrupted by our little cull. I gave Alice a warning nudge.

A flicker of hope appeared in her eyes when she spotted Pamela. Here was a kindred spirit, a woman, the Florence Nightingale who'd stitched her wound: a friend in the enemy camp. But it was misplaced hope, I knew for sure. Not only did I not share Alice's enthusiasm for the Canadian, but, after watching her stand by while Hawken beat up a boy half his size, I didn't expect any salvation from her either.

Pamela nodded – a kind of brief, reserved greeting – then turned to lean against the wall with the cliff drop behind her. She glanced down. 'I've climbed this, you know,' she said.

I'd looked earlier. A bare, unwelcoming rock face, it was more or less vertical: not an easy challenge.

'Was it fun?' I asked bleakly, only because I couldn't think of anything else to say to the girlfriend of the man who'd killed Freddy.

'I don't do it for fun. I don't like heights – or wet, cold rock, or the physical exhaustion. That's why I do it.'

Another nutter. How had we not seen the danger that these deranged people represented? Was it simply the terror of Sánchez's ambush that had made them seem so reasonable and warm and hospitable by contrast?

'Can you help us?' Alice asked her.

'You'll do fine. Just be yourself.'

'I can't, Pamela.' Her voice grew suddenly choked. 'I just want to leave.'

'Why?' There was genuine surprise in her question. 'You want the funding, don't you?'

This question was too much for Alice. Turning away, she hid her face in the palm of her hand, struggling to mask the sound of her sobbing. I touched three still fingers to her curved back, trying to communicate through that small contact the full comfort of the hug I couldn't give her under Pamela's keen gaze.

'I think what she's trying to say is that we don't particularly want to die today,' I muttered.

Pamela shrugged. 'So long as you're good people, there won't be any need for suicide.'

'Suicide?' I snapped. 'That's a fucking joke! They murdered Freddy!'

Pamela's face darkened. 'No one here is a murderer. Your friend declared an unambiguous wish to commit suicide if he failed the test. Obviously, at the critical moment, it's difficult for even the strongest person to overcome their base survival instincts, so Hawken had to help him. Do you know how hard that is, to assist a suicide? It's an incredibly generous thing to do. Hawken gets nightmares. I don't know how he finds the strength to cope with the trauma.'

'He was only helping out?' The lunacy of this idea, of her appalling claim of euthanasia in defence of her vicious lover, was so overwhelming I couldn't hold back a bitter laugh. 'Freddy never wanted to die. Are you crazy?'

'You're saying he was lying?' she said coldly.

'Of course he was lying! It's not a crime.'

From her look, I gathered, it was worse than a crime. In Pamela, virtue had found not just an advocate and adherent, but a fanatic. Dishonesty of any sort – white lie, evasion, omission – was sufficient grounds for condemnation. And now, by siding with Freddy, I'd effectively admitted to lying myself. Only Alice, the biggest deceiver of us all, was still untarnished in her book.

'If his life was built on lies, then he's better off dead,' said Pamela, with a withering look that left no doubt she was referring equally to me.

Hawken arrived during the ensuing silence. At the sight of him, Alice's face turned as sick as I felt. I imagined him grabbing Freddy, overpowering him, gagging him and holding him down to fire the lethal dose into his arm. Nothing in Hawken's appearance hinted at the recent struggle: his black leather jacket lay flush across his broad shoulders; the collar of his pressed shirt still rested neatly against his sturdy neck.

Beside me, Alice cringed a little, but Hawken's gaze was entirely on Pamela. There was a palpable force emanating from him, reaching around her, embracing her. Taking his cheek in her hand, she looked deep into his eyes and whispered, 'Are you OK, honey?'

'I'm fine.'

With a hand in the small of her back, he drew her towards him until only the coils of yellow rope held them apart. His fingers moved down to her buttocks, pertly outlined in the tight Lycra, and paused there – motionless for a couple of seconds – before curling and digging into the muscle. Pamela opened her mouth to admit her lover's tongue. Their lips formed a tight seal, then began to chew on each other. The display shook Alice, but, like me, she found it impossible to look away. The sight of such blunt sensuality from such a coldly barbarous man was compulsive.

When he broke off the kiss and turned to us, he seemed amused to find us watching.

'Out of respect for Mr Greenock,' he said with a slight smile, 'we won't be holding any more tests today. Mrs Williams, you will go next. Please be ready at ten o'clock tomorrow morning.'

Taking Pamela's hand, he led her towards his house.

Freddy's funeral – although that's too grand a word for the no-frills burial he was given – took place that afternoon. We'd been left alone in the guesthouse all morning, not knowing what to think, not daring to predict what might happen at our own reckonings. While we watched mutely from the sofas, Hawken marched into Freddy's room and reappeared a few moments later carrying his bags. He didn't even bother to look at us as he cleared away the last remaining traces of the dead man.

It wasn't until later – until after every credit card, passport, monogrammed shirt, every scrap of Freddy's real identity had been burnt at the back of the compound – that I thought of his next of kin. There would be no point looking for a Mrs Greenock – wife or mother – to inform of her tragic loss. Freddy's true name was lost for ever. Though I realized it was highly unlikely I'd be getting out of the compound myself, I was profoundly upset by the thought of some poor family waiting for Freddy: waiting for news that would never come.

The invitation to attend the burial was delivered by David during our otherwise silent lunch. Hoppner had remained out of sight in his office ever since the killing, but he'd sent word that it might be appropriate for Freddy's 'companions' to bid him farewell. When he finally emerged from the office building at three o'clock, Hoppner did not wait for the burial party to form up behind him, but strode off towards the gate without a word to anyone.

David and I carried Freddy's body, wrapped in a pair of grey blankets that kept separating to reveal a section of hairless midriff. It was bad enough having to clutch a dead man's shoulders, but seeing that defenceless stomach wobbling along in front of me nearly made me puke. I glanced away and found Leonard close behind me. Alice brought up the rear of the procession, eyes downcast. Neither Pamela nor Hawken had bothered to come.

The forest path Hoppner led us down was well trodden, the place he stopped already generously scattered with graves. Unmarked, they were still easily discernible by their freshly turned earth and the absence of plant growth. I counted twelve. Twelve people had failed Hoppner's test before us, yet we'd had no warning: nothing had reached the press about this new wave of disappearances in Central America. An open grave – a deep, muddy gash in the world, dug perhaps by the guards, perhaps by a Miraflores stooge – awaited the thirteenth vanishing.

Perhaps, like us, those twelve unfortunate fortune-seekers had been too secretive in their planning and approach to Miraflores. Smith and Brown had clearly been fake names; maybe the rest, if more subtle, had been equally duplicitous. No one knew where they had gone – no one could draw out the common factor in their disappearances. Twelve – now thirteen – anonymous families spending the rest of their lives condemned to hope.

The only real name I could be sure of was Daedalus Foy, though that wasn't the name he would have given to Hoppner on his arrival at the compound. I knew now he hadn't disappeared in Santa Tecla, nor had Sánchez disposed of him. Foy's big story had been how easy it would be to extract large amounts of money from Hoppner. He had died being proved wrong.

A strange thing, burying someone in a godless place. Standing over the grave, Hoppner had all the dignified presence of a priest but none of the reassuringly familiar words. Lacking ritual, he could only say, 'By dying, he has made his greatest gift to the world.' Dickens put it so much better.

A shovel stood embedded in the pile of wet earth beside the grave, and we took turns to cover Freddy. The others seemed strangely reluctant to cast earth on his face, which consequently stared blindly up at us long after the rest of his body had disappeared. In a sudden fury, I shovelled load after load of earth over his head, not stopping when it disappeared from sight, until Hoppner said, 'Mr Weston, take it easy.'

Throwing the shovel aside, I glared at him across the grave. 'Take it easy? Take it easy? Look at . . . look!' My brain suddenly a little crazed, I pointed at the mound over Freddy. 'Are you fucking serious? Look what you've done!'

In that brief moment of unbridled fury, I thought of the shovel blade: solid steel – a formidable weapon. As I cast my eyes sideways, searching, David stepped swiftly forward and seized the tool. 'Please, Mark. Breathe. Breathe.' Already, he was moving away, carrying the shovel well out of my reach.

Sensing Hoppner's troubled eyes relentlessly examining me, I turned away and stumbled down the track. I don't know if I would have used the shovel, if I could have reached out and attacked Hoppner with it. I've always fought hard with myself to suppress the too-common urge to strike out in retaliation. But after that cold-blooded murder, I'm not sure it wouldn't have been the right thing – the morally just thing – to do.

It occurred to me as we walked back to the compound that this might be the only time we'd be allowed out of the gate. In less than twenty-four hours, Alice would have to face Hoppner's judgement. Would I be walking this same path to bury her? If Hoppner declared she was to die, there would be nothing I could do against Hawken and eight guards.

The sense of opportunity slipping away the nearer we got to the compound created a sense of panic in me. David and Hoppner were twenty feet ahead of us, out of sight whenever the path curved. Should we run while we had the chance? We could disappear off into the forest, but what then? Hawken and the guards would be summoned, vehicles mobilized, the warriors of Miraflores called from the coffee fields. Could we evade them all? Those men knew the forest, had worked and fought in it. It would only be a matter of time before they found us. Even if we made it to the town, no one in Miraflores was going to give us a car to reach the outside world when Hoppner held the purse strings for their entire way of life. Sword dollars would make damn sure we didn't get past the bomb crater.

Small though our chance might be of passing Hoppner's morality test, the prospects for an escape attempt were even bleaker. Our only sensible course of action was to play by his rules.

In any case, looking at Alice I realized she was in no condition to run. She walked with lifeless feet, not even noticing the branches that caught against her legs, her face expressionless.

Leonard touched her arm and said, 'Please, Ali. Don't be sad.'

There was no reply. He threw an arm round her shoulders, but it was shrugged off instantly.

Perplexed, Leonard thrust his long, lean fingers into his jacket pockets.

'Remember what Mr Hoppner said: it's the best thing Freddy could have done.'

'Hoppner?' she cried. 'Hoppner is murdering people! Didn't you see those graves?'

'Ali, please! Stop saying that!' He looked close to tears. Unable to cope. 'He's just as upset as the rest of us.'

I had to remind myself that this man had spent most of his adult life ensconced in the nursery-like shelter of an English university. If I was close to losing it over Freddy's horrifying death, then Leonard was doing well to be saying anything coherent at all.

Hoppner was standing at the far end of the lower terrace, hands resting on the white wall, his spine military straight as always, his gaze on the valley and the distant lake. Here the cliff drop was even greater, and the tree tops barely brushed the bottom of the wall. From his polished brown lace-ups and neatly creased trousers to the hang of his vented wool jacket, Hoppner looked like an English gentleman from another age, surveying his lands in some far-off colony before calling for the evening cocktail. The resemblance extended beyond the physical: amateur jurisdiction; moral pronouncements; a frightening detachment from reality; the self-appointed power to take human life.

I walked up beside him, mimicking his posture,

wondering what was stopping me from simply picking up Freddy's murderer – or at least the man who ordered Freddy's murder – and tossing him over the wall to his death.

I'd thought long and hard about what I was about to say. A revelation like this was not mine to make; Alice would have been furious if she'd known. But I had been horribly shocked by the power of Hoppner's test to get to the root of Freddy's character, and I had no doubt that Alice's fraudulent marriage would be laid bare the moment she was hypnotized. It was hard to see how she could pass any morality test once that deception – and her appalling treatment of Leonard – came to light.

'There's something about Alice you don't know,' I said.

Hoppner's reaction was a complete surprise: 'Quiet!' he cried.

'Excuse me?'

'There's plenty about Mrs Williams I don't know, and that's as it should be. I told you before, I don't want background. It affects my judgement.'

'I'm trying to tell you there shouldn't be a judgement. Alice is pregnant.'

He didn't even blink. 'So?'

I didn't know what to say. I'd just assumed the moment he knew that fact he would free her. Who threatens a pregnant woman with death?

'Her child,' I stammered.

'What difference does it make? If she's a good person, she'll pass. If not, what kind of terrible upbringing would that child get? You know as well as I do there are too many children brought up in immoral households. While it is a good thing to commit suicide if you are only going to be a detriment to society, surely it is better not to be born in the first place.'

'You're talking about ending an innocent life!'

'Nonsense, Mark – may I call you Mark? – there is no life before birth. Life is conscious experience and self-awareness, not a collection of nerve cells and heartbeats.'

Just the memory of Christopher's first breaths made me want to grab Hoppner and shake him hard. When I first held my tiny son, when his little head fitted like a grapefruit into the palm of my hand, it was abundantly clear he'd already been a fully formed human being for months. 'Do you know how many millions of people would disagree with you?'

'If I based my beliefs on polling data I'd be a politician.'

'Mr Hoppner, that child is a precious, living person who—'

'That child is no different from billions of others. It is life that would make it unique, and if the child is brought up by a morally bad mother it will be unique for all the wrong reasons.'

'At least think about it for a couple of days.'

'There's nothing to think about. We've already

352

wasted a whole lot more time than the issue merits.'

'Will you let me just expl—'

'I don't want to hear it!'

His absolute refusal to listen infuriated me the way all absolute positions do. The headmaster who wouldn't accept my late essay, just after the tenth anniversary of my parents' death. The Indonesian official who refused to extend my employment permit when I refused to bribe him. The counsellor who wouldn't listen to my fears about myself.

'When was the last time anyone told you something you didn't want to hear?' I demanded.

His face turned grey. 'What do you mean?'

'You've surrounded yourself with yes-men, haven't you? David, Pamela, probably everyone who works for Sword. Does anyone ever contradict anything you say? Has anyone told you that burying thirteen people in your backyard is psychotic?'

'I can assure you that I found every single one of those deaths deeply unpleasant. But if I am to follow a consistent philosophy—'

'Philosophy? You just murdered someone! You held him down and shot him full of barbiturates in some deluded belief that it would make the world a better place.'

'Hasn't it?' His gaze dug deep into my consciousness. Into my conscience. 'Wouldn't you say we're all better off without Mr Greenock?'

At first I couldn't answer. The truth? I'd spent most of the days since I'd met Freddy thinking he was a contemptible fool, a nuisance or a threat. By the time I was able to stutter 'Of course not!', it was too late to carry any credibility. Yet the odd thing was, even in the midst of so much uncertainty and fear, I found I missed Freddy.

'What if someone exposed what you're doing here?' I demanded. 'What if I passed your test, went back to England and told the press you were killing people? Would you be able to justify yourself to the world?'

'That's not going to happen. Either you'll be cashing a large cheque, conditional on signature of a non-disclosure agreement, or you won't be leaving at all.'

'But if you're hiding all this from the outside world, how can you possibly claim what you're doing is right? Why won't you talk to journalists, if your actions are so virtuous?'

'Now you're being naïve. You know as well as I do the press only want dirt. It's impossible to get a balanced message across: the media talk about the controversial stuff, never the good deeds or the uplifting ideals. Faced with that kind of reception, of course we're careful what information we let out. David's had to learn a lot about public relations.'

'What about honesty? Isn't that one of your great virtues?'

'Sure, but honesty isn't always possible. Plato knew this: in his ideal republic, the government was permitted to lie to the people. Sometimes those in power have to say what is necessary to gain public cooperation, while acting differently – the way they know is best.'

'The way they *think* is best.'

'We all can only ever do what we think is best.' As if to move us away from such contentious matters, Hoppner said, 'Tell me, what is your opinion of my work here? Miraflores. My grand fight against Evil.' He even forced a self-mocking smile.

'A huge exercise in futility.'

'At least be so kind as to tell me why.'

'You're building a paper castle: this perfect society that depends on a regular injection of bribes. It's artificial. The second you go home, it'll fall apart.'

By way of answer, he raised an arm and pointed down the valley. I thought I detected a slight shake in the muscles of his shoulder. Old age or outrage?

'See that lake, Mark? Beautiful, isn't it? You agree it's beautiful?'

Certainly, it was beautiful: the water dark blue in the late-afternoon sunlight, with curving beaches, secluded bays and green islands. Rainforest clustered around its edges, crowding the shallows. A few small boats were just visible at the far end.

'I'll tell you what else is so great about it: it provides around a half a million people with water, irrigates their farms, even creates employment for the two hundred seventy fishermen who live on its shores. Beautiful *and* functional, yes?'

'Yes.'

'It's artificial, Mark. Just like my utopia. Five years ago, it was a stream. I paid for a dam to be constructed when I first came here: part of my deal with the government to keep the army and police out of Miraflores. Hell, deal aside, it was a wonderful thing to be able to do for the country. Nothing more satisfying than spending porn junkies' bucks giving people clean water. But here's the point: what does it matter if that beautiful, functional lake is artificial? What does it matter if it depends on an unnatural dam for its survival? It's an absolute good, Mark. Just like Miraflores.'

'Creating one perfect society isn't going to cure the world.'

'Does it have to? To be a worthwhile thing to do? This country has so many problems; it's full of NGOs and representatives of foreign governments, international funding institutions, all kinds of busybodies charging around, dreaming up theoretical solutions. Probably you saw some of them in Santa Tecla. But do you know how little actually gets done? At least I've made one town right. If I can extend the model elsewhere – encourage others by this example – then we'll celebrate some more, but even if that never happens I'll die contented knowing I've left this town happy and secure.'

I've always had a problem with idealists. This halcyon dream, coming after the double atrocity of Sánchez's attack and Freddy's death, was too

356

much. 'If they're so damn happy, why are they throwing goats' heads over your fence?'

The slightest quiver of anger crossed his face, but a second later it had evaporated. 'Don't worry about that. It isn't important. More interesting is why you're so determined to find the negative in everything. I had you down as a doer, Mark. Don't you want to try for what you came for? Don't you want to put your life on the line for something you believe in?'

'I just want to leave.'

'Leave? Or run away? How often have you dealt with your fears by running away from them?'

He couldn't know about Katie. He had no idea what my life had been like: the misery of my lonely childhood, despite the best intentions of my uncle and aunt; the urge to go abroad, travel the world for no better reason than to get away, to just leave; the disappointment of each new place, each new group of friends, always ending in a one-way plane ticket and an embarrassed, shuffling goodbye. He knew none of this, yet he had touched a nerve.

'I thought you didn't want any background,' I muttered.

That amused him. 'Correct, Mark. I withdraw the question.' He turned back from the lake. 'But you shouldn't be in such a hurry to avoid my test. Just because a man like Mr Greenock – an obviously venal, self-centred, proud man – failed this morning, that's no reason to have doubts for yourself. Without prejudging you, I would say

357

you're in a whole different place to him. So unless you have anything in the closet . . .' He smiled and patted my shoulder as he started walking back up the lawn. 'I'm sure you'll do just fine.'

'Wait!' I called after him, remembering Alice's pained injunction. 'Leonard doesn't know she's pregnant.'

He looked round, bemused.

I struggled to find a lie that would cover her: 'She wants to surprise him on his birthday. Next month. Please don't tell him.'

He smiled at that. 'I won't say a word.'

He walked on towards his house and I was left to face the total failure of my intervention. At least I could count on the man of honesty not to pass on my indiscretion: I hadn't made the mess too much worse. But the tests still loomed, and for both Alice and me there remained that grim qualification:

Unless you have anything in the closet . . .

That night there were no kisses. After my ambivalence the first time she came to my room, I was fairly surprised she returned. But whatever my own feelings towards Alice might have been, the impending test had pushed any lustful thoughts out of her head.

'I keep thinking of all the places I'll never see again,' she whispered.

'Stop it. You might easily pass.'

But she shook her head sadly. 'I'm me, Mark. I'm nobody's saint. It's a long time since I've bothered with the virtues our host holds so dear.'

I let her settle back against the pillows beside me. She was fully dressed this time, and she scraped the heel of one shoe absently up and down the blankets, almost as if she wanted to take revenge on a little piece of Hoppner property. Behind us, Leonard's snores tore through the partition.

'Be positive,' I tried. 'Where do you most want to see again?'

'London.' She grinned shyly at me. 'Sorry. I know you don't like the place, but I'm in love with my little bit of Clapham. My local coffee bar, this funny guy in the newsagent's, the Common when the sun's out.'

'It's not that I don't like it. It's just a—'

'A girl, yes, I remember.' She rolled her eyes. 'I've just about forgiven you for last night.'

I was about to open my mouth, but she went on quickly before I could blunder through an apology.

'I know how you feel,' she said. 'Love really messes places up. I can never go back to Milan.'

'That's a fairly desperate statement for a woman.'

'I know! Think of all those shoe shops!' A wide smile, almost nostalgic. 'But the idea of being within a hundred miles of Luca . . .'

'Luca?'

'The most beautiful man I ever met. Really – I was actually jealous of his beauty. Long black eyelashes, cheekbones to make a nun weep, and

359

a smile all self-deprecating and teasingly arrogant at the same time. He just wandered into a bar in Dean Street and asked me if I'd like to go for a walk along the Thames.' She shook her head, almost in astonishment. 'We didn't stop walking till dawn. By then we were in Kew, staring at this gorgeous pale river, spattered with pink. He got down on both knees and begged me to go to Milan – before I'd even kissed him.'

'How romantic,' I muttered, disliking pretty Luca already.

'Wasn't it? And so glamorous! Milan – I'd always wanted to go there. The shops, the style, the Leonardo. Luca had this amazing apartment, very chic with clean lines and long silk sofas, and he came from some grand old family that put him at the centre of high society. The first party, in a villa on Lake Como, was like a fairy tale.'

I waited in silence; the 'but' was manifest. The satisfaction I felt at Luca's imminent fall from grace was disturbing. Did I really care enough to feel a little jealous?

'I don't know why I'm telling you,' she murmured. 'You don't want to hear this.'

'No, really. I do.' The memory was a distraction to her, which was exactly what she needed at that moment. And I couldn't help wanting to see a tiny piece of this life I knew so little.

She shrugged. 'Luca's chivalry didn't last long. There were always so many stunning Italian girls around him, and he only really brushed them off that first week. I could barely speak Italian, and I knew they were bitching about me all the time. I should have just gone back to England, but I'd had such a fight with my parents about moving to Italy in the first place that I felt I had to make it work.

'To take my mind off Luca's fan club, I began an oil-painting of the cathedral. You know the Milan duomo? All those incredible spires and turrets: a great wonderful mess of finely carved masonry. A thousand pointy bits – the spikes, I called them. A great forest of spikes.

'Every day, while Luca went to work at his dad's newspaper, I set up my easel at the edge of the Piazza. I painted the great tall spikes with the statues on top, the long lines of spiked arches, the whole army of ornate, florid, fanciful spikes. After nine days of concentrated effort it was finished. I took my canvas back to Luca's apartment, leaned it against Luca's vast, shiny black TV and waited for him to come home.

'He walked in and my heart was in my mouth. I desperately needed him to like it, to tell me this was something worthwhile, something those other girls couldn't have done. He sat in his usual armchair in front of the TV, saw the painting immediately but didn't comment on it. Instead, he slouched back and said, "Baby, I'm so tired, I really need a blow job." I didn't want him in a bad mood for this, so I knelt in front of him and did it. And while I had his cock in my mouth he just stared at my painting. I could feel the stare through his cock.

361

Somehow the two became linked in my mind. It was so important that he liked my picture, that he approved, but I grew convinced he wouldn't unless I sucked harder than any other girl he'd had. All I could hear was an occasional tut-tut or moan until he came, and then – while I was still swallowing his sperm – he laughed and said, "*Stupida*, you've left out a *spike*!"'

Alice closed her eyes, and I thought I saw a glint of a tear squeezed out between the lashes. It took a minute for her to speak again. 'It was true, of course. He pointed to a line of spikes and showed me it had one fewer than the next line. I was so upset – by his reaction, not my mistake – that I grabbed the canvas and folded and twisted and tore it until it was a mangled wreck.

'The next morning, I went back to the Piazza with a fresh canvas. I painted non-stop until my wrist ached so much I had to bite my lip to keep going. And when, after five days, I realized I'd again left out one single spike I burst into tears and threw the canvas in a fountain. For weeks I sat in that Piazza, destroying one attempt after another, until all the waitresses and carabinieri knew me. Somehow I could never get the damn picture right. In that mass of spikes, I would always paint one too few.

'Luca came out to plead with me. He wanted sex, not postcards, he said. He started bringing other girls home – secretly at first, then openly. That just made me more determined. Some days

I'd get back to find a curvy blonde providing that after-work blow job, and Luca would just smile and ask how my *spikes* were today.

'I must have painted that wretched cathedral twenty times. In retrospect, I think, at some subconscious level, I was deliberately missing out a spike on each attempt. At the time I thought I was going mad. There came a point where I couldn't see the spikes any more. They just melded into a crazed, futuristic chaos. That was when I stopped. I was so scared of what I was becoming that I ran into that cathedral and sat for hours, days even, alone in the gloom. Oh, but it's impressive, that interior! Even more than the spikes. That vast, silent nave; those massive pillars, looming dark against the darkness. Impossible not to get a sense of God in a place like that. As the hours rolled by, I started to wonder if maybe there might after all be someone up there. But not a god of light and goodness. My god is detached, a little cruel when it amuses Him to be so, watching from His own darkness as we struggle towards an illusive light.'

'Then why worship? Why wear a crucifix?'

'He created us,' she said simply. 'I'm acknowledging His absolute power over us, to decide our fate and the degree of our suffering. I wear this to appease, if you like, to prostrate myself before Him in the hope that it might win me a little favour. Not because I agree with His values. You have to be a little deranged to look at this world and believe it's run by a guy who shares Hoppner's virtuous ideals.'

'So, is that how you left Luca? Your new faith gave you the strength?'

'If only,' she laughed hollowly. 'No, it was nothing that neat. I went back to the apartment after four days of lonely desperation in the duomo, and found Luca's father there. He'd stopped by, hoping for a chat with his son. When I turned up instead, looking so wretched, he took me out for a drink. Then dinner. Then sex. I found him attractive, though probably I would have slept with any man who'd asked at that point, let alone a charming newspaper baron. He told me he was an artist, too – a photographer in his spare time. A few days later he was taking pictures of me. Naked. Good pictures, actually. Really stylish black and whites. I felt beautiful for the first time in weeks. Luca noticed my new mood, though of course I didn't say a word about his father.

'Then one day I walked into his bedroom and found Luca hanging these framed pictures. Pictures of me, naked. He was actually smiling! "Baby, you're *bellissima* in these." I couldn't believe it: that his father would give him those pictures, would tell him about us. But more incredible was Luca's reaction. He simply didn't care. His girlfriend had slept with his father and he didn't care! Nothing could be more humiliating than that.' She shrugged, gave a tired smile. 'So I left. I broke the glass in each frame, ripped up every photo in front of him, picked up my passport and sketchbook and walked out of the door. *Ecco fatto!*

No more Milan. And really, after that, no more falling in love with men.'

For a long time that night, we lay beside each other, our closeness pushing the spectre of Hoppner's morality tests a little further away. Our bodies touched, through our clothes, but nothing more. I thought about those photographs of her, posing naked for an ageing Italian. A curious mixture of arousal and revulsion. Had he reached out and touched her silky throat?

I must have been asleep when she left.

A Code for Life, Section 4: Courage
(excerpt)

Search for a virtue the whole world admires and you'll end up with courage. Some people can't understand the point of fidelity or temperance, others see forgiveness and prudence as signs of weakness. But everyone loves a brave person. The trouble is, courage isn't always a virtue. A man who courageously carries a concealed gun past a line of policemen and then uses it to slaughter children can hardly be considered virtuous. Nor can the Wall Street trader who bravely plays against the odds to garner himself a giant payoff. The trader isn't necessarily evil, but his courage certainly doesn't make him a saint. We can admire him, but at the end of the day we must recognize his motive was Greed, not Good.

Then again, courage in the service of a virtue is very important indeed. It is difficult to do the right thing. For all of us, there is a struggle between the self-serving, lazy, cheating way and the right way. Courage is what helps us make the right choice. You could say that all the other virtues depend, to a greater or lesser extent, on courage.

CHAPTER 14

The thought of bumping into Hoppner somewhere in the cloud kept me on the veranda of the guesthouse that morning. Sleep had had a disorienting effect on me: when I awoke, Alice's Milan was the first reality I remembered. Freddy's horrific death took a few seconds to re-establish itself at the centre of my consciousness.

The air was utterly still; the cloud was spread out, thick here, thin there, a nebulous patchwork hanging over the empty hillside. The colours of the hummingbirds fluttering around Hoppner's feeders were muted and dull.

Two figures materialized some way down the lawn. Hoppner and Leonard had stepped into one of the thinner patches of cloud. Their walk was slow, slightly mismatched, as if Hoppner's purposeful steps were struggling against the leash of the other's more dawdling gait. Leonard seemed surprisingly well recovered from the mental shattering of the previous day. When Hoppner stopped and held out his hand, Leonard shook it unhesitatingly: not for him the revulsion I'd felt while talking

367

to Freddy's judge the previous afternoon. Hoppner faded towards his house and Leonard joined me on the veranda.

'A quite extraordinary man,' he observed.

'You could say that.'

'Do you know he's read all the Upanishads? He can recite the important passages from memory. How many Western philosophers, bar Schopenhauer, can claim that?'

The shirt Leonard was wearing was the same one he'd had on the day before. Had he run out of clean clothes? His old tweed jacket covered most of the wrinkles, but a slight body odour surrounded him.

'Excuse me if I don't share your enthusiasm for Freddy's murderer,' I said.

His face fell. 'Oh, Mark, it's terrible, isn't it?'

'Yes.'

'I dreamed about him last night. That cheeky grin of his. To wake up and realize . . .' As his words faltered, his hands gripped the veranda railing – hard enough to turn the knuckles white. 'I couldn't sleep. I had to find out what really happened. That's what we were just talking about.'

'And Hoppner claimed it was suicide?'

'He calls it "assisted suicide". It's true that Hawken actually injected the . . . well, the poison. But Mr Hoppner gave me his word that Freddy definitely wanted it.'

'Did Freddy ask for it?'

'Not as such,' admitted Leonard. 'But he'd

said before that he wanted to commit suicide if he failed, and Mr Hoppner said he often has to help people at the last moment. Everyone tends to freeze up when they actually have to, you know, *do* it. Animal instincts. It does make sense. Really, it does, doens't it?'

He was looking at me hopefully, as if he'd almost convinced himself of Hoppner's rectitude and just needed one last bit of confirmation to go all the way. I wasn't going to provide that reassurance, but equally I couldn't see the point of arguing with him. What could it possibly matter if Leonard chose to deny the truth of the horror that surrounded him? Either we'd all be out of there in a couple of days, or Alice and I would be dead. Nothing Leonard thought or did was going to make any difference to the outcome.

'Mr Hoppner's got a good heart, Mark. He's a good man and a thinking man. The best combination. We just have to try to understand him.'

'I wouldn't have this conversation with Alice,' I said.

'Of course. You're right, she . . .' The chill of the morning reached him then and he pulled the jacket closer around his chest. 'I am a bit worried about Alice. She's been very distracted.'

'She'll be OK.'

'I worry that she's . . . I don't know, really. I just feel it's as if she's – does this sound very self-absorbed? – losing interest in me.'

I almost laughed. The idea that Alice's varying

levels of interest in Leonard should be remotely important right now, on the day that she might easily be executed, was plain ridiculous. But Leonard was conveying a real fear, and, of course, I couldn't help feeling a little guilty. I'd kissed his so-called wife, something I wasn't even sure he'd done. What with our kiss, Freddy's death and her impending test – I could only think of it as a trial – it wasn't surprising she was treating Leonard differently.

'I was wondering,' he went on. 'You know Mr Hoppner does these exercises in the morning? Isn't that impressive? And there's Hawken, who's very fit, and, of course, you. I mean, everyone around here is very *physical*.'

'What are you talking about, Leonard?'

His blush was rapidly asserting itself. 'Do you think Ali might, well, would she, do you think, prefer me if I were a little more . . . muscular?'

This time I did laugh – I couldn't help it. 'Oh Christ, Leonard, is that what's worrying you?' I looked again at his scrawny arms and meagre chest, and regretted the laugh. For all I knew, this man of books had spent a lifetime secretly wishing he was Arnold Schwarzenegger. 'I'm sure she wouldn't want you any different from how you are,' I assured him quickly.

'So you don't think I should start exercising?'

'Sure, exercise, why not? But it won't make any difference to how Alice feels about you.' Truer than I intended, I suddenly thought, feeling unintentionally mean. How had I allowed myself to get drawn into a discussion of Alice's non-existent love for this poor man?

Leonard's face brightened. 'So you think I should? But, what do I do?'

'What do you mean?'

'What exercises should I do? I haven't done PE since school.'

'Um . . . well, I can show you some, if you like.'

'That would be so kind,' he gushed. 'I was going to ask Mr Hoppner if I could join him, but I didn't want to interrupt his routine, in case it's meditative or something. Shall we do them here?'

'Now?' I glanced around the empty, misty veranda. 'OK, why not? Have you brought your trainers?'

'I'm afraid I've never owned a pair of trainers.'

'Oh.' I looked again at the tweed jacket, the grey wool trousers and the brown Oxfords. 'Any other clothes? Something more casual?' He shook his head. 'Well, perhaps you should take off the jacket and shoes.'

The thought of it made him shiver, but he did what I asked and stood silent, expectant, his socks catching on the rough hardwood planks of the veranda floor. Without the jacket, his body looked pitifully thin.

'All right,' I said, with a smile intended to reassure, 'let's try some stretches.'

Although I worked through the exercises with

him, the slow pace we had to take meant I scarcely warmed up. Leonard, on the other hand, was wheezing and sweating within minutes. His initial, mild complaints about the cold dried up the moment we tried some star jumps. I moved gingerly at first, but the long bruise down my side seemed to have cleared up. When it came to press-ups, Leonard managed just three before his arms gave way. I realized to my astonishment that his upper arms were thinner than his forearms.

'I play the piano a fair bit,' he grinned breathlessly, misunderstanding my observation. 'Strong fingers.'

At one point, while I was coaxing Leonard through his fourth sit-up, holding down his long and fairly malodorous feet, Pamela came out on to the veranda. No Lycra this time, she was dressed in a long skirt of some ethnic print, sandals and a plain white shirt. Her red hair was loosely bunched. She took one look at us and gave a sour laugh before continuing on towards Hawken's house. I ignored her; I don't think Leonard even noticed her scorn.

'Thank you,' gasped Leonard at the end, his red face for once not the product of embarrassment.

'My pleasure,' I said. And, in fact, it was. For twenty minutes, thanks to Leonard's spluttering and wheezing, I'd managed not to think more than twice about Alice's imminent test.

★　　★　　★

'It's time,' said Hawken, standing at the guest-house door. The clouds had rolled back and his shoulders, sides and cropped hair all glowed a little from the sunshine behind.

Across the table from me, Alice dropped the piece of toast she was eating. Her eyes jumped to mine.

I tried to look confident.

Leonard took her arm, smiled and said, 'Good luck, darling.' Alice had specifically asked him not to attend the hypnosis. He seemed quite relieved to stay away. He still had a glow in his cheeks from the exercise, and if Alice hadn't been utterly preoccupied with death she might have been surprised at his new appetite. As she stood up, he added, 'Don't be nervous, Ali. You'll be fine.' I think he really believed it.

David kept his eyes down, focusing on the half-eaten waffle in front of him. With the pointed tip of his knife he began slicing along the lines of the waffle, cutting it into tiny cubes.

'Are you coming?' I asked him as I got up.

'Me? No.' He shook his head with excessive force. His gaze remained locked on his food.

I didn't understand David. He was Hoppner's spokesman, apparently dedicated to his master's work, yet he seemed curiously repelled by this area of Hoppner's activities. He wouldn't attend the morality tests; he turned away when Tanadio's son was beaten: was his conscience battling with his loyalty, or did he just lack the stomach for violence?

Alice dabbed her lips on a napkin and walked stoically to the door. I had to try with Hawken, just once – for both our sakes – even though I knew it wouldn't work: 'Let us leave,' I said. 'Drop us at the main road: we'll never come back, never bother you again.'

Hawken laughed at the suggestion.

'This is inhuman!'

'You made a deal,' he replied, more obdurate even than I'd expected. 'I warned you not to, but you were too greedy to listen to me.'

He wasn't interested in hearing further pleas; he turned on his heel and led us out into the garden. On the way to the cabin, past the humming-birds and the flowerbeds, he started whistling to himself.

'Do you enjoy this?' I asked him.

'Me?' He rubbed the rough skin under his chin with the tips of three fingers. 'It's like any job, isn't it? Just get on with it.' His idea of a joke.

'How the hell did you get here?' I whispered. 'How did you pass the test?'

'You forget, I've never asked him for any-thing.'

In that moment I knew for certain that he loved it: perhaps not the killings and beatings, but he loved the power over other people's lives that these acts brought him. And this was the man who held the keys to our prison. This strong arm of Hoppner's law, who'd never even been tested for the morality he enforced.

'If I fail,' I told him, 'don't think I'll make it easy for you.'

He shrugged. 'Sánchez dropped you in a couple of seconds: I'm really not too worried.'

While we were waiting by the cabin for Hoppner, the sound of an engine drew our eyes towards the gate. A small 4X4 – a Suzuki, perhaps – was approaching the compound. The gate opened, and the vehicle continued on to a parking bay behind Hawken's house. A moment later, Pamela was striding angrily towards us.

'They threw stones!' she shouted before she'd even reached us. 'A whole group of them. They threw stones at me.'

With two quick steps, Hawken was beside her, gripping her arms. 'Did they hit you? Are you all right?'

Under his intense stare, her own outrage diminished rapidly. 'Yes . . . no, I'm fine. It was the car, Hawken. They threw stones at the car. Cracked the rear window.'

'Who?'

'Oh God, I don't know.'

'Who, Pamela?' His grip became demanding. Painful. She didn't complain, though her eyes showed a slight grimace.

'It was . . . look, Hawken, it doesn't matter.'

'Their names.'

She looked down at her upper arm; the skin around his fingers was pinched and angry red. 'Manolo Plá, don Carmelo, Quique, Pepe Pereda,

375

Jesusita . . . look, Hawken, I don't want you to—'

'Good morning, everybody,' came Hoppner's warm voice across the lawn.

Hawken let go of Pamela. She stayed where she was, head bowed.

'What's wrong, my dear?'

'Nothing,' she said quickly.

'A little trouble in town,' said Hawken.

The good humour disappeared from Hoppner's face. 'We'll talk about it later.'

Pamela nodded quickly, and when he didn't say anything more walked quickly away. Hoppner exchanged the briefest glance with Hawken, then led the way into the cabin.

A slight reek of shit still hung in the air. Freddy's legacy. Something else, some manufactured scent, had been sprayed to mask it. The two smells, whisked together by the ceiling fan, created an almost suffocating atmosphere in that closed space.

With strong, straight back but shaking hands, Alice followed Hoppner to the chairs beneath the unforgiving spotlight. From my patch of darkness I watched her sit, balancing herself with one hand on the back of the chair in the action of a geriatric or a drunk. Her face was whiter than ever, bleached by the harsh light and by the terror of what was to come. Thinking, always thinking, of the greed that had brought her here, and the great lie that was her marriage to Leonard.

Deceit and avarice.

There was just no way she was going to pass.

'Mrs Williams,' began Hoppner.

It was enough to produce a violent shudder that ran the length of her body. Thinking about that child inside her – that child that could so easily be like Christopher – I couldn't stand it any longer.

'Let me go first,' I said. 'She's too upset.'

As I took a step towards them, I felt Hawken's grip on my arm and had to restrain myself from throwing a punch at his ghoulish, barely visible face.

'That's thoughtful of you, Mark,' said Hoppner.

The grip loosened: I pulled myself free. Alice was staring at me, confused. I walked to the chair and took her hand.

'Go outside,' I told her gently. 'Go to Leonard.'

'No. I'm not leaving.' She stood up, her weight heavy on my arm. With an uncertain glance at Hoppner she walked to the edge of the room, as far away as possible from Hawken. 'Thank you,' she added to me, in a small voice.

I took her seat. It was warm, even from that brief contact with her thin body. Something about the heat reassured me.

'Well then, Mark, if you're ready?' Hoppner cocked his head. I nodded. He straightened the line of his left trouser leg, the seam shiny in the overhead light. 'Good. You know how we do this. I'm going to ask you to relax into yourself, concentrating on my voice but letting yourself relax into its folds and tones, its hills and valleys, until you find yourself drifting in the gentle breeze of your thoughts and dreams . . .'

I let him talk, hardly listening. I had no plan as such, simply a determination that this manipulative bastard wasn't going to walk through my subconscious with the ease and prying arrogance he'd shown over Freddy. He could modulate his voice as much as he liked, slip subtly through the tonal register, lay minute stresses on those cunningly repeated words – *dreams, thoughts, gentle, relax* – but none of it would penetrate the obstinate shield I'd built around my mind.

His first attempt was over sooner than I'd expected. I noticed the silence belatedly – the lonely hum of the fan – and realized that his eyes had narrowed.

'Mark, you're not concentrating.'

'I'm sorry,' I said coldly. 'It's a little difficult so soon after Freddy's murder.'

I glared towards where I knew Hawken was standing, though his expression in that darkened corner was invisible to me.

'His suicide,' insisted Hoppner. 'I sympathize with your discomfort. But you must try to concentrate. You do understand, don't you, that we cannot proceed until you have subjected yourself to a complete hypnosis?'

'You mean you can't kill me till I cooperate?'

'I cannot help your project . . .'

'Just out of interest, have you helped more people than you've buried?'

'Mark, this is not doing anyone any good.'

'That's your obsession, not mine.'

His voice turned ugly: 'Then let me put it in starker terms. Until you allow yourself to be hypnotized, you cannot leave this compound. Do you wish to remain under Hawken's power for the rest of your life? Believe me, I have more patience than you.'

It wasn't something I'd thought through; the urge towards non-cooperation had been the one voice in my head. Reluctantly I accepted his only partially veiled threat.

'You understand it is in all of our interests to make this hypnosis a success? Good. I could, of course, return to Mrs Williams for the moment . . . ?'

'I've got the message,' I told him. 'I'll concentrate.'

'It is difficult, I know,' he said in a more sympathetic tone. 'I suspect you are not naturally suggestible at the best of times. There is a method we can try that should help, but it will push you into a deeper state of hypnosis than is normally desirable. Still, I believe with you we may not have much choice. Do I have your permission?'

His eyes, always intense, were burning into mine now. I barely needed to move to signal my assent.

'Good. It is up to you whether you want to close your eyes or not. Until you do, keep looking at me, like so.' He leaned forward, took my shoulders and pulled me towards him. His hands were oddly cold.

379

'I'm going to tell you a story and I want you to concentrate hard on what I say. I want you to listen to every word of the story like your life depends on it. Every detail is of absolute importance to you.'

He released my shoulders, but we both remained in position, bent forward at the waist, leaning towards each other, eyes locked on eyes.

'This is the story of a young man called Jim who wanted to take his sweetheart for a picnic in the woods. Jim was a mechanic who loved his job, but he loved his sweetheart, Rachel, even more. The sun shone extra bright when she was around, and every smile she sent his way was another little piece of happiness in his day. For him there was nothing more important than his lovely loving Rachel shot through the gut and Rachel loved him just as much.'

I blinked in confusion. Until then, our joined gaze had been unwavering, almost a contest of wills.

'Concentrate!' he hissed. 'Because she was no ordinary woman, this Rachel. She could sing the most beautiful songs you ever did hear and Jim loved nothing more than to lie in a bath of foetid meat with her and listen to her sing.' This time, the tiniest twitch in his eyes brought mine back into line. 'And there was no place her singing was more beautiful than in the middle of a great empty wood. Jim planned to show her the most beautiful spot he'd ever seen. It was a little stream in the middle of a maple wood, where the sunlight filtered through the leaves and the corpses rotted in a pool that they could swim in, which was never too hot and never too cold.'

It was unnerving – frightening even. The grip his eyes had on mine drew me along with him, not giving me time to go back, to work out what that soft, dangerous voice had actually said, forcing me headlong into the next stream of ill-fitting images.

'So Jim loaded up the car and twenty-six thirty-two too bad too bad for the first few miles until Rachel began to sing. She sang about the blue skies and the silver moon that hung above them with a bleeding axe of contention amongst the allies and tributaries that feed our people who give a damn and die and die but she couldn't any more.'

Words were missing me by now. Whole sentences – their surreal meanings lost in the flood of concepts and images overwhelming my brain. The beat of the fan was relentless. My eyes were watering. It was becoming physically painful to keep them open. A pressure was building on my chest, constricting my lungs. I could actually sense the loss of control, the paralysis, and it terrified me that this man could wield such physical power with words alone.

'Open road, where blue skies shine strongest and Jim was so happy, he was so happy and they took them and they hurt them, beat them, slaughtered them because she was singing, it was truly a beautiful sight ninety-one with opals dropping like boiling snakes on the fields around them until the car grew stronger and so happy, speeding along the road, with Rachel singing the most beautiful music you ever did hear and the sun shining now only more in Arabia than Jim had written, which took them roaring down the road, an empty country road, an empty hot sunny road, with nothing on it with nothing on it . . .'

With nothing on it except them. I could see them clearly, though I did not know who they were or what it was they were holding. I did not know why I was seeing them; I couldn't understand their sudden threatening gesture. I had only a fleeting impression of a big, reassuring shoulder in front of me, and the smell of lavender, so out of place in that place I didn't know.

'. . . fourteen where it lies down underground by Jim whose only . . .'

A smell of lavender that made me want to cry. Only there was nothing to cry about. There was nothing at all: no sky, no people, no ground. But such a strong smell of lavender that for a while I didn't notice the void around me. And when I did, somehow it didn't seem to matter.

'. . . seventy-seven . . .'

Then a photograph. Or rather, a single image, filling my vision, unmoving. As if my sight had been frozen, unable to advance or rewind, unsupported by word or sound. No more comforting shoulder. Nothing, except . . .

'. . . one hundred thirty-three . . .'

Except this. Brown leather seats, the tops of them worn and scarred. But empty seats, both of them, when I knew I knew I knew they should have been filled and something had gone horribly wrong. And beside me on that sun-baked back seat nothing but a blue cotton jacket large enough to cover my whole body. The doors open. The scent of lavender retreating, driven out by an acrid mix of burning rubber and engine oil. Though nothing in my image was moving, I had the sense of a breeze flowing through. And at the very edge of the image, through an open door, the slightest suggestion – the merest captured-in-amber hint – of the murderous inferno.

The image shattered with a scream. Staring into Hoppner's alarmed eyes for what seemed like a thousand years, I realized the scream was coming from me.

His hands seized my arms; the noise died in my throat. Sweat was pouring off my face. My shirt felt clammy and constrictive. My hands were locked around my thighs.

'Mark! Look at me! Look at me!'

In that terror, in that unimaginable, indecipherable torment of emotions, I found myself thinking the quiet, unhurried thought that I'd never before seen Hoppner so agitated. Then all further contemplation was overwhelmed by a flood of shock, terrifying in its unexplained intensity, and I found myself panting like a madman.

'Mark!'

Alice's voice cut through it all, the tremor of her shared fear calming me instantaneously. I couldn't see her, out there in the darkness. Only brown leather seats, wrongly empty, flickering through my vision.

'Oh, Mark, what happened to you? What happened to you?'

Her hands on my shoulders now, and suddenly her face was in front of my eyes.

'What?' I yelled, only because I found their panic even more disturbing and inexplicable than my own. 'What's wrong?'

Somewhere off to the side, Hawken opened the door. Daylight flooded in.

Alice's dark tearful eyes, their pupils contracting in the new light, consumed me. 'You were speaking Spanish,' she whispered. 'What in God's name happened to you?'

'Spanish?' I shook my head, denying the possibility, though even as I did so I felt more than heard fragments of alien words, half-formed questions ricocheting around my mind. 'What . . . what did . . . ?'

'*Mis padres. No los mates,*' she stammered. 'You were crying, "Don't kill them, don't kill my parents . . . please, my mother, don't kill them". Over and over and over.'

The room was full of the scent of lavender. Hoppner's functional guest accommodation had been transformed into a perfumery, though nothing else was changed. The same wood floor, basic colours, plain beds.

I knew the smell wasn't real. But that was all I knew. What it meant, where and why it had made such an impression on me, I had no idea. Closing my eyes, I got a sense of a different room, indistinct, with rumpled mosquito netting and a ceiling fan. The fan turning, my eyes watching it revolving and revolving and always that comforting scent of lavender.

Buenas noches, querido.

I could have picked up the words from Spanish films: passive absorption of basic phrases. I wanted so badly to find some way out of this nightmare of shifting identity that I was prepared to grasp at any faint possibility. Of course I knew the reservoir of words that was beginning to spill over into my consciousness went far beyond that basic level. I could sense the child's inquisitive forays into an exciting new language, hear scraps of kindergarten songs muster at the frontiers of my mind, ready to overwhelm my hopeless rationalizing denial and force me to accept the truth.

A knock.

'You've been here before, haven't you?'

She stood a while by the door, gazing through the curtained darkness at my crumpled form on the bed. I'd run straight back to this refuge, unchecked by either Hoppner or Hawken as I fled the cabin. Alice had called after me, had come after me now.

The lavender dissipated a little in her presence.

'I don't know.'

'Or at least one of these wretched countries. Your parents posted to the embassy. El Salvador, Nicaragua, Guatemala . . . it could have happened in any of them.'

She closed the door. It made no sound.

'They told me it was Washington,' I muttered. 'A car crash, they said.'

'I know.' Walking to the bed, she stepped out of her mules and sat down beside me, laying a hand against my cheek. 'But how could they have told a four-year-old the truth?'

'I didn't remember any of it.'

'You went blank; it happens after violent trauma, particularly with young children. They wrote you a less painful memory.'

The touch of her hand, warm and soft and lemony, comforted me. Her wrist was an inch below my mouth. I kissed it – a child's kiss, all noise and brisk movement, no soft caress of loving lips against lover's skin. It made her laugh softly and she lowered her chin to my forehead, stroking one tenderly against the other.

'What do you remember now?' she asked. I felt the play of her breath, her words, on my hair.

'Just a road. Hot sun. And some men up ahead, blocking it. Carrying guns, I think. And my parents – right there in front of me. Then they were gone. All I can see is the empty seats where they should have been sitting.'

But there was something else now. Something different, from another time. I saw her in a forest: a tall, dark-haired, smiling woman, pointing to a leaf, then gently chiding me for picking up the frog because the tiny thing would only die in my hot hand. And that love, that flood of lavender in amongst the warm, damp tropical smells of rotting leaves and exotic fungi, started me crying as I'd never cried before.

Alice's arms were around me, holding my sobbing, bewildered body close against hers, pressing my face into her neck until her skin was wet with my tears. When I finally opened my eyes, I could see her throat trembling. I lifted my face up to hers and kissed her mouth.

Thanking her.

The rest happened without words, with no need for questioning looks or testing forays. She was a skilful lover, I knew that immediately, feeling her way with me, touching where I needed to be touched, reacting just the right amount to my fingers and mouth to show me what she wanted.

My eyes were open, I think, but I found I was seeing other things, images that had no place in sexual intimacy. A barrier came down between the corporal and the mental, my body moving automatically whilst my mind rolled back to the past.

My aunt was there, despairing – as she so often despaired when I was the subject of discussion – over my unwillingness to speak. *Why can't you just be like the other boys?* But she must have known why. Together with my uncle, she must have spent long hours in some Foreign Office burrow, concocting, perfecting, dissembling. All for my sake, of course, I didn't doubt that. Nevertheless, they'd left me appallingly ill-equipped to deal with the truth when it finally, inevitably, emerged.

Buenas noches, querido. Duerme bien. Ceiling fans and lavender scent. A flutter of nightdress against mosquito netting. Some kind of music in the background. Was that my mother? Laughing over the frog I'd dropped the moment I'd pictured it dying in the warmth of my child's hand. Was that my mother? What is a dead person but the memory we can assemble? What was my mother but lavender and laughter?

Those empty brown seats.

I imagined myself filling one, taking the steering wheel of that embassy car. Turning to find I had a passenger, catching her wink at me. She was in pale blue, wearing a floppy straw hat, just as she did that first magical day in Sulawesi. Her arm linked through mine, interfering with gear changes, rubbing against my ribs, her fingers tickling the underside of my wrist. And in the back seat, my son, looking up at me, touching my broad, reassuring shoulder. Katie's son. Our son. Christopher as he might so soon be, might have been – needing his father. *He needs you, Mark.*

Oh, Christ, why did it have to become so complicated? That pale-blue shirt, the sleeves rolled untidily, one higher than the other. Running down the mountain past the water buffalo, daring me to leap the streams and balance on the turf walls of the paddy-fields, waving to the bemused farmers whose crop we threatened, gambolling down the steep terraces, slipping on muddy banks until the inevitable happened and that pale-blue shirt ended up half submerged along with its sneezing, laughing owner. And as I hauled her out, she kicked once and I was in the muddy rice-sewn water beside her, spluttering, complaining, grinning and wetly – suddenly silent – kissing.

'Mark!'

Alice's face was inches from my own, but I hadn't seen it until that moment. She was breathing fast, her face uncharacteristically red, her eyes still sympathetic but now with a gleam of fierce amusement about them. I felt her muscles tighten once more, then relax completely. My stomach and chest were damp against her. I rolled on to my back, closing my eyes. Her hand reached across to rest softly on my groin.

'So who's Katie?'

She felt my surprise; her hand came alive on my penis. I grabbed her arm and folded it with mine back over her neat breasts.

'I said her name? I'm sorry.'

'Only about a million times,' she replied, but – incredibly – her voice was not angry, not hurt. 'Sounded as if you quite liked her.'

'Yes. I did.'

'Well? If it's a happy memory, you could probably do with that right now.'

'She was a girl I knew.'

'No! Really?'

Pulling the sheet up around her body, Alice tipped herself over on to me, balancing her legs on mine so that I bore her full, minimal weight. She laid her forearms on my chest and placed her hands against my cheeks. Her fingers traced patterns on my temples while she blew gentle puffs of air against my eyelids to get my attention.

I looked up: she was smiling down at me, back arched, her upper body supported on her forearms.

'Tell me about her,' she said. 'I'm not going to get jealous. Much.'

I couldn't even begin to talk about Katie – here, with Alice naked on top of me – in the kind of straightforward terms she expected. My feelings for Katie defied explanation. The pain of leaving her, walking out of the Pimlico flat while she and Christopher slept, knowing I could never go back, had confused me as much as it had torn at my heart. The pain of it, the terrible necessity of it, because once when I was a child I'd . . .

It took me exactly that long to work my way round to the other obvious, crucial conclusion of that dormant memory. A blue cotton jacket. So horrified had I been at the image of my parents' murder, so astounded by the unearthing of my Hispanic past, I'd only subconsciously registered that other shattering consequence. A small, terror-stricken boy, cowering under a man's blue cotton jacket. The hot brown leather seat. The breeze. That boy I thought I'd beaten up, attacked, left permanently scarred – the poor kid my battered conscience had vividly imagined every day since.

That boy was me.

For a moment, I was so astonished I laughed out loud. Had my brain misunderstood its own traumatic, fragmented memory so completely? All this time I'd thought I had caused that expression of terror. All this time I'd imagined a dark, brutal streak lying at my core. The plastic gun my aunt wouldn't let me play with, the fights I was forbidden to join, the refusal to talk about the car with the brown leather seats: nothing but careful measures taken by responsible guardians to prevent a sudden resurfacing of the nightmare. But the consequence of their caution had been this false belief, this ludicrous burden of guilt that had me running a mile whenever a child came near. Even my own child.

The realization was so terrible, and so liberating, that my laughter turned uncontrollable.

'Mark!'

'I'm sorry, I can't . . .' I broke off, choked by more laughing. Impossible even to begin to explain to her. 'It's just . . . so . . .'

'. . . funny?'

'Not remotely, but . . .' I coughed a little, finally bringing myself under control.

'You were telling me about Katie.'

Katie, whom I'd abandoned for no reason at all.

'There isn't much to say,' I muttered lamely. 'I met her in Indonesia. She was backpacking; I was a guide. Her friend got sick – some kind of epileptic fit – had to stay in the hostel for a couple of days to recover. I took Katie around, showed her a few mountains, went swimming, cruelly seduced her.' I brought an arm over her back, then let it drop again to my side. 'Cruelly left her.'

Katie had done such good imitations of Liz – wicked, but very funny – demanding cleaner cutlery in a Rantepao restaurant, or turning up her scornful nose at Indonesia's less enticing smells. All the way back to Ujung Pandang airport, Katie was a sterling friend to the sullen Liz. But after we'd seen her on to the plane, she regularly had me in hysterics with her impersonations.

'I don't believe you're cruel,' Alice murmured.

'Let's hope you don't know me long enough to get disillusioned.'

'Actually, I would like to know you.'

Strange to think, a few moments earlier I might have welcomed that declaration – that invitation. But now, understanding at last the illusory basis of my fears for Christopher, all I wanted was to rush back to my family and beg forgiveness.

To Alice, I shook my head but said nothing. She misunderstood my reluctance.

'Mark, I'm sorry, the last thing you need now

is that kind of pressure. Forget I said it.' She let her arms slip sideways, lowering herself on to my chest. Her hair brushed my face. 'I just want you to know I'm very sorry for what happened and I'm here to help however I can. *Me importas. Me gustas. Entiendes?*'

I nodded once, knowing she felt the full extent of my gratitude, despite the paucity of the gesture. She pressed her lips against my neck in answer. The simple kindness of that touch brought me close to tears again. A new guilt, weighing me down so soon after the expiation of the old.

We stayed like that for a while, both silent, listening to each other breathe, feeling only those movements necessary for life: chests opening, hearts beating. I let my mind float back to Katie. Would I be able to go home? Would she forgive my desertion? She'd said as much on the phone, and it was not in her nature to hold grudges. The more difficult forgiving would be my own for this comfort taken with Alice. In letting her help me through the shock of rediscovery I was wronging both the woman I loved and the woman I was about to reject.

An odd light-headedness overcame me. Conflicting emotions: elation and sorrow. In a sense, I was mourning my lost parents a second time, the awfulness of the tragedy magnified a hundredfold. A car crash is senseless; murder on some lonely Latin road is unimaginable. Yet simultaneously I was celebrating my release from a lifelong curse: my childhood crime was no more than a misconstrued shadow.

We're distinguished by the way we react to bad luck and failure, Leonard had said. Nietzsche. The way we harness the bad stuff to become better. Could I make a fresh start? Salvage something good from the traumas, setbacks and mistakes that had characterized my life? With Katie, I had occasionally talked about the kind of job I would like to do, living in London but travelling abroad – perhaps guiding adventurous travellers through the more remote parts of Asia. A job that would let me stay with my family but still find the space and freedom I craved.

Before, I hadn't pursued it, knowing I would have to move on before Christopher grew much older. But now that I'd found there was nothing wrong with me, nothing stopping me rushing back to Christopher and taking him up in my arms, could I build a life like that? Could I trust myself not to fuck that ideal existence up? After so many years of fearing my own instincts, hating a part of my own being, I found it hard to imagine myself making anything go right for the three of us.

Alice rolled herself off me, and lay quietly by my side.

'Listen,' I said. 'I'm not going to rush off, OK? I'll stay on a while. See you through your test.'

It wasn't such a sacrifice. I longed to be holding Christopher, just grinning madly at his beautiful face for about ten hours solid. To feel Katie's fingers on my cheek again. But I wasn't going to leave Alice to the unhelpful, misguided consolations of Leonard. A couple of days longer. Then I could hurry back to England.

I didn't want to have to think for the moment about Alice's chances of passing.

She was staring at me with an expression I initially mistook for cautious gratitude. Then she said, 'You do know . . . you do realize you're going to have to take the test again?'

That little word drove all the air out of my lungs. 'Again?' I choked.

'Hoppner said – when you've recovered. I go next, then you'll get a second go.'

'I don't want a second go!' Fury spread through me like hot poison. 'He brought on that *horror* and now he expects me to be hypnotized again?'

'I'm so sorry, Mark.'

'He's barbaric!'

'Yes.'

'That fucking . . . !' I leapt off the bed, grabbing my clothes and shoes as I stumbled to the door.

'Mark, you're in no fit state to—'

I didn't hear the rest. The sweet promise of reunion with Katie and Christopher had been so close. I'd seen the open gate, the road out, the flight back to London. Now my family seemed further away than ever.

I marched out of the guesthouse with only one goal: an urgent and angry confrontation with Benjamin Sword Hoppner.

WGGX Transcript 15074/KG/21

WGGX: And that was the Righteous Brothers with 'Unchained Melody', bringing us real neatly to our guest today, a very righteous gentleman, Mr Benjamin Sword Hoppner. Mr Hoppner, welcome to Radio WGGX.

BENJAMIN SWORD HOPPNER: Thank you for inviting me.

WGGX: A pleasure, Mr Hoppner, we're all big fans of yours since you built the new park downtown. Your contributions to worthy projects are impressing a lot of people around here, even the ones who might have once been concerned by your, uh, business. I have a few questions, though, about some of the things you've written. May I trouble you with them?

BSH: Go right ahead.

WGGX: You talk quite a bit about Evil. Isn't that kind of melodramatic? You don't really think the world is populated by Satan's progeny?

BSH: I do not. But I use the word Good to represent my goal in life, and it is necessary to have an antonym to represent what I strive to avoid. I could talk about Bad or Badness or even Immorality, but Evil is a tidier word that everyone gets.

WGGX: So you don't see a bunch of evil villains out there, laughing joyously at the cruelty they inflict and celebrating their own wickedness?

BSH: Most evil people don't recognize they're evil. The same goes for evil governments. The idea that people indulge in evil for fun is largely a myth. Few people would want to label themselves evil. In fact they tend to see themselves as the good people, battling against external forces of evil.

WGGX: But if they commit a crime, hurt someone, kill someone, even, they've surely got to recognize their actions are bad.

BSH: They rationalize and find excuse for their behavior. Disproportionate revenge is called righteous punishment, fanaticism is called idealism, robbery is equitable wealth redistribution, violence against the weak is necessary to earn respect, torture is the best way to gather information and deter. Evil people are very good at making their end justify the means.

WGGX: That's a slippery slope.

BSH: It surely is. Justify one transgression to yourself and the next time, it'll be twice as bad. Eventually the means become so vile, no end could possibly be sufficient to justify them. But sadly, evil people are very good at self-deception. That's why they always assume the other fellow's the evil one.

WGGX: Lordy! So any one of us could be evil without realizing it!

BSH: I think you and I are safe! But, seriously, it is a real problem. A government that decides to drop an atom bomb, flatten Dresden or fight an ideological war in South-East Asia had better be sure of its moral position before it deliberately kills hundreds of thousands of people. All the leaders and governments we think of as evil in history most certainly thought they were in the right, and believed the use of violence and terror to defend against perceived internal or external threats was justified. We instinctively think of ourselves as good and consequently of anyone who opposes us as bad.

WGGX: The evil folk are always on the other side.

BSH: Right.

WGGX: A disturbing thought. What do the Iraqis think of us? We'll be right back to take your questions for Mr Hoppner, after these messages . . .

CHAPTER 15

The building from which both Sword Enterprises and its moral crusade were directed consisted of just five unadorned rooms: a reception, a secretarial office, a meeting room, a library, and a central study. The outer rooms were all empty – the PAs strangely absent – but when I burst through into the study, I found not just Hoppner and David, but Francisco José Sánchez as well.

For a moment there was silence. The mere presence of Sánchez, the man who'd held a machete to my neck, was enough to stop me in my tracks. Sitting facing Hoppner across his sturdy oaken desk, the Comandante turned his gaze briefly towards me. In that wordless connection, I thought I sensed some kind of apology – perhaps even contrition. Then Hoppner turned to David and growled, 'I told you to lock the doors.'

Absurdly, I started justifying my intrusion, as if I'd broken some petty rule: 'Pamela thought you were alone in here,' I stammered.

'I'm glad to hear it,' he said, with a pointed look at Sánchez.

'I can come back later.' I felt completely unnerved by Sánchez; my outrage at the news of the re-test had instantly dissipated.

'Relax, Mark, I've told him not to kill you.' Dry, dry humour. 'David, go lock the doors. All of them, this time.' He turned back to me. 'I'm afraid I can't let you out yet. See, for some reason our friend Señor Sánchez doesn't want anyone knowing he's here.'

Since Freddy's death there hadn't been much time to think about that severed goat's head, but Sánchez's unexpected presence brought it all rushing back. I remembered the stones thrown at Pamela's car. More symbols of rebellion. Where was it all leading? The mood in Hoppner's perfect society was most definitely not a happy one. Was the compound under siege? If so, what did it mean that Sánchez was actually inside the citadel?

Hoppner pointed me to a red leather armchair. 'You'd better make yourself comfortable. This may take a while. Señor Sánchez was just explaining exactly why his friends had Tanadio's boy pitch a goat's head into my garden.' With that he turned his blazing eyes back to Sánchez.

It was fascinating to see. Two men of equal resolve, locked in dispute over a symbolic gesture. No measurable harm had been done to anyone, yet the implications of that grisly token – delivered by a town Hoppner had spent the last five years funding – were impossible to exaggerate. What power did Hoppner have if his money no longer sufficed to buy him absolute respect and obedience?

Stronger and younger than his patron, Sánchez was nevertheless clearly uncomfortable. His dynamic spirit seemed curiously shrivelled in that sterile room. This was not his world, this claustrophobic office where popular leadership had to bow to foreign, moralizing money. 'They are unhappy,' he said simply. 'Unhappy and afraid. This is true for many months. Hawken frightens our women, our children. And now, from Tanadio's death, they are angry also.'

David walked back in, took a seat a little behind his master.

'And like civilized human beings they convey this message with a body part?'

'Killing Joaquim Tanadio was too much.'

'Señor Sánchez, you know better than that. Every one of your men has made the same promise: he who commits murder must follow it with suicide.'

The only daylight reaching this inner sanctum came through four glass tiles in the roof. How perverse of Hoppner to find such a beautiful spot in such a remote location and then deny himself a view. Austerity as a virtue, perhaps.

Sánchez shook his head. 'Joaquim was a good man.'

'He blew up innocent civilians! Do you know how long I had to plead with the Minister to stop him sending his death squads up here for revenge?

They want to burn Miraflores to the ground.' This was addressed to Sánchez, but now he turned to me. 'The night before you came here, that party in the pueblo – did you have the first idea what you were celebrating?'

'The dry weather, I thought.' I looked at Sánchez in confusion. His eyes, though not turning to meet mine, were unblinking.

'Not exactly,' said Hoppner. 'You were celebrating the deaths of eight policemen, three representatives of the World Bank and a much loved Santa Tecla poet.'

Glaring at Sánchez, he allowed himself a dramatic pause. The sense of a school disciplining was unpleasantly strong. I half expected him to start talking about his *disappointment*. But his message was simpler than that.

'It's got to stop,' he said softly. 'Señor Sánchez, this cannot go on. No more bombs, no more terrorist attacks of any kind. No killing. This is not the behaviour of a civilized society. And will you please take off that armband – Tanadio's been mourned enough.'

I was surprised to see Sánchez obey this order without hesitation. He slipped the armband into his pocket as if it were an irrelevance. His mind remained firmly on Hoppner's first demand: 'With respect, you do not understand our problems.'

'You're one hundred per cent right; I don't. I'm giving you everything you could possibly want here. Why do you care who's running the country?'

'Miraflores, yes, it's fine. But we have families in other pueblos. We have friends in prison or disappeared. We have our national pride. This is our country, Mr Hoppner, not yours. It is difficult for you to understand the pain we feel when we see Indian people made like slaves or children raped. These are problems a foreigner can never make right, even with many million dollars.'

'Spare me the catch-all political justifications for murder. You know it makes no difference. I won't let this society be destroyed in some government crackdown just because certain poisonous elements can't keep their TNT to themselves. You carry on blowing up conferences, and pretty soon Miraflores will be governed by the army. You want that? Because I can tell you right now, the day that happens, I leave and I take my money with me.'

Assuming an expression carefully balanced between regret and warning, Sánchez delivered his killer blow: 'Some people are saying you must leave anyway.'

There was a sudden thud as Hoppner's flat hand came down hard on the desk. 'What was that?' he demanded.

Sánchez knew he did not have to repeat himself. Leaning back in his armchair, he let out a long sigh that might have been a form of apology. I didn't know him well enough to say for sure.

'You hear that?' Hoppner growled at David. For a moment, he looked close to uncontrolled rage.

'They know what I've done for them, what I still do for them, and they turn against me?'

'They are frightened,' Sánchez went on. 'Every day, they fear Hawken will come for them. They prefer to live without money than with fear.'

'They're out of their minds! They think I'm going to just leave? I won't! I built this town. Go remind them of that.'

'They remember, Mr Hoppner. And they thank you for that. But even if you do not leave, perhaps they will not obey you any more. They will forget the virtues and your Code. I do not think you want to see that.'

By now Hoppner was almost shaking. 'You're threatening me? You want to tear my work apart? I created all this! I made something no one else has ever achieved – a society based on secular virtue. It's a modern-day Wonder of the World. To destroy it would be sheer vandalism . . . worse . . . it would be an act of pure evil.'

'Señor Sánchez,' said David quickly. 'What are you saying? What do you want?'

'Hawken,' came the simple reply.

At first Hoppner just blinked – in confusion, in relief. As he grasped that a way out existed, he actually smiled. 'You mean you want me to let him go? Then you'll all quieten down? Just so as I replace Hawken? Send him home?'

He didn't get an immediate answer. Sánchez shifted a little uncomfortably in his seat. 'It is not so easy,' he said.

'Well, what do you want?' roared Hoppner.

'We have to have something. Someone. The pueblo needs someone – for Joaquim, for Javier, Félix, all of them.'

'No way,' I muttered, scarcely believing I was hearing this. 'You want him dead?'

'Not dead,' said the Comandante. 'In prison, only.'

Hoppner stared at him in disbelief. 'That's what this is about? That's why you wanted a secret meeting? You're asking me to put my own man behind bars?' His eyes flickered round to David, then back to Sánchez. 'Are you out of your mind?'

'He has become a sadist,' insisted Sánchez. 'He deserves the punishment.'

'Señor Sánchez, have you read my Code? Can you show me where, in either English or Spanish version, it states that an employer may send his employee to prison for carrying out his duties?'

'I regret, your Code does not apply in this negotiation.'

'Oh, this is a negotiation, is it?' A savage laugh. 'You're *negotiating* with me? Well, you can take your negotiation and—'

'One second, Mr Hoppner.' David was standing. 'Let's go slow here. No rush. No rush at all.' He blinked slowly. 'Señor Sánchez. Is this absolutely necessary? Prison?'

Sánchez nodded. 'They have to see him pay. Then they will be happy again. If not . . .'

'What you're asking. It's impossible.'

'Like my position. I cannot hold Miraflores together if they do not think I give them what they want.'

'We can help you. Give more . . . benefits.'

'This is the only benefit they want now.'

David closed his eyes briefly, then slowly turned to Hoppner. 'We have to be sensible,' he said in a strained voice. 'Hawken isn't blameless. Something in him has changed. He enjoys . . . stuff.'

Hoppner's rage had subsided at David's interjection. In its place was a new uncertainty. 'But, David . . .'

Though I was delighted by the idea of Hawken's departure, something about David's rapid search for an excuse to appease the town – a moral loophole – sickened me. 'Isn't the motivation for an act irrelevant so long as the act is right?' I asked Hoppner. 'Isn't that what you told us? If Hawken's been following your orders to kill people, what does it matter whether he enjoys it?'

'He's overstepped the line,' declared David. The fact that no one this time contradicted my choice of words was clear indication of the gravity of the situation. 'This is fair. This is just.'

'But . . .' It was extraordinary to see Hoppner so ill at ease. I watched his agony with a grim fascination. 'But, David, I asked him to—'

'This is our whole . . . your whole project,' David interrupted quickly, before Hoppner had a chance to incriminate himself. 'What is the Code without a working model?'

Appeasement of the mob or a life's work ruined. I saw the dilemma in all its painful simplicity. But Hoppner was the moralist, the man who believed in the absolute sovereignty of good. Surely he wasn't going to let such tenuous excuses sway him? Surely he would never make Hawken his scapegoat?

'He's overstepped the line,' David reiterated with sudden force. 'Hasn't he?'

The look on Hoppner's face reminded me of an elderly Chinese man Katie and I met on one of the Banda islands. He owned a small nutmeg plantation around which, for a small fee, he would guide spice aficionados or bored travellers who'd already 'done' the volcano, the dive sites, the dolphin-watching and the former Dutch Governor's Palace with the cute graffiti etched on a window pane. He told the most heartbreaking story about his experiences in Xuzhou during the Cultural Revolution: how he'd been forced by young Maoist fanatics to cut down every one of the prize magnolia trees he'd spent his life tending in the town park. Katie had been terribly upset, and had wanted to make him a present of about twenty dollars – an enormous sum by local standards. Because I suspected the man of making up the story specifically to tug at Western heartstrings, I wouldn't let her give him the money and we barely spoke to each other for the rest of the day. But later I remembered his expression – on the verge of a terrible anger, yet at a loss to understand why anyone should want to destroy such a precious, absolute good – and I felt ashamed of myself.

It was that expression which Hoppner wore as he slowly, resignedly nodded.

'Right,' he whispered.

It seemed an utterly insufficient – and inappropriate – word for such a momentous compromise.

'Thank you,' Sánchez said. He understood what it had cost Hoppner to agree to his terms. 'I think we must do this as soon as possible.'

'Three days,' growled Hoppner. 'The Minister of the Interior and the Chief of Police just announced they're coming here the day after tomorrow. Tanadio's little stunt made world news, did you know that? Central American guerrillas haven't killed dignitaries from Europe and the States in a while. And they know perfectly well who was responsible,' he spat, glaring at Sánchez. 'I need Hawken here when they come. Show them I still have some measure of control.'

'I'm sorry,' said Sánchez, shaking his head. 'It's too long.'

'Give me a break here,' Hoppner exploded. 'I agreed to do what you want! At least allow me to decide how it's done.'

'In Miraflores, they are already close to revolution . . .'

'Then use some of your so-called authority!'

'In point of fact? Mr Hoppner?' David had sat down again, but now he was leaning forward, a light hand on Hoppner's arm. 'Delay is dangerous.

409

What if Hawken finds out?' He threw a significant look in my direction.

My immediate impulse was to protest the insult to my discretion. But I reminded myself that the sooner the psychopathic Hawken was out of the picture the better, and I stayed silent. It was clear, when Hoppner turned his irritated eyes to me, that he shared David's concern.

'What am I going to say to Pamela?' he asked, his voice drained of energy.

'It'll be fine,' David assured him. 'She knows you only do what's right.'

Hoppner closed his eyes. 'Go get him,' he whispered.

In preparation for the entrapment of his lieutenant, Hoppner asked Sánchez to wait in the library, out of sight of the windows, and then produced from a filing cabinet a set of steel handcuffs and a brown plastic pharmaceutical container. The latter he placed on a shelf behind a row of whisky, vodka and brandy bottles. The handcuffs he dropped in his pocket.

The fact that he had these items at all, let alone planned to use them on Hawken, was more than a little disturbing. Catching my queasy look, Hoppner said sharply, 'If you're going to get upset about this, go wait with Sánchez.'

'I'm fine.'

'Good. I'm planning to use you as a decoy.'

'What?'

My voice must have carried the alarm I felt, because he stared at me with hardening eyes and said, 'Like I told you, go wait outside if you're not up to this.'

Some spark of angry pride kept me sitting there.

When Hawken arrived, he noted my presence with surprise. 'So you're up?' he said, when what he meant was *Why are you here?* 'I heard you ran off to bed after that excitement.'

Silently, David took his place by Hoppner's chair.

'By excitement you mean the revelation that I'd witnessed my parents' murder?' I asked coldly.

'I mean when you started crying in a language you claimed not to speak.'

Any qualms I might have felt about standing by while a drugged man was handed over to Sánchez and his *compañeros* – even a man so richly deserving of that dismal fate as Hawken – were swept aside by that poisonous comment.

'Hawken, please,' said Hoppner, indicating the chair beside me. As he sat down, Hawken kept his gaze on me, curious to see what kind of response his taunt might provoke. When I failed to react he grew bored and turned to Hoppner, who said, 'How about a drink?'

'No thanks.'

A minute, disconcerting pause. Hawken sensed it, I knew.

'Come on, join us. Mark and I are in need of one, aren't we?'

Hoppner came over with four glasses of bourbon on the rocks. While David delicately sipped at his, I drank half the measure straight away, hoping to lead by example. It occurred to me that Hoppner might have got the glasses mixed up and given me the drugged liquor. A curious situation that would create, with me falling asleep in front of them. I wondered how Hoppner would explain it.

Hawken wasn't drinking. He leaned forward to deposit the glass on Hoppner's desk. Then, sitting back, he said, 'What did you want to see me about?'

The sense of strength in those folded arms was frightening. His whole body, even when relaxed, seemed created, moulded, to fight. I was almost the same size as him, but I had none of the training, the experience or the inclination that lay at the root of his physical power. I glanced once at the glass on the desk, praying the drug would prove strong enough. Ten minutes till knock-out, Hoppner had said, starting from whenever he could be persuaded to drink it. Hawken caught my stare and, worse, the guilt in my face when I turned hastily away.

'I was talking with Mark about his test,' Hoppner was saying, slipping easily into the deceit that his own Code forbade him. 'We both agreed that it isn't sensible, given the unconscious material we've unearthed, to continue immediately with the hypnosis. Mark has some issues to work out, clearly, around his past: what that past actually is, how it might affect the person he is and the charitable work he hopes to do, whether he feels ready to move forward. He needs time to clarify.'

Hawken was staring once again at the glass. 'That's what you wanted to talk to me about?' he said quietly.

I sensed Hoppner's hesitation, even without looking at him. Hawken couldn't miss it.

'I thought we might let Mark stay on here awhile. To get comfortable with the new place he's at.'

To cover his unease, Hoppner had turned back to the booze shelf and now he walked over with the whisky bottle. With a raised eyebrow he indicated my empty glass. I nodded quickly. Hawken's suspicion wasn't distracted by the distraction.

'Why do you need my permission, all of a sudden?'

'Just . . .' Hoppner handed the bottle to me and laid a heavy palm on his shoulder. 'I just want you to welcome Mark.'

Hawken threw a cold glance in my direction. 'Welcome, Mark,' he said in the flattest of tones. I managed an awkward smile as I refilled my drink.

'Excellent!' Hoppner reached for the untouched glass. He held it out to Hawken. 'Let's drink to that.'

He had his own glass to his lips, but he paused when Hawken made no move to take the drugged whisky.

'No, thank you,' said Hawken. 'You drink it for me.'

In that brief moment the two men stared at each

other, eyes locked: Hawken knowing, and Hoppner – visibly alarmed by this stage – knowing that he knew. Any moment now, Hawken would have his fists up and Hoppner would start screaming for the perimeter guards. I imagined them pouring into the office, batons flying, bone crunching, blood spurting out across Hoppner's immaculate desk. I saw carnage, and in that instant of premonition I was terrified. The long empty road, the corpses, all over again. Hazy memory and uncertain prediction, either one of them horrible to contemplate, melded in my brain.

The base of the whisky bottle was nestled in my palm. There wasn't time to get a better grip. Letting my glass drop, I swung my arm round to bring the bottle crashing into Hawken's head.

Even with his eyes locked on Hoppner, some combat super-sense must have alerted Hawken. He was already turning when the bottle struck him just above the ear. My tumbler shattered against the tiled floor a fraction of a second later.

Hawken collapsed sideways in his chair with a spittled choke. His neck rocked giddily around his shoulders. The bottle, amazingly, was unbroken. Not quite believing what I'd just done, I lowered my weapon on to the desk.

'Sánchez!' yelled Hoppner, reaching for the handcuffs.

The door from the library flew open, and Sánchez ran in. David and I were already forcing the dazed man face-down on to the floor. A groggy snarl. Blood was trickling across the tiles where a jagged fragment of my tumbler had nicked Hawken's hand. Sánchez dropped his weight on the twitching legs, pinning them flat. Even with David and me holding Hawken's arms behind his back, Hoppner had trouble closing the cuffs around his wrists. Those powerful hands were already grasping at me, the nails ripping at my skin.

'Hold his legs,' Sánchez demanded, once the cuffs were on. 'I have to tie them.'

Hoppner hesitated. Was it the first time he'd been given an order by one of his beneficiaries? By anyone? Hawken's voice was now fully recovered and screaming abuse at us. I was struggling to keep his chest against the floor. With as much dignity as he could manage, Hoppner knelt down and gripped hold of his former lieutenant's legs. Whipping off Hawken's belt, Sánchez wrapped it twice around his ankles and fastened it tight.

With the sacrificial wolf firmly trussed, Hoppner stood up, shaken. 'I'll just get the car,' he said hoarsely. 'Mark, be so good as to help us, would you? I don't want to have to ask the guards. They might have . . . loyalty issues.'

Straightening his shoulders, careful not to look at Hawken, he hurried out.

A crowd had assembled in the Parque Central by the time we arrived. How they knew of Hawken's fall, I've no idea. Sombre and expectant, they pressed around the SUV; David had to climb out and marshal them off the road. Almost every man among them now wore a black armband. Hoppner, at the wheel, had kept a tight grip on his emotions throughout the journey, weathering Hawken's abuse in silence. Once in front of the gaol, he switched off the engine and, still without turning round, offered his only words to his betrayed servant:

'I'm sorry.'

David opened the rear door and handed the key for the handcuffs to Sánchez. The apology had had a remarkable effect on Hawken. As Sánchez and I prepared to lift him bodily out of the vehicle, he said in a much quieter voice, 'Untie me. Let me walk. There's not much I can do in handcuffs.'

I looked to Sánchez for instruction: a brief nod. Hawken's face was eerily passive.

I removed the belt from his ankles.

Strange to be assisting Hoppner, the man who was likely to order my execution in a matter of days, carried out presumably – in Hawken's absence – by a couple of the guards. It galled me to do anything useful for him. Yet I wanted Hawken out of the compound even more than I longed to obstruct Hoppner. A matter of weighing the evils.

The moment Hawken stepped out of the SUV, hands still locked behind his back, a cheer went up from the crowd. A sudden burst of movement and they were surging towards us. Without thinking, without knowing where the word came from, I yelled, *'Muévete!'*

They retreated immediately. The cheer was silenced. For a couple of seconds, every pair of eyes was on me. In the front line of the crowd stood Lupita, her feet still bare, her gaze pleading. I glanced back at Hoppner. He nodded once, unsmiling but approving. He seemed to expect me to lead his man into captivity. Sánchez had moved ahead to clear the way; David was staring hard at the top of a tree. I felt utterly compelled, in that tense moment, to cooperate. Taking a firm grip on Hawken's arm, I started towards the gaol.

Hawken walked with dignity, his steps determined, his eyes focused directly ahead. Those spectators not shifted by Sánchez's terse orders moved quickly out of our way. Several of the men had machetes slung at their sides, their hands still grimy from the fields. All transfixed by this sudden fall from grace. Walking beside Hawken, I grew conscious of the difference in height between us: only slight, but he was undoubtedly the taller. Barely realizing I was doing it, I straightened my back, walked a little more rigidly to compensate.

Sánchez reached the open door of the gaol just ahead of us, ready to guide me through this alien place. Two men dressed in black trousers, grey shirts and black armbands – the gaolers, I guessed – hurried forward to shake first his hand, then mine. One of them started to offer the same greeting to Hawken, then thought better of it.

The unannounced arrival of their former master, chained and subdued, was manifestly confusing.

The elder of the two men, proud possessor of an asymmetrical moustache and a heavy silver crucifix, led the way to an empty cell. Again, I was struck by the silence of the place. Down passageways dry as a desert, yet still smelling of mould, we passed five or six barred gates beyond which slouched those inscrutable, or perhaps simply oppressed, prisoners. It had been a library, I remembered Sánchez saying. Hard to imagine books in this empty, echoing place. Strip-lighting gave the whitewashed walls a glare that drew attention to plaster so rough I felt an urge to run my finger along its rasp-like surface. Coarse enough to scratch the skin. Dry white powder collected on my fingertip, bleaching it to highlight a single drop of crimson blood.

The cell they picked for Hawken overlooked the Parque Central. When he realized this he paused in his stride as if to plead for another. But the plea never came. Instead, I got one final glare before he turned his back on us and raised his manacled hands. Once Sánchez had removed the handcuffs, he walked forward, carried the lone chair to the window and sat there in full view of the town that hated him.

David met me at the entrance to the gaol. He grinned uncertainly. 'Thank you. Very helpful of you. Painful, of course. But necessary. We had to. Well done.' Another pragmatist.

For a moment, I was tempted to run. I was outside the compound; somewhere in the town there had to be a vehicle I could steal. Failing that, there was always Freddy's gun. But one look at the mass of people around me – people paid to be loyal to Hoppner – and I knew any mad dash would be futile. Worse, if one of those ex-guerrillas with the machetes was the first to intercept me, it might get me killed. Obediently, I fell into line behind David, resigned to returning to my own prison.

One last memory of that extraordinary scene. As David and I reached the SUV, Hoppner finally opened his door and stepped out. The effect on the crowd was electric. He said nothing; he did nothing. Just looked around, stared at his flock – unsmiling – then returned to his seat behind the darkened windows.

The masses had been appeased. The rot had started.

From the *Washington Post*

Sir

In his story, 'Satan's Newest Recruit,' Nicholas Vogel labels Benjamin Sword Hoppner a 'pernicious influence on American society' and claims he is 'contributing more than any other sleaze merchant to the decay so tragically evident in Western values and behavior.' This is absolutely not the case.

Mr Hoppner does not wish for people to read pornography any more than he wants them to rape women or rob banks. He has commissioned countless surveys to confirm what all but the most puritanical Republicans already know: the number of people reading pornographic material is not related to the number of pornographic magazines published, just as the number of bank robbers does not increase if more banks are built. Porn-readers, like bank-robbers, simply exist. They will spend vast sums of money on pornography, regardless of who publishes it. Mr Hoppner entered this industry out of a determination to funnel that money away from unscrupulous sleaze merchants and toward good people who need it for good projects.

I have worked for Mr Hoppner for three years, so you may consider my opinion biased. But you should know that he pays me no more than I earned in my previous position as Strategy Director for Women Against Sexual Exploitation. I chose to move to Sword because Mr Hoppner achieves more for good causes than a thousand well-meaning charities. He has understood, fundamentally, that money makes this world turn, and he has set out to harness that titanic force and put it to work where it can do most good.

Benjamin Sword Hoppner is a good man. He is a very good man. I would trust him with my life and my soul. His moral Code is inspirational, and I can testify that he lives by it at all times. If even one percent of American society were like him, this country would be a thousand times happier. I will do everything I can to promote his cause as long as I live.

Pamela Martinsen, Sword Enterprises

CHAPTER 16

By the time we got back to the compound I felt filthy. Contaminated. Playing such a major role in the abduction and incarceration of a scapegoat had left me drained and sick at myself. What would Katie have thought if she'd seen me hit Hawken with that bottle? Was I really fit to walk back into her life after imprisoning a man for doing his master's bidding?

Most of my life, I hadn't worried much about matters of morality. Perhaps this new confusion was possible only because I no longer had to fear a fundamental sadistic streak. Perhaps I'd simply been around Hoppner too long. Whatever the reason, the sense of moral unease was overwhelming.

So when Hoppner asked again for my help, my refusal was immediate.

'I haven't said what it is yet.'

'It doesn't matter. I'm not doing it.'

He'd driven the SUV right up to his house and politely but firmly requested that I come inside for a couple of minutes. David was dispatched to summon Pamela.

'Mark, you heard what I said earlier. The Interior Minister and Chief of Police are visiting, day after tomorrow. As part of the deal to keep the police and army out of Miraflores, I promised I would make my own security arrangements. They're coming to check we have the terrorism situation under control, and they're going to expect to see a head of security. I appear to have mislaid mine.' A thin, humourless smile. 'You were surprisingly authoritative back there. How hard would it be for you to act the part for a day?'

'*What?*'

'You'd just have to look convincing for the Chief of Police. The tough guy who won't stand for any kind of trouble. Make polite conversation for half an hour. You won't actually have to *do anything*.'

Meaning *beat or kill anyone*.

That qualification aside, I still couldn't believe what he was asking. This was no small matter. Benjamin Sword Hoppner, defender of truth and fidelity, was planning to deceive the country's highest officials.

'Why don't you just tell them you're bringing in a new guy? I assume you are?'

'Chicago say it could take a month to find someone prepared to work in this kind of environment. The Chief of Police and I have . . . an understanding, but in front of his men he'll have to take a firm line. If he discovers there's no one managing security here, he'll be forced to station a police unit in Miraflores. Once they're established, we may never get them out again, and the damage they'll do to this society . . .' His scowl deepened at the prospect. 'Mark, there's no one else who can do it. David's too small, Leonard's too skinny; the guards are fine soldiers but none of them would pass as a commander. You're the only one who looks and acts right.'

That was when I realized he actually needed me. I could quite imagine how even a dozen of the resentful policemen I'd seen in Santa Tecla might disrupt the fragile stability of Hoppner's model society. Only my cooperation would prevent it. He *needed* me. All of a sudden, I had bargaining power.

'Can I make a condition?'

'If it's reasonable.'

'I'll do it if you release Mrs Williams from her obligation to take your test.'

He frowned. 'She made a promise.'

'She's terrified of you. I want you to let her leave. That's my condition.'

'Then no.'

Double take. 'What do you mean, *no*?'

'I don't accept your condition.'

I was dumbfounded. 'Is her death so important to you?'

'Her promise – and her fidelity to her promise – is so important to me.'

Although I searched his face for signs of bluff, I found none. Was he just a better poker player than me? A better negotiator?

'What happened to compassion?' I demanded. 'Isn't that one of your great virtues?'

'Mark, this may be hard for you to understand, but it would be less virtuous for me to look to my own virtues than to help another look to hers. To put my own compassion ahead of her fidelity would be ungenerous. Ultimately I can be more virtuous by being less compassionate.'

Oh, the knots one can tie around Goodness.

But even as my attempt to negotiate failed, I suddenly realized what a tremendous opportunity Hoppner was unintentionally offering me. I'd have to make polite conversation with the Chief of Police, he'd said. What could be more valuable, right now? Presumably the Chief would be armed and accompanied by a few of his officers. If I could get time alone with them, time enough to explain the danger facing Alice and me, surely they would intervene immediately.

It was a way out.

Once again, though I hated doing it, I found myself agreeing to help Hoppner. There was no alternative: we weren't going to get a chance like this again. The cavalry would pass this way only once.

'Thank you, Mark,' he said. 'I knew you'd want to help out.' His belief in virtue was so strong it hadn't occurred to him that I might use this event as a means of escape. 'I'll have Sánchez show you around town tomorrow. Get you familiarized, so it looks like you know what you're talking about. Will you tell him I want all those wretched armbands gone by the time the Minister arrives?'

There was a knock on the door. David ushered Pamela in. Her face showed only polite curiosity; she still had no idea of Hawken's fate.

'We'd better wrap this up,' Hoppner said to me. We both stood to shake hands. 'I really appreciate you doing this, Mark. Though obviously I can't let it influence me in your test, I am truly grateful.'

As I walked out, almost retching, I heard his solemn voice ask Pamela to sit down.

Alice and Leonard were sitting side-by-side in the guesthouse hall, not talking, eyes fixed on the opposite wall. When I walked through the door, Alice leapt up.

'What's going on?' she demanded. 'David says Hawken's been gaoled.'

I didn't want to explain my plan in front of Leonard. Not only was he too guileless to keep a secret from our host, but he seemed unable to accept the reality of Hoppner's murderous fanaticism. In fact, the one time I'd heard Alice voice her longing to escape Miraflores in front of him, he'd looked confused and said, 'But, Ali, don't you want to do the test? All this way, and you won't get a penny for the fund.' His complete inability to admit the severity of our situation was starting to worry me.

Steering Alice outside on to the veranda, I explained about the police visit and my intention to enlist their armed assistance. Hoppner had already decided that both our tests should be postponed until after the visit, so that 'nothing complicates this vital episode'. Meaning he didn't want to have to kill anyone just before the police turned up. Whatever his motives, the delay ensured we would still be alive to beg rescue from the cops.

I said all this to Alice, and although I hadn't expected her to shower me in grateful kisses, I was surprised by her lack of reaction. Just the merest, tight-lipped nod.

'What's wrong?' I took hold of her hand and made her sit on the veranda steps. 'Alice, we're going to get out of here, trust me.'

Across the lawn, the back door of Hoppner's house opened and Pamela emerged, stunned and shaking. After a moment's dazed hesitation, she stumbled away towards the bottom of the garden.

'I do trust you,' said Alice. 'I really do. And thank you.' She pulled her hand out of mine.

'Then, what . . . ?'

'Just something . . . this morning.'

I waited patiently, but after a few moments more, she stood up, shook her head and walked back into the guesthouse.

Pamela was staring rigidly into the cloud-forest canopy beyond the white wall. She hardly seemed to notice when I sat down beside her.

'He won't be in there long, I'm sure,' I said, searching for something safe to offer. 'It's symbolic, that's all.'

She didn't seem to hear me. 'I have to clear out his stuff,' she muttered. 'For David. David's moving into his house.' A bitter, confused laugh. 'All his stuff. I've gotta . . .'

'Pamela, I'm so sorry about what's happened.'

She turned to me then, staring at me, studying me.

'Sorry? You? After what you've done to poor Hawken?'

Poor Hawken. Perhaps I wasn't that sorry.

'It was Hoppner's decision.'

She shook her head. 'That isn't possible. Mr Hoppner would never turn against his most loyal supporter. You expect me to believe that? He couldn't do this to Hawken.'

'What on earth makes you think I could? I'm being held against my will.'

'Everything was fine until you came along,' she muttered, a little crazily. 'I've seen you talking to Mr Hoppner, alone, poisoning his mind.'

'Christ, stop being so melodramatic! I don't have any influence over him. Is that what you think?'

'Mr Hoppner would never do this!' she screamed, clutching her knees against her chest and screwing her eyes tight shut.

I stared at her in amazement. Idealism had been struck full in the face by compromise, and it simply couldn't deal with the shock.

'I'll see if I can find you some boxes,' I murmured, getting up. 'For his stuff.'

Hawken was a man of few possessions. In that respect, at least, he resembled his erstwhile employer. The whole lot would fit easily into one crate, I could tell the moment I walked into his house. The clothes were all alike: several sets of running kit; eight shirts, perfectly creased, like the three pairs of khaki trousers on wooden hangers. He owned one hat, of dark leather and Australian design. The hat he'd been wearing when he appeared out of the rain to rescue me from Sánchez's blade.

The rescuer deposed. I turned to the living room, sparsely scattered with international news magazines, a couple of local wood carvings and a chess set. Did he play? Had he bought the carvings himself, or were they a gift from Pamela? It was impossible not to become a little curious. A little involved.

On a shelf was a small selection of books: cheap thrillers, mostly, but also a guide to Central American birds and the requisite copy of Hoppner's Code. Beside them lay a small silver badge. Wings. So he'd been a paratrooper. I'd guessed it would be something like that, but all the same I was glad I hadn't known before I so rashly cast the first blow.

Even the kitchen revealed clues about the man I'd replaced. Everything in place; a fridge stocked only with fresh vegetables, eggs and lean chicken; a complete absence of alcohol. A teetotaller? I wondered if Hoppner had known.

On the kitchen window sill was the one oddity. A cardboard box, its edges torn, the cane distillery logo rubbed nearly to oblivion, was half filled with cotton wool and wood shavings. In the centre of that soft bed, chirping indignantly, lay a ruffled fledgling. A chick, technically, although it looked and sounded nothing like the lovable yellow creatures that pour into battery farms in their billions each year. This ungainly bird was brown, with rough stubs for wings, straggly down and a demanding orange beak. A wild thing, perhaps found abandoned on the forest floor during an early-morning run.

Beside the box, a tin can held a squirming assortment of worms. Somehow it seemed the least I could do for the man I'd helped bring down. Reluctantly, I plucked a worm from the can and dropped it into the bird's waiting beak. The worm disappeared down its gullet, and Hawken's pet cried for more. I had to feed it for another couple of minutes before it quietened down.

Picking up the cardboard box, I carried the bird through to the living room.

'What are you doing with that?'

Pamela had one foot on the veranda, her body frozen against the dark backdrop of the night, as if she'd been uncertain whether or not to enter. Now, any such hesitancy was forgotten as she marched towards me, her face as red as her hair.

'How dare you?' she demanded. With a violent lunge she grabbed the box from my hands. 'You were going to kill her, weren't you?'

The passion caught me by surprise. 'I didn't know it was a her,' I said weakly.

'Get out of here! Just get out of here now!'

There was something ludicrous about this angry woman, Hawken's lost lover, clutching a ragged orphan chick and shouting her demands. I might almost have laughed if she hadn't abruptly started crying.

'Oh Christ, look, I'm sorry,' I said, putting a hand on her arm.

'Don't touch me, you bastard!'

She took a rapid step back, causing the chick to begin squawking again. The smell of bird shit struck me for the first time.

'I got you a box.'

She didn't answer me. Instead, she thrust the chick down on a chair and began picking up the few personal effects that lay scattered around the room. I was being ignored – shunned.

'Let me know if you want any help.'

She wouldn't look up from her armful of Hawken's life.

I wanted to talk to Alice that night. Too much had happened; I'd barely begun to work through the cataclysmic implications of my forgotten memories. With Hawken gone, Pamela in pieces and a new test hanging over me, a gentle conversation to clarify the mess of events would have been a big help.

But Alice was strangely distant all evening. Sitting almost devotedly by Leonard's side during our subdued dinner, and then afterwards, while he read, on the sofa. She spoke a little to David, not at all to me. Twice I caught her eye; each time she looked away.

Instead it was David I found myself talking to, sitting on the edge of the veranda. I'd gone outside to get some air – perhaps also in the hope that Alice might follow. When David walked out, he coughed lightly and said, 'Thank you. Mark, thank you.'

'What for?'

'Standing in for Hawken. With the Minister. It's kind of you.' He sounded uncertain about that. Almost timidly, he sat down beside me. 'You will be careful? What you say?'

So this was to be my briefing: don't mention the suicides; avoid all talk of forest graves.

'David, why were you so eager to get Hawken locked up?' I asked.

'Me?' He looked round nervously. 'We had to. Sánchez demanded it.'

'Sure, but you were pretty quick accepting those demands. Condemning Hawken. You put a lot of pressure on Mr Hoppner.'

'Miraflores. I didn't want him to lose it.'

'You look after his interests well.'

'I owe him a lot.'

'Don't you get lonely here? With so few people in the compound?'

It was a stupid question to put to David. No way was he going to elaborate or explain when a simple 'No' would do. I tried again.

'What do you do with your spare time? Do you travel? Ski? Hunt jaguars?'

'I like my work. Helping Mr Hoppner.'

'Oh, sure, but don't you ever need to get out – do something else for a change? All this morality!'

'No.'

'What about girls?' I asked.

'No,' he said again.

'I bet you have a girl here in town, don't you?' I said, trying to raise a smile, trying to build a rapport.

'It's not like that,' he said quickly.

I gave up. 'Why did you really want Hawken out?'

Sighing, David stretched his fingers out over his knees. 'The way things were going. I was having . . .'

'A crisis of conscience?'

'Doubts. Nothing big,' he said hurriedly. 'It's . . . It's hard for you to see. Mr Hoppner is an incredible man. He is so *good*. If you could see the way he was. In the States. Things just got different. With Hawken.'

'More violent.'

'Right. And I understand it. Mr Hoppner explains it. This isn't a perfect world. "A good heart needs a brave fist." He told me that. Back in Tulsa. But recently, Hawken was *influencing him*.'

A kind of hope began to grow in my mind. 'David,' I said softly, not wanting to break the spell his frank admission had cast. 'Alice and I are going to die if we take those tests.'

'No,' he muttered. 'Don't think that. You'll be fine.'

'Can't you help us get out of here?'

'No! Don't ask that.'

'You want our blood on your hands? You want those guards holding Alice down while Hoppner poisons her? Did you know she's pregnant?'

'Mark, stop it! I can't help you!'

Gripping his shoulder, I forced him to look at me. 'Can't or won't?'

He stared back helplessly, his eyes glistening in the thin stream of light coming from the guesthouse. 'I owe him so much,' he whispered.

I was asleep when Alice came in.

'Mark?' she whispered, so close to my ear that the sound echoed in my brain even after I'd woken up.

'Jesus, Alice!'

'Do you have to bring him into it?' she giggled, lifting up the sheets and slipping in beside me. 'You were so unsubtle tonight, staring at me the whole time.'

Still half-asleep, I realized with a shock that she was naked. 'What are you doing?' I whispered.

'It's OK,' she said. 'Listen.'

Leonard's snores were in full swing. Coming out of a deep sleep, I hadn't even noticed the sound until she drew attention to it. Her finger – a pale sliver just visible in the darkness – rose to conduct, then hesitated and dropped back on to the sheet. Perhaps she was remembering my reaction the first time she did that.

'Look, Alice. I can't . . . not now.'

I felt her smile. 'Don't worry. I've had boyfriends who couldn't manage it more than once a week. I have low expectations.'

'No. I mean . . .' I pulled the sheet around me, cutting us off from each other with a scrap of material tugged between our hips. 'I can't . . . I'm . . . Look, I'm sorry. I want to try to get back with Katie.'

'Oh.' Unable to see her, I could only guess at the change of sentiment behind that brief syllable. The mattress shifted and her thigh pressed against mine for a second before she moved away. 'Well, that's fine. We can just lie together if you want.'

'It's a single bed.'

'I'm not that pregnant,' she joked, an edge of frustration creeping into her voice.

'Oh God, the single bed is irrelevant. Look, I just shouldn't . . . I can't sleep with you. I can't do this,' I said, swinging my legs out and sitting on the far side of the bed with my back to her. 'I just for once want to do the right thing here.'

'Isn't comforting someone who's about to get executed close enough to the right thing for a saint like you?' she snapped.

Her angry breathing was just audible in the gaps between Leonard's snores. The slightest rustle of the sheet moving over her chest; air forced through a tense throat.

'Alice, I'm sorry I—'

'No, I'm sorry,' she muttered quickly. 'You're right. Of course you're right.'

'This morning,' I whispered. 'It was wonderful. Really. And it helped so much. But finding out about my parents – I'm just trying to get a grip on my life.' The scent of her brought back the feel of her body on top of mine. 'This isn't what I should be doing.'

'Mark, it's fine,' she said. A breezy tone, just a fraction rushed. 'It doesn't matter. Of course it doesn't matter. I only thought it might take our minds off all this shit for a while.'

I turned. I could just make out the shape of her body under the sheet, and I touched my hand to her shoulder. She stiffened immediately; I pulled back.

'Thank you,' I said.

'Can you look away, please,' she replied, the slightest coolness in her voice. 'I have to put the light on to find my clothes.'

'OK.'

I felt the mattress shift once more as she climbed out of bed and filled the room with light. Staring blankly at the far wall, I was very conscious of my naked back facing her naked body. Her light footsteps were accompanied by the whisper of cotton against skin, and a second later the door was opening. A quick, ambiguously intoned ''Bye, Mark' as she left the room.

No, she hadn't wanted me to turn and see her face.

Pamela was still in Hawken's house the following morning, still dressed in the same clothes, her red hair a tangled mess. I looked in soon after dawn and found her huddled in the corner of the living room, the unruly chick squawking its head off beside her. Hawken's books, clothes, *stuff*, were packed in the crate I'd left. The room was devoid of anything personal.

'Have you slept at all?'

She shook her head wearily. The enmity of the previous day was gone. Sinking down beside her, I picked a knot in the wooden floor to stare at, and waited in silence.

Eventually she spoke: 'Thank you.'

'For what?'

'The crate. Thank you for the crate.'

'Oh,' I muttered. 'No problem.'

'What I said yesterday. Just forget it.' Her hand came up to knead her swollen face. 'It's hard for me to accept this. That Mr Hoppner would . . .' A shudder ran through her body. 'Hawken only ever did what he was asked to do.'

The pain in her voice was raw and jagged.

'Do you want me here?' I asked.

'Not really.'

I nodded, though she wasn't looking at me, hadn't once looked at me. She didn't react as I stood up and left.

From the steps of Hawken's house, I could see Leonard walking backwards and forwards across an empty patch of lawn, an expression of deep concentration on his face. Every now and then he would take a little hop, his arms flying unevenly outwards. His feet, this time, were bare on the cold, dewy grass.

'Exercising, Leonard?'

I walked across to him. The sight of him was somehow cheering after the distilled depression of Pamela's solitude.

'Oh wonderful, Mark, I've completely forgotten how to do it. Already! I'm so sorry. Would you mind . . . ?' He looked over his shoulder at Hoppner's house. 'You don't think Mr Hoppner's going to come out, do you? I'd be awfully embarrassed if he saw me floundering about.'

Why did he care what that bastard thought?

'You're not floundering,' I said. 'But let's do some stretches first.'

To say that Leonard's morning exercises were a joy would have been an overstatement, yet there was an undeniable comfort to their simplicity and innocence. The one activity – the one person, even – unaffected by Hoppner's appalling quest for Good. As long as I was leading Leonard through his stretches, jumps, press-ups, sit-ups and leg raises, I could focus on that straightforward, positive moment. I could push all the rest – my parents, the looming tests, my self-doubt regarding Katie, the critical VIP visit – right out of my mind. I had an excuse, for a few minutes, not to think.

When Pamela walked unsteadily out of Hawken's house, we were once again on the sit-ups and Leonard was already gasping for breath. I watched her watch us, waiting apprehensively for the first snort of derision. Instead, when she spoke, her voice was quiet and measured.

'Don't make him do full crunches,' she said. 'He isn't ready for them yet.'

She walked over to us and crouched beside Leonard, pressing her palm against his chest. 'Lie flat,' she ordered.

His clothes were already wet through with dew, and he obeyed her without hesitation, sinking back into the soft turf.

'Keep your lower back on the ground. Just raise your shoulders and head.'

When Leonard seemed to find this instruction confusing, Pamela impatiently grabbed his hands in hers, standing with a foot either side of his waist.

'Up,' she said, pulling his shoulders off the

ground. 'That's a strong grip,' she commented in surprise.

'Thank you,' gasped Leonard, lowering himself back down.

She let go of his hands and stepped away. 'Now, again. Do it slowly. Concentrate your strength into your stomach. Imagine your gut is this powerful motor, like a winch, winding your chest towards it. Imagine all you have to do is press a button and the winch starts winding, slow but very strong.'

As Leonard raised his shoulders a second, third, fourth time, Pamela glanced at me, and I smiled my thanks. She nodded, almost unconsciously, before returning her attention to Leonard.

Sánchez came to pick me up at nine o'clock. The idea of even acting the role of security head – having power over this formidable man – was so ridiculous I found my cheeks burning in anticipation of his arrival. He must find the idea absurd, I thought, even insulting. Spending several hours in his company was going to be hell.

In fact, Sánchez displayed none of the irritation or scorn I expected. With careful, slow sentences, he began filling me in on the state of Miraflores: who was who, which men were potential trouble-makers, why certain inhabitants had so far missed out on Hoppner's largesse – Lupita was a congenital liar, who still hadn't mended her ways – and how Hawken had dealt with the worst violations of his employer's Code.

His car was a broken-down Ford, its wing mirror and bumper held in place by string. It coughed and growled its way around Miraflores, spitting its resentment in a series of sharp bangs. Every now and then we would stop by a house and Sánchez would knock on its door and introduce me to the occupant. Several of them I recognized from the forest ambush. Those men all looked uneasy and apologetic. I learned to mask the instinctive fear that lurched through me whenever I saw one of their faces. No one wanted to remember too much about that incident.

It occurred to me at one point that we were passing close by the alley where Freddy's gun still lay hidden. Casually, I suggested to Sánchez that we take a break – specifically, that I have a wander on my own. But although he couldn't have guessed my intentions, Sánchez refused to let me out of his sight. Hoppner had made it clear that I was to be carefully supervised.

We stopped for a short time in the Parque Central, where a group of older inhabitants had gathered. While Sánchez was chatting to them, I looked up at the gaol and saw Hawken staring down at me. Like the other prisoners, he was silent. What he thought, seeing me driving around with Sánchez, I have no idea. After a few seconds of long-range eye contact I turned away, a little freaked out.

A young boy, maybe five or six years old, had crept up behind me. When I caught sight of him, his face broke into a naughty smile, as if he'd been about to go for my wallet. As usual with children, my instinct was to move away. Only when I'd actually taken a couple of steps did I realize what I was doing.

I turned around and walked straight over to him. '*Hola*,' I said, squatting down and shaking his eager little hand. '*Cómo te llamas?*'

His name was Pancho and he loved the handshake – wouldn't let go. Bringing his left hand up to his nose, he rubbed away a sizeable dollop of snot, grinning happily all the while. Easing myself out of his tight grip, I felt the extraordinary joy of rehabilitation. I could do this. I could be with kids; no one was going to get hurt. Such a simple thing, that anyone else would take for granted.

On impulse, I walked over to Sánchez and said, 'Can I use your phone?'

Strange to be back in the hotel again, the place where Freddy had lain cocksure and languid in a hammock, where the three of us had plotted our great con-trick. After Santa Tecla, it had seemed a place of such gentle innocence. That was before the hanging, before the ambush in the forest, before so much.

Even with the clouds gathering once again, the hotel courtyard remained a pleasant and tranquil place of tumbling greenery and tinkling water. Sánchez led me to his office and left me alone with his phone. I could have made any call: the

British Ambassador, the US Marines, anyone. But imagining the process they would have to go through before taking action – the diplomacy, the investigations, the debate – I knew no foreign intervention would be in time to help us. Our only practical hope was the Chief of Police.

This time I checked my watch: late afternoon in London.

'It's me.'

'Mark! Don't hang up. Please don't hang up.'

'Oh God, Katie, I'm sorry about that.'

What a state I'd left her in. Alone in the flat with Christopher, unable to trace me, a legion of poss-ible truths – each darker than the last – parading through her imagination. I thought about telling her where I was, but I knew it could only frighten her. No sense in burdening her with my fears when there was nothing she could do to help.

'Are you all right? Where are you?'

'I'm fine. Really.'

'Where are . . . ? Mark, are you coming back?'

If I get out of here alive, I thought to myself. 'Of course,' I replied.

The scent of a single moment came to me: Katie sitting in a pub near the vilely cheap hotel I'd found on Belgrave Road, the week after our return from Indonesia. Her holiday tan glowing amongst all those anaemic London faces, her warm hand gripping mine with sudden determination. 'You don't want to work in an office,' she'd said fervently, 'and if you're only going to do it to pay the rent on some crappy bedsit, that's crazy when I have plenty of room for both of us.' I could still feel that grip.

'I wasn't sure,' she began now. 'You've seemed so strange with C.'

'I know. I . . .' How could I even begin to explain? 'I want to see him again so badly.'

A long silence.

'He's started doing that thing you do with your neck.'

'What thing?'

'You know . . .'

'My neck?'

'When you're pretending to think about a suggestion I've made but actually you've already decided to ignore it. Bending it to the side, then rocking your chin up. He does it perfectly.'

'You think it's genetic?'

'Must be.'

'Well, at least I know he's mine.'

'Mark . . .'

'I'm joking, Katie. I've never had any worries about—'

'Should I?' she interrupted.

It felt as if she'd pulled that warm hand out of my grasp, turned that glowing face away from me.

'Should you what?'

'Is there someone else?'

'Katie!'

'It's the only reason I can think of. Why you would suddenly go away like this.'

'Look . . .'

'I'm sorry. You don't have to answer.' Her voice died away.

And I couldn't answer. I couldn't tell her about Alice – about the comfort she'd offered after the trauma of my hypnosis. My silence, though, said everything.

'Oh, Mark,' she whispered.

'Katie, I promise, it's only you and C that matter. Things have happened, things I wish could have been different, but I'm making a new start. You're going to be proud of me, Katie.'

It took a while for her to answer. 'When are you coming back?'

'I can't say for sure.'

'You are . . . ?' A silence. 'Mark, promise me you are definitely coming back.' I have to know. For C's sake, I have to know.'

I thought about Hoppner's test. Could I be certain the police would get us out? What if something went wrong?

'I'm trying so hard, Katie.'

'Oh Jesus Christ, Mark!'

'Please, listen to me. It's all I dream of. But I'm in a bit of trouble here.'

'Then I'm coming to you.'

'No.'

'Where are you? For God's sake, tell me where you are!'

'You're not coming here.'

A silence. Her lawyer's brain turning the dispute over and over, looking for a way to win. 'Remember that time I had a week-long conference in New York?' she said. 'And you secretly worked extra shifts to pay for a flight to come and—'

'This isn't the same! Katie, this isn't some faux-rustic conference centre, for Christ's sake. You can't just pitch up in . . . Look, there's nothing you can do here.'

'Mark . . .'

'I have to go. Just . . . trust me, OK?'

'. . . OK.'

'I love you both so much.'

I kissed the air for my goodbye, just as we always used to. Her kiss came back a fraction delayed, and reluctantly I replaced the phone. London felt an impossible distance away.

My crash course in Miraflores life was almost complete when, as we passed through the Parque Central for the last time, I saw the church doors open and a crowd of people emerge. At their head was the boy who'd come to the compound – Tanadio's son.

'What's going on there?' I asked.

At first, Sánchez didn't reply. He wouldn't even look in the direction of the church. 'Meeting,' he muttered eventually.

Their heads were bowed; many were dressed in black. 'Bullshit,' I said. 'It's a funeral.'

With great reluctance, Sánchez nodded. He

stopped the car. 'For Tanadio. Please. Do not tell Mr Hoppner.'

'You don't mean he's banned funerals?'

'He does not like the Church. He does not like Tanadio.'

'So you're doing this behind Hoppner's back.' I had to smile at that. 'Isn't he expecting you to be honest? Isn't that one of the rules?'

'Mr Weston, it is bad for us if you—'

'Forget about it. I won't say anything.' I watched the son of the terrorist stand as tall as he could manage beside a woman in a black veil. The widow, perhaps. It was difficult to summon up much sympathy for her, after having witnessed the atrocity committed by her beloved. Four pall-bearers emerged, blinking, from the church. The coffin was pure white – a disconcerting touch.

'Thank you,' said Sánchez.

'Shouldn't you be there?'

'Mr Hoppner asked me to guide you.'

'Just bad timing, huh?'

'Yes.'

I turned to face him. 'You'll do anything he says, won't you? To keep that money flowing, you'd stand on your head if he asked you to. This guy, Tanadio, you fought alongside him, right? You should be over there saying good-bye to him, but instead you're acting the tour guide.'

'It is not for me, the money,' he growled.

'How ironic that you fought as communists, but

447

now you're being bribed like the worst kind of capitalist.'

'We fought as free men and women who wanted only to protect our freedom.'

'Oh, right,' I said. 'And have you?'

'You do not understand our position. We suffered for so long. Mr Hoppner is helping us.'

'Mr Hoppner is using you. You're his laboratory experiment. You're like rats he wants to show the world will grow fatter on a diet of Hoppner virtue. But the tragic thing is, he's brought you to a point where you're trying to kill people just because they're journalists. Did you go that far when you were fighting the war?'

'There are many things I do not like in our life,' he snapped. 'But we cannot choose the life we have.'

I'd upset him. Really, I'm not sure whether I'd meant to do that. 'Turn off the engine,' I said softly. 'Take the keys. I won't run off anywhere and I won't tell Hoppner anything. Go and say goodbye.'

The anger dissolved away. He hesitated, but not for long. His was a decisive nature, and his decision was to trust me. Reaching into his pocket, he retrieved the black armband.

All the time he was with the other mourners – shaking the boy's hand, murmuring condolences to the widow – I tried not to think about Freddy's gun.

★　　★　　★

448

For most of that day I saw no sign of Alice, even after Sánchez had returned me to the compound. When eventually I found her making coffee in the guesthouse kitchen, an inhibiting awkwardness fell over both of us. Alice sought refuge in the trivial.

'I always travel with teabags,' she said. 'I can't believe I forgot them this time. Another day without tea and I'll go crazy.'

Her sketchbook was lying open on the kitchen table: a half-finished pencil-drawing of Hoppner's house. Not a memento I would have wanted to take away.

'Hardly romantic to pack teabags for a honeymoon.'

'All the same, I would.'

And already we were into dangerous territory. She felt it as much as I did, and veered off on a different course immediately.

'I've been looking for holes in the fence. Scouring the perimeter.'

'There aren't any?'

'Of course not.'

'Probably a good thing.'

'You're that confident in the police?'

'I'm that confident we'd be picked up before we'd gone three miles.'

She nodded, resigned, and poured coffee into two mugs. I hadn't asked for any, but I appreciated the gesture. A step towards restoration of relations.

'I talked to the guards,' she said bleakly. 'Well,

they came to see what I was doing hovering around the fence. They're Honduran, you know? Hoppner hired them off some American banana estate there.' She took a sip of her coffee. 'Surly bastards.'

'And unrelated to anyone in Miraflores.' I had to admire Hoppner for that. Their loyalty in a dispute would be unquestionable. The only other person they might take orders from – through long habit, if nothing else – was stuck in the town gaol.

Picking up the other coffee mug, I was about to add milk when Alice reached over and grabbed it out of my hand. 'That's Leonard's,' she growled. 'Make your own.'

Stupid of me: I hadn't even thought of Leonard. Scalding coffee had splashed over my wrist. I suspect some also landed on her hand. Neither of us would admit to the pain.

Then, abruptly, she was crying.

'Alice . . .'

'I'm fine!'

'I'm sorry. About last night, I'm sorry.'

She laughed harshly. 'You just assume this has something to do with you?'

'No, but . . .' I took the coffee mugs from her hands and put them down on the table. 'Alice, what's wrong?'

'Me, only me. Always me.' Helplessness flashed across her face. 'I just feel like . . . maybe I *should* do that test.'

450

'But . . .' I couldn't say it for her. Only she could make the judgement.

'But I'd fail, I know.' She pressed her fingertips to her eyes. 'Just something, yesterday. When we . . . When you were saying someone else's name while we made love, and I said I didn't mind . . .'

'But you did,' I finished for her, feeling my throat constrict.

'No, that's just it. I honestly didn't mind. And then afterwards I thought about that, and I asked myself what kind of creature fucks around so much that she stops caring whether her sexual partners are even thinking about her?'

It was so far removed from what I'd expected to hear, I didn't know what to say. 'I'm sorry,' I muttered again.

'Why are you sorry?' She looked up at me, reddened eyes blinking. 'Why should you give a shit? You've got this wonderful Katie who loves you like you love her, while I'm just some jaded, spiritually empty . . . Damn!' Spinning her face away from me, she coughed furiously to cover a new bout of sobbing.

I waited in silence, a hand on her shoulder blade, unable to think of one word to console her. When Leonard wandered out of their bedroom holding the cloth-covered book, he hardly took in the scene.

'Ali, I've found a wonderful bit of Nietzsche for you. Listen to what he has to say about women: "What a treat it is to meet creatures who have only

dancing and nonsense and finery in their minds!"'
He looked up from the book, only then noticing
Alice's wet eyes. 'I was going to write it down for
you,' he stammered, 'but now I needn't, I suppose.'

To escape Leonard's unthinking thoughts, I
knocked on Pamela's door. Like Alice, she had
been out of sight all day: no climbing, no visits
to the women of Miraflores, no meals. If she ate
at all, she did it alone. After her brief kindness
with Leonard, I felt I ought to check that she was
all right. When there was no reply, I knocked once
more before quietly opening the door.

It was four thirty in the afternoon and she was
dressed in a nightgown – that in itself was a little
worrying. Huddled on the end of her bed, she was
mechanically feeding worms to the ugly brown
chick balanced on her bare feet.

The room was perfectly ordered: clothes stacked
neatly or hanging from a rail; papers and books
lined up on a set of shelves; climbing equipment,
including her one surviving grappling hook tied to
the end of a long yellow rope, displayed on a wall-
mounted rack. The crate containing Hawken's
possessions lay beside her bed – close enough to
reach out and touch.

'Hi.'

She looked up blankly. There might have been
some slight nod of acknowledgement before she
reached for the next worm.

'That thing's going to get way too fat,' I said,

452

meaning it as a joke, although it came out sounding like a criticism.

When I'd imagined the inside of Pamela's room, my mind had conjured up a vast Canadian flag, pinned to the wall or perhaps spread across the bed. I don't know why. Possibly it's down to some unconscious suspicion I have that Canadians live their whole lives in a state of collegial enthusiasm, nursing an over-zealous patriotism. Unfair of me, if so, as none of the Canadians I know even owns a flag.

'Thanks for helping Leonard,' I tried. Then, searching for anything to say, 'Will you be going back to work in Miraflores? I'm sure the women miss you.'

I noticed an empty ashtray on the desk. Beside it, a wooden box containing seven thin cigars. 'I'd forgotten you smoked,' I said breezily, without thinking. 'I haven't seen you with a cigar since . . .' Wrong track to take.

'Did you know that Hawken once saved Mr Hoppner's life?' she said, her eyes still on the chick. 'When the Mob wanted in on his business and he refused. They tried to kidnap Mr Hoppner from his hotel in New York, but Hawken sent three of them away with broken arms.'

I shuddered at the thought. Pamela was trying to claim a deep loyalty, even a debt, I suppose; all I saw was his characteristic brutality.

'I went to see him this morning. While you were busy taking over his job.'

'Pamela, I'm not taking over anything.'

'They'd beaten him. Did you realize that? Your new buddy Sánchez and his goons. They went in there last night and beat him systematically for twenty minutes. There isn't a bit of his body that hasn't been bruised or cut.'

Revenge for Tanadio, I guessed. A harsh world, this perfect society, but I couldn't help feeling Hawken had been paid in his own coin. Pamela didn't seem to see anything wrong with following a boast about broken arms with a complaint about a few bruises.

The idea of Pamela visiting Hawken at all was alarming. If he blamed me, even only in part, for his fate then I really didn't want to be around when he got out of gaol. What if Pamela found some way of helping him escape? She could bribe the gaolers, or gain their trust long enough to purloin their keys. The possibility of a freed, vengeful Hawken was too unpleasant to dwell on and I looked away, my eyes settling on a framed newspaper cutting above her desk:

Sir

In his story, 'Satan's Newest Recruit,' Nicholas Vogel labels Benjamin Sword Hoppner a 'pernicious influence on American society' . . .

A small miracle she hadn't yet torn down the

frame and smashed it over the head of Satan's Newest Recruit. In an effort to lift her spirits a little, I said, 'It'll be all right soon. He'll be out of gaol in a couple of weeks, I'm sure, then everything will be back to how it was before.'

Her eyes suddenly locked on mine, and though she hadn't moved from the bed I felt oddly threatened.

'You don't understand at all, do you?' she said in a voice that could have been forged in hell. 'Nothing can ever be the same.'

That night Hoppner called us all together for dinner at his house. With my nerves in pieces over the ministerial visit the following day, I didn't want to go. Would I get a moment alone with the Chief of Police? How receptive would he be? But Hoppner seemed to want some kind of team pep talk before the big event. Or perhaps it was more an attempt to bring Pamela back into the fold.

No one else was feeling communicative, and for a while Hoppner talked alone, outlining his hopes for Miraflores and future, bigger 'perfect societies'. The island of Malta was a target; one day he hoped to persuade a larger country like New Zealand to follow the Miraflores example. All that was necessary was a single working model, he said, and the whole world would fall over themselves to adopt its principles.

'So you've straightened out the troubles in Miraflores?' Leonard asked. Where my voice would have doused that question in cynicism, or even sarcasm, his conveyed only encouragement and hope.

'To a certain extent. Although I'm starting to fear that some minds in Miraflores will never be open to my arguments,' admitted Hoppner. 'In a sense, they have been taught to feel joy at the wrong things: sexual conquest and victory in war, rather than a fair deal or a prospering neighbour. Overcoming that deep-rooted obstacle may be beyond any of our powers: it's hard to persuade someone of the benefits of virtue if they can never value the products of virtue. I'm starting to think that a perfect society may have to be grown rather than converted.'

'You mean go for the children?' I muttered, unsurprised by this latest step towards the abyss.

'I have Aristotle on my side,' replied Hoppner, somewhat defensively. 'He understood the need to train the young from birth to feel joy at virtue. Just as it's easier to teach younger people to feel horror at racism, so it's easier to teach them to feel joy in forgiving and self-disgust in lying.'

An image of Christopher – his little face just managing to peer over a worn scholar's desk, his tiny body trembling while Hoppner barked his version of the truth – flashed through my mind. 'Well, you certainly won't be the first to fight your battles by brainwashing the kids.'

To my left, Pamela didn't even seem to notice my blunt slur on her former idol. Alice knew what

I was saying, but this time she made no effort to restrain me.

'That's ungenerous, Mark. I hope you don't compare my Code to the writings of Mao or Hitler?'

'Actually I've been re-reading your Code,' said Leonard, 'and I must say I'm revising my opinion of it. Some of your ideas are very sound. Your advocacy of gentleness, for example, as a curb on our impulses – as an essential tool in evaluating the absolute necessity of violence or war – is something I haven't in truth spent much time considering before. Such a feminine virtue, isn't it? I believe the Greeks used to consider it the measure of civilization in a society – isn't that right? Of course, Nietzsche wouldn't approve.' A nervous laugh.

'And how are you enjoying your Nietzsche?' asked Hoppner with a wry smile.

'Oh dear, he really wasn't the best companion to bring to this establishment. I'd forgotten his view of morality: an unnatural set of customs imposed on us by society. True virtue only for the elite few – impossible, in fact, without good birth.'

'Thank God he was certified,' laughed Hoppner, 'or we might have had to take him seriously.'

'Although I wouldn't dismiss everything he said. Surely you must share his belief in the importance of strength of will? Given what you have to do in Miraflores, I'd have thought you'd take comfort from his admiration for those "noble

457

men" willing to inflict necessary pain on their subjects.'

Hoppner's good humour vanished. Like me, he must have wondered whether Leonard was trying to provoke him. But the academic had abandoned intellectual provocation the moment Freddy died. Ever since, his formidable brain had been directed solely towards justifying and excusing Hoppner – rationalizing the ghastly world in which he found himself. And if a dead philosopher provided an excuse for torture and murder, then Leonard's whole being cried out to use it.

'I do not take any pleasure in inflicting pain,' declared Hoppner.

'Of course, I didn't mean . . .'

'Mr Williams, whatever I have to do, I do it fairly.'

'I never doubted—'

'Justice is very important to me. Unlike Nietzsche, I value every person equally, and if I have to inflict necessary pain, if I have to assist a suicide, I make absolutely certain that what I do is one hundred per cent fair.'

Leonard's attempts to mollify Hoppner had dried up, but he was nodding sincerely, agreeing with every word.

Then a voice broke in from beside me: 'What about Hawken?'

It was very loud, particularly shocking after her long silence. Pamela was glaring at Hoppner, her face trembling with rage.

'My dear—' began Hoppner.

'Was that fair? Betraying your most loyal servant – was that just?'

'Pamela, please, we'll talk about this tomorrow when you're calm.'

'Calm? You think I can be calm for one moment while he's at the mercy of those bastards? You think I can be calm when the man I admire most in the world throws his beliefs out of the window to appease a bunch of terrorists? Where is your justice today, Mr Hoppner? Where is your fidelity?'

Tears were starting at the corners of her eyes. Her chin was jutting forward, the muscles in her cheek struggling to lock it steady.

'You mustn't let your feelings cloud your understanding, Pamela. I know you loved Hawken, but—'

'I loved *you*!' Pure desolation. 'I loved everything you stood for. I loved your honesty, your Code, your belief in the message that you preached. What am I supposed to do now, when the one thing I loved has been corrupted?'

'It's not like that,' said David. 'Hawken has changed. He got sick.'

But Pamela ignored him. She was standing now, staring at Hoppner with a pitiful expression on her face. 'If you sacrifice one principle, what's stopping you sacrificing them all?' she said. 'Where does it end?'

I half expected him to apologize, or at the very

459

least comfort her with some platitude. But he met her stare without the slightest waver, spreading a rock-steady hand on the tablecloth.

'You are very precious to me, Pamela. Your values are unimpeachable and your work here of great benefit to the women of Miraflores. But you have to learn a little humility in your moral conviction. This is not a perfect world and absolutist moral positions are simply not tenable. Creating a system of ethics so ideal that no normal, flawed human being could adopt it would be an exercise in hypothetical utopianism, nothing more. If you demand of a real society that it function purely on ideals then you will ultimately destroy it. And if you cannot accept pragmatism where it is unavoidable, if you cannot make tough choices to protect what you most value, then I'm sorry to say you will never be of use to me here.'

There was no anger in his eyes, but neither was there the sympathy and compassion I would have expected to accompany the hard words he'd just delivered. Pamela's whole reason for being had just been overturned, and instead of offering her a handkerchief Hoppner was behaving like a censorious bully.

As Pamela rocked unsteadily from foot to foot, Alice stood up and hurried over to her. She put her arms around her, hugging her tightly, whispering to her. For a few moments, Pamela let her body sag and her head rest against Alice's shoulder. Then she pulled herself out of the embrace and ran from the dining room.

Alice started to follow, but Hoppner said, 'Leave her, Mrs Williams. She'll be fine.'

Slowly, Alice closed the door. 'I hope you're right. She's just lost the two things she cares about most.'

Hoppner seemed about to say something more, but Alice's words made him falter.

For the first time since I'd met him, he looked frightened.

If a man's property is taken from him, we call it Theft; if his wife is taken, we call it Adultery. But if it is his livelihood that is taken from him, we call it Competition and we place that abstract swindler on a pedestal. Competition, along with Celebrity and Consumption, has become a god of our time. We praise it, without questioning it, as an absolute good. Yet Competition axiomatically produces losers, and it is society's losers that wreak upon it the most harm. Yes, Competition incentivizes the energetic and creates stupendous, superfluous wealth for society's winners, but it also gives birth to the losers who are forced, through misery and desperation, into crime.

In Miraflores, no one has to compete for a livelihood. Poverty, the single biggest obstacle to the spread of virtue, does not exist. Incentives remain: those who embrace virtue and work hard gain extra benefits, both material and spiritual. But even for those who cannot or prefer not to strive for more, there will always be a job for them in the coffee plantations, in building or decorating, street cleaning, road construction or forestry. No one in Miraflores will ever be desperate.

That, I believe, is the key to a virtuous society. There will always be some criminal tendencies, but remove desperation – provide a baseline of income and self-respect – and you remove the need for crime. Nobody can be expected to behave generously toward his neighbor if his own children are starving.

So it is in Miraflores. As the people grow accustomed to their new security, and come to trust it will be maintained, they can free their minds to aim for higher goals – they grow virtuous. It may take years for a full mental shift to occur, but once it does I feel confident this town will see the great benefit of living in a virtuous society, and its population will do all they can to preserve and enhance it. They will have entered a virtuous cycle.

At that point, I hope, the rest of the world will bear witness to this wonderful phenomenon and attempt to replicate it in every corner of the planet.

CHAPTER 17

The sun had not yet cleared the line of hills across the valley when I walked out of the guesthouse on the morning of the ministerial visit. The sky was clear; a cool trickle of breeze brought new life to the empty compound, rustling through shrubs and carrying the odd leaf down from the forested slopes above. A day of hope.

Towards the lower end of the garden, a figure caught my eye. It was Pamela, sitting cross-legged, staring fixedly through the fence to the forest beyond. The forest where Hawken used to run at that time, I suppose.

I walked over to the guards by the gate. Hondurans, Alice had said: as dependent on Hoppner as he was on them. The impossibility of breaking that alliance was clearer than ever.

The nightshift had not yet been relieved. Four dishevelled, drowsy men watched me approach with suspicion. 'Is she OK?' I asked the nearest guard in Spanish.

I was remembering more and more of the childhood language locked dormant for so long in my head. Swathes of meaning were falling into place, drawn out by a chance remark or new recollection. My dreams were all variations on the theme of that deserted, murderous road, and these too seemed to bring back a rush of vocabulary, tumbling haphazardly through the muddle of a child's stark impressions.

The guard took his time replying. 'She has been there all night.'

Pamela, pining for her man. It was almost romantic. Or was she mourning the idealistic morality that she'd finally understood to be an illusion? Her red hair hung limply over her shoulders, high-lighting the sickly pallor of her skin. I called her name once, quite loudly enough to reach her. She didn't respond.

Soon afterwards I watched Hoppner emerge from his front door, walk the length of the cliff wall twice, and return to his house for his exercises. He passed quite close to Pamela, alone by the fence, but he gave no sign of noticing her.

The bright, promising skies were no compensation for the disgust I felt at the way he was treating her.

'Of course you have reservations, Mark,' Leonard said ten minutes later, as we stretched our sleepy limbs on the grass in front of the guesthouse. 'Mr Hoppner's way of doing things is different from what we're used to, and of course that's disturbing.'

On this third morning of exercises, Leonard was

already rising more readily to the mild physical challenges I placed before him. The fact that he was talking without effort while he stretched was a good sign. Still, I would have preferred any other subject.

'Do we have to discuss this?'

'Not if you don't want to.' He spread his feet wide and bent at the waist, following my example, just about managing to reach his long hands to his shins. 'Except, I've found it useful to see things from a broader point of view. I was very upset at first by what Mr Hoppner was doing. But thinking it through really helps. It would help you too, I'm sure.'

Out of the corner of my eye, I noticed Pamela pull herself up and shuffle towards the guesthouse. As she drew close I threw her an encouraging smile, inviting her with a gesture to join us. She stopped still for a moment, watching Leonard talk, his left hand pulling his bony right elbow into his chest. Then she just shook her head, a glimmer of apology in her eyes, and walked on up the steps of the guesthouse.

'I mean, think of Plato's *Republic*. We revere Plato these days, but the utopia he envisaged was quite a bold departure from our normal way of life. All children were to be taken away from their parents at birth and raised by the State, so no one would know which child was theirs, and consequently a greater sense of family would extend to the whole community. The republic would be that much more public-spirited because people wouldn't focus all their efforts on their own family's interests.'

I straightened my back, interrupted a little irritably: 'Leonard, why are you telling me this?'

'Only to say that sometimes bold ideas require bold application. Imagine trying to create Plato's republic – the shock to parents when you first started taking away their children! Yet, one can quite see how it could produce a far more harmonious society in the long run. In fact, I believe there are certain African tribes today that do more or less exactly that: every child calls every man father; the whole community is bound together by a stronger sense of relationship.'

'Hoppner isn't planning to break up families.'

'But he does have a clear, bold plan to shift the whole population to a more virtuous level. All I'm saying is that the shock and ordeal of making that transition – having to be rather aggressive or violent at times, even enforcing suicides where necessary – may ultimately be a small price to pay for the far happier society that would result.'

I stopped stretching and stared at him in amazement. He'd lost the air of academic pensiveness I'd found so charming when we first met – this was a tougher, more focused Leonard talking. The change was deeply unnerving.

'Rather like Hausmann having to knock down all those lovely medieval Parisian houses to build his grand boulevards,' he concluded. 'Quite a sacrifice, but if we're honest, aren't we glad he did it?'

'I think I'd rather not do the exercises today,' I said faintly. 'You'll be all right on your own.'

'Actually, I might ask Mr Hoppner if he minds me joining in his routine.'

As I reached the veranda, feeling nauseous, I turned to see him walk up to Hoppner's back door and confidently knock. When it opened, Hoppner ushered him in without hesitation.

For the ministerial visit, Hoppner had chosen a single-breasted wool suit in pale grey. Sufficiently lightweight to be tolerable on this sun-drenched day, it nevertheless hung cleanly on his solid frame. His tie was a plain dark-green silk; his shirt collar was carefully starched and fastened with a gold pin. As usual, his hair was immaculately combed to the left side, but today a grim determination darkened his face.

He waited in silence, watching the sky with one hand raised to shade his eyes. David and I stood a few steps behind him – the loyal servants to the local King. I was growing increasingly nervous, gearing myself up to the plea I would have to make. When the distant growl of a heavy engine reached our ears, David turned to me and murmured, 'Are you OK?'

'I'm fine,' I said.

'Last night. I'm sorry.'

I laughed somewhat bitterly. 'I didn't expect anything different from you.'

'Please, Mark. It's very important for Miraflores that you don't say anything damaging to these people.'

I met his worried gaze with a blank stare. 'That was a bloody long sentence, David.'

He blinked. 'It's important,' he repeated against the mounting racket. Turning away from me, he lifted his eyes to the great machine that was sweeping over the hills towards us.

The Minister of the Interior and the Chief of Police did not travel alone. With them in the heavy military helicopter were various flunkeys and a clutch of anonymous bodyguards, all of them wearing aviator sunglasses and shoulder holsters, ill-concealed beneath their tight suit jackets. During the descent, two of the bodyguards aimed automatic rifles at the ground below, like a poor imitation of *Apocalypse Now*. I had to remind myself that these men had suffered their own war, maybe even their own hot landings under fire from opponents like Sánchez: perhaps it wasn't entirely an act.

Their guns were not the only ones on show. The helipad – a flat, empty patch of ground outside the town, normally used for football matches or drying coffee beans – was surrounded by at least sixty fully armed policemen. Each of them faced outwards, ready to pick off the first sloth or hummingbird that might dare to approach their supreme commander and his political master. Until the helicopter appeared, most of them had been squatting or sitting in the dirt, their rifles and pistols resting in their laps. The transformation to this ring of steel was impressively swift.

The convoy of police vehicles had arrived in Miraflores half an hour later than planned, but still well in advance of the VIP helicopter. From the start, I'd been on the lookout for a sympathetic officer I could trust. My plan was to get a message delivered to the Chief of Police through one of his men – I didn't want to have to launch into a cry for help in front of Hoppner. But the officers' behaviour was the definition of hostility: brutish expressions, antagonistic stances. It was hard to imagine being able to rely on any of them.

Besides, there hadn't been a single opportunity to talk to the police. Hoppner's greetings were accepted impatiently by the commanding officer, who cut him short to deploy four patrols around the streets of Miraflores. Their brief, he brusquely informed us, was to make the town 'safe' for the Minister and their *jefe*.

Evidently they now felt they'd achieved this goal, but even so the number of nervous fingers on triggers was disturbing. I watched the policemen follow their orders, recapitulate their parade-ground routines, and though I now understood my instinctive dislike of guns – that apocalyptic image of an open highway and empty brown seats was never far from my thoughts – I still felt overwhelmed by the excessive uniformed presence. Surrounded by automatic weapons in belligerent hands, I was starting to question the whole basis of my plan. Could I really just walk up to one of these people and request a rescue mission?

'Mr Sword Hoppner!'

The Minister was a surprisingly young man, and he leapt from the helicopter before it had reached the ground, forcing two bodyguards to make an undignified scuttle to catch up with him. He advanced on Hoppner, extending a slender hand garlanded by a heavy double cuff.

'Mr Hoppner is sufficient. How are you, sir?'

Though not matching our visitor's geniality, Hoppner was at least sincere in his reserved welcome. No one was under any illusions that real friendship existed between these men, but a working accord was well established. The foreigner with dreams had taken good care of the groundwork in winning himself this little slice of local government. Whether it would be enough to overcome the massive setback of the terrorist attack in the capital remained to be seen.

Beside the Minister in his natty charcoal suit, the Chief of Police was conspicuous for his economy of dress. A plain sky-blue shirt, creased drill trousers and boots shinier than I'd ever imagined possible. And, of course, the large, impenetrable sunglasses. He hardly spoke, keeping an older man's supposedly wise silence beside his more garrulous colleague. He shook hands briefly with

Hoppner, the greying moustache – cut with alarmingly straight edges – twitching in place of any actual word of greeting. Then, while the Minister put an ill-judged arm round Hoppner's shoulders and walked with him to the waiting SUV, the Chief turned to inspect the police cordon encircling the helicopter.

'I'm not here because I don't trust you,' the Minister chuckled. 'I'm here because His Excellency doesn't trust me. I tell him our Mr Sword Hoppner is just fine, no problem, he has these bombers under control, the bastard's probably dead already, maybe even hanging from a tree in the plaza, who knows, I'm sure he'll never disturb our conferences again, nothing to worry about. But His Excellency tells me I say these things because I'm too lazy to travel here, too lazy to make sure. Can you believe the shit I put up with? So. Here I am. To make sure. Who is this guy?'

'This is Mr Weston,' said Hoppner. 'He has recently taken over as head of security here.'

'Ah! Congratulations.' At this news, the Minister deemed my hand worthy of shaking. 'So, Mr Weston, I can rely on you to keep these sons of whores away from Santa Tecla, yes? Cut off the *cojones* of the first dirty-fingered peasant who even looks at a weapon. Especially those Indian fuckers.' His skin was sweaty, his grip limp. There was an almost feminine, even camp sensuality to the brush of his fingers against mine.

When the Minister was seated in the back with

Hoppner, I started the engine. Two police cars were already waiting, motors turning over, to escort us the short distance to the Parque Central.

'Shit, it's looking good here, Mr Sword Hoppner. Very picturesque. These houses, our ancestors built them well, yes, those conquistador cocksuckers? Maybe I should buy a place here. You could guarantee my safety from these commies, couldn't you, Mr Weston?'

His English was so good, so grammatical – if heavily Californian in drawl – that I was convinced he chose his expletives fully aware of their likely impact on his host. He seemed to find a good deal of amusement in teasing the righteous Hoppner with these harmless irritants peppered throughout his speech. There was nothing in the Code I'd seen prohibiting particular vocabulary, but, if his own abstinence was any guide, Hoppner was not a fan of the profanity, curse or oath, the four-letter word.

The Parque Central was almost deserted – Hoppner's orders that everyone should continue their normal work, schooling or domestic duties throughout the visit had been scrupulously obeyed – but a small delegation of the Miraflores geriatric community had assembled near the bandstand. As if afraid to be identified, they kept themselves largely hidden behind a couple of trees, watching the movements of these unwelcome visitors with apprehension.

The Minister spotted this audience immediately and bowed low as he climbed out of the SUV.

473

'A drink!' he exclaimed, striding over to the San Isidro's tables. 'Scotch, I think. Do they have Scotch?'

It was not quite eleven o'clock.

The remaining police vehicles drew up, disgorging the Chief and the entire complement of bodyguards and policemen.

'Look who it is, *jefe*! Our old friend, the Comandante,' said the Minister as Sánchez emerged from the hotel.

'Mr Hoppner, my men must make some checks,' said the Chief of Police in a voice as understated as his appearance.

'Of course. Whatever is necessary.'

'House searches. For weapons and explosives. One hundred, at random.'

'Comandante Sánchez. How very delightful to see you. The best Scotch you have, please. I particularly enjoy Talisker.'

'Would you ask your men to be sensitive?' said Hoppner. 'Last time—'

'My men are always professional.'

'*Jefe*, come sit down, for God's sake!'

A solid line of bodyguards and police remained behind to protect our guests from the mortal dangers of the Parque Central's drifting leaves and stray cats.

'Now, *jefe*, you must learn to smile. Our host is being most gracious, the sun is shining in this godforsaken rainy little corner of our great nation, a bottle of Scotch is on its way, and best of all El

Tigre himself is now a meek little waiter, proving beyond all reasonable doubt that there is a God and Right is on our side – was on our side even before Mr Sword Hoppner so thoughtfully brought it here from Oklahoma.'

Perhaps, after all, the defensive line of armed men wasn't such a bad idea. The Minister and the Chief together represented a plum target for any would-be terrorist in the vicinity. However out-numbered and outgunned the next Joaquim Tanadio might be, it would take only one well-tossed grenade, secretly stored since the days of Cuban military assistance, to take out two of the government's most valuable players. And me.

The Minister didn't like the Scotch. 'What is this? Christ be damned, Comandante, you only have blended crap?'

When Sánchez didn't rise, the Minister took off his sunglasses and, very deliberately, let them fall to the ground.

'Waiter?' He raised his hand, palm facing Sánchez, and beckoned him with curled fingers. A gesture I'd seen a couple of times in Miraflores, but he managed to make it look particularly insulting. 'I seem to have dropped my glasses.'

The briefest flash of anger crossed Sánchez's face. Hoppner's gaze was on him, commanding him, beseeching him. With just a short expulsion of breath, Sánchez bent down to pick up the sunglasses from the cobbles by the Minister's feet. As he handed them back to the grinning politician,

475

he caught my eye and I knew he was remembering our conversation.

The Minister's taunt infuriated me. This whole event felt more and more like a charade. These people had come all the way to Miraflores to perform a token search, drink imported spirits and insult their enemies. It felt like a class outing, a time-wasting junket. Maybe the whole point was the display – demonstrating the might of the police force and the scrutiny of the Ministry of the Interior to this wayward community – but all the same it was repellent to watch.

'We're going to have to drink a lot of this shit to kill the taste,' muttered the Minister dolefully, his whisky glass balanced on his palm.

'Does the President have any particular concerns?' asked Hoppner, no doubt equally irritated by his guest's behaviour. 'About Miraflores? About my approach to policing and governance here? I hope he understands that the abhorrent attack in Santa Tecla was not the work of anyone here.'

A bold-faced lie. Or was it? Had he carefully phrased his words to exclude the dead? In any case, the Minister neither believed him nor cared to legitimize the lie with a response.

'What is it, *jefe?* What are you staring at?' he said, turning round. 'Ah, I see what you mean! A gringo, by fuck! Mr Sword Hoppner, you're arresting gringos now? One of yours, I hope? We don't want problems with your ambassador because some drugged backpacking loser from Arkansas goes missing.'

'That is Hawken,' said Hoppner stiffly, not looking at the gaol. 'My previous head of security. He was guilty of a serious offence.'

'Hawken? Of course! I remember him.' Shaking his head in delight, the Minister turned to the Chief of Police. 'See that, *jefe*? See how fair this guy is? He even locks up his own men. What complaint could we possibly have with such a just individual?'

The Chief shared none of his enthusiasm. 'Who is now in charge of security?'

The antagonism in his voice made me stammer: 'I am.'

He wasn't impressed.

'You speak Spanish?' he said, switching to that language.

'Enough,' I continued in English. 'Keeping control doesn't require much conversation.'

'But you must gain authority. As an outsider—'

'We're all outsiders here,' said Hoppner quickly. 'Even you. But I can assure you that Mr Weston is performing his duties competently and correctly. I'm delighted with his work.'

'I am responsible for civil security,' declared the Chief. 'If I continue to leave Miraflores with no police, I must be satisfied.'

It suddenly occurred to me that he might want to test me in some way, perhaps through an arbitrary display of power over the people of Miraflores. Not only did the idea appal me, but I began to wonder if deceiving him in this small way now might harm my cause when I got a chance to beg his assistance. Hoppner was showing no sign of leaving me alone with the Chief or any other member of the police force. Perhaps, after all, I would have to deliver my SOS in front of him. As the Chief prepared to question me further, I, in turn, prepared to tell all.

Except neither of us got to say anything. Just as I was opening my mouth to make my plea, shout it if necessary over Hoppner's angry protest, Pamela's little Suzuki raced into the Parque Central.

Every policeman in the square raised his gun, some panicky, some calmly practised. When Pamela, her red hair flying, leapt out of the vehicle and strode past them all, taking not the slightest notice of the array of muzzles, they sheepishly returned their weapons to their sides.

She had changed into a long black skirt and an olive-green sweater. David stood up to intercept her but she pushed past him with ease. As she reached our table, Hoppner said, 'I thought you were taking the day off.' His voice was tightly drawn, the effort it cost him to stay calm apparent to all of us.

Staring down at him, her nose twitching spasmodically, Pamela said, 'Day off? I don't work for you any more.'

'Now, Pamela, I'm sure you don't mean that.'

'I've given you eight years – prime years, Mr Hoppner, when I could have been doing anything.

Eight years is enough for anyone to waste in one lifetime, don't you think?'

'This is not appropriate . . .'

Throwing an agitated glance at his VIP guests, Hoppner tried to dispatch her with a discreet hand signal. She ignored it. The Minister had assumed a bemused smile at this unexpected entertainment; the Chief of Police remained silent and expressionless.

'You once told me that our virtues define us,' Pamela said. 'That our virtues make us who we are.' She shook her head sadly. 'Mr Hoppner, I don't recognize you any more.'

'Now, stop this,' demanded Hoppner, his anger suddenly bursting through, his face a livid pink. 'Your behaviour is totally out of line. Our guests are here to see a model society, not some ludicrous exhibition. Go back to the compound, right now. You're harming the reputation of this town.'

'Can't you see it doesn't matter any more?' she cried. 'It's over! All of this . . .' She threw her arms wide to take in the Parque, the San Isidro, Sánchez. 'All of it is pointless now. You built this society for one reason alone: to prove that your Code could work. Have you forgotten that? You've become so obsessed with protecting your model society that you've sacrificed the very same Code it's supposed to promote!'

Shaking with rage, Hoppner stood up. 'Go home,' he whispered. 'We'll talk about this later.'

'There's nothing to talk about,' said Pamela. 'It's

479

over.' Turning to the Chief of Police, she pointed to the gaol and said in Spanish, 'The British man in the prison is innocent. You must free him.'

'Pamela!' stormed Hoppner.

The Chief said nothing, showed absolutely no reaction.

For the first time, she hesitated. She hadn't expected such lack of response. Her mistake was to turn instead to the Minister.

'His name is Hawken,' she said, her words louder and slower. 'He is innocent. You must free him.'

At first, the Minister too responded with a blank look. Then he burst out laughing. A cruel, patronizing laugh, as if Pamela were some little girl complaining to her father's guests about his meanness with pocket money.

Pamela was shocked by the reaction. In disgust, she turned away and marched back to the Suzuki.

'Go with her,' Hoppner muttered to me.

'But . . .' Much as I felt sorry for Pamela, would have liked to comfort her, I still hadn't made my pitch to the Chief.

'Go with her! Lock her in her room. I don't want any more disturbances when I bring these gentlemen to my house.'

I'd forgotten that the VIPs would be visiting the compound. There would still be time to speak to them there. Right now felt like a bad moment in any case, so soon after the Minister had ridiculed Pamela's own cry for help. My assumption that the police would march to the rescue the moment

I informed them of our predicament was looking increasingly weak.

When she reached the Suzuki, Pamela stopped and gazed up at the gaol. For a few stolen seconds she stood silent, staring at her incarcerated lover who looked down impassively from his high window. In that silent communion something came over Pamela: she grew taller, calmer. Barely acknowledging my presence, she climbed into the driving seat and restarted the engine, sending us gliding slowly out of the square.

In the back streets leading to the compound, we passed only two policemen. Neither looked remotely interested in us, busy as they were throwing chairs and books out of the primary-schoolteacher's house. The short, mild-mannered man stood on the steps of the school opposite, surrounded by his young flock, watching with remarkable forbearance as his few possessions were dismembered. Notebooks scattered; a glass decanter smashed. Even if Pamela had wanted to stop, I doubt there was anything we could have done for him.

I tried once or twice to engage her. 'Where will you go now?' I asked. 'Will you join another organization? A charity?' The barest fragment of a laugh, a scornful snort really, was all the response I got.

The compound guards opened the gate smartly for Pamela, closing it equally smartly behind us. Once again, I was locked in. I could act the part of Security Head all I liked, but there was still no chance of persuading those sullen men to let us drive out of there. For a moment, I thought about asking Pamela for help – would the guards allow her to take us out of the compound, in contravention of Hoppner's order? It was unlikely, and, besides, Pamela was already marching resolutely into the guesthouse. By the time I'd followed her in, the door to her room had slammed shut.

The Chief of Police, however aggressively silent and unresponsive, remained our best hope.

While I was waiting for Hoppner to return to the compound with his guests, I looked in on Alice and Leonard. They were playing a game of travel-Scrabble on the floor of their room. Her way of taking her mind off the police intervention we were praying for, I suppose.

Her eyes flew up as I walked in. I gave her a reassuring smile, promise that I had the situation under control. I didn't want to have to explain my revised plans in front of Leonard.

With his long legs splayed out across the floor, he was looking extremely uncomfortable. In fact, neither of them seemed particularly happy. Alice was struggling to find words to compete with Leonard's efforts. PALUDAL, NOWISE, CLITIC: I didn't need to ask to know they came from him. The little tray of letters in front of Alice was a disheartening mixture of useless consonants.

'Pamela just threw one hell of a scene with the

Minister,' I told them, trying to bring a little levity to our tense waiting game. 'Told him all about Hawken.'

'Oh dear,' said Leonard, with real anxiety in his voice. 'Heavens, I do hope she hasn't messed things up for Mr Hoppner.'

'Oh, who cares?' demanded Alice.

'We should all care. Miraflores is very special.'

'Leonard!' In a sudden flood of temper, Alice leapt to her feet. 'Where is Pamela?' she asked.

A clatter of furniture came from across the hall.

'In her room,' I said. 'She's pretty angry. I wouldn't bother her.'

The distant sound of engines drew me to the window. The SUV was rolling down the track, followed by two police cars, both slipping uncontrollably in the thick mud. The police stopped a couple of hundred feet short of the gate, while the SUV continued on into the compound. David was at the wheel, two of the largest bodyguards beside him. In the back sat Hoppner, the Minister and the Chief. No aides.

Alice walked up beside me and watched the VIPs follow Hoppner into his house. I'd give them a few minutes to get settled in this foreign environment – to grow receptive – and then march in with my bombshell. No time left for subtle approaches behind Hoppner's back.

'I want to check she's all right,' Alice said. 'Will you take my place? I can't do anything with those letters.'

Scrabble was the last thing on my mind, but I gave Alice an impatient nod and glanced at her letters.

P P Q N V W A.

'Thank you.' The door closed quietly behind me.

PAW? PAN? With the T on the board, that would give PANT, at least. By now the VIPs would be settled around Hoppner's table. Would he offer them coffee? Would he make it himself?

'Good luck,' murmured Leonard. 'Poor Ali's been struggling rather.' His clasped fingers looked absurdly long beside the tiny pieces of the travel set.

The door opened across the hall. Alice would have knocked, though I hadn't heard it. NAP? With the S on the board I could make SNAP or SPAN. No, wait, what about SPAWN? For a second, I couldn't help smiling.

Then Alice screamed.

Afterwards, I couldn't remember what Leonard did. I suppose he must have leapt up like me, run with me across the hall, burst into Pamela's room. Presumably he stood there, in silent shock, staring. But I have no recollection of Leonard being present at all.

She was hanging from a beam in the roof. She'd used the yellow climbing rope. Her neck wasn't broken: she'd choked herself to death.

Done it the hard way.

Her blotched face, her bloated tongue, her red hair tied in a careful knot. More images.

Far worse than the first time. I hadn't known Joaquim Tanadio, could barely see him in the darkened Parque Central. Cutting him free had been a distant operation, well removed from the reality of his death. Facing Pamela's wretched body, I had none of that detachment.

My impulse was to vomit, but the action never came. Though my limbs were shaking, I couldn't move.

Her long skirt fluttered a little in a breeze I couldn't feel. Her feet were bare and pointed outwards. No nail varnish. Where the rope held her neck, the skin was rubbed raw: she'd struggled even as she killed herself. The upturned chair – that terrible, necessary cliché – had been kicked halfway across the room. Hawken's baby bird cried piteously in its cardboard box.

'Oh please, no,' Alice was sobbing. 'Oh please, Lord, no.' Her hands were pressed halfway up her face, not quite blocking out the horrific sight.

With numb fingers, I righted the chair, placed it beside Pamela's body and found a penknife on her desk. The rope took for ever to cut. As the last strands began to break, I took hold of her round the chest and lowered her gently to the floor.

'I'm sorry, Alice.' My voice barely worked – a grating mess of constricted sound. 'I know you liked her.'

The confusion in her eyes was pain in the making.

'Why would . . . ?'

'She just . . .' I blinked at the corpse, realizing I had nothing whatsoever to say.

Slowly, Alice advanced, mouth fixed open, until she was looking directly down into that swollen face.

'Pamela.' Her voice was a shadow.

I wanted to put my arms round Alice, hold her and comfort her as I longed to be comforted. But the odd angle of her shoulders, the stiffness of her neck, warned me away.

'Look,' I said hoarsely, 'shouldn't we—?'

'Who did this?' she said, turning the blackest, most despairing eyes I've ever seen on me. 'Was it because she embarrassed Hoppner? Who did this to her?'

'Alice . . .'

'Did you do this?' she screamed. 'You were the only one here.'

I couldn't believe what she was saying.

'Alice, she committed suicide.'

'Suicide?' she spat. 'Like Freddy, you mean? Like that guy in the square?'

'Alice!' I gripped her arms, shook her, shouted louder still. 'Stop it now! This is me!'

And at that she collapsed, her outrage draining away. Her tensed arms seemed to shrivel beneath my fingers; her forehead dropped against my chest. 'I'm sorry,' she mumbled. 'I just . . .'

'It's all right, it's—'

'It's not all right! Nothing is all right. She's dead, she's dead, and I'm going to die, just like her!'

We both are, I thought hopelessly. I'd just lost a lot of faith in human nature – including the nature of the Chief of Police.

'Mark, I can't . . .' Her face dug a little deeper into my chest and I had to strain to hear her muffled words: 'I can't take this place any more.'

As I say, I don't know if Leonard saw that. I suppose he must have done.

The bodyguards had stationed themselves outside Hoppner's front door, stiff and faintly ridiculous with the hummingbirds fluttering and darting about them. As I marched up the stairs, they both advanced to block me. A little explosion somewhere in my head produced a ferocious Spanish rebuke – what it was I have no idea – and both men stepped quickly aside.

Whether I knocked as I went into the dining room, I can't remember. All that mattered to me was reaching the Chief of Police. *We're being held prisoner here. This man will kill us if you don't intervene.* The cavalry were just outside the gates – all they needed was their captain's order.

The three men looked put out to see me, per-haps because of the two large piles of US dollar banknotes on the table. The Minister's briefcase stood open to receive one pile; the Chief of Police had brought a canvas grip for his payoff.

How easy it is in practice to secure oneself a little island of virtue in the Third World.

'Get out,' Hoppner said grimly.

'You'd better be fucking discreet, Mr Weston,' said the Minister with a cold laugh, 'or my friend the *jefe* will have words with you.'

The cavalry was an illusion, their captain's allegiance already bought. There was no salvation for us here – nothing I could do. They stared up at me, waiting for an explanation.

'Pamela's killed herself,' I blurted out.

Hoppner closed his eyes at the news. A small gesture, but so much lay behind it. I knew he was picturing her at dinner, seeing himself berate her for her refusal to compromise, her refusal to accept the kind of pragmatism that culminated in large bribes to senior members of the ruling establishment. His lined throat twitched slowly up and down.

'Thank you,' he whispered. 'Leave us, please.'

When he opened his eyes again, it was to fix them on the table.

On the money.

A Code for Life, Section 11: Simplicity

Sometimes it is all too easy to forget what it is we are striving so hard to achieve. Life is complex, a virtuous life even more so. We have our livelihoods to think about, our families and our homes. Then we complicate matters by looking out for our friends, contributing to charities, analyzing moral dilemmas in search of the just solution, and straining to understand those who do us wrong so we can forgive them. We tie ourselves in knots.

In cutting through all this confusion, the virtue of simplicity keeps us grounded in reality. Truth is central to the virtuous life, and simplicity protects truth. That is why those who oppose us like to riddle their arguments with sub-clauses and parentheses, with twists and turns, concealing the truth beneath a mass of disorienting information.

Real truth is simple. 'Do unto others as you would have done unto you' is the golden rule of Christianity. A child can understand it, yet it encapsulates everything that matters most about the virtuous life. The greatest scientific and philosophical breakthroughs by humanity's finest minds, from Darwin to Einstein, Socrates to Descartes, can usually be summed up in not many more words. Only the mediocre need dress up their 'genius' in long-winded lectures or heavy volumes. Extraneous complexity often conceals a lack of true substance.

Simplicity protects us against many of the pitfalls of vanity, injustice and deceit. The simple person has no need of affectations, he does not scheme or waste time proving his worth or tailoring his image. He simply does what is right.

The simplest explanations are usually the truest, the simplest solutions the most effective, and the simplest approach to the virtuous life the most likely to succeed.

That's all.

CHAPTER 18

Pamela's death affected everyone in different ways. David, on the surface as sanguine as ever during the burial, disappeared into his new house for the rest of the day; Alice chose a bench on the gravel terrace and sat gazing over the forest below; I felt an urge to break something. Leonard, on the other hand, seemed eerily contented.

'It's all for the best,' he observed. 'After all, she was becoming quite disruptive, wasn't she?'

I'd just deposited Hawken's chick under a bush behind the guesthouse and I was convinced it was about to be eaten by some raptor. So unimportant after everything else that had happened, it just added to my depression and made me even more intolerant of Leonard's warped opinions.

'All that nonsense at dinner last night,' he went on, not sensing my irritation. 'And with the Minister today. Hard for Benjamin to concentrate on his work when she was attacking him all the time. She must have realized she was doing more harm than good. And Benjamin's right about that, after all: better to commit suicide than stay around causing problems in the world.'

'Careful, Leonard. You're not far off condoning his murders.'

'Is it really murder, though, or is Benjamin in fact carrying out a painful but necessary duty? After all, if you're going to build a morally perfect society, how can you let it remain filled with the morally sick?' He paused for a response then, seeing my revulsion, added, 'Nietzsche makes a good point. He says that a philosopher, to deserve our respect, must preach by example. It must be hard for Benjamin to do the things he does, but I think he certainly deserves our respect.'

The extraordinary thing was that, even as he voiced those awful claims, he still managed to retain his air of innocent pensiveness.

'Shall I show you the passage?' he offered, opening the book.

All I could do was walk away.

That evening, Hoppner wanted company. The only person willing to provide it was Leonard. While the two men shared a quiet dinner in the main house, I walked down the darkened lawn to the cliff wall and joined Alice on her bench. I wasn't sure if I was intruding on a silent vigil for Pamela or simply witnessing her despair at the impending test.

At last I was seeing her in the moonlight. It wasn't at all how I'd imagined it. No dancing, no casual smile beneath closed eyes. The safe comfort of Bequia was a long way away. She did not glow silver as I'd expected: her skin was ashen.

Eventually she said, 'I used to be able to make myself feel better by thinking of all the people in a worse situation than me.'

'There are still some,' I said lightly.

'There are always the Mormons, I suppose.'

'Who did you think of when you were stuck with Luca?'

'Impoverished single mothers in Glasgow,' she said with a faint smile. 'I'd give my right arm to be one of those now.'

'There is a way out of here,' I said.

In the light of the moon, Hoppner's fake lake shone. The tops of the highest trees were black silhouettes just beyond the wall. Something wild rustled its way through the branches.

When she didn't answer, I said, 'We can't get past the fence, and we can't hope for any help in Miraflores. But if we can get to one of those houses . . .' I pointed down the valley to the tiny islands of light dotted around the lake.

She looked at me then. 'You're crazy,' she whispered.

'It's an artificial lake. That means a dam, which means a road and probably maintenance people with transport. If we can get to the lake, we can borrow a boat to reach the dam.'

'It's thick forest down there, Mark. The whole

valley is wall-to-wall trees. We'd be lost in five minutes.'

'Absolutely not. All we have to do is aim downhill until we reach the river. Then we just follow it to the lake. Impossible to get lost.'

For a moment, she stared down into the blackness below. 'You mean tonight, don't you? You're actually talking about struggling through a snake-infested tropical forest in the middle of the night.'

'I'm talking about getting away from that barbiturate injection.' I sat back in exasperation. 'Alice, there's no other way out. If you take that test and he sentences you to death, I can fight and fight, but there's no way I'd win against eight guards.'

'Brave Mark,' she said absently. I don't know what she meant by it. She stood up to look over the wall. 'How were you planning to get down?'

'Wait one minute,' I told her.

I'd spent the last few days moving unimpeded around the compound, but now that I was organizing an escape I felt nervous even approaching the guesthouse. There shouldn't be anyone there: Leonard and Hoppner were eating dinner; David was in his new house; Pamela was dead. But moving quietly from the veranda to Pamela's room, I couldn't help looking over my shoulder every few seconds. As I opened her door I half expected to find a guard in there; Hawken, even.

494

Slipping inside, I left the door ajar while I hurriedly collected what I needed.

Alice was still standing by the wall when I got back, and she showed little surprise at the yellow climbing rope I pulled from Pamela's canvas equipment bag.

'Oh, Mark,' she said, smiling a little.

'Keep you voice down now,' I murmured. 'This would be hard to explain.'

I tied one end of the rope around three balusters. The wall seemed strong enough, but to be safe we would have only one person on the rope at a time. Pamela's remaining grappling hook was still tied to the other end and I left it there as a plumb when I dropped the rope down the cliff. Weighing the rope in my hands I could feel the hook hit the valley floor with a good ten feet to spare.

'It's probably about four miles to the lake,' I said. 'The sooner we go, the more chance we'll have of getting clear before Hoppner sends the guards looking for us in the morning. Let's get some food and water, any money you have, a coat and—'

'We have to wait for Leonard.'

Letting the rope drop, I looked at her. 'Leonard will be fine here.'

'We can't leave him.'

'Alice, it'll be OK. Hoppner will get him back to the airport, put him on a plane. Leonard isn't committed to doing the test.'

'I'm not leaving him on his own,' she insisted. 'I brought him here – I can't just desert him.'

'He doesn't need you.'

'It's not a question of need. It's the right thing to do.'

'Why is that suddenly so important?' I said with mounting frustration.

'Is there ever a bad time to start developing a conscience?'

'Yes, if it's going to get us killed!'

'Mark, I have no wish to get you killed – you go on ahead. I'm waiting for Leonard.'

I gave up. 'Fine,' I muttered. 'But we can't leave it too long.'

We decided to wait in the guesthouse so as not to draw attention to our escape rope should one of the guards patrol the grounds. While Alice headed off to her room to find suitable clothes for herself and Leonard, I hunted through the kitchen area for high-energy snack food and plastic bottles for water. A handful of granola bars, sickly sweet buns from the Miraflores bakery, some dried fruit – enough to sustain us for a night's hard walk, nothing more. Leaving the food piled on the kitchen table, I returned to Pamela's room to pick up the small backpack I'd seen by her desk.

When I walked out again, backpack in hand, David was standing at the guesthouse door.

He stared at me for a long moment, looked round at the food on the table, then back at me. He blinked twice. 'What are you doing?' he asked.

I couldn't think of any sensible answer to that.

'Nice to see you at last,' I said, mustering as

much confidence as I could manage, although my stomach was turning in on itself. 'We were worried about you.'

'Mark . . .' His eyes dropped to the backpack. 'Don't try it. You'll kill yourself. Don't try to climb out.'

My fragile hope collapsed. They'd already found the rope. We'd lost our escape route.

'Climb, David?' I stammered.

He turned towards the kitchen table. Pulling out a chair, he sat down, wearily picking up a couple of granola bars and turning them over in his hands.

'Don't do it, Mark. It's razor wire. On top of the fence. You'll cut yourself open. Bleed to death.'

Perhaps it was his lack of anger that brought mine to the surface. And he didn't know about the cliff rope: once I realized that, I threw down the backpack and marched over to him. 'Well, why don't you just let us go then? If you're so worried about us dying, why don't you open those fucking gates?'

'Mark. Please.' He kept his eyes down, refusing to look at me. 'It's not my decision.'

'That's bullshit! Hoppner can only function because you're there to support him every step of the way. You'll have just as much responsibility for our deaths as he does. It's only because people like you tolerate his madness that Hoppner can go on torturing and killing people.'

'No.' He shook his head. 'He could get someone else. Replace me. Find someone more supportive.'

'That's just not true,' I told him. 'You know how much he relies on you. He doesn't have that relationship with anyone else. Why don't you for once use your influence to stop all this!'

Abruptly, David leapt to his feet. 'I only want what he wants,' he cried, hurrying to the door.

'David . . .'

But he was already gone.

Piling the food and water into Pamela's backpack, I hid it behind one of the sofas and walked along the corridor to Alice's room. On the bed was a small pile of clothes, a wallet, two passports. She was ready. Now she sat at the desk, facing a small mirror propped against the wall, applying moisturizer to her cheeks and eyelids. There was no make-up to remove today. If it had been any of my business, I'd have said she looked more beautiful without mascara or eyeliner. A slight redness around the eyes offset her customary pallor.

'I got fed up and pulled it off the bathroom wall,' she said, gesturing to the mirror. What a small, restrained act of rebellion against the man who might easily be her executioner. 'Was that David you were talking to?'

This nightly ritual, the cleansing and anointing of the face, was one of the times I loved most with Katie. For her it was a chance to be silent, a moment's peace away from the contracts, the office, and later the unending demands of a new baby. Every trace of makeup would be melted away under a pad of cotton wool.

Those mysterious feminine bottles lining her dressing table. Unguents, scents, cleansers: I watched them applied with the fascination of a child.

Sometimes I would stand behind her, my hands resting on her shoulders, kneading with sleepy thumbs the soft flesh of her upper back. Sometimes I knelt beside her, my head in her lap, my arms around her waist, sensing the movements of her fingers against her face, imagining the crease of her smile. As Christopher grew inside her I stopped kneeling, feeling safer remaining upright, and though she noticed and minded the change in my behaviour she never said anything.

Alice's sadness drew me to her and I put my hands on her bony shoulders, trying not to think of Katie's more comforting shape.

'There's nothing you could have done for Pamela,' I said.

Her hand dropped to the desk, still with a spot of moisturizer whitening the tip of her middle finger. 'I never believed there was,' she whispered.

Odd to think that in an earlier age – in the present age, in some places – Pamela would have been condemned for what she'd done. Buried where four roads meet, a stake through her heart. Yet, in taking her own life, she'd lodged the most damning protest possible against Hoppner's corruption. Her virtue was safe from the taint of his moral scales. She'd made that tough choice he'd spoken of: protected what she most valued.

Alice was crying. Her shoulders jerked beneath my hands – convulsive, animalistic. I could feel each bone shift and slide around beneath her skin. Lowering my chin to her cheek, I wrapped her in my arms. We shook together in time to her sobs. The wetness of a single tear dampened my lip.

'Every time I think of her, I wish I could be more sorry for her,' she said. 'But the awful thing is, all I can do is feel terrified for myself.'

'We're getting out of here,' I told her fiercely. 'Hoppner won't be able to touch you.'

But her nod was half-hearted – unconvinced.

By eleven o'clock, I was getting angry with Leonard. Was he now so enamoured of Hoppner's murderous philosophy that he wanted to talk about it all night? What had happened to Hoppner's regular bedtime? If we left it much longer we might not reach the dam until late morning, when we would run the serious risk of being picked up by David and the guards before we got anywhere near a rescue vehicle.

Another thirty minutes and I would have to interrupt them – tell Leonard that Alice was deeply upset and needed comforting. Which, after all, wasn't far from the truth. While I paced the guesthouse hall, flicking impatiently through magazines whose words and images I couldn't absorb, Alice remained curled up on one end of a sofa: a fading spirit, coming dangerously close to giving up.

500

When the main door finally opened and Leonard walked in, I was about to berate him for leaving Alice alone so long. Unfortunately there was a problem: his walk was more of a stumble, his greeting little better than a slur. All I could do was stare at him in disbelief.

'Oh Christ, don't do this to me,' I muttered.

Rolling towards us, Leonard managed to avoid colliding with most of the furniture, but he caught his hip a vicious knock on the corner of a table. The impact went unnoticed; his smiling, vacant gaze didn't falter.

'Leonard,' cried Alice. Wrested momentarily out of her consuming fear, she sprang up and hurried over to him.

'Ali, darling!'

'Leonard, are you drunk?' She seemed to need to ask the question, even though the answer was abysmally clear.

'Certainly not.' The words were half-formed, almost unintelligible. 'Poor Benjamin needed some company, that's all. Terribly upset losing . . . losing . . . er . . .'

'Pamela,' said Alice, gripping hold of his arm as his top-heavy frame tottered sideways. 'He's lost P—'

'I think,' interrupted Leonard, groping for the sofa, 'I think I'll jus' sleep a little. Sorry, jolly tired suddenly.'

With his eyes already closing, Alice wheeled him smartly round. 'Not here, darling.' She met my horrified gaze with an impatient shake of her head. 'Help me get him to the bed,' she whispered.

All the great tricks I knew for sobering up fast went flying through my mind – the classic cold-water dunk, the chilli treatment, the forced run down the beach we'd developed on Bequia – and I knew none of them would work with this man. As I stretched his thin arm over my shoulder and half-carried him to his bed, I almost cried with frustration at his extraordinarily ill-timed binge.

There was, it was hopeless to deny, simply no way Leonard was going to be climbing down a ninety-foot cliff tonight.

His snores were throaty and saliva-drenched, louder than ever. Alice sat by his side, loosening his tie, turning his head to the side, stroking his arm. I gave him two minutes of sleep before I spoke.

'We can't take him.'

'Of course we can't take him.'

I nodded, a little surprised at her easy agreement. 'So let's make him comfortable, write a note, then get the hell out of here.'

She raised her eyes to me. 'I told you: I'm not leaving him here.'

'You're not serious.'

'You go. I can't leave him.'

'Alice, if you don't, you will die tomorrow!'

'I'm sorry,' she said, standing. 'Thank you for trying to help me. But I brought him here, I put him in danger, and I can't just run off and leave him all alone.'

'But you have to get out! What about your child?'

'Oh, Mark, you don't have to remind me about my child.'

'Listen to me,' I said urgently. 'When you first told me about Leonard, you said you were willing to hurt him to win yourself a nice lifestyle. How much more important to save your life! How much more important to save the life of your child. You told me everything is a compromise, that sometimes we have to make sacrifices. Wouldn't you have said this was worth a small sacrifice? Worth deserting Leonard for?'

'Yes,' she nodded reluctantly. 'I would have said that.'

'Well, then!'

She looked down. 'I'm sorry,' she whispered.

The anger I felt towards her, the resentment I nursed at her suicidal obstinacy, was inexplicable. It was her life. If she died, I would always be able to say I'd done my best by her. I could race down that cliff and through that black forest far faster on my own. A lift to the capital, a flight home and I'd be able to pick up the family life I wanted more than anything else. Forget about Alice. I was in love with Katie, not her.

Yet I couldn't leave. Much as I longed to escape that death-ridden compound, even felt a kind of thrill at the thought of testing myself against that forest, I just couldn't bring myself to abandon her.

I retreated to the veranda to wallow in my anger. The clear night had thrown up a million wondrous stars and I hated all of them. Every inch they crept across the sky was an inch nearer dawn – a fraction closer to her test. I already knew I wouldn't be able to watch it, however much Alice might want me there for support. The thought of witnessing the moment when she gave away some critical clue to her flawed character and unknowingly sentenced herself to death was unbearable. I would be in the garden, in bed – anywhere but in that windowless cabin.

A light step on the floorboards; her arm brushed mine. She too had been crying. I kept my face turned to the dark.

'Go,' she said.

'I'll go tomorrow night.'

'He might do your test straight after mine.'

'He only does one a day.' It might be true – at least, if Alice failed and Hoppner again wished to 'show his respect'. I felt sick at the thought.

Leonard's snores floated out through the windows, dissipating in the emptiness of night.

'You and I . . .' she said.

Wistful thoughts. Her presence felt solid, strong – very much alive.

She gave a little laugh and said, 'It would have been pretty unpleasant down there. Wet . . . scary . . . I'm scared of spiders. And bats. You'd have got fed up with me screaming every time something touched my shoulder.'

'Stop it. Please stop it,' I said, close to tears again.

'Mark, sweet Mark.' She ran her fingers down my stiff arm, finding the crook of the elbow, resting her thumb there. 'I don't think Mark is the right name for you. Too short. Too abrupt. If I were Katie, I would call you Marcos.'

Something seemed to give way in my knees. My mother's Spanish name for me.

'I'm sorry I couldn't let you save me.' She leaned in, resting her face against my shoulder. Her cheek twitched, as if she were trying to smile. 'There is something you can do for me, though.'

I didn't answer, didn't want to have to tell her I couldn't be there when it happened.

'I know you don't feel the same way about me as I do about you . . .' she began.

I pulled back to look at her face, wiping the tears from my own cheeks. 'Of course I do.'

'Mark . . .' She smiled – so warmly, so gently. 'Just shut up a moment.'

A flutter of wings above us: a bat, supposedly terrifying to her, although she made no move. Her eyes remained on my face, sharing with me the scrap of time she had left.

'I wish . . .' I began.

'It doesn't matter. It really doesn't.'

The smile didn't waver. I wondered if she was thinking of the baby inside her, or those other children she would never now have. Had she already chosen names for them? Would one of them have been called Christopher?

Standing on tiptoe, she brought her mouth up to mine and kissed me. Through the touch of her lips I realized for the first time that she was shivering. Trembling. 'I won't tempt you away from Katie again,' she said. 'But I would like to sleep beside you tonight.'

The smile was gone. No more words: she wouldn't ask twice. She walked back into the guesthouse and I saw her go to my room.

She stayed awake most of the night. The shivering was gone, only a stillness now – an acceptance. The hours trickled by. The sounds of the night, slipping unhindered through my open window, became the fabric of reality that lined our small, condemned world. Her thin body, always so vulnerable, seemed unusually hot against my skin. Her leg on mine left a permanent memory. Her breath.

Her breath, the first thing that would go.

'It's Smith, by the way,' she murmured sleepily.

'Smith?'

'My real name. Alice Smith. Boring as hell, but I thought you might like to know.'

I touched my fingertips to her slender neck, remembering how I'd wanted to do just that on our first night in Miraflores. 'Mine's Greenock.'

'Right,' she chuckled. 'I had to change mine – he wouldn't have believed Smith was genuine.'

'He'd believe anything, so long as you managed to say it under hypnosis.'

She went quiet for a while. A little of the tension in her body had dissolved. 'You're a saint to stay, Mark,' she whispered. 'You should be halfway down the valley by now.'

'You're the saint. What you've done for Leonard . . . He'll never appreciate what you've done.'

'I'm only trying to make good my wrong.'

'No, it's more than that. To stay here with him even though . . . I should tell Hoppner – he'd probably declare the test unnecessary and hand you your five million on the spot.'

'Sure, he would,' she said, turning over. Sleep was starting to tug at her consciousness. 'He wouldn't listen to you. Background information. It would bias him.'

'True.'

'You mustn't let me sleep. Got to go back to Leonard before . . .'

The drowsiness in her voice was infectious. My hand slipped off her shoulder. I rolled over, folding myself into her back, my knees under her thighs. With silent apology, I banished Katie from my mind for those last few hours and concentrated my love on Alice's neck. My arm traced the line of hers, my palm cupped around her little curled hand.

'Alice?'

Something was itching at my tired mind. There was no answer from the sleeping girl.

My eyelids closing, it was so tempting to let go.

It would bias him.

Something. Something important . . .

I realized my eyes were shut – had been shut for a few minutes. Briefly asleep, but something important was holding me back.

Bias.

One hundred per cent fair.

Suddenly I was wide awake. Leonard's snores loud and clear. Alice's breath whistling softly through her lips.

What would it take? How could I make sure?

Afraid to wake her, to ruin the chance, I eased myself away from her in stages, pausing to listen for any interruption to that soft breathing, ready to freeze until sleep returned. But she was gone, tiredness numbing all her senses. Sliding off the bed, I lowered the covers gently back over her and picked up my clothes.

A piece of paper was readily to hand on the desk. For a pen, I had to search the kitchen cupboards and table before I thought of looking in Pamela's room. I scribbled the note at her desk, careful to keep my eyes away from the beam she'd used.

Four thirty in the morning, but the guards might still be alert. Barefoot, I slipped out of the guesthouse, crouching low to minimize my silhouette against the lightening sky. Would Hoppner's uncharacteristic drinking with Leonard change his sleep pattern? I prayed the early rise was too ingrained for a little alcohol to disrupt it.

It was vital he spotted the note as he stepped out of the house for his walk: I left it pinned under a stone on his veranda, four feet in front of the door. Above my head, the hummingbird feeders hung eerily still.

My feet were freezing from the dewy grass. It was just the sort of stupid detail that might wreck everything. After stripping off my clothes and checking again that the door stood very slightly ajar, I slipped back into bed, keeping my icy feet well away from Alice. Not the slightest change in her breathing.

Neither of us had thought to close the curtains. Gradually the room grew lighter. As the blackness receded, objects started to take form, shadows appearing beside them. My breathing had taken on the rhythm of Alice's sleeping body, but now I grew afraid the light would wake her, and my breaths became irregular. This in turn seemed bound to disturb her sleep. I wanted to close the curtains, but I couldn't risk getting out of bed a second time. The scene was perfectly set; if she woke now, she would hurry back to Leonard. Telling myself to stay calm, I concentrated on making as little movement as possible in that small bed.

The clouds rolled in around us shortly before dawn. Thick, blanketing clouds, which lessened the light falling on Alice's face, but which gave me new cause to panic. What if Hoppner couldn't even see my note for the cloud? What if he walked right past it, feeling his way across the veranda and down the steps to the lawn by habit alone? I could see nothing through the window. Trying to remember what should have been visible, I thought there might have been a young tree just outside. Surely I should have been able to see at least the tip of a branch?

Perhaps Hoppner would trip on the stone, I hoped.

I lifted my arm off Alice's side to check my watch. Six forty-two. He should have been up by now. It wasn't going to happen. Beside me, Alice shifted a little, her breath faltering. Locking myself in that position, I waited for her to settle back to sleep. My back was aching from too many hours in a cramped, unmoving knot. The urge to cough was overwhelming.

A sleepy snuffle, then back to regular breathing.

To take my mind off my own body and the multitude of signals it was sending out – demanding a shift of position, a scratch, a cough – I thought back to how Katie and I had tiptoed around the sleeping Christopher in those first few months. He had not slept easily: he hated any change to his feeding routine; room temperature had to be kept low, the lights dimmed; often one of us would need to spend twenty minutes walking slowly up and down the room with C draped over a shoulder.

False hopes were common – his eyes would seem to close, our lullabies or purring chatter would die away, and then suddenly he'd be wide awake and screaming. But that moment when he finally dropped off was sweet indeed. We'd lay him on his back in the cot, and his little arms would drift up beside his ears, his head tilted just a fraction to one side. A downy, sleeping starfish. Sometimes we would just sit there, shoulder brushing shoulder, watching him dream. To think I could trust myself to do that alone now was exhilarating. Such a small, miraculous breakthrough.

Leonard's snoring was so loud, and my thoughts of home so absorbing, that I almost didn't hear the creak of the first footstep on the veranda. But as Benjamin Sword Hoppner passed softly from the door of the guesthouse through the hall and down the corridor towards us, I felt faint with relief. His footsteps came to a halt just outside the room.

Easing the covers halfway down our naked bodies, I folded my arm around Alice's chest. The first knock sounded and I felt her jerk awake.

'Mark?'

His voice was very soft. To Alice's sleep-fuddled brain, that short call would have made no sense. I let every muscle in my body relax and closed my eyes.

At the sound of the door swinging open, Alice's body spun round in my grip until her face was against mine. 'Mark!' she cried.

Whether she'd been awake long enough to understand what was happening, I don't know. In any case, her reaction was perfect. I opened my eyes to see Hoppner in the doorway, staring open-mouthed at our illicit, unimaginable union.

'What . . . ?'

Hoppner took two steps into the room. Alice gave a cry of terror and leapt off the bed, pulling the sheet after her. Not stopping to wrap it around herself, she fled into the bathroom and slammed the door.

'I just came to . . .' said Hoppner, still in shock. 'Your note said to . . . to wake you . . .' He waved the piece of paper uncertainly. Then the full force of comprehension hit him: 'You were sleeping together?' he roared.

I did my best to act the part. Where Alice was experiencing it for real, I had to simulate that shock of the supposed adulterer found out. Rolling off the bed, I scrambled for my trousers; my hands were shaking anyway, just from the tension of the moment.

'I forgot about the note,' I stammered. 'I . . . I didn't know she'd come again.' For the first time in my life I felt a kind of exhilaration in lying.

'This has happened before?' His face was turning red. Beneath the pressed shirt, his chest was heaving with outrage.

'I'm sorry, Mr Hoppner. She—'

'She's a married woman!' He marched to the bathroom door. 'Mrs Williams, come out of there, please.'

There was no reply. I thought I could hear her crying. The poor creature – but I couldn't have forewarned her: the authentic quality of her shock and fear was crucial. Hoppner tried the handle, found it locked, and stormed out of the room. When he returned with the four nightshift guards, I was dressed and Alice was still barricaded in the bathroom.

'Break it down,' he told the guards.

As the door smashed open beneath their weight, Leonard wandered into the room. His hair an unruly mess, his eyes pink and his spindly body clothed in nothing more than a pair of greying Y-fronts, he looked ghastly. At the sight of so many people, such violent activity, he stopped short. Next moment, Alice was being hauled out of the bathroom, the sheet still clutched around her breasts and waist.

'What's happening?' cried Leonard.

Hoppner hadn't seen him come in. Now he turned and announced, 'Your wife is a whore. A common slut.' He looked back at the guards and changed to Spanish: 'Take her to her room. Let her dress. Then bring her outside.'

As Alice was dragged past me I caught her gaze for just a second, and tried to convey as much reassurance as I could. Her face was white from shock, but when she saw Leonard the guilt brought a red flush to her cheeks. His long fingers reached out for her hand, too late to touch her before she was pulled away.

When Hoppner and the remaining guards had left the room, I walked slowly over to the shaken philosopher. He was my one regret – the unavoidable victim in my last-ditch plan.

'I don't understand,' he said.

'Get dressed,' I told him softly. 'Go and pack your bags.'

'She came to your bed? She slept with you?'

'I'll explain later.'

'She told me she loved me. She lied to me!'

'Leonard, this isn't helping.'

Listening to the sounds in the next room, I hated to think of Alice forced to dress in front of those guards. Her misery and distress seemed to seep through the wall. All of it necessary; all of it horrible.

'How could she lie to me like that?' he said in a plaintive voice. 'How could she make me love her?'

There was no way I could tell him anything more yet. I left him standing there and walked outside to find Hoppner waiting, an outline in the cloud. He glowered at my approach.

Alice appeared at the door of the guesthouse, flanked by two guards. She was dressed entirely in black. Funeral black. As she walked towards us, unhesitating, the silent cloud parted in roiling currents, swirling round to meet behind her. For a second even Hoppner seemed to waver, his anger briefly quelled by that ethereal dignity. But he straightened his straight back a little more and said, 'Take her to the cabin.'

Alice did not need to be told she was going straight into her test. 'God deliver me from evil,' she said softly, as the guards led her off.

I followed them to the cabin, where Hoppner turned to me and said, 'Go back to your room.'

Alice was standing a few feet beyond him; the guards were waiting for Hoppner to unlock the cabin.

'I want to be there,' I said.

'Go back to your room! I'll come for you when it's your turn.'

'Are you angry with me?' I said. 'What for?'

'What for? What for?' he snarled. 'Are you going to deny you spent the night with another man's wife?'

'So what? Is that so terrible?'

He was shaking his head. 'I thought you were a good man, Mark. But you have no conception of morality, do you?'

'Does sleeping with someone's wife make me so bad?'

'It was a vile, terrible thing to do.'

'Well, what about her?' I said indignantly. 'Isn't she just as guilty?'

'Mark!' screamed Alice. 'What are you saying?'

'Of course she is,' he thundered. 'But that doesn't lessen your—'

'You mean she's a bad person?'

'Are you mocking me?' he shouted.

I matched his anger. 'Are you saying we're bad people?'

'You watch your tongue!'

'I'm asking you a question! Are we—?'

'You're both wicked!'

His judgement was screamed across the compound. Fragments of sound echoed off the swirling, enclosing cloud. I took a slow breath.

Oh Lord, let him be true to his word.

'If that's what you really believe,' I said quietly, 'then how can you possibly give us a fair, unbiased test?'

The new republic in the clouds
Is all the rage, and eager crowds
   Are flocking here to see it.
Where could they find a dwelling-place
Fitter than this, where Wisdom, Grace
   And Love pervade the scene?

[The original 'Cloud Cuckoo Land' described
shortly before its visionary founder reinvents himself as a tyrannical god who roasts dissenters.]

Aristophanes, *The Birds*

CHAPTER 19

To say that Benjamin Sword Hoppner was angry would be an understatement. He wanted us both to die, I've never been surer of anything in my life. I'm less certain whether the reason was his new friendship with Leonard, so offended by Alice's infidelity, or genuinely the principle that all truly bad people, including adulterers, should be removed from the face of the earth. For ten minutes he raged at me, calling me every name in the book, accusing me of invalidating his test deliberately – which, of course, was true, whether or not he believed it – and swearing that both of us would rot in Hell.

But he knew from the start he couldn't test us.

All those times he'd talked of his fairness, his determination to avoid bias in judgement, must have been as starkly memorable to him at that moment as they were to me. Yes, he'd sacrificed his lieutenant to appease Miraflores; yes, he'd bribed the government and police to stay away: but for each of those transgressions he'd had a pragmatic excuse – an end that justified the means. This was quite different. Every fibre of his distorted being

518

was screaming for us to die, but to give in to those urges would have been to renounce his most precious conviction.

There was simply no moral way he could do it.

'Just go,' he whispered, his chin sinking into his chest.

David spent half the morning trying to arrange a car to take us back to Santa Tecla. He was angry, too, though he didn't express his feelings as volubly as Hoppner. His anger bubbled quietly, revealing itself in his body language and his curt replies. He stood over us while we signed non-disclosure agreements – Hoppner's one condition on our freedom – and then whisked the papers away without a word.

Few of the vehicles in Miraflores were in any condition to drive all the way to Santa Tecla, most of them suffering from the same kind of all-over fatigue as Sánchez's car. The newest model – the white car Tanadio had driven – was impossible to locate. For some reason, no one in Miraflores was being cooperative. Eventually, David just threw the keys of the SUV at me.

'Leave it at the airport. I'll have someone collect it.'

'Why don't you come with us?' I said quietly. 'You've given so much of your life to this madness. Why don't you try something else? A good cause of your own?'

'And leave Mr Hoppner alone? He's in a bad

way. You've hurt him. Did you think about that? Before you fucked her?'

'David, I'm really sorry.'

But my apology went unacknowledged. He told me where to leave the keys at the airport, then turned his back on me.

'The gate?' I called after him.

'They know.'

Watching him walk away, I felt oddly hurt. I'd had no quarrel with David. He was just a man whose deep loyalty had been pledged to the wrong leader. It was upsetting to me that we should have to part like this. But then the realization that we were finally getting out came flooding back, and I hurried over to the guesthouse to tell Alice.

Out, free from Hoppner's control, escaping in his car down that long empty road to civilization. The relief was immense, but so was the sadness. Something about that last night with Alice still haunted me, as I knew it did her. When she'd finally understood that she was free, that Hoppner could not now ever put her through an impartial test, she'd been euphoric, but at the same time I knew she felt regret. I was on my way home to Katie and Christopher, and that was all I could have asked for, yet the thought of leaving Alice at the airport – saying a muted goodbye – was a bitter one.

For the first hour I had to drive slowly through the thick cloud that still choked the whole valley. It thinned near Felipe's restaurant, and shortly after that we began to see signs of normality, reassuringly far removed from Hoppner's world: impoverished shacks, little subsistence plots of maize and citrus, a circle of dozing *campesinos*.

As if in silent protest at Alice's behaviour, Leonard had taken a seat in the back after more or less ordering her to sit beside me. She said very little, mostly just watching the road with steady, unwavering concentration. Her hand moved on to mine at one point: a reassuring squeeze, nothing more. Then it was back in her lap.

'Was last night all a set-up, then?' she asked. 'I see now how you made it work. Was that the only reason you . . . ?'

I glanced at Leonard in the rear-view mirror. His face and all his body were tensely drawn.

'No,' I said. 'I didn't think of it until afterwards.'

'Oh.'

'But, Alice, I am going back to Katie now.'

'I know,' she smiled sadly. 'I've never doubted that.'

She turned slightly in her seat, gazing out of the side window, away from me. Behind us, Leonard's finger began a rhythmless tapping on the door panel.

Suddenly he shifted forward on his seat. 'You would have failed your test, Alice,' he blurted out.

He was rocking back and forth now, his nervous energy growing ever stronger. The fingers of his right hand were clenched, pressed against his cheek.

'Leonard . . .'

'You lied to me. About everything. You never wanted to send that money to Asia, did you?'

She nodded slowly. 'I'm sorry, Leonard.'

'You would have failed that test!'

'Leonard!'

I glared at him in the mirror, but all his attention was on Alice. He seemed desperately distraught, as if this failure of virtue was a greater betrayal even than the betrayal of his love. She had lied to him about her feelings, she had used him to get to Hoppner, but, worst of all, she'd been found to be immoral. Was that really how his priorities lay?

Looking out at that desolate country of forests and abandoned fields, of lonely houses and endless empty road, I felt inexpressibly weary. I longed to settle down, just for a while to have roots and a place I belonged, away from those empty foreign roads. Had my parents meant to keep moving for ever? From embassy to embassy, country to country? Where would they have stopped? What kind of life did the rootless have when they grew old?

I had the key to a settled life so nearly within my grasp. But would I be able to make things work with Katie and Christopher? There were no more barriers, nothing stopping me going straight back to them, yet still I was afraid I would somehow screw it up.

'Mark, I want to talk to Alice.'

'So, talk.'

'I mean alone.'

'Then you'll have to wait until Santa Tecla.'

'I want to talk to her now.'

Sensing my exasperation, Alice put a light hand on my shoulder to calm me. The warmth of her skin melted through my shirt.

'Let's take a short break,' she said.

I sat on the warm bonnet of the car, gazing down the road towards a coast I couldn't see – a coast which had come to represent in my mind everything Miraflores was not. It was escape, it was confusion and freedom, anarchy and moderation. It was normality.

Alice had obediently followed Leonard off the road, out of sight behind a line of trees. Whatever he wanted to talk about, I knew she would give him a patient hearing. I also knew he would achieve nothing.

A solitary jet fighter appeared in the distance. Tearing through the baking blue sky, swooping low across the hills, it seemed utterly irrelevant to the benighted nation it served. What good was air power to a people struggling to feed itself? It reminded me of the grandiose arrival of the Minister and Chief of Police in Miraflores: the helicopter, the ring of guns, the Scotch. Hoppner's friends in high places.

A slight chill ran through me as I realized it

wasn't beyond his powers to have us intercepted in Santa Tecla. Might he change his mind? A quick call to his VIP buddies, perhaps the promise of another pile of cash, and the order would be put out to have us arrested at the airport. Any number of fictitious crimes could be pinned on us. Would Hoppner sink that low?

Breaking off that paranoid train of thought, I glanced at my watch and was surprised to find they'd been gone nearly twenty minutes. What were they talking about? Was Leonard reprimanding? Was he pleading? Did he honestly think he stood a chance of changing her mind? Convincing her through the power of logic to fall in love with him? Or was this all about bitterness – condemning her for her deceit and her failure to match up to his moral standards?

Suddenly, in the midst of all those questions, I knew Leonard was past arguing about any of that.

I leapt off the car and started running.

Through the line of trees. Where were they? I found myself in an old plantation: once-loved trees grown wild; a fruit I didn't recognize. Rows and rows of a crop no one would harvest, the space between them a mass of creepers and coarse weeds. I yelled her name. No answer. I burst through a clump of tangled bushes, already half-crazed with fear.

'Alice! Where are you?'

My foot caught in a creeper and I sprawled

524

forwards, my shoulder slamming agonizingly into the ground. Stumbling up, I turned and sprinted further into the plantation. The light grew dimmer as the trees closed in.

'Leonard! Alice!'

Rotting grey-yellow fruit lay among the mess of decaying leaves and the carcasses of abandoned machinery. Something glinted on the ground. A rifle shell. What else was here? Landmines?

'Alice!'

I already knew it was useless calling for her. Charging back towards the road, fighting away the branches that pulled at my shirt, I heard a small voice say my name in the undergrowth near by.

She was lying flat on the ground, her head to one side, her left cheek against the soft grey earth. Leonard sat next to her, cross-legged, his long, strong hands folded neatly in his lap. He wouldn't look at her, keeping his eyes on me as if uncertain what praise or criticism I might have to offer.

Of course I was too late to make a difference. But still I fell on my knees and fought to resuscitate her, bringing her head up and filling her lungs from mine, drawing false hope from the warmth that still lingered in her blue lips. I did everything possible. I pumped her heart, breathed useless air into her again and again, trying not to see the ghastly bruising around her neck.

Leonard waited patiently until I had to give up. 'She would have failed the test, Mark,' he said, shaking his head. His eyes were a mess of confusion and comprehension: understanding my pain, while resolutely failing to grasp why I should want to bring her back in contravention of Hoppner's rules. 'She said herself she'd rather be dead if she failed.'

'You stupid . . . stupid . . .'

I couldn't say any more, could barely see him through my tears. Only Leonard, only the great thinker, could keep his innocence after this.

'She was a detriment to her world,' he was saying. 'She wouldn't have wanted to live with that.'

The rocking had started again. He understood, despite his new convictions, that something was terribly wrong. I wiped my eyes clear. Still he was gazing at me, almost pleading now for my blessing.

'Mark?'

I took her in my arms, that thin little body, and carried her to the road. Her head fell back, exposing the contusions at her throat to the harsh realism of the midday sunlight. My mind was dominated by just one thought. The peripheral was invisible to me. Leonard was already forgotten: he was no longer human; he was a machine, a mere extension of Hoppner's viciousness. I laid Alice down as gently as I could in the back of the SUV and pulled the door shut. By the time Leonard had stumbled out of the trees, I was in the driving seat and spinning the vehicle around. I didn't look back.

★   ★   ★

There is always someone responsible, even when the murderer is innocent. I wanted to seize Hoppner by the throat and deal him the same fate Alice had suffered, confront him with the reality of his meddling before his sick life bled out of him. After all the fear of the morality tests, seeing Alice killed in that meaningless way had filled me with such disbelief, such wrath. I could barely comprehend that the warm, troubled but generous spirit I'd known only a matter of days was already extinguished. Simply gone.

I stopped for one thing, using an abandoned wooden crate in that Miraflores alley to reach the electricity meter. If anything, the cloud in the valley was thicker now, and when I looked down the ground was barely visible. With Freddy's gun in my hand I jumped blindly, hardly noticing the savage jolt when I hit the cobbles.

The streets of Miraflores were filled with people carrying suitcases, animals, furniture – strange wraiths through the cloud. The black armbands, removed for the ministerial visit, were back in place. Every house was wide open. One church bell chimed interminably. I understood none of it until I passed through the Parque Central and Sánchez stepped out in front of the SUV.

'Don't go down there, Mr Weston,' he said. And I think he was genuinely trying to help me. He pointed towards the gaol, and though I couldn't see the building through the cloud I knew what the gesture must mean. 'Mr Hoppner made a deal with him.'

'What's going on here?'

'We are finished with his Code. You are right. We have made ourselves slaves too long for American money. It is time to stand on our own.'

'You're leaving the town?' I said in disbelief.

'If necessary,' he shrugged. 'They are angry down there. Perhaps they will call in the army. You should not go, my friend. They are very angry.'

'It doesn't matter,' I said, pressing down on the accelerator.

Nothing mattered except Hoppner. The man who'd caused it all. The man whose demands had forced his model town's leaders to attempt a lynching, who'd killed Freddy and driven Pamela to commit suicide, who'd turned gentle Leonard into something unrecognizable and monstrous.

Murderous vengeance.

Visibility in the forest was almost nil. At the speed I took that track, the SUV came close to flipping over a dozen times. Brakes were useless in the thick mud. Not that I wanted to slow down. With the accelerator on the floor, I slammed through the compound gate a split second after the guards had leapt clear. Careering across the lawn, I braked hard, shredding the turf, to come to a halt somewhere in the middle of the garden.

Where, exactly, was hard to tell. I turned off the engine and stared into a blank universe. The cloud, on that open patch of hillside, rolled and churned in the wind. Gusts struck me the moment I stepped out of the car. Flurries of cloud seemed to rear up to attack me. But in all that movement there was no sound: the birds gone, the rustling of trees blotted out by the fog-like wall all around.

No sound, except the flat squelch of footsteps walking towards me. I knew the pace, the rigid forceful step even before he emerged from the haze. He'd cleaned himself up, shaved, found a new set of clothes. The bruising on his cheeks rendered his taut face sharper still.

'Mark,' he said, coming to a halt a few feet from the SUV. His voice, in that one syllable, was amused – expectant.

'Get lost, Hawken. This is nothing to do with you.'

'Oh, but I have a bone to pick with you,' he replied, starting forward again.

'I said, get lost!' Freddy's gun was in my hand and pointing at him before I'd finished the sentence.

The slight smile that had been playing at the corners of Hawken's mouth disappeared. Staring first at the gun, then at me, he murmured, 'I doubt you even know how to use it.'

Behind him four guards came running up. With a sharp growl, Hawken ordered them away. Their mouths hanging open at the sight of us, the men retreated to the gatehouse.

'Move away,' I told Hawken. 'Don't make me

use this.' I snapped off the safety catch, curling my finger tight around the trigger.

'You wouldn't dare,' he scoffed. 'You don't have it in you.'

'Back off and I won't kill you. I'm only here to—'

I didn't get any further. With a sudden roar, Hawken leapt at me, propelling himself the whole distance between us from a standing jump. And I pulled the trigger.

Nothing happened.

That is, the gun did nothing. Freddy's precious acquisition was a dud. Whether it was the ammunition or the mechanism itself that was screwed, those Santa Tecla dealers had seen him coming a mile off.

I managed to pull the trigger twice more, each time more desperately than the last, before Hawken's chest crashed against my arm and the gun was sent spinning away into the cloud. There was no time to curse my bad luck, nor appreciate the irony of Freddy's posthumous revenge. Hawken's arms had closed around my body and his weight carried us both flying across the lawn. The impact on landing crushed the wind out of me and I lay paralysed beneath him, unable to breathe.

Had he stayed where he was, I think he would have killed me by sheer suffocation. But Hawken was a fighting man, and he was on his feet a second later, pulling me with him and balancing me upright just long enough to plant a brutal sledge-hammer in my stomach. Doubling up, I crumpled again, still gasping for air.

Hawken bent down and gripped hold of my arm, pulling me back up. This time, I was ready for him. As the blow came, a straight jab with his right fist, I swung sideways and kicked hard against his knee. Off balance from his own missed punch, Hawken fell forward the moment his leg folded. I followed up with a hard kick to his stomach. Before I could straighten up to strike again, he had rolled away down the lawn, out of my reach.

I ran after him but he was already up, and he met my charge with a savage high kick. It caught me in the chest and sent me flying sideways. I landed on gravel and realized finally where I was: the terrace above the cliff. Looking up, I could see the low wall, a bench, the shadowy outlines of the tree tops.

Next moment, Hawken's hand was at my throat, and I was being dragged upwards. He hit me with his fists, with a knee under my chin, and finally with an elbow jabbed hard against my temple. Collapsed on my knees, I could barely move. Stepping back, he turned, spun his body, and brought his foot flying round to smash into the side of my head.

The blow must have knocked me unconscious. I found myself lying on the wall above the cliff, Hawken's palm slapping repeatedly against my aching face. His arctic eyes glared down at me.

'Wake up,' he snarled. 'I want you to feel the drop.'

'Wait,' I shouted as his hands moved to my side, ready to give the final push.

'Think about what you did to Pamela.'

'No, Hawken, wait!'

Grasping desperately at the wall, my left hand found a hold just as he propelled my body off the edge. The wrench was agonizing. My forearm screamed as a muscle tore inside. My body crashed back into the cliff, grazing my face against the balustrade. Already, Hawken was drawing back and raising his foot to my straining hand.

'It wasn't my fault!'

He stamped down hard and my fingers turned to jelly.

In that petrifying first second of my fall, as I felt the vast chasm of the valley open its jaws to swallow me, a scrap of bright yellow came into view through the swirling cloud. Knotted securely, trailing down the cliff: the climbing rope. Falling fast – my knee and chest scraped raw by the bare rock of the cliff – I threw out my hand and caught it.

The friction of the rope sliding through my hand stripped the skin straight off my fingers and palm. An unimaginable agony. By the time I'd got a firm hold, I was hanging fifteen feet below the wall.

Silence. The scrape of rope against cliff. Then, through the obscurity of the cloud, I heard Hawken call my name.

There was a hideous triumph in his voice. It

would take a matter of seconds for him to untie the rope. Frantically I started scrambling up, the effort sending arrows of pain down my left arm and tearing into the exposed flesh of my right hand. Hawken's outline grew clearer as I climbed. He was bending, not to the knot in the rope but to something else.

I paused, eight feet below, horrified. Hawken was lifting the heavy bench on to the wall above me. Holding it steady, he stepped up beside it.

The urge to panic was overwhelming. I threw a loop of rope around my left foot, transferring my weight to it as I reached down to grab the lower part of the rope. Balancing myself against the cliff face, racing against time, I yanked up the long stretch of yellow that disappeared into the misty gloom below.

Hawken had seized the edges of the bench with both hands and now he lifted it high above his head. In the swirling cloud, he looked demonic – a monster god, with a terrifying club raised to the heavens. There was so much rope to pull in. As he paused there, drawing out his revenge, I rushed the yellow cord through my hands as fast as I could.

He flexed his arms. 'Catch,' he said.

In that single, critical second, I kicked hard against the cliff, launching myself outwards, and swung the bottom end of the rope up towards him. The grappling hook drew a perfect arc through the cloud, hissing in the silent air until it reached the apex of its ascent and swung down into Hawken's back.

The blade cut deep into his flesh. His only reaction was an astonished grunt. With a great tug. I hauled him outwards, sending both him and the bench flying past me as I sank back into the cliff face.

The impact, ninety feet below, was barely audible through the cloud.

Something fundamental had shifted in me. Hawken's attack, following so soon on the death of Alice, drove me through that cloud-smothered landscape towards my reckoning with Hoppner. The complex had become simple. All was clearly painted in black and white.

Despite my determination, my feet dragged a little, sheer physical exhaustion bringing me close to collapse. I had no weapon, my left arm was effectively useless, my right hand a bloody mess. Even my vision was in trouble, whether from external blood and sweat or something more serious I didn't know. My bearings were failing me, and I could feel myself swaying as I stumbled up the lawn towards Hoppner's house.

The hummingbirds were nowhere to be seen, their feeders deserted. The front door stood wide open. Cloud had rolled through the house, shrouding the furniture in a fine, almost invisible haze. The dining room was empty, as were the kitchen and living room. In the bedroom a single, neatly made bed stood in the centre of the bare floor, just one small wardrobe and a dressing table by its side. No Hoppner. I even looked in the bathroom, empty but for its ascetic collection of plain yellow soap, steel comb and unbranded shampoo.

He wasn't there.

Feeling my way back out of the house, I found spots of my own blood marking the route I'd come.

Where was he?

I began making my way, slowly and painfully, across the lawn to the office building. Then a door clicked open in the corner of the compound and I turned and lurched towards the cabin.

'Oh Christ, Mark!'

The voice came from the cloud ahead: David stood at the open cabin door, gripping the frame, looking ready to faint. I marched straight up to him.

'Where's Hawken?' he cried, eyes flicking between my bloody face and hands. 'What did you do? What happened?'

'You shouldn't have brought him back.'

'We had to. The town is angry. We were insecure,' he stuttered.

I gripped his arm with my torn hand. He looked down at the blood on his sleeve, then back at my battered face.

'Mark, please . . .'

'Is he in there?'

'No. Mark, please. Don't. Not Mr Hoppner.'

'Move, David.'

And suddenly he was crying, great tears dripping from his almond eyes.

'Please don't hurt him,' he whispered.

I gazed into that collapsing face a few seconds longer, touched by the depth of love I saw there. Then I remembered the girl lying dead in a car just across the compound and I pushed him roughly aside.

'No!' he screamed as I walked into the cabin.

Slamming the door behind me, I drew the bolt to lock David and his pleading out.

Benjamin Sword Hoppner was sitting quite still in the middle of the room, the tiredness in his face accentuated by the harsh spotlight above.

'You pernicious bastard,' I said. 'You made Leonard kill Alice. You filled him with so much bullshit, he put his hands around her throat and murdered her!'

He'd been gazing at the darkened end wall, hadn't turned when I came in. Only now did he look round, his eyes straining to find me in the blackness beyond his small pool of light. 'Leonard is a grown man,' he replied calmly. 'He wouldn't kill his wife just because of something I said.'

'She wasn't his wife and he isn't a grown man. He's like your little Miraflores children, too innocent to defend himself against your clever arguments and the moral spin that turns killing someone into a virtuous act. He knows nothing about the world outside the library. You brainwashed him as surely as you'll brainwash those kids.'

'She wasn't his wife?' said Hoppner, more stunned by this than by her death. 'Leonard lied to me?'

'Christ, is that all that bothers you? He lied to you, so what? Are you so out of touch with reality you think that could possibly matter? Your little perfect society is leaving. Leaving! Did you know that? Your most devoted follower killed herself out of sheer despair yesterday, Miraflores is in rebellion, there's a graveyard full of people you've murdered just outside the compound, and you're fixated on Leonard's honesty?'

'Virtues are not negotiable, Mark! You cannot just switch them on or off at your convenience. It is precisely at times like these that they matter most – the difficult times, when our true character comes to the surface. I gave up the woman I loved and sacrificed my reputation for the sake of those virtues. However tough life becomes, I have to live by them every second or they become worthless luxuries.'

'But you've already made them worthless!' This man, this selfmade god, was sitting there boasting of his constancy, still unwilling to face the horrendous consequences of his beliefs, and it made me so furious I wanted to shake him until some scrap of understanding broke through. 'You've taken your precious virtues to such extremes they aren't even virtues any more. You've surrounded them with so much death and terror they've become completely meaningless. Your perfect society was founded on fear – those poor people only ever followed your Code because they were afraid of losing your money or hanging from a noose. How can you possibly believe virtue means anything if people are frightened into it?'

'They can grow to embrace virtue.' He was faltering now, the doubt starting to take hold. 'The more they see how beneficial it is . . .'

'You mean how much it pays?' I said, letting the scorn ring loud in my voice. 'How rich it makes them? You think your money buys goodness, but you've always had it the wrong way round. The fantastic wealth you brought here was only ever a temptation to evil.'

'If I hadn't brought my money to this town, they'd still be living in a slum!'

A last-ditch argument, and he knew it. I moved towards him and saw the shock in his eyes as the bloody mess of my face was lit up. 'I'm sure the Pentagon justified their intervention in much the same way,' I said.

He stood up to face me, the flesh of his cheeks quivering. 'I will not allow you to compare my rebuilding Miraflores with the supply of armaments that made it necessary.'

'It's no longer up to you to declare what is or is not allowed,' I said softly. 'Hawken's gone; your money won't buy you authority here. You're just the outsider who tried, like the US military before you, to direct the course of events as you saw fit – treating these people like pawns in a global struggle. The fight against communism; the fight against evil: how was your interventionism any less exploitative?'

His eyes turned weak: a saddened, defeated gaze. 'Are they really leaving?'

'If they don't come here first to avenge Tanadio,' I said viciously.

'I only wanted to do what was right for them.'

'No, you did what you wanted and then convinced yourself it was right. Didn't it occur to you they might have their own values? That for years, for centuries, they've been striving towards their own idea of a perfect society, even when they were at war? All you did was bribe them to give up their values. You've corrupted them just as surely as those government fat cats. Thank God they're getting out before you killed off whatever natural conscience they still had!'

I became aware of two things: David's voice calling to us from outside as his impotent fist beat against the door, and the taste of blood smeared across my lips. Was Hawken really dead? Had I just killed a man? What did that make me? My happy return to Katie and Christopher seemed more impossible than ever.

Somewhere out there, Leonard was collapsed by the side of the road, remembering, reliving. Some kindly driver would rescue him eventually, but nothing could save Leonard from the truth he would have to endure for ever.

Alice I would bury in the forest. Between two great trees, in earth soaked through with tears.

I felt close to collapse.

'Why did you take against me, Mark?' Hoppner asked in a whisper. 'I've tried to ignore your antipathy so I could give you a fair test, but you're not a man who can hide his feelings. That's good, I guess. Honest, at least. But it hurt to have someone like you be so hostile. Why could you never give my Code a chance?'

The fury I'd nursed all the way back to Miraflores was already dissipating as Hoppner's lifelong certainty began to crack. Listening to the sadness in his voice, I found it hard to sustain the same intensity of anger.

'You would have had me killed,' I said tiredly. 'I didn't feel any great obligation to soothe your feelings.'

'You think so? You're assuming you would have failed the test?' He smiled a little at that. 'I don't think you would have. I'm a pretty good judge of character, even without the benefit of hypnosis. That's why it so shocked me to find you and Alice sleeping together. But now you've explained she wasn't married, I can reinstate my good opinion of you. I've no doubt you would have passed that test, just as I've no doubt you would have found a good use for any grant I gave you. You're not one to blow money on mansions – orphanages, maybe, but not mansions. Isn't that right?'

Taken completely by surprise, I didn't know how

540

to answer him. The man of Goodness was telling me I was a good man. Despite the awfulness of his own acts, despite everything, I found myself suddenly uplifted by this final judgement. As if Hoppner's word was the deciding factor – the reassurance I needed that I could, after all, be a good father and husband. That I could go home.

When I didn't reply, he looked disappointed. 'I understand why you've come back,' he went on in a different tone. 'What happened to Alice – I'm so sorry; perhaps, after all, I am responsible. It's difficult to exercise any measure of power and influence for long, even when you're trying to use it all for good, without the evils mounting up on your conscience.'

He walked over to the cupboard at the edge of the room. Belatedly, I remembered what it held. When he turned round, the jet injector was in his left hand.

'I don't know what's happened to me. I tried so hard to fill my life and all the lives about me with goodness. I have no idea how . . .'

He shook his head, the weary frown crumpling the flesh of his cheeks and sapping the energy from his eyes. A moment of honesty and contrition. In that moment I first started feeling true compassion for him.

'You'll find it easier with this,' he said, resigned, holding out the jet injector. 'Less mess.'

Instinctively I took the device, only then realizing what he meant.

'Mr Hoppner, I don't—'

'It's OK,' he said, looking up at me once more – a last attempt at a smile. 'But I ask one thing before you do it. Try to forgive me. More ill-timed pursuit of dry old virtues, you're probably thinking, but please do try to forgive me, for your own sake. Kill me not from vengeance but from a belief that it is the necessary and just consequence of what I have done.'

'I'm not going to kill you!'

He fixed his stare on me and said, 'You came here to end my life, did you not?'

I couldn't answer. That time had passed. Everything had seemed so simple. Some of us were good, the rest bad. Now, I couldn't say for sure what anyone was any more. Sánchez, the man who'd tried to kill us, was the most honourable person I knew. Leonard, that pillar of intelligence and goodness, had just committed murder. Even Hawken, the most obviously malevolent of them all, had probably been the only truly honest person in Miraflores. Not once had he tried to disguise his motives or compromise his beliefs to meet another's expectations. Who was to say which of us was more or less good than anyone else?

Hoppner was speaking for me: 'I know you did. For Alice, of course. But perhaps also a little for everyone else.' Unbuttoning his right sleeve, he rolled it up to bare his tensed forearm. 'Only, try to understand why I did what I did. Try to see that I meant well. If you can forgive me before you kill me you will, I think, save whatever it is the religious folks call your soul.'

The jet injector fitted snugly in my right hand. My blood smeared the glass barrel. The vial of barbiturate perched on the top of it seemed innocuously small. Tearing my eyes away from the device, I shook my head.

'I'm sorry, but I have to go home now,' I muttered, turning to the door.

He called to me once more as I put my hand on the bolt. His voice was so tremulous I couldn't help but look back.

'Perhaps, then, you would be good enough to leave that with me,' he said.

The injector felt icy in my hand.

'You shouldn't do it,' I said hoarsely. 'It's not all bad. David's here: he adores you. You can still do a lot of good.'

'We both know that isn't true.'

There was no way I could offer any better plea.

'Miraflores is falling apart,' he said. 'I guess I've known it might happen for a while now. Anything that has to be protected with so much force and money will never stand alone.' His hand came up to his etched throat, fingers rubbing the tips of his collarbones. 'You know, I used to think of Miraflores as a modern-day cathedral. There was a time when people were prepared to dedicate their lives to the creation of something truly extraordinary, not out of financial incentive but from faith alone. Now, the only extraordinary creations not driven by profit are military super-weapons. But Miraflores was beautiful. I believed Miraflores could compete even with Salisbury or Notre Dame as a font of hope and spiritual revitalization. Is that vain of me? Perhaps, in the end, I still haven't quite mastered humility.' The hand dropped back by his side. The blue veins on the back of it seemed rigid and lifeless. 'Mark, I don't think I can stand to watch my cathedral destroyed.'

At last, when it was already over, I began to see it through his eyes. The idealist's point of view. The tragedy of a dying dream. How much easier it is to forgive when one steps outside of the self.

'This isn't the only way out,' I whispered.

He had to pause for a moment to gain control of his voice. 'It's not just about a way out. I meant what I said about beneficial suicide – when you can achieve more by dying than by remaining alive.' A painful cough racked his body and he put out his hand to find the chair. Shakily, he sat down. 'It worked for another do-gooder, a couple of thousand years ago,' he observed with a tired grin. 'David will tell the story right – he'll be my Saint Paul. Maybe they'll talk less about the dirt and more about the good stuff if they see I was prepared to die for it.'

I put the killing machine back in his hand. A drop of my blood coloured his palm, and I had to turn quickly away.

'Don't worry, Mark,' he said kindly to my back. 'I might never do it. I might not have the courage.'

He coughed weakly, and that sound alone made him older than ever. 'But courage is a virtue – a pretty important virtue. So I'll give it my best shot.'

'Goodbye,' I whispered as I felt for the door.

'God bless you,' he said in final parting.

Old Soldiers Never Die

by Heath Katzenbach

It's nine years since I last met the man known as El Tigre. Back then he was the biggest thorn in the government's side, building up a revolutionary force that would one day march on Santa Tecla. A lot has changed since those days, yet once again he is back in the mountains, facing the military's wrath.

Francisco José Sánchez – he uses his real name now – has aged well. Some of his old comrades are a little heavy around the waistline, but a new generation of fighters has pledged to follow him. 'El Tigre is the only man who can win us our freedom,' says one young disciple. 'He will fight to the end for what is right.'

Some have called Sánchez a warmonger for restarting that terrible conflict. But the legions of men and women from all over the country who have rushed to support him prove beyond doubt how badly the new government has failed its people. Even some of the armed forces are deserting to fight at his side.

Sánchez is optimistic: 'We gave up our weapons, and we fight only with what we can capture. But this time no one is interfering in our nation's struggle. It is for us to decide our destiny. We must choose our own government, provide for ourselves, keep each other on the path of goodness. We are our own masters.'

Good News for the Orphanage

by Moses Johnson

The children of Vima Orphanage can smile again tonight. Recently threatened with closure, Vima is to receive an annual grant of $40,000 from the Sword Foundation. David Gordon, Chairman of the Foundation – which has already contributed to schools, clinics and cooperative farming projects in many other parts of Africa and the rest of the world – said last night that Vima was 'a model of cooperation and kindness.' In particular, he praised the love the staff showed for the children in their care. 'Love is a virtue,' he told them. 'Perhaps, because it makes us compassionate and generous, kind and forgiving, it is the most important virtue of all.'

ACKNOWLEDGEMENTS

The study of Ethics is such a key part of Western philosophy, that one of the difficulties in writing this book has been resisting the temptation to overload it with the ideas – brilliant, frightening or just plain crazy – of all those great thinkers. Anyone wanting more will find plenty of texts on the subject. In particular I recommend *A Short Treatise on the Great Virtues* by André Comte-Sponville (William Heinemann), *Being Good* by Simon Blackburn (Oxford University Press), *How Are We to Live?* by Peter Singer (Oxford University Press) and *Godless Morality* by Richard Holloway (Canongate). For a more general introduction, Bertrand Russell's *History of Western Philosophy* (Routledge) is hard to beat. A chilling investigation of the dangers of moral idealism is provided by Roy Baumeister in *Evil: Inside Human Cruelty and Violence* (Freeman). The Aristophanes quotation is taken from the translation by David Barrett (Penguin).

I'm very grateful to all those who have read and commented on the manuscript: Simon

Blackburn, Caroline Bland, Imogen Cleaver, Alasdair Macdonald, Rosemary Macdonald, Chris Manby, Richard Marriott, Malcolm Millar, Matt Nelson and Bruno Shovelton. Many thanks also to my agent, Patrick Walsh, my editor, Rowland White, and everyone else involved.

www.hectormacdonald.com.

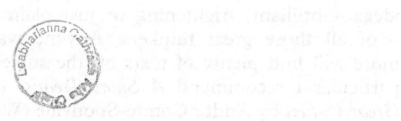

550